THE CAMELOT CODE

SAM CHRISTER

SPHERE

First published in Great Britain in 2013 by Sphere

A CIP catalogue record for this book is available from the British Library.

ISBN 978-0-7515-5091-7

Typeset in Bembo by M Rules
Printed and bound in Great Britain by
Clays Ltd, St Ives plc

Papers used by Sphere are from well-managed forests and other responsible sources.

MIX
Paper from
responsible sources
FSC® C104740

Sphere
An imprint of
Little, Brown Book Group
100 Victoria Embankment
London EC4Y 0DY

An Hachette UK Company
www.hachette.co.uk

www.littlebrown.co.uk

THIS BOOK IS DEDICATED TO SOME VERY SPECIAL FRIENDS. THANK YOU ONE AND ALL:

Andy Freeman, Maria Mares, Mike Monaghan, Vladimir Cucuz, Nattalia Azuul, Anna Ka, Hemanth Kumar, Astrid Burton, Michael Betts, Pablo Monti, Arn Đed de Gothia, Maria Del Carmen Triadani, Arantzazu Herrera Peñate, Ana Rackovi, Sharmistha Ghosh, April Stone, Jeanette Holland, Emicar Balmaceda, Silvia Milzoni, Tony Emery, Patricia Connolly, Siladitya Basak, Roxana Popa, Christina Pougoura, Shane Nelson, Serdar Aditepe, Henri Rantalankila, Nikki Petty, Andrew Evans, Barbora Vörösová, Sónia Alves, Diana Vass, Aida Ali, Richard Dave Gomersall, Caroline Peruzzi, Šárka Měřínská, Ivancescu Razvan, Tatjana Antic Jasic, Läle Oo, Eric Nelson, Emily Henshall, Negrea R. Cristian, Corrina Fawcett, Sneha Ravikumar, Cristina Ionela Bulea, Tom McMurdo, Tanaya Patankar Lampard, Elina Emilova Chausheva, John Dalton, Lara Larisimo, Ricardo del Valle, Nikolas Sofikitis, Marcel Kortekaas, Laura-Maria Borti, Cheryl Dalton, Rachel Taylor, Jose Luis Zenteno Cesar, Betka Nosková, Daniel Komor, David Vilhena Marquez, Susan Percival, Aja Tafilaj, Dawn Wylds, Sravan Kumar, Coenraad De Kat, Julie Dring, Alina Coman, Denise Smith,

Michelle Marchant, Ann Christin Siljan, Yve Fanor, Ana Velicaru, Pat Taylor, Natasha Kemmer, Anita Abramczuk, Kostas Iordanou, Corinne Mudd, David Price, Monika Nabrdalik, Paula Marland, Jorn Urup Nielsen, Ralph Siebenaler, Ray Stacey, Dawn Denson, Ilona Griffiths, Florence Ruffin, Debbie Ward Yexley, Sharon Wilson, Richie Shemilt, Marcel Kupka, Debbie Hyde Hart, Henriette Irving, Carole Wright, Terry Parrish, Jan Saunders, Sarah Nicholls, Adrian Titley, Leonie Dargent, Audrey Atkinson, Martin Elliott, Stuart Turner, Jamie Mileham, Niamh Dunlea, Danni Carr, Calum Murray, Rachel Hadingham, Pat Gough, Czar Ngaosi, Allwyn Jose, Lindsay Jane Chant, Sara Jackson, Nuno Silva, Casey Yandek, Paul Nuttall Royrogersmcfreely, Shane Barrett, Kay Podboj, Pam Scholl, Clare Davies, Belfast Dave, Jenny Wood, Sladjana Vasic, Prowting Leila, Dilyana Dimitrova, Jackie Nash, Matthew O'Connor, Val Tunnicliffe, Dave Watson, Anna Ó Máille, Helen Branson, Paula Dixon, Valérie Navon, Fiona Gebbie, Carolina Camacho, Donna Rail, Evgeny Chirskov, Helen Turvey, Micka Sinette, Meyer Thorsen, Niels Søndergaard, Jovana Joe Tepavcevic, Amir Isakovi, Medina Kleine Maus, Sabrina Ikpodo Abnukta, Anne Sofie Sandholdt Jørgensen, Emma Kathryn Reitbauer, Rui Costa, Maria João Barros, Valérie Lascoux, Bas Peelen, Michael D. Gonzalez, Hilary Bancroft-Thain, Richard Shipman, Angela DeMarte Frear, Mark Womble, Nikola Nakov, Renzo S. P. Tomassi, Gareth Jones, Tantor Jane, Marija Kvajo, Čuturić Paul Stafford, Margret Jonker, Jason Cr, Peter Van Den Bussche, Jude Thompson, Sherry Potter, Chris Parry, Keli Grejs, Pedro M. Baptista Costa, Alexandra Svjetska, Huiloo Ho, Denny Stribling, Sarah Diedrich, Carmen Forján,

Julie March, Neville Dawkins, Aleksandar Ilic, Paul Bendon, Graham Smith, Dawn Bushell, David Taws, Danish Hasan, Gerrie King, Richard Daniels, Adam Stockwell, Lainey Everett, Theresa Bruton, Lukasz Semla, Sarah Bennett, Tim Busbey Sévana Topalian, Michele Cockram, Darryl Bastian.

THE CAMELOT CODE

PROLOGUE

The sight of blood

WALES, GREAT BRITAIN

Behind ancient, castellated walls, high in the solar chamber in the eastern tower, the screams of the innocent pierce an old man's dreams.

Myrddin draws his near-skeletal frame from the rough wooden cot lodged under a narrow slit of a window. Without looking at any timepiece, he knows it is midnight. That the fragile earth spinning beneath the waxing moon is once more being shaken by a storm of evil.

The pull on him is strong.

He wraps his tall, frail form in a thick blue robe and descends a spiral of timeworn steps. At the foot, he catches his breath and braces himself for what is to come.

Again a powerful force moves him.

He shuffles across the dark hall and opens the huge, arched doors at the end.

ANTIQUES ROW, KENSINGTON, MARYLAND

Blood from the stab wound in his stomach oozes through Amir Goldman's fingers and spatters the dark floorboards of the antiques store he's owned for thirty years.

The widower sinks to his knees. He's dying and he knows it. His deep sadness is not the loss of a few more years. It's that he's been robbed of redemption. Denied the chance that his mundane, miserable, scrape-a-living life might amount to something.

Greatness had been within his grasp.

If he hadn't been greedy, this would never have happened. Instead he'd have closed a deal that the antiques world would have spoken about for centuries. His name would have ranked alongside Gildas and Malory, Geoffrey of Monmouth and Chrétien de Troyes. The big secret would have been out.

And Amir Emmanuel Goldman would have outed it.

Which, he guesses, is why he's dying.

The Chamber of Prophecies is cold and perfectly circular, lit by a crescent of virgin candles made from the fat of animal sacrifices.

The flames flicker as Myrddin enters. His gaze rises to the vaulted ceiling then falls to the twelve unique stained-glass windows beneath it. Each depicts a man whose existence is as mythical as his own.

He makes his way to a giant font, fashioned from Irish rocks more than five thousand years old.

In the water he sees his straggle of white beard and hair, arrow-slit eyes and creased leather skin stare back at him.

The surface trembles and corrugates. Tiny ripples become waves. The Font of Knowledge rumbles and shakes. Myrddin grips the wide bowl to stop it breaking.

This is what *it* wanted.

Him.

Raw energy flows into his hands and arms. Seeps into his skin, his blood and organs. Builds in power until he feels like his skin will split and burst.

Myrddin's mind fills with unbearably bright light.

The vision is starting.

Now he must endure it. Suffer it, in all its painful clarity.

The knifeman kneels beside the bloody floorboards and touches Amir Goldman's face comfortingly. 'Don't fight it. It'll be over in a minute.'

The old storekeeper feels weak and dizzy. Through blurred eyes, he watches the man watching him.

The killer-in-waiting backs away from the river of red at his feet. He lifts an arm to check the passing time then resumes his patient posture.

Amir's agony is everywhere now. He slurps for the last dregs of oxygen. His knees curl up. He is foetal and bloody. A fatal parody of how he entered the world over seven decades ago. A grandfather clock beats a soothing tick. His tired eyes close and he counts the silence between the clicks.

'Amir?'

The hurt is fading now, stroked away by the brush of the pendulum, as soothing as his dead wife's hand, a touch he's not felt for twenty years.

'You still alive, old man?'

He hears a chime and lets go of his last breath. Frees it like a tiny bird from a cage.

'Amir?'

His eyes shut. The pendulum swings. His wife's hand

strokes his face. Her skin against his. He's waited so long for her kiss and the warmth of her love.

Across the blood-stained boards, the door opens. A brass bell pings. Amir Goldman's killer slips into the night.

Death is coming.

Myrddin sees the old enemy on a far-off shore.

He rides a silent brown beast, one that moves with noiseless hooves and many giant mouths to swallow men whole. There's a flash of blue in Death's deceitful hand. The burnished steel of a blade peels pink flesh and raises a torrent of red.

Myrddin's heart prickles with pain. He clutches his chest and sinks to the icy floor, struggling fπor breath.

He must warn the others.

Thousands of miles away, a man has been murdered.

The Keeper of Time killed in the Cave of Past and Present.

The gates of evil are open. A fresh cycle of bloodletting has begun.

PART ONE

The true mystery of the world is the visible, not the invisible.

Oscar Wilde

1

FBI HQ, SAN FRANCISCO

A murky fog rises from beneath the Bay Bridge and crawls towards the giant federal buildings crowded near the choppy waters.

Mitzi Fallon stares out from the glass belly of the FBI skyscraper. '*Some* weather,' she says to no one at her side. 'I move from LA, for what? To start my morning in the mist, like a freakin' gorilla? Sheesh.'

Heads turn as the muttering brunette, dressed in grey slacks and a new white top, hauls a box of personal belongings down a thousand miles of corridors.

She shoulders open a door marked: HISTORIC, RELIGIOUS AND UNEXPLAINED CRIMES UNIT and surveys a small but empty open-plan room with four desks. Tucked in the corner is a tiny office created by a floor-to-ceiling glass partition and a barely visible swing-in door.

Mitzi dumps her stuff on an empty desk and reflects on

why she's uprooted herself and two children to join a unit dubbed 'The Unsolvables'. Some of it's down to the pay rise and relocation cheque – money's tight when you're raising two teenage girls on your own. Part of it is the opportunity to widen her horizons and work with the FBI in a new multi-agency task force. If the truth were known, most of it is about starting afresh. Quitting town. Getting away from Alfie.

Her Alfie.

Alfie Fallon.

One-time love of her life, turned drunk, turned wife-beater.

The lieutenant unpacks. First out of the bubble wrap is a 'World's Best Mom' mug, then a pile of framed photographs of her twins, Amber and Jade. A favourite of her and the girls at Disney gets a kiss before it's put in place.

The thirty-nine-year-old crosses to a spotless desk that has only one item on it – a thin, stainless steel nameplate proclaiming its missing occupant to be JONATHAN BRONTY. She's been told the squad's only man was once a priest in a tough downtown district in LA. 'Well, Father, if your soul is half as clean as your desk I'm sure you're going straight to heaven when the big day comes.'

She puts the nameplate down and drifts to the next workstation. It's heaped with files and documents. Teetering near the edge is a row of old reference books and the proclamation: VICTORIA CANTRELL, UNIT RESEARCHER.

Adjacent is a third desk, that of LT ELEONORA FRACCI.

Mitzi inspects a tube of expensive foreign hand cream, a gorgeous brown Achille Pinto silk scarf and two small blue Murano glass fish used as paperweights. She picks up a silver-framed photograph showing a strikingly beautiful woman in a smart Carabinieri police uniform, flanked by her small but proud mother and father.

The office door opens.

Stood there is her new boss, unit head Sandra Donovan.

'Quite a looker.' Mitzi returns the photo to Fracci's desk. She nods to her cardboard box. 'I think I'll sit over there, just so no one thinks me and the lovely Eleonora are part of a before-and-after commercial.'

Donovan doesn't laugh. The forty-four-year-old's sense of humour is as short as her masculine haircut. She extends a hand and grips hard. 'Good to have you on board, though we didn't expect you until tomorrow.'

'Hey, if that's a problem, I can gladly go home.'

'No. If you're on the payroll, you're on the clock. Personnel are useless. Come to my office; we can talk there.'

'Where's everyone else?'

'They're out on a case. Will be all day. It's something the cops downtown have been struggling with.'

Mitzi follows her into the small area behind the sound-proof glass. 'Anything interesting?'

'Maybe.' She slides into a chair behind her desk and gestures to Mitzi to sit. 'Week ago cops found a woman's body buried in her own back garden. Homicide has been grilling the husband ever since.'

'Sounds like a domestic.'

'They thought the same. But this is a weird one. Forensics found multiple semen samples on the corpse and none are the husband's.'

Mitzi frowns. 'But why call in this unit? What's historic, religious or unexplainable about a rape-homicide?'

Donovan manages a smile for the first time. 'The vic was a witch. A full-blown black magic priestess.'

2

ANTIQUES ROW, KENSINGTON, MARYLAND

Detective Paddy Fitzgerald, the cop everyone calls 'Irish', stands outside the antiques store on Howard Avenue, eating a large Danish. At his feet is a bucket of black coffee still too hot to hold let alone drink.

He isn't going into that stinking hole of a crime scene until he's finished his breakfast. The stiff in there has been cooking all weekend and from what one of the CSIs has told him, there are enough blowflies to lift him off his feet.

Calliphoridae.

He hates them with a passion. Hates their noise and their way of hanging around even when he's batted the fuck out of them.

Irish sends uniforms to canvass for witnesses and tries the

coffee. Still too hot. He puts it back down on the sidewalk and inspects the gathering crowd.

Human blowflies. Every bit as bad as the bloodsuckers inside. To say nothing about the press. Those cocksuckers are even worse. His vitriol has been sparked by the sight of Tommy Watson, an idiot from the crime desk of the *Washington Post*, with a long rap sheet for misquoting police.

The reporter raises a hand and with it his voice, 'Hey, Detective.'

Irish ignores him.

'You got a minute for me?'

He dusts pastry flakes off an unironed blue shirt that testifies yesterday's dinner included meatballs and tomato sauce.

'Come on; give me a break, Irish. You got a quote I can use for the online edition?'

'Yeah, I got a quote. Tommy Watson don't know his fat, lazy ass from his chicken-shit elbows – and if he wasn't screwing the ugliest broad in Dispatch he wouldn't even know to be here.'

'Screw you, Lieutenant.' He flips him the finger.

'Screw you, Tommy tiny dick.' He looks up, as he pulls forensic overalls and shoe covers from a police bag. 'What? You don't think Big Brenda told us about Tiny Tommy?' He laughs and starts to suit up.

A hanging bell rings as he opens the door of Goldman's Antiques and a sign saying CLOSED clatters against the reinforced glass. The light inside is nicotine-brown, as though tainted by too much contact with dark wood, dust and history.

The floorboards bend and creak as he walks a non-contamination route marked out by the forensic teams. The place smells of beeswax polish and brass cleaner.

And death.

The air is fat with the stomach-turning stink of it.

A young, male crime-scene photographer is up a short aluminium stepladder. He's shooting video of the body, its relation to the entrance, the register, the showroom and the small restroom that, by the look of it, also gets used to make hot drinks.

Medical Examiner Cherrie Archer is on her knees, searching for defence wounds and trace on the hands of the cadaver. Over the stiff, curled fingers, the thirty-three-year-old blonde sees Irish shuffle towards her. He's six-foot-plus but slouches and seems smaller. His dark, curly hair is specked with grey and looks like he slept the night in a cardboard box. Every time Cherrie sees him, she remembers that half a decade ago he had a brain sharper than her skull saw.

Then came the incident.

The one no one talks about.

Not divorce. Not the death of a partner. Not a clichéd crash into drink and ruin.

Something worse. Far worse.

She tucks a curl of hair back into the hood of her white Tyvek suit. 'I'm just about to start, Detective. Want to join me?'

Irish's knees crack as he bends beside her. 'That's the best offer I've had today.' He corrects himself, 'Come to think of it, it's my best offer this year.'

3

HRU CRIMES UNIT, SAN FRANCISCO

Mitzi hears them coming down the corridor laughing and joking. The way colleagues do when they're comfortable with each other.

She feels very much the new girl. Undoubtedly they'll be nice as pie to her. Then someone will call a contact in LA and learn her husband used to beat her. Someone else will discover she stuck a gun to his head, had him jailed and then banned from coming within a mile of her or their kids.

'Hi there!' she says as they enter the office. 'I'm Mitzi Fallon – from the LAPD.' She sticks out a grin and her hand.

'Jon Bronty,' says a man with chestnut-brown hair. 'People just call me Bronty.'

Mitzi notices he's of medium build, not much taller than she is. Maybe five ten. Somewhere around thirty, trim but not muscular and, despite old-fashioned brown cords and a scruffy green shirt, has a comfortable way that she imagines some women – or maybe men – might find attractive.

'This is Eleonora – Eleonora *Fracci*.' Bronty pronounces the surname with melodramatic accentuation.

'Ciao *'itzi*.' The brunette from the Carabinieri photograph is wearing a pale-pink blouse and short brown skirt that shows off ridiculously toned legs.

'It's Mitzi with an *M*.' She tries not to sound too annoyed. 'Not itzi as in "itsy bitsy".'

The Italian looks baffled. '*M*— itzi?'

'Close enough.'

A young, mousy woman in jeans and a Big Bang T-shirt flashes a set of teeth braces. 'Victoria Cantrell – Vicky. I do research. Research and coffee.' Her voice says New York – Brooklyn. '*Lots* of coffee.' She gives a nervous giggle. 'They drink it all day. Would you like some?'

Mitzi would. She'd like a long tumbler of vodka to go with it. 'Sure, that'd be great. Thanks.'

The youngster looks pleased. 'How d'you take it?'

'Black, no sugar.' She pats her hips. 'Can't afford the calories.'

'Exercise,' suggests Eleonora. 'It is the only way to kill calories. I take sugar *and* cream but I do gym and kill the calories. You should come.'

'Honey, the only gym I could do in a morning is one spelled J-I-M, and he's going to have to be tall, rich, handsome and not mind taking on two teenage girls.' She spins round one of the framed pictures. 'These are my calorie killers.'

The room is silent. Silent enough to tell her that no one else has kids.

She repositions the photo.

Sandra Donovan appears from behind her glass partition. 'Are you ladies playing nicely?'

Mitzi and Eleonora stare through her.

'Good. Then how about someone updates me on the Satanists?'

Bronty pumps a green bead of germicidal gel into his palms and rubs his hands clean as he talks. 'The victim's closet was full of black magic paraphernalia. Witches' robes, candles and spell books.'

'Nothing in the husband's?' asks Donovan.

'Not a thing. He wasn't into it, or didn't know.'

'*Bullshit*,' says Mitzi.

'You don't know the case,' snaps Eleonora.

'I don't need to. If she was being nailed by Satanists, hubby knew it. She'd be weird in bed. Ask any married guy.'

'Maybe she *should* know the case.' Sandra Donovan can't help but enjoy the friction between them. 'Give her the briefing notes, Eleonora.' She turns to Mitzi. 'It's going to be interesting to see what you make of it.'

4

BRITISH EMBASSY, WASHINGTON DC

The British Embassy lies less than three miles north-west of the White House, in palatial grounds on the southern side of the US Naval Observatory and east of Dumbarton Oaks, the research centre renowned for Byzantine studies.

The building, the first erected on Embassy Row, boasts seven main bedrooms, all named after past ambassadors. The current occupant, Sir Owain Gwyn, stands patiently in the Howard and Halifax Suite while his valet dresses him.

Every article of clothing has been handmade by trusted tailors and carefully checked by the middle-aged servant before his master is allowed to wear it.

From laundry to skin, it is the valet's job to know exactly who has washed, ironed and delivered it back into his care. Even then, the rigorous routine is far from over. Most items are X-rayed, others are subjected to toxicity testing. All are dusted top-to-bottom with a hand-scanner to ensure no microscopic trackers have been sewn into their fabrics.

'Your under-armour, sir.'

'Thank you, James.' Forty-two-year-old Owain comes from a long line of tall, broad, dark-haired Welshmen. At almost six foot six, her Majesty's ambassador in America has to become a contortionist to get into the proffered garment. Although it looks like a combination of vest and long johns, it is a unique piece of clothing, fashioned from state-of-the-art grapheme, a fine mesh of carbon atoms that, according to the manufacturers, is 'strong enough to support the weight of an elephant balancing upon a spike'. He wears it to protect him, not from gymnastic mammals but from bullets and bombs.

'Comfortable, sir?'

The roll of Owain's warm brown eyes gives away the fact that he is not.

A buzzer sounds.

The flat-screen monitor above the door shows the output of eight security cameras around the residence, including the adjoining room where a tall, sandy-haired man in a sharp grey suit is waiting.

The valet knows his time is up. 'Is there anything else, sir?'

'I'm afraid I'll need you early tonight for my farewell charity dinner, say five?'

'That's not a problem, sir. Might I be so bold as to say something personal?'

'Feel free.'

'I'm sure the government of the United States will miss you greatly. I think you have done amazing things in your work here, sir and it's been an absolute pleasure to serve you. You'll leave quite a hole.'

'For all of a week, James. Then the hole will be filled and I'll be forgotten. But thank you for your kind comments. You should get off now, make the most of the rest of your day and the short time we have left in Washington.'

The former guardsman gives a courteous nod, takes a neat military stride to the door and pulls it open for the ambassador.

Owain greets Gareth Madoc, a childhood friend and former army colleague, with the Welsh equivalent of good morning, '*Bore da*.' He waves at a breakfast trolley. 'Do you have room and time to have a *crempog* with me?'

The former soldier smiles. 'I *always* have time for a *crempog*.'

The two men go back to a life before knighthoods, international postings and politics. Their history stretches beyond the green valleys where they were born to the intertwined genealogy of two clans who lived and fought together in days long before Romans ruled Britain.

Madoc leans down to the lower tray of the trolley and lifts out a wicker breadbasket covered by a starched white cloth. 'A little surprise with your breakfast.' He grasps the square of cotton and jerks it away, like a magician performing a table trick.

Owain stares at the basket's contents. He carefully removes the single object and handles it with reverential respect. He turns it over in his scarred hands, then kisses it. 'Who recovered this?'

'George.'

'And the rest?'

'Still missing.'

Owain winces. 'Were there casualties?'

'Unfortunately, yes.'

The ambassador flinches then passes the ancient relic back. 'I am late. Please make sure it is returned to its proper place. We need to talk this afternoon about what's still missing and what we tell the others when I meet them.'

5

NORTH BETHESDA, MARYLAND

Irish bangs on the apartment door for the second time. 'Police. Open up!'

He stands to the side and slips the safety off his gun. Sophie Hudson is only a store assistant at Goldman's but she called in sick on the day of the murder. If she's mixed up in this killing, anything might happen and Irish doesn't want that 'anything' to include a doped-up boyfriend with a spray-and-pray Mac-10.

There's a click. The door opens barely six inches.

A croaky voice spills through the crack. 'I'm not taking the chain off. Not until I see some ID.'

Irish flips out his badge and holds it to the gap.

She could be buying time. The killer might be climbing out a window and down a fire escape.

'C'mon lady, open the door, or I'll do it for you.'

The slab of cheap, blue-painted MDF closes and reopens without the chain. A small woman in a short nightdress steps back so he can come in. She's five six, a little plump and looks disorientated. Without make-up, her nose is Rudolph red and her long dark hair a mass of rats' tails.

'Sophie Hudson?'

'Yeah. What's this about?'

'Lieutenant Fitzgerald, Washington Homicide. You work at Goldman's in Kensington, right?'

'Right.' She's quick enough to add together Homicide and Goldman and realize it equals something bad. 'Is Mr Goldman okay?'

Irish goes Hawkeye. Now is the very second a killer or accomplice has to put on the best performance of their life.

'No, he's not. And he never will be. I'm sorry to say, he's dead.' He holds back the rest of the details.

Sophie's hand goes up to cover her open mouth. 'Oh, my God.' She stretches out a bunch of fingers to the arm of a sofa, steadies herself and then sits.

It seems she's forgotten she's in a short nightie and Irish sees more of a young woman than he's done for many a year.

The cop averts his eyes and walks to the back of the apartment. He runs water in the tiny galley kitchen and takes a tumbler to her.

'Thanks.' She looks dazed.

Seconds pass before she takes a drink and puts the glass on a side table. She pulls a tissue from a pink box with flowers on it and blows.

Irish can tell the cold is genuine. But that doesn't mean she wasn't involved in the crime. Even killers and accomplices come down with flu. He glances at his notebook. 'The answerphone in the store shows that you called Saturday around seven a.m. and said you were sick and couldn't make it in.'

She holds up a tissue. 'Been dying most of the weekend.' She is instantly horrified by her unintentional pun. 'I'm sorry. What happened to Mr Goldman?'

'He was murdered in his store.'

He watches her face for twitches and her hands for tension. 'So you were sick on Saturday but went in Friday. What time did you finish?'

'A little after four. He sent me home early because of the cold.' She bites a nail.

'That was kind of him.' Irish's tone hints that he still needs to be convinced she's telling the truth. 'Did anything happen during the day that was different, or anything strike you as unusual in any way?'

She hesitates and chews the last of a hangnail.

'He said he had some business happening. I guess he was referring to the cross that he bought.'

'What kind of cross? A Nazi cross? Wartime stuff?'

'No. Mr Goldman was Jewish. He wouldn't touch anything like that. This was Christian.'

'Catholic Christian or just Christian Christian?'

She gets to her feet. 'I made a drawing of it.' She goes to the back of her room and brings him a sheet of A3 notepaper from her bag.

Irish regards it with scepticism. 'Why did you sketch this?'

She looks embarrassed. 'Mr Goldman kept the cross from me and that made it intriguing. But he's forgetful. He sent me to the safe to get an item for a customer and I saw it. Only a glance, but it was interesting, so I made the drawing. It looks kinda weird, don't you think?'

Irish isn't thinking about the cross.

He'd missed the safe.

Hadn't seen one anywhere. Searched behind the counter, wall panels, back rooms, everywhere.

'You said "safe" – did you mean as in a lock-up box or a wall safe?'

She smiles for the first time since she heard the knock on the door. 'You couldn't find it?'

'No.'

'Mr Goldman would have been pleased. It's not a regular safe. It's fitted into a wall and hidden behind a panel in the grandfather clock.'

6

SAN MATEO, SAN FRANCISCO

Ruth Everett waters a long, wide bed of flowers at the front of her twenty-acre ranch. Through the spray rainbow, she sees the battered station wagon of her older sister raising dust at the end of the drive.

The two of them have always had an up-and-down kind of relationship, and since Mitzi moved in with her kids. Actually, it's been more down than up. She hopes it won't be long before they find a place of their own and she and Jack get their privacy back.

The two women share their mom's dark hair and good cheekbones, and these days pretty much the same 'fuller woman' body shape as the catalogues so kindly call it. But Ruth is tanned, toned and dresses like she has her own personal stylist, while Mitzi often looks like she got dressed in a thrift store.

Ruth watches the old car stop at the top of the drive, its long tail of brown dust wagging in the faultless blue sky. Her sister gets out and slaps the Ford's door shut. Birds scatter from trees and a rabble of butterflies desert a buddleia.

She locks off the yellow nozzle on the end of the hosepipe as she approaches. 'So how did it go?'

'Jury's out.' Mitzi looks tired. 'There's an ex-priest with OCD, some Italian glamour puss who's angling for a slap and a cute kid who makes crap coffee.' She takes off her unfashionable, police-issue shades.

'You being harsh?'

'Yeah, I probably am. I hope so, anyway.'

'How about I open a bottle of wine?'

'How about I jump in the air and click my heels?'

Ruth smiles and hands over the hosepipe. 'Spray a little while I get it.'

'Sure.' Mitzi twists the nozzle too much and decapitates several roses. 'Where are the girls?'

'They've gone into town with Jack to get stuff for a barbecue. I think they had it in mind to soft-soap their uncle into buying treats.'

'Yeah they would. That's the kind of sneaky thing my daughters do.'

Ruth drifts inside and Mitzi plays the water spray over the

yellow roses, pink chrysanths and startlingly blue ceanothus. It's a nice feeling. After living out here at 'South Fork', as she calls it, it's going to be hard moving the kids to the kind of shack they'll be able to afford. Still, they're holding things together and Jade is kicking up less than she used to. The first few months after she threw Alfie out were bad for everyone but especially Jade. She's always been closest to her dad and still misses him. As time goes by, Mitzi will probably let them visit the creep more, but right now one weekend a month is as much as she can stomach.

'Sis, you're still drowning things.' Ruth has reappeared with a glass of Sauvignon Blanc.

Mitzi twists the nozzle off and drops the hose. 'Sorry. I was never good with growing stuff.'

'You grew the girls good.'

She takes a glass from her and settles on a teak bench turned white by the sun. 'You think?'

'Yeah, I think.' Ruth clinks her bowl of golden wine against her sister's and sits beside her. 'I wish my fifteen years of marriage had two gorgeous kids in it.'

'Hey, you've got all this.' She waves a hand at the giant spread of land. 'And you can have my two any time you like.'

Ruth smiles. 'I guess so. What about you and your new home?'

'I scanned the papers today; there are a couple of places out at Serramonte and one across the San Mateo bridge that I'm going to fix to see at the weekend.'

'There's no rush.'

'Thanks. But I'm driving you nuts. I can tell. And I need to get the girls settled over the summer and into school for the new term.' She sees Jack's SUV kicking dirt at the end of the long drive. 'Looks like they're back.'

Both women take final sips of wine, then wander over to where the garages are.

The big Porsche Cayenne halts and the girls burst out the back doors swinging store bags.

'Uncle Jack bought us those trainers that we saw.' Amber opens her bag for her mom to see. 'Look, *Prada*.'

'They're *so* cool,' adds Jade.

Mitzi's in shock. She couldn't have afforded one pair, let alone two. 'That's real kind, Jack. You've spoiled them, thanks.'

'My pleasure. You got a big hug for your brother-in-law. How you doing?'

'I'm doing good.' She surrenders herself to his open arms and he pulls her a little too tight and intimate for her liking.

'Let's get that barbecue going,' grins Jack as they break. He picks four bags of groceries out of the back of the SUV and winks at Mitzi as he heads to the house.

7

ANTIQUES ROW, KENSINGTON, MARYLAND

It's early evening when Irish reaches the crime scene with Sophie Hudson. The streets have emptied and shadows on the tree-lined sidewalks softened.

The old man's body has been moved. The wet squad has scrubbed away the blood and cleared the blowflies.

A uniformed cop opens up for them. Beyond clouds of industrial-standard disinfectant, Irish still smells death.

Sophie wobbles slightly as they enter. He puts a reassuring arm around her. 'It's okay; we'll be outside again in no time – just open the safe for me.'

She nods and leans on him for support. The strange odours disorientate her. There's a sickly sweet smell she doesn't recognize. Irish feels her apprehension rise with every step.

Sophie stops and looks down. Areas of dark wooden boards near the counter are lighter than anywhere else. They've been washed. Scrubbed hard.

This is where the strange smell is coming from.

She can't go forward. Can't step nearer the place where *it* obviously happened.

Irish feels her go rigid. 'Come to the side. We can walk round. Don't look down. I'll watch out for you.'

She lets him waltz her stiffly to the skirting boards and behind the counter. Only when she's near the register does she realize she's been holding her breath. A long sigh escapes.

'You're doing really well, Sophie. Really well.' Irish can see the clock now. A grand casket of mahogany, with a face as white and cold as mortuary marble. There are minute and hour hands of black sculpted iron and a big brass pendulum swinging low.

Sophie gets down on her knees and flips open the tall oblong panel at the foot of the timepiece. Behind it is a small metal safe eighteen inches high by nine wide.

She types a six-number code on the keypad, hears a familiar click and pulls open the door. Inside are two pull-out shelves, each two feet long, extending beyond the back of the clock and into the part of the safe that is cemented into the load-bearing wall that the timepiece is bolted to.

Sophie lifts them out. She stands and puts the trays on the counter.

'It's not here.' She looks up at Irish. 'The cross has gone.'

8

BRITISH AMBASSADOR'S RESIDENCE, WASHINGTON DC

Scrupulously polished mirrors around the vast, opulent ballroom reflect the dazzlingly dressed figures of more than two hundred of the world's richest and most powerful people.

Sir Owain Gwyn insisted that his farewell is also a charity occasion, which is why movie stars, musicians, politicians, magazine editors, sportsmen and women have all paid $10,000 a ticket to attend the Ambassadorial Ball for the Disabled and the Homeless.

The deep bass of a brass gong draws eyes to the small stage where the Vice President of the United States, Connor Anderson awaits their attention.

'Don't worry, everybody, my speech is going to be *very* brief.' The fifty-year-old white-haired Texan lets the last of the noise subside before he continues. 'Sir Owain is leaving us, returning to the service of Her Majesty the Queen. On behalf of the American government and its people, I can't thank you enough for what you've done while you've been on duty here in our country. Your diplomacy and your hard work will be remembered forever.

'Sir, you have made a special relationship between our countries even more special. But you and I, and President Renton, who regrets that he cannot be here tonight, know that you have achieved even greater things that for security reasons we cannot speak of. Ladies and gentlemen, it is a sign of a truly exceptional man that what he does privately, without public credit, outshines the work that most of us do publicly and crave recognition for. Sir Owain Gwyn we raise our glasses to you; we thank you most sincerely for all you have done and wish you the greatest of success in your new posting back in your homeland.'

The room resounds with hearty toasts of 'Sir Owain!'

While the audience applauds, the vice president half-turns to an assistant and lifts from a velvet cushion a gold, white and red medal. 'On behalf of the United States Department of Defense, it is my honour to present you with this decoration, the Legion of Merit for exceptionally meritorious conduct in the performance of outstanding services and achievements.'

He holds aloft the rare neck order and even louder applause breaks out as the British knight stoops to duck his head into the loop of red ribbon.

It takes more than a minute for the clapping to stop.

The dark-haired diplomat cradles the medal, one of the highest ever awarded to a foreigner. 'Most unusually for a Welshman, I find myself stuck for words.' His soft brown eyes blink as camera flashes explode. 'I'll always treasure this and also the wonderful memories that at the end of tomorrow I will take back to Great Britain. I will leave behind a country that has become my second home and one I love dearly. The Gwyns have had ancestors here since the Mayflower docked. Rest assured that even when I am thousands of miles away, America and its great people will remain close to my heart. Thank you. Now enjoy yourselves.'

A band breaks into dance music and almost drowns the applause as he steps away from the small podium.

Gareth Madoc, who's also his right-hand man in the US, takes him to one side. He cups his hand to his mouth so no one can lip-read the news he breaks to the ambassador. 'We've just got new intelligence on a terror strike.'

'Where?'

'Here in America. New York, to be precise.'

Owain looks across the ballroom. 'Then I should stay and not fly back tomorrow. We can rearrange my meeting with the others.'

'No, it's important that you stick to your agenda.'

'Why?'

Madoc hesitates. 'There were complications with regards to the recovery of the relic.'

'The old man's death?'

'Yes. Believe me, it is best if you are out of the country as this unfolds.'

9

SAN MATEO, SAN FRANCISCO

The girls are finally asleep and Ruth and Jack have gone to bed.

Mitzi is in Miss Piggy PJs – a Christmas present – but not ready to rest. For the past two hours, she's gone back and forth on the witchcraft case. Donovan gave her a set of the case files and now she's word-blind. Nothing she looks at makes sense any more.

She creeps downstairs and runs a glass of chilled water from the dispenser on the front of the giant fridge fitted neatly in the corner of Ruth's lavish oak kitchen.

She takes her drink out onto the patio and hears crickets crackling in the darkness. Her presence triggers security lights that pick out the redwoods, giant sequoia and oaks standing sentry on the edges of the property. A vast tract of lawn is broken by a broad-leafed maple, some California laurels and a lot of Ruth's flowerbeds.

The patio door slides open. Jack stands there in just his boxers, hairy gut sagging over stretched elastic. 'Let me guess: you got so hot thinking about me you had to come out here to cool off?' He grins and sneaks down on a steamer chair next to her. A newly popped bottle of beer drips condensation in his meaty hand.

'You wish.' Mitzi hopes to hell he's not got anything stupid on his mind.

Jack stretches out and swigs the beer. 'You want some?'

She can tell he's still drunk from dinner and raises her glass of water. 'I'm good, thanks.' She gestures to the lawns. 'Your garden looks as pretty at night as it does in the day.'

He swings around on the steamer and catches her eye. 'So do you.'

Mitzi laughs him off. 'You've had too much to drink.'

He stretches out a hand and grabs hers. 'Seriously, Mitz.' I've always been attracted to you. Even when I met Ruthy, it was you I wanted to be with.'

She pulls her hand free and stands. 'I'm going to pretend I never heard that.'

He gets up and slips between her and the door. 'Why?

Don't tell me you don't feel the same way. I've seen how you look at me. How you've *always* looked at me.'

'Back off, Jack. All you've ever seen is what's in your mind.'

'Hey' – he sounds offended – 'a woman like you should be grateful for attention from a man like me.'

Mitzi can't believe her ears. 'What?'

He lumbers into her personal space, puts a hand to her cheek and breathes beer into her face. 'I've been good to you and your girls. No harm you being a little good back.' He pulls her close.

She flips her arms outward and pushes him away. 'This never happened.'

He grabs her again. 'But it should.'

Mitzi whips his wrist behind his back and slams him against the wall. She kicks out his right leg, so he's left spread-eagled and eating brickwork. '*Never* happened, Jack.' She pulls on his wrist and gets a grunt. 'You never said anything and you never ended up like this.' She kicks his leg wider until he face-slides down the wall.

The patio door makes a loud shushing noise as she slides it open, enters the vault of a lounge and slams it again. Before heading to the stairs, she takes one look back at the sorry heap out on the terrace and then heads to bed.

What she misses on the way up is her sister.

Ruth has been stood in the shadows of the lounge watching them both.

10

KENSINGTON, MARYLAND

Irish sits alone at the bar drinking whisky.

He can't be bothered to eat. Couldn't care less about going home.

What he wants is to get blind drunk.

He needs the alcohol to flush the toxins of murder out of his body. Clear his head of the images of the old man with his staring eyes and his opened-up stomach twitching with maggots. And he needs it quickly, before the fragile dam walls in his memory break and the other horrors burst through.

The ones from the black day.

It's eight years since he took a deep breath and lifted the lid of a crappy chest freezer in a suspect's basement. He'd expected the worst. Knew it would be bad. But nothing had prepared him for what lay inside.

'Again.' He slams the shot glass down. 'Double.'

The bartender knows better than to expect manners. Tomorrow or the next night, when Irish comes in sober, he'll tip him big and apologize. Which is more than most people do.

The cop raises a hand to acknowledge the arrival of another pale amber vial of Slaney Malt.

Everything is still too clear.

He welcomes the tingle of the ten-year-old whisky against

his lips. It goes down his throat like a trail of lit petrol then starts a comforting fire in his gut.

Sophie Hudson's face swims to mind – the moment when she realized the cross was missing. How can a man get killed for a crucifix? How much could it possibly be worth? Who would buy such a thing and what would they do with it?

He feels the start of a sneeze and grabs a handkerchief from his pocket. The explosion is so hard it leaves blood on the dirty cotton. Must have picked up a cold from the damned store clerk. It's the last thing he wants.

'Again.' Another bang of glass on wood.

The bartend gives him a dark look as he pours another.

'Amir Emmanuel Goldman.' Irish raises his refill high. 'God bless you and' – he grasps for something appropriate – 'and may your fucking lousy killer rot in hell.'

He throws back the whisky and bangs the glass down.

Now he waits. The shot hits his stomach like gasoline in a volcano. His head rocks. Vision blurs. Tongue goes numb.

Drunkenness. At last, it is coming. Horribly late. But like a much-loved friend, always welcome.

Irish pulls out a wad of dollars and peels off too much. He slaps it down. Climbs unsteadily off the stool pushed up against the long brown bar and heads for the door. He's going to make it.

The freezer lid has stayed closed. He'll survive another night.

11

WALES

The pull of the moon is strong.

Ebb and flow. Like the rush of a tide hitting a shoreline, then creeping back out to sea.

Myrddin feels the elemental shift as he arthritically descends the stairs in the ancient tower. His bare feet slap cold well-worn slabs. His thin and mottled hands scratch cotton-candy hair that covers his head and face in almost equal measure.

Once more he's been disturbed. Jarred from his sleep in the early hours. His mind filled with doubts and demons.

A rumbling cough breaks from his lungs and escapes as an echoing hack down the dark, stony passages.

He pushes open the heavy door to the Chamber of Prophecies and savours the oaky creak it makes and the clang of iron latch and lock as he closes it behind him.

This is his Chamber. Only he has ever come in here. Only he can divine the meaning of the visions that are channelled to this sacred spot. To the Font of Knowledge that stands on the tomb of the great one.

The musty midnight air is stirred by the swish of his long and lavishly decorated robe. His long fingers find the curved rim of the receptacle and he peers down into what seems an abyss.

The still liquid begins to tremble.

The augur sees shapes in the fractured surface, like clouds

blowing in a stormy sky, swirling and spinning, spiralling and disappearing. Clouds torn and eaten by a monstrous black bird with a stomach full of flesh and bones.

Beneath the drifting grey islands, there is a woman with two faces. She is near a great lake, hiding in silence behind a giant shield of wood, wanting to be found by one but not another. She is full of love and confusion, the sun of the heart at odds with the moon of the mind.

The old mystic's legs sag. He understands what the vision means. Knows who the woman is and whom she is going to betray. The consequences of the act are clear to him.

Darkness sucks oxygen from his lungs and starves his brain of thought. He slips shoulder first into the stone, then collapses onto the sacred tomb beneath it.

The world sways around him. He floats out into the blackness, like a small boat pulled from shore by the tides of an ocean.

12

HRU CRIMES UNIT, SAN FRANCISCO

Most of the city is still sleeping when Mitzi heads in to work.

She likes that she missed the rush hour. The great red bridge is almost empty and all the more magnificent for it.

Most of all, she likes that she's not starting her day with an awkward face-off with Jack.

She spent most of the night wondering if she should tell her sister. But tell her what? That her husband was drunk and made a pass? That he said he'd always preferred her to Ruth? Either of those things was likely to end their marriage and create a rift between her and Ruth.

Hopefully, he got the message.

She takes a coffee to her desk and starts up the desktop PC. Her mailbox is jammed with spam and a couple of messages from ex-colleagues wishing her the best in the new job.

Before she starts work, she browses the *Huffington Post*. It has features on 'Bondage for Beginners', 'Ten Reasons Why Women Like Bad Boys' and 'How Wearing Rubber Knickers Can Help You Lose Weight'. She works back to front, dismissing the pants story out of hand – she'd have to wear a truck tyre to lose the amount of weight she wants to. Bad boys are the last people she needs in her life. And she's damned sure she doesn't want her wrists wrapped up in cling film while some masked stranger spanks her with fifty-dollar paddles.

About an hour later, there are noises in the corridor.

Eleonora breezes in with wet hair and no make-up. She's dressed head-to-toe in Fendi. A tailored military jacket in jade, and matching beltless pants cling to every perfect inch of her legs. A zesty yellow top is paired with a structured handbag in the same striking colour. She's on her phone and drops a retro Diadora gym bag beside her desk while she talks intently.

Mitzi silently curses. It's just not right that Eleonora looks that good.

The Italian finishes and glances across the desks. '*Buongiorno*, 'itzi. How are you?'

'It's Mitzi. M for motherfucker, then *itzi*. M-M-M-itzi.'

Eleonora laughs. 'I am sorry. M for M-itzi. How are you?'

'I'm good. Now let me guess, you've been to the gym and you're feeling absolutely amazing.'

'No, I feel like shit. I always do after gym. Did you know Michelle Obama goes at four-thirty a.m. every day?'

'I don't even want to think about four-thirty, let alone go anywhere at that time.'

Eleonora fingers her wet hair. 'Guess I look a mess, yes?'

'I wish I could say yes, but you look like you're just about to strip off and model for *Sports Illustrated*.'

'That's a magazine?'

'It's a magazine. Guys say they buy it for the articles, but they're not fooling anyone.'

A flash of mischief illuminates Eleonora's face. 'Aah, now I understand. Men, they are such simple animals.' She grabs her purse. 'I am going to the restroom, then maybe I buy coffee before I meet Bronty. You want to come with us?'

'Where are you going?'

'Bronty called last night. He met a priest who introduced him to someone in the Church of Satan and he knows our dead woman, Rea Masters.'

'Knows as in sexually?'

'No. I don't think so. Though of course it is possible. Bronty said Rea started in the Church of Satan then found herself at odds with the grotto she joined.'

'Grotto? You make it sound like Santa Claus.'

Eleonora sits on the edge of her new colleague's desk. 'That is what they call the covens, or lodges. You know the Church of Satan's founder lived not far from here. For maybe thirty years it was run from San Francisco.'

'Anton LaVey. He wrote the Satanic Bible, right?'

'*Si*. After he died the Church switched to New York.'

'Hell's Kitchen?' jokes Mitzi.

Eleonora misses the pun. 'You want to come with us?'

'Yeah, thanks, I'd like to ride along.'

The office door opens and Donovan sticks her head in. 'Got a job for you, Fallon.'

'I thought I had a job – this witchcraft case?'

Her boss hands over a sheet of paper. 'This has got your name all over it. Just in from Washington.'

Mitzi takes the paper and looks at it. 'What is this? Some kind of cross?'

'Congratulations. I see why you made lieutenant and why you're so valuable to HRU. It's a cross that has been linked to a murder. The detective in charge has asked for our help. I said you'd be on the redeye and arrive tomorrow.'

'That could be a problem. I need to fix childcare.' She nods to the two girls in the photo on her desk.

'It *won't* be a problem,' says Donovan. 'Life fits around the job, not the other way round. Fracci and Bronty are working Masters, so you had better be on that plane – or find yourself another squad.'

13

WALES

The stone of the chamber floor makes for a cold pillow, but Myrddin gladly endures it until he feels some strength creep back into his limbs.

The seer's head throbs and his bones crackle with arthritis as he gets to his feet. He knows what has to be done. His task is far from finished.

Myrddin eyes the Font of Knowledge, aware of the dangers it contains. For many years, the ancient receptacle has drained his energy and spirit. It has taken from him and given to him in equal measures. Each experience has left him fuller in mind and less in body.

He grips the bowl of the font. Braces himself for what is to come, tilts his head back and closes his eyes. 'I am here, old friend. Standing firm and tall, ready for you again. Write your page of history and leave me fit to carry it to the fingers of the world, that they may turn it and move on.'

The stone he holds trembles. A slight vibration at first, then a deep rumble. A growing thunder beneath Myrddin's feet. Then the energy. Different this time: not slow and building. A sudden jolt. Electrifying. His mind fills with white. Snow white. Virgin white. Angelic white.

The vision comes.

A baby who becomes a man who becomes immortal. A child who grows faster and stronger than any human ever has. A young man who faces the world with the wisdom of a centenarian.

Myrddin knows this man.

He sees him surrounded by people but alone. He is caught in a moment of doubt. Trapped between the holiest and unholiest of men. He is troubled by two women. One very much known to him and one a complete stranger. Both are in danger; both will see death.

Death. This time the old foe comes with a long list. He seeks out brothers and sisters, men and women. Seeks them out randomly and specifically. Some for good reason, others just for the joy of seeing their blood in the snow.

The pure white snow.

It's falling now. At first, just flakes on the seer's flushed cheeks. Cool, like the kiss of a maiden. Now heavier. Splashes of icy rain, chilly enough to start the shivers.

An avalanche.

A deadly whiteout erupts inside the seer's mind. Knocks him to the ground. Covers him. Buries him. Suffocates him. His hands slip from the font and he stumbles backward. This time he doesn't fall. The vision is complete. He understands and knows what he must do.

A new phase of the Arthurian Cycle has begun.

14

KENSINGTON, MARYLAND

Twenty-three-year-old Dwaine Velez wishes he'd taken a leak before he got in his Ford Wagon.

If that little bitch's pops hadn't turned up shouting the odds 'bout *the sanctity of his daughter* he'd have been able to use their goddamned bathroom. Instead, he ended up hopping down the drive with one leg in his pants and the rest of his clothes thrown all over the shrubs.

Un-fucking-dignified. That's what it was.

Still, it had been worth it. She was a peach. These girls out in the sticks don't get much action and when they do – man, they make the most of it.

He heads south down Connecticut Avenue, back towards

the Capital Beltway, dark eyes scanning for a place to pull over. Jay-Z is rapping on the radio – 'Bring it On' from *Reasonable Doubt*, the album that propelled him from being a punk who'd put a cap in his brother, to one of the world's most bankable music stars.

Dwaine drums fingersticks on the steering wheel and gets thinking. 'Hey fella, I sure as hell would like to teach your lady some tricks. That Beyoncé has one fine booty.'

The song hits the chorus and the voice from the radio answers.

The young contractor laughs. 'I can hang. Man, can I hang. And bro', let me tell you, no way would she ever come back to you after she's spent a night with me.'

Up on the left he spots some trees, and maybe the last chance to relieve himself before rolling out west to help fix some drains in McLean then on to a backed-up septic tank just north of Washington.

What a life. Eat your heart out, Jay-Z.

He parks on Beach Drive, crosses the near-deserted carriage to a clump of trees and a long track called Rock Creek Trail.

Dwaine is desperate. The burly six-footer is spraying overgrown grass within a split-second of getting his fly down. Every time he thinks he's going to stop, another round of tequila shots and bottled water comes from somewhere.

Must be the sex. Sex always makes him pee like he's a fire hose.

A thought hits him. A bad one. He hopes to hell that bitch

hasn't given him something *nasty*. Dwaine looks down at the boiling soil.

'Fuck, man!'

The shock is so much he wets his legs. He stumbles backwards. Staring up, through a thin layer of puddled earth, is a man's face.

He's been pissing on a dead guy.

15

ENGLAND

A windy six-hour flight from Washington brings Owain Gwyn back to British soil, or, to be more precise, the blacktop runway at Heathrow.

A VIP escort team meets him airside and whisks him through diplomatic channels to his waiting helicopter. The armour-plated Bell is quickly in the air, covering the one hundred and thirty miles west to his country estate in Somerset at a cruising speed of more than two hundred and fifty miles an hour.

From the window of the ten-million-pound thirteen-seater, he watches the deep green of the lush English countryside slide beneath him. Mile by mile his spiritual connection renews. By the time he sees the Somerset Levels he feels whole again.

Glastonbury.

No other town triggers so many mystical associations.

The Isle of Glass. Joseph of Arimathea. The Holy Grail.

As the former British Ambassador to America looks down upon Glastonbury Tor, tales of history and legend blur in his mind. This is said to be Avalon, the place where Excalibur was forged. Where Arthur, the warrior king, was brought after being savagely wounded in battle by his mortal enemy, Mordred. Where some believe he died and others maintain he was 'born again' and rose to become immortal.

The helicopter circles a grand estate and begins its cautious descent. Owain Gwyn is back where he belongs, where his ancestors fought and died for freedom and Christianity. Back home.

He checks his phone as the descent begins. He has several missed messages but there is only one that truly interests him.

The one from Myrddin.

16

ROCK CREEK TRAIL, MARYLAND

Booze seeps through Irish's bloated pores as he stands over the buried corpse. He uses his stained hanky to wipe alcohol slick from his forehead.

The crime scene is only a mile from Amir Goldman's

store. Given that the most exciting thing this hick-town settlement ever sees is the traffic signal changing, he's willing to bet his pension that they're connected. Not that his pension's worth that damned much.

For once, he's arrived at a scene ahead of the ME and has already briefly interviewed the guy who apparently came here for a leak and splashed more than his feet.

He takes out a small camera bought more than a decade ago, with half the pixels of the one built into the new-fangled smartphone that he doesn't know how to use. He shoots off three-sixty degrees' worth of surrounding shots so he can always revisit the body and scene. CSIs will get better ones, but the process of doing it opens up his mind.

Irish concentrates harder than a chess player and picks his way around the scene, careful not to trample evidence underfoot, shift bushes, or knock any trace from thorns or branch snags.

Through the lens, the dead guy's head looks like a dropped paper plate on the grey-brown soil. He's been buried in the shallowest of shallow graves, face up, along a rough track that cuts through a copse of trees starting near the rest stop. There's not enough flesh above ground to tell much about who he was. Dark hair. Hazel eyes. A big nose that he probably got teased about at school. He was probably mid- to late-twenties with fifty years still to burn.

The way Irish figures it, this is the only place the killer could have sunk him. The roots of nearby trees and bushes are too big for anyone to dig either left or right. It's hurried and messy. Whoever did it was hoping the burial would buy him time. Meaning he's not local and is long gone.

Even though the cop's head is pounding from a hangover, he has a good idea of what's gone down. The antique store had been a two man job. After the old man's death they'd stopped and rowed. Things got out of hand and one killed the other.

Irish picks up boot prints: deep heel marks made in soft soil. Deep because the victor was carrying the body of the loser. He sees two drag lines. Parallel tracks right up to the shallow grave. And another set of footprints, smaller than the boots made by the poor schmuck who found the body.

Irish walks past the body. The path loops back onto the road and he can see a single set footprints heading that way.

The killer's.

17

SAN MATEO, SAN FRANCISCO

Jade and Amber are playing Swingball on the lawn when Mitzi pulls up. They're belting the roped ball at each other and splitting their sides laughing as it lashes back around the centre pole and they swipe at nothing.

'I'll play the winner,' shouts their mom, as she carries a bunch of flowers from her car towards the back door of her sister's house.

'It'll be me,' boasts Jade.

'No way,' Amber adds a Williams-sisters grunt to her backhand return.

Mitzi finds Ruth in the kitchen chopping vegetables. Red, yellow and green peppers cover a butcher-block island. 'Hi honey, I'm home!' she jokes.

The look on her sister's face confirms her suspicions that this is going to be a tense meeting. 'I brought you some flowers. Lilies – of some kind. I don't know which, but they're pretty.' She offers the bunch of purple, pink and cream trumpets.

'They're Longiflorum and Aurelian hybrids. Thanks.' Ruth opens a cupboard door, brings out a vase with a wide fluted neck and fills it three-quarters with water. 'You were out early this morning.'

'Yeah. First day at work had my head spinning.' Mitzi takes a beat then plunges into the big request. 'They want me to go to Washington to help on a murder. Would you mind looking after Jade and Amber for a couple days, till I get back?'

Ruth looks around for scissors. 'When do they want you to go?'

'Kinda now. Late flight tonight, gets me there at stupid o'clock in the morning.'

She finds the scissors in the dishwater, cuts the flower stems at a slant and drops them into the vase. 'I saw you.'

'Saw me where?'

'Last night, with Jack. I saw you both.'

Mitzi turns cop and goes on the front foot. '*And*?'

'Huh, is that all you can say? *And*?'

'*And*'s a reasonable question—'

'It's not a question; it's a conjunction.' She slams the scissors down on the marbled worktop. 'I saw Jack pawing you.'

Mitzi waves a dismissive hand. 'He was drunk, Ruth. Men paw when they're drunk. They paw anything. Shit, if you'd had a dog and it had been up on the back porch instead of me, he'd have most likely pawed the hound instead.'

'I didn't just *see* you – I heard you as well.'

'Good. Then, you heard exactly what I said to him. I told him he was drunk and should behave. That was it. Nothing happened and I went to bed.'

'Nothing? You threw him at the wall.'

'Yeah, well, he'll live.' She moves towards her sister. 'Don't make too much out of this. Man plus drink equals something stupid. Every time.'

Ruth is in a bad place, doubts circle her marriage like buzzards over road kill. 'I heard him say how he'd always liked you.' Her voice slips towards a sob. 'Liked you more than me and—'

'Jeez, Ruthy, give this up!' Mitzi holds her by the shoulders. 'When guys are juiced, they say all kinds of shit. You know that. It's a lesson learned on prom night and remembered every time you walk in a bar or club. Right?'

She nods. 'Still, it's best you go. I'll look after the girls while you're away, but when you come back, I don't want you staying here. I want you out, Mitzi. I'll pay for a motel – anything – but I don't want you under my roof again, not anywhere near my husband.'

18

ROCK CREEK TRAIL, MARYLAND

Soil falls in clumps from the corpse as the ME's team lift it out of the shallow grave and rest it respectfully on a thick plastic sheet.

Irish squints to get his first full look at the vic. He has dark hair and is well-built. He's dressed in a blue linen jacket, faded denims, a white T-shirt with the word DIESEL across the chest and ankle-length suede boots. His skin has been paled by death – dried out, cracked and creased by mud and earth.

Cherrie Archer, the examiner who worked Amir Goldman's case, uses a soft brush to clear insects from dead eyes. She looks up at the detective and anticipates his question. 'Right now, all I can tell you is what you can see. He's male, late twenties, well-nourished, around a hundred and seventy pounds. Looks perfectly fit and healthy, except for being strangled to death.'

'No gun or knife?'

'Not that I see.'

Irish had expected a weapon. 'Did the unsub use a ligature?' He works his way around the pit so he can stand next to her and the body.

'I don't think so. The body's quite dirty, though.' She leans across and inspects the neck from several angles. 'I can't see any ligature marks, but look here . . . ' She points. 'There's bruising, abrasion, as though he's been held from behind in a very strong choke hold.'

Irish bends over the corpse. 'I see it. How would it have been done?'

'Stand up and turn away from me.'

He does as he's told.

Up close, Irish's odour of sweat and alcohol is worse than the corpse's. She ignores it while she uses her right arm to demonstrate a v-shaped lock on him. 'The assailant probably jammed his head in the crook of his arm and then swung him up and over his hip.' She leans a little so Irish can feel the choke.

'Whoa, whoa, enough. I get it!'

She lets go. 'You okay?'

'Yeah.' He rubs his neck.

'Hold a person long enough like that and they choke out. Keep doing it and they die.' She moves back to the body. 'I used to be a soldier. Learned close-combat skills along with medicine in the Marine Corps.'

'I see.' Irish carries on nursing his neck. 'I guess not many guys took first dates too far with you, then?'

'Not many.'

He turns his head left and right to free the cricks in his neck. 'You got any gloves? I want to go through his pockets.'

She dips into her coveralls and produces a spare vinyl pair. 'Are you sure you're okay? You look pretty pale.'

'Yeah, I'm fine. Apart from being half-killed by you, I picked up a cold, that's all.' Irish stretches the gloves and works his fingers inside. Truth is he feels weak as a kitten and wants to sleep for a year.

The vic's jeans yield a squashed carton of cigarettes, a

Zippo lighter, sticks of gum and the corner of a newspaper. There is a Washington phone number written on it. Irish pulls out his cell and calls it. The techies told him there's a facility to record calls but he can't remember how to do it.

The call beeps out and trips a message service.

An old voice, slow and precise, rolls down the line. 'This is Amir Goldman; I'm not available to take your call. Please leave a message after the tone – and be sure to visit our showroom in Kensington, the antiques capital of DC.'

Irish hangs up and looks at the scrap of paper. The dead man lying in front of him no doubt called Amir to check he was in the store. Then he turned up and killed him. 'I need this bum's prints, ASAP.' He peels off his gloves and dumps them on the sheet. 'Thanks, doc.'

19

THE BRONX, NEW YORK

Nabil stinks of garage grease. He hates the smell almost as much as he hates America.

It rides with him now, an unwelcome passenger in the cab of the white flatbed truck that he's 'borrowed' from work to get home. Even in here, he can't get away from it.

The twenty-four-year-old parks outside a verminous

brownstone apartment block and climbs filthy stairs to the sixth floor. There's no point trying the lift; he can't remember when it last worked – doubts it ever will again.

He lets himself in to his short-term rental and slams the door so hard it makes the frame tremble. Hopefully, it pisses off the old guy next door who beats on the paper-thin wall every night.

He goes straight to the squalid kitchen, pulls a ready meal of Mac and Cheese from the refrigerator, forks the top and puts it in the microwave. While it cooks, he sticks his phone to his ear and speed-dials the only number on the handset.

'It's Nabil. I'm home.'

That's all he says. All he ever says when he enters the apartment.

But it's enough. It's what's expected of him. A coded phrase to let them know he's alive.

Safe.

Not captured or killed.

20

GLASTONBURY, ENGLAND

Gwyn's ivy-covered stately home has ten bedrooms, two dining rooms, a library, drawing room, study, orangery, two reception and living rooms, a ballroom, gymnasium, indoor and outdoor pools and more than thirty acres of heavily fortified and constantly guarded grounds.

He and his wife have a live-in chef, who has previously held two Michelin stars. All vegetable produce is grown in the house's gardens, fish comes from the private lakes and meat and poultry from the estate's farmland. It's quite a place to come home to.

Outside the mansion's great arched entrance door are the figures of waiting footmen and his wife, Jennifer. Lady Gwyn's waist-length blonde hair is being blown by the down draft of helicopter blades and her silky amber dress sparkles in the bright sunlight.

Within moments of the copter's door being opened, Owain's in her arms. Holding. Kissing. Reconnecting.

She takes his hand and hurries him inside, away from the noise of the dying motors.

'There's a call,' she says in the quiet shade of the marbled hall. 'It's from Gareth, he says he couldn't get through while you were in the air.'

He takes it on an encrypted phone.

'I'm sorry not to give you any time with Jennifer,' says Madoc. 'I've just had a message from Antun. Things are changing. The cell commander is nervous. A target has been fixed.'

'Does he know where and when?'

'Wall Street, tomorrow.'

'Wall Street? Are you sure?'

'I'm sure. More importantly, he's sure. I'm going to send

you the details of where they're plotting up, so you can talk to the Americans.'

Owain checks his watch. 'I've got the Inner Circle meeting in an hour.'

'It'll be after that.' He takes a long pause. 'Are you going to tell them everything?'

'I have to, Gareth. We have no option. Our old "friend" has left us with no choice but to issue the mandate.'

21

KENSINGTON, MARYLAND

Irish is at the bar; a bottle of beer and a whisky chaser stand at his elbow.

Two women in their forties sit on stools around him, glasses of white wine in their hands.

Sarah Cohen has short brown hair and a wide mouth. Suzie Clark is a bleached blonde with strong blue eyes. They work stores either side of Goldman Antiques and for the past hour Irish has been buying drinks in return for information.

'I was away when those uniformed police came by,' explains Sarah. 'Getting my things from my *ex*'s place.' She emphasizes the past tense. 'Which means I'm available.'

'Not for long, I'm very sure.' Irish lays on a little charm as he eases a notebook out of his jacket. 'So tell me again what you saw on the night Amir died.'

'I was going away Saturday morning. Had the day off and was headin' to Atlantic City for a birthday party. I saw a man come out of Amir's around ten-thirty p.m. and shut the door behind him.'

'Why did that catch your eye?'

'Coz he pushed on the handle to check it was locked properly. Like you'd do if you own the place.'

Irish writes before he asks the next question. 'And how did you say he looked?'

'Handsome,' she says. 'Muscular. Tender side of thirty.' Her face lights up while she pictures him. 'Tall and clean-shaven, very dark hair. Looked real nice.'

'Did you notice what he was wearing?'

She thinks for a minute. 'Blues. A blue jacket and jeans. Not a jean jacket, something smarter.'

Irish takes a swallow of his beer. The description fits the stiff dug up in the woods. 'What'd he do then?'

'Crossed the road, got into a big brown car and pulled away.'

Suzie taps her on the arm. 'Tell him 'bout the noise.'

She obliges. 'There wasn't any.'

'Probably an 'lectric vehicle,' adds Suzie, keen to prove she's worth her free drinks. 'One of those high-breeds.'

'You mean hybrids,' says Irish. He turns back to Sarah. 'You see the make, or recognize the type?'

She shakes her head. 'I'm not good with cars. Not like I am with men. It was a big, boxy thing.'

'Probably an SUV,' suggests Suzie authoritatively. 'Sports Utility Vehicle.'

'Thanks,' says Irish. 'I know what SUV means.'

'I watched it go,' adds Sarah. 'A few seconds later a car started and drove after it. Took me clean by surprise because it hadn't any lights on. It was silver. Like a limousine but not as big.'

Irish downs his whisky shot. 'Like a pimp's car?'

Sarah pulls a sour face. 'No. Classier. It had one of those glass roofs. I could see street lights reflecting on it when it drove off.'

'Two or four doors?'

She has to think. 'Four.' Something occurs to her. 'Oh, and I might be wrong on this, but the licence plate was weird.'

'How so? You mean out-of-state plates?'

She looks embarrassed. 'It sounds stupid now. Forget I spoke. I'm really not sure I'm right and don't want to say the wrong thing.'

'Say it,' urges Irish.

'I don't think it was a DC plate. I'm not even sure it was American.'

He waves the barman over and makes a final note. An out-of-state plate spells only one thing.

Trouble.

The kind that can be near-on impossible to investigate.

22

GLASTONBURY, ENGLAND

A swarm of helicopters cover the sprawling green grounds. Chauffeured cars crunch the long gravelled drive. Armed guards shadow eleven men and women into the stately home and usher them through cool, marbled corridors to a door marked Wine Cellar.

Two former SAS men flank the big black slab of oak. They check credentials before allowing anyone to descend the stairs. Once below ground the visitors use fingerprint- and retina-identification systems to enter a huge windowless and bombproof room.

At the centre of the secure space is an ancient, circular table. It is marked with heraldic crests and Christian symbols. The circle itself is more than just a design that ensures no one has prominence – it is a Eucharistic symbol: a representation of the holy host.

The delegates of the Secret and Sacred Order of Arthurians take their places.

They are all highly successful executives, CEOs and owners of philanthropic businesses that also fund the SSOA. The organization is dedicated to peace, freedom and an endless fight against terrorism and evil.

Like Britain, the country where it is headquartered, the SSOA is governed by two distinct authorities, one chosen and one hereditary. Today's meeting is of the Inner Circle – an operational body made up of chosen delegates. They have been picked, not only because of their immense wealth and power, but also because they are so passionate about the central aims of the SSOA that they are willing to die – or kill – for them.

While the Inner Circle formulates and implements policy, it can't do so without reference to a much larger and even older authority.

The Blood Line.

The BL is comprised of members who are direct descendants of the Knights of the Round Table.

Beneath these two bodies, is a hidden army of modern-day knights. A secret force, spread internationally. Recruited almost exclusively from national military and intelligence bodies. Its uniform is the anonymity of every day clothes and its camouflage that of suburbia and average life.

Today's agenda, like the briefing paper, is written in Arthurian Code. The rotational cipher was created centuries ago on two wooden wheels marked with letters and numbers. The outer contained numbers and the inner letters. The base code would always be A and 1. But every day someone would spin the wheels and then record the random number that matched A. So if A aligned with 6, then the day's code would be known as Plus Six. Modern Arthurians have special digital token codes that need alphanumeric logins to retrieve the pass codes of any documents sent to them.

Circle secretary Lance Beaucoup, reads the minutes of the

last meeting. He is mid-thirties, tall, dark-haired with the broad shoulders of a swimmer and the waist of a gymnast. His voice has a Gallic lilt.

'Does anyone wish to comment?' asks Owain.

The room is silent.

'Then take them as passed, Lance.'

There's an awkward silence. One filled with expectancy and fear.

The Frenchman continues, 'We come to the issue of our *trusted* colleague. Our absent friend.'

All eyes fall on the empty twelfth seat at the table.

'It is now clear,' says Owain, 'that Angelo Marchetti has broken from our order. He has a secret life beyond his secret life. One of gambling, cocaine and crime. Angelo has been siphoning off money. His own accounts have been forged and he is personally bankrupt.'

Mutterings break out.

'Please – I haven't finished.' He waits until silence has been restored. 'He has stolen several artefacts from the Order and may have fled the country. From what we have been able to discover, he used local crooks to sell a number of burial crosses that he himself had looted. A religious dealer of dubious repute in America was approached and he acquired one cross. He was killed two days ago by Marchetti's men. We aren't sure why.

'We now have a complication,' continues Owain. 'I've harboured suspicions about Angelo for a while so had him followed the last few weeks.' He nods across the table to a young Englishman. 'George tailed his men as they drove away from the dealer's in Maryland. He'll tell you the rest.'

George Dalton, a slightly built man with a trimmed dark beard and pale blue eyes, gives his account of what happened. 'After the killing, two men left the scene. They stopped on the outskirts of Kensington and went into a copse. Only one of them came out. He drove south and pulled in at an all-night diner about a third of a mile east of Dupont Circle. I watched him eat at a booth by the window. When he returned to the car I tackled him. Unfortunately, he was more skilled an adversary than I expected and had a knife.' George raises his arm to show his bandaged hand and wrist. 'I'm afraid it was a very close-quarters encounter and he was killed. I recovered a Knight's Cross from the glove compartment of his car.'

Owain interrupts. 'There are still two crucifixes missing and possibly other artefacts that we don't yet know about. We presume Angelo has now lost faith in his minions and is personally trying to sell the crosses. I think we can all guess to whom he will eventually turn and what the consequences of that could be.'

Fresh mutterings break out and Lance takes this as his cue. 'As of this moment, Angelo Marchetti is expelled from our Order and we are issuing an alert for his capture and permanent exile. You should put whatever bounty you wish on his head and treat this as a matter of utmost urgency.'

Owain sees their sadness. The man with a death warrant

on his head had been a friend and comrade to them for many years and his betrayal is hard to believe. 'Be in no doubt – Angelo poses the biggest threat to our existence for centuries. Do not hesitate to act resolutely in this matter. We have no room for forgiveness, emotion or error. Strike swiftly; our chance may come but once.'

23

INDIANA AVENUE, WASHINGTON DC

Police HQ is an imposing slab of sandstone and glass set among a collection of other similarly striking buildings that belong to the fire and justice departments, the district court and Department of Labor.

Up on the command corridor, the name etched on a door halfway down says CPT. ZACH FULO. Irish raps on it.

'C'm'in!' The words are spat out by a voice of grit and glue.

The cop opens the door and hesitantly steps inside.

A lean black man looks up from a desk layered in paperwork. 'Take a seat, Lieutenant; you're late.'

'Traffic was bad out of Maryland. Sorry for the delay.'

'Traffic's bad everywhere. A guy your age should have learned that by now.' His dark eyes tip to a document in his manicured hands. 'HRU – that's Historic Religious and Unsolved, right?'

'Yes, sir.'

'What the hell they doing asking about one of our cases?' He holds up the paper.

Irish stares at the FBI badge and realizes one of the top brass there must have written to him. 'I asked them, sir. Given this has since kicked up into a double homicide I thought it it might be wise.'

'No, Lieutenant. *Wise* would be asking me first. *Really wise* would have been solving the case already.' He screws up the paper and throws the ball at him. 'You're an idiot, Fitzgerald. Just in case you're in any doubt, idiots are at the opposite end of the spectrum to the wise.'

'Captain, this crime is linked to some old cross that's probably a valuable artefact. The HRU has the infrastructure to help us work all that out and find the kind of unsub prepared to kill for that kind of thing.'

'Me. I'm prepared to kill. And guess who my victim's likely to be? Now get outta here. I want a full report on my desk by seven in the morning, so don't get too wasted tonight.'

Irish hauls his injured pride out of the captain's office and back to his desk.

He pulls open the bottom drawer and grabs a box of tissues. The cold Sophie Hudson passed on still has him honking snot and blood. He sticks a wad of tissues in his pocket and pulls out the second thing he's after.

Scotch.

He unscrews the top of his emergency bottle and takes a long swallow of the cheap whisky. Doesn't stop until he feels its hot fingers choking his throat. Then he screws the top back, drops the bottle in his drawer and kicks it shut.

The office is deserted. A gap between shifts. He powers up the computer and finds what he hoped for in his mailbox.

A message from Traffic.

He'd told his old friend Billy Puller about the murder he was working was in woods off the south end of Rock Creek Trail, close to where the east-west Capital Beltway crosses Connecticut Avenue. He said he was interested in any brown SUVs and silver saloons that hit that intersection from ten p.m. onwards on Friday night. Ten being the earliest time the ME thought Amir Goldman could have died.

By the time he's read the first line of Bill's mail, his heart's already flipping.

Irish – we searched traffic cams and found a brown Cadillac Escalade hybrid heading south to Washington, followed a few cars back by a silver Lincoln. They were timed joining the southbound interstate at 11.04.32 and 11.04.47 respectively. Vid tech has strung together some clips for you (see attachment). Both vehicles come off north of Dupont Circle and then we lose them.

Couldn't make out the plate on the Lincoln. The Escalade has a cloned registration – rightful owner is in Annandale.

Call me – I'll give you full details.

Hope it helps,

BP

Irish opens the attachment and presses play.

The footage is good quality. An Escalade heads down a slip road. The overhead camera shows the driver. He's alone. Late-thirties, maybe early-forties. Clean-shaven. Broad. Light hair.

Five cars back, a Lincoln pulls out to the middle lane, stays there and doesn't zip on by. The kind of thing you do when you're following someone and don't want to be noticed.

Irish studies the traffic. The Escalade is doing about sixty. So is the Lincoln. He sure as hell is tagging him.

No sooner do the Dupont signs come on screen, than they both indicate and take their wagon train off the interstate and out of view.

Irish digs out the Scotch for a celebratory belt then rewinds the footage and plays it from the top. This time he sees the small stuff. The Escalade is badged as a hybrid and the Lincoln has a panoramic glass roof. Both vehicles fit with the descriptions Sarah Cohen gave him but the driver of the Escalade doesn't. He has light hair. The victim in the woods was dark-haired. This must have been the driver parked up outside Amir's store and the winner of whatever altercation broke out when they drove off after Goldman's murder.

Irish figures that, given the timing of the footage, the guy he's looking at on screen is almost certain to be the killer.

The Lincoln comes into view again. It's an expensive model. One of the new ones.

'Ho–lee shit.' He hits pause. 'Rule Friggin' Britannia.'

A broad smile breaks out across his face as he stares at what is unmistakably a diplomatic plate.

24

VIRGINIA

The second semi-final of *America's Got Talent* is playing on the new fifty-inch flat-screen in the family lounge. Sword-swallowing dwarves compete with gymnastic nuns for a place in the last show. TV doesn't get better than this.

At least not when your brain is aching from stress and all you want to do is sit in front of the tube with a drink and snacks.

Ron Briars has had a rough day. Right now he's wondering if he should have got 3D as a bigger reward for all that hard labour.

Sixty-inch, 3D, internet equipped. Home cinema, surround sound. Sport certainly would have been a blast on that baby.

But – as usual – he'd given in to his wife's demands and settled for something a bit smaller. More fitting with the layout of the room, the French windows and fireplace. Not that either him or his teenage son can even begin to understand how the fireplace or windows have anything to do with a TV.

Ron's cell phone rings.

Wife and child stare accusingly at the BlackBerry as it rudely buzzes and flashes on the side table next to his iPhone and almost empty glass of French red.

Not many people have the number and those that do are very important. White House-important. Chief of Staff- or even President-important.

Ron smiles apologetically, gets up and takes the offending phone to the den. A glance at the display shows the caller has withheld the number.

The head of the National Intelligence Agency answers with caution. 'Hello.'

'Tole Mac.' The voice is calm and measured, almost without accent but clearly British. 'That's Tango. Oscar. Lima. Echo. Mike. Alpha. Charlie.'

Seven letters and two words agreed by the NIA and the party on the line as a means of identity verification.

The caller is a trusted source. About as trusted as they come.

The principal security advisor to the President of the United States reaches quickly for pen and paper. 'Clearance noted. Please, go on.'

'Denny's Garage and Body Shop, opposite Leonard Gordon Park in Jersey. You have between midnight tonight and sunrise. No later. Four men are sleeping inside with enough explosives to rip up half of New York. One entrance, a roller door and it is alarmed. We wish you good luck.'

25

GLASTONBURY, ENGLAND

The Inner Circle disbands and the armour-plated helicopters and cars disperse.

Only Beaucoup and Dalton stay behind. They're working closely on leads relating to the missing crosses and whereabouts of Angelo Marchetti.

Owain and his wife dine alone. Not in the plush summer room that overlooks the croquet lawn, or in the conservatory that opens out to the rose gardens and southern lake.

They eat in the wild. Out at the summit of Glastonbury Tor, where the sun sets cherry-red across the soft, green, rolling hills.

Hundreds of feet beneath them, armed guards patrol the hill and ensure the couple have their brief moment of privacy. Anyone wishing to climb the very public place will be politely paid off with whatever it takes – thousands of pounds if necessary.

The contents of the wicker picnic basket are as exceptional as the ancient landscape. Rustic bread and Welsh cakes baked within the last hour. Buffalo mozzarella, beef tomatoes and green and black olives delivered that morning from Tuscany. Fresh cockles and shrimps from the nearby coast. Homemade pheasant pâté and an '82 Lafite from the Rothschild estate in France.

They sit at the top, where thousands of years ago there was a monk's retreat and then a sacred chapel. From here they can pick out Great Breach Wood, Polden Hills, Brent Knoll and West Mendip Hills.

But Owain and Jennifer see much more. They see the ghosts of Shamans, Druid priests and necromancers. They see St Patrick strolling the land looking for converts. Saxon hermits hiding in the hillsides. Celtic tribes massing. Roman armies marching. The roots of civilization growing.

And they see Arthur and his Queen arm-in-arm, the Knights of the Round Table assembling and the holy goddess Fortuna stretching her sword-holding hand up from the cold water of the lake.

For almost a minute, Jennifer watches her husband stare into the distance. Normally, being here relaxes him, helps him unwind. But today the tension is still there, etched in grooves across his head and in words unspoken. She intertwines her fingers with his. 'What are you thinking?'

It takes him a second to return from distant thoughts. 'Many things, but nothing for you to worry about.'

She tugs his hand. 'Don't patronize me. What's troubling you?'

'Josep Mardrid.'

She shudders at the mere mention of the name. 'What has he done now?'

'He and his corporation grow more ruthless by the week. Currently, his bankers are buying up huge stretches of land in the Democratic Republic of Congo, Niger and Togo. Among others.'

'Why is that so bad?' Jennifer asks. We've invested out there and a lot of the charities I support are busy there.'

'He's trying to create a slave trade just like his family did generations ago. In Togo he's been paying armed gangs to terrorize farmers and destroy their crops. Hundreds of men and their wives and children have been injured, some killed.'

'That's terrible.'

'The gangs rape teenagers of either sex. They break the bones of babies and children, then Mardrid has his suited bankers move in and make the beaten men derisory offers for their businesses. He is emerging as a third-world baron in cocoa, cotton and coffee. In time, he'll do the same in cattle and will then control all the major food chains.'

'What will you do about it?'

'Anything and everything I can. If necessary, we'll fight fire with fire. If we don't, then nothing will be grown or raised without him getting his share.' Owain puts his arm around his wife and kisses her. 'Let's not talk about him. He only makes my blood boil and we have so little time together. I have to leave for London tomorrow.'

She squeezes up to him. 'I don't want you to go.'

'Neither do I. But I have so much to do. And so little time in which to do it.'

His words sting her. 'Have you spoken to Myrddin? Is he worrying you as well?'

'No, I haven't. And no, he's not worrying me.' Owain doesn't mention that the old man has already insisted on coming to see him. 'But I really don't need to speak to him to know something bad is happening. I feel what he feels. I always have done.'

Jennifer lifts his fingers to her lips and kisses them. She knows he's right. Things are about to change. And not because of what her husband has said, or what Myrddin might believe, but because of the very thing that she is keeping secret.

26

JERSEY CITY, NEW YORK

The CTU rendezvous takes place at 0100 hours on the south side of Leonard Gordon Park, a six-acre spread of popular recreational land off Manhattan Avenue.

It takes Operational Commander Paul Bendon less than a minute to remind the six-man assault unit and two-man bomb-disposal team of the layout of the building and in particular where the four terrorists and their cache of explosives will be positioned inside it.

While Bendon speaks, a miniature drone hovers silently over the single-storey building. High in the starless night sky, it constantly relays thermal images formed from the men's body heat to the tiny screen embedded in the visor of his full-face protective mask and helmet.

The commander runs a final check with two surveillance operatives hidden close to the target building and then gives the 'go' signal.

The unit slips silently from the blacked-out van and shifts stealthily across the corner of the park towards John F. Kennedy Boulevard. The body shop is in sight.

The metal roller door is down all the way and anchored from the inside. The three front windows and the back two are closed and have sturdy wire mesh over what is certain to be reinforced glass. The walls are white pebbledash over thick breezeblock. The roof is bitumen, plasterboard and cheap wooden joists – all too thin and noisy to risk anyone walking on.

It means Bendon has had to plan another way in.

The team with him is the best there is: MacNeish, King, Kupka, Parry, Cavell and Elliott have been in more than a dozen raids at least as dangerous as this. When it comes to badasses, they're off the scale.

Bendon waves MacNeish forward.

The thickset operative slips into position, raises an Arwen launcher to his shoulder and chugs a series of brick-penetrating rounds through the mortar.

As the payloads empty CS into the body shop, a small explosive charge blows out an architectural weak spot between the roller door and the window. King rolls in two flashbangs.

Kupka and Parry are through the hole and into the smoke before the dust has had a chance to rise, let alone settle. Bullets spray from CTU carbines – not the normal deadly lead but unique tranquillizers that penetrate and discharge on impact.

There's a volley of enemy fire from low in the far corner. A round smacks Elliott in the shoulder and spins him. Cavell returns fire.

It seems like all hell is breaking loose. A wall collapses and part of the roof falls in. Parry shouts, 'Out! Out!'

More of the roof comes in. There's another wild burst of gunfire. A crouching terrorist breaks cover and runs through the mist.

Bendon sees him. He's heading into the other part of the body shop. The place where the pits and the explosives are.

A burst from the commander's Heckler and Koch hits the terrorist in the back and drops him in the dirt. Bendon kicks the man's weapon away and snags him with fast-tie plastic cuffs.

Another bomber breaks from the mist.

Kupka is close enough to smash a forearm into his face and knock him flat. He tilts his gun and shoots tranquillizer into the man's chest.

There's silence now.

Everyone strains and concentrates. Thermal recon showed four people – they've only hit two.

The team sweeps the fog with their weapons. One by one, calm voices speak into Bendon's earpiece.

'Clear south.'

'Clear east.'

'Clear west.'

'Clear north.'

He picks through the rubble. Chunks of brick and breeze-block shift beneath the soles of his boots. Down in the pit he sees the store of bombs and bomb-making materials. There are stacks of PBX, plastic bonded explosives. Some small devices are already completed, others still need to be assembled. Alongside them are dozens of detonators, bags of binding materials, packs of plasticizers and several canisters of cyclotrimethylene.

Bendon waves the bomb-squad boys forward and steps outside. Two of the cell got away when the roof fell in but his men are after them. He picks up the radio in the van and links through to CTU control. 'Two captured. Two escaped but the information was a hundred per cent accurate. The place was a bomb factory. A big one. Tell Director Briars his informant delivered, again.'

27

GLASTONBURY, ENGLAND

The black Jaguar arrives in the dead of night.

Armed guards leave the warmth of their security lodge, peer briefly through the bulletproof glass then respectfully wave the limousine past.

It travels a short way down an unlit track to an old gatekeeper's cottage. The driver, a large man with military haircut gets out and opens the back door for his passenger.

Myrddin struggles to extricate himself from the plush seating. His long spine is bent and stiff from the arduous journey, his mind already on the return trip he must make soon after daybreak.

The cottage smells of damp and is as sparsely furnished as his chambers in Wales. There are no curtains or carpets. In the middle of a rough wooden table stands a wicker basket of cold meats and cheeses, along with a vintage bottle of single malt whisky and two glasses.

Outside he hears noises. Feet on gravel. Attentive voices of the gate guards.

The door creaks open and Owain Gwyn enters. 'It is so good to see you!'

They embrace warmly.

'How are you, my dear, dear boy?' asks Myrddin as they break.

'I am well. Though I feel terrible about you driving all this way. You should have used the helicopter.'

'*Fuh.*' He flaps a hand dismissively. 'Horrible things. You know I am too old to fly.'

Owain laughs and then points around at the bare room. 'I always feel bad when you stay out here in the cold like a hermit. We could make you so much more comfortable in the main house.'

'I *like* to live like this. Besides, I have the whisky to keep me warm.' He uncaps the bottle and pours two glasses.

Owain sits at the table with him. 'When we get to Wales, let me bring people in and refurbish your chambers and the solar. Central heating, damp proofing, electricity. Bring you some of the comforts of the twenty-first century.'

He shakes his head. 'Shelter alone is a luxury. Anything more builds a barrier between me and the spirits I wish to converse with.'

Owain raises his malt. '*This* is the only spirit I want any contact with.'

They touch glasses and drink.

Myrddin puts his whisky down and cuts to the purpose of

his visit. 'I have told you of some of the recent things that have broken my sleep. Have any of the visions yet made sense to you?'

'Sadly, yes.'

'Specifically?'

Owain is pained to explain, 'Angelo Marchetti, a member of the Inner Circle has been stealing artefacts and money. It's a long story, but as a result, men he recruited were responsible for a murder in America – the owner of an antique store—'

'Ah, this is the Keeper of Time.'

'It would seem to fit your prophecy.' He freshens their glasses.

'But only one dead?'

'No, there were more.'

'I foresaw the brown and silent beast that bore Death and his disciples.'

Owain nods. 'One of the men we pursued was in a brown hybrid SUV – that's a vehicle that runs silently on electricity as well as petrol or diesel.'

'As old as I am, I know what hybrid means.' He turns his sad eyes up at Owain. 'There is something I have not yet told you.'

'Then, I suppose now is the time to tell it.'

Myrddin is almost afraid to speak the words. 'I have seen *the child*.'

Owain looks shaken.

'He is coming.'

'You are certain?'

'I am. He is coming and with him, there will be a river of blood that will flow from country to country, continent to continent.'

28

DULLES AIRPORT, WASHINGTON DC

The redeye from San Francisco leaves late. When it lands almost three thousand miles away, there's no gate available. One of those nights is turning into one of those days.

Redirected into a freed-up bay, there's no ground crew to operate the air-bridge. By the time the passengers sleepwalk off the Airbus, it's almost half past eight in the morning and Mitzi is already two hours behind schedule.

'Thank you, have a nice day,' says a smiling stewardess.

Mitzi glares as she glides past. She'd been made to fly cattle-class by the FBI and hasn't slept a wink. Her only good fortune is that she's travelling with only a trolley bag, which means she breezes through security.

In the arrivals hall, she finds a scruffy, middle-aged taxi driver holding a piece of cardboard with her name on it. He looks about as pissed off as she feels.

'*Fallon* – that's me.' She waves a hand.

'You're late in.'

She can't believe his attitude. 'Yeah, well, shit happens. Stick it on the bill. And while you're doing that, add another ten dollars because I need some coffee before you drive me anywhere.'

He laughs and shakes his head in disbelief that he has to wait even longer. 'There's a Dunkin' Donuts, a Green Leaf or a Guava and Java, all within a minute of here.'

'Dunkin'. The other two sound expensive and I'm in no mood to talk lapsang souchong to some spotty student.'

'Can I take your bag?'

She notices that he smells of booze and looks like death. 'I got it. Do I really look so weak that I can't roll a trolley bag?'

'No, you don't. But you're sure as hell snappy.' He leads the way to the coffee shop. 'I was just being polite.'

'Yeah, well, in your case *polite* would be having a shower after a night on the beer.'

'I worked late last night so didn't get home to change. I'm sorry. I'm having something of a bad time at the moment.'

'Yeah, well, bad time is no excuse for bad smell. My bad time runs all the way back to LA via San Francisco and courtesy of enough men smelling of liquor to know the score.' She catches that maybe she's whipping him too hard. 'Listen, I'm sorry I kept you waiting. Remind me when you drop me off and I'll make it up to you with a good tip.'

They arrive at the donut stand and join the queue. Mitzi flips open her purse. 'You want coffee? I'm buying.'

He looks pleased. 'Why not? Dunkaccino Medium. Could manage a strawberry cheese Danish if you can stretch that far.'

'You're joking, right? *Strawberry cheese*? They *really* do that?'

'Strawberry cheese, or apple cheese. Take your pick.'

Mitzi goes strawberry plus a double espresso. She pays for everything and he picks up the bags and coffee from the counter.

'Let's sit a while and eat these,' he motions to a table. 'I don't like to move around when I have food or drink.'

She studies her watch. 'Not sure I have time for batting the breeze. I should have met someone an hour ago.'

'I know you should. A cop, name of Fitzgerald.' He pulls out a chair for her. 'You just met him. Sit down and he'll brief you while we eat.'

29

GLASTONBURY, ENGLAND

The rear lawn of the mansion glistens with morning dew.

Two figures, both dressed head-to-toe in white, tread the turf in the sharp morning light.

They nod respectfully, then fill the dawn air with the savage swish of steel.

Sir Owain Gwyn and Lance Beaucoup first crossed swords at the Olympics when France fought Great Britain. In battle, a great friendship was forged and Lance subsequently joined the Order.

Steel slashes air. Knees bend. Toes tap. The men spin and lunge and whirl, elegant figures in dazzling bright breeches and vests. Behind the foil facemasks, neither of them blink. To do so would be costly.

Across the lawn, an electronic scoring box beeps and echoes thinly.

First blood to the Frenchman – a fine feint followed by a lightning jab to the shoulder.

Owain counters aggression with guile. His giant feet go light. For a second, he has the speed of a featherweight. He parries, then lunges.

Lance dances backwards, ropes in his aggression and tries to stay patient. He counters and parries. Backs off again.

Owain lunges.

The Frenchman flicks away the epee blade and catches him low in the abdomen.

Another beep. A second point to the younger man.

They touch blades. The dance begins again. One that in ancient times would have ended in defeat, death or, worst of all, dishonour. Feet fly back and forth across the damp turf like scampering pups.

Lance cuts low, then high.

Owain blocks.

Both blades slide down to the bell guards. Eyes and muscles lock.

Owain leans in. Hurls his foe backwards. Lunges again.

The Frenchman deflects the blade downwards, steps to one side, stabs upwards.

A third beep.

'Stop!' Owain pulls off his mask in despair. 'You are still

too good for me.' He sounds breathless. 'I can't be humiliated any more.'

'Then use your right arm, *mon cher ami*.'

'If I do, then my left will never learn to be an equal.'

Lance lifts his forearm to wipe sweat from his brow. 'Your right is so good, your left will never need to hold steel.'

Owain puts his arm around his friend and leads him back to the house, where breakfast is being prepared. 'Did you hear anything further about last night's activities in New York?'

'Yes. We got intelligence around four this morning. Two captive. The Americans will interrogate them later today. One of the others, the bomb-maker and Antun escaped when CTU stormed the building.'

'Antun is a good man. Is he injured?'

'No, not at all and he thinks his credibility is good enough for him to stay in.'

'That's dangerous. Very dangerous.'

'Isn't everything that we do?'

'Al-Qaeda is depleted in people, not in thought. Make sure he does not underestimate them.'

'I will.'

Lance raises his sword. 'Would you like to try your luck one final time?'

A glint comes into Owain's eyes. 'I would. But not with these knitting needles. I have broadswords and body armour. How about a brief session with those, before breakfast?'

The Frenchman's eyes twinkle. 'I thought you would never ask.'

They walk back, talking of their shared passion, of ancient swords and historic battles. Owain glances towards the old gatehouse. The black Jaguar has left. Myrddin has already gone.

30

WASHINGTON DC

Irish briefs Mitzi over their airport breakfast.

He tells her in detail about the two deaths, the witnesses who've been interviewed, what few forensic clues they have and the footage of the Cadillac Escalade hybrid and its tag-team chum, the Lincoln.

When they're done, he rolls her bag to the car and drops it in the Ford's trunk.

She climbs in the passenger side and lets out a yell. 'Holy Christ, what a mess!'

The footwell is filled with trash.

'What you got down here, apart from dysentery and Ebola?' She looks closer. 'Old cans of soda. Screwed-up bags and wrappers from Subway and McDonald's. A newspaper or ten.'

'I like to read.'

'I'll buy you a book on hygiene.'

'Not many people get in that side.'

'I can see why. Where did you say we're going first, embassy or to see the store girl?'

'Embassy. It's more important.' He looks her way. 'Outta interest, how did you end up in this weird FBI squad?'

'I worked a case related to the Turin Shroud. You know what that is?'

'Course. I was brought up Catholic. Used to be an altar boy. What d'ya reckon – is it fake or for real?'

Mitzi laughs. 'That's a long story. Anyway, after dealing with a lifetime's worth of history, religion, politics and tricky Italians we got a result. I used it for a wage hike and a ticket out of town.'

'You like the new job?'

'Too early to say. So far, it beats the hell out of chasing gangs across Compton and Linwood.' She checks her watch. 'I've got a researcher showing a picture of your cross to history professors and theologians this morning. Give her another hour or so and I'll call in.'

'I pray she strikes lucky.'

'You not picked up any more?'

'Only that it was worth a lot of money. Amir, the old man I told you about, was scraping together every dime he had and borrowing more to buy it.'

'Looks like your bosses made the smart move calling us in then.'

'Ha.' He shakes his head despondently.

'Ha? What does *"ha"* mean?'

'Means my bosses don't really approve of you being here. I made the request without asking them.'

Mitzi raises an eyebrow. 'Do you like having your ass kicked?'

'It's a tough old ass and it's been kicked so much I don't feel the pain no more.'

They pull up at the main entrance of the British Embassy. Both cops clock the plethora of surveillance cameras and heavy-duty guards with machine-guns and sniffer dogs.

Irish winds down the window and dangles his ID for a gate guard. 'We're investigating a major crime and need to speak to the ambassador, or one of his representatives.'

The security man lifts the road barrier. 'Park over there and we'll do some checks, then I'll take you round to the rear entrance. One of the consular officials will come and speak to you.'

'Thanks.' Irish drives through and parks in a visitor space.

Mitzi gets out and takes in the red brick and ivy, the grand windows and pristine gardens. '*Not bad*. I guess at a push I could live here.'

31

THE BRONX, NEW YORK

Nabil Tabrizi has been a cell commander for only eighteen months. The bomb factory was his first big responsibility. One he screwed up.

He knows the CIA didn't simply get lucky. His operation was taken out two days before they were ready to blow up Wall Street. Someone acted on top-quality information. Possibly from the inside.

Brought up in The Bronx, he is outwardly as much a New Yorker as most. But his heart has been with al-Qaeda ever since he was bullied at school for being Muslim. Long before his cousin was beaten to death by rednecks because he bore the same name as Khalid Sheik Mohammed, one of the masterminds of the World Trade Center attacks.

Nabil meets his contact in a back room of a lawyer's office near Stan's Sports bar, a ball's throw from the Yankee Stadium. The thin, black-eyed man sits in the shadows.

'You have been compromised from within, Nabil.' The words hang in the musty air. 'You do realize that, don't you?'

'Yes, I do, Imam.' He knows he must be both contrite and focused if he is to survive. 'I am very sorry this has happened.'

'Do you have any idea who it might be?'

'Not Abbas or Samir. They were both taken by the authorities. And not Tamir; he was killed.'

'Who does that leave?'

'Halem and Malek are the only others. Malek was the bomb-maker, so I don't think it was him.'

'Then it may be Halem. But who is least known to you?'

He has to think for a moment. 'Samir and Halem.'

'This Halem, has he run?'

'No. He is still around, which is why I think it may not be him.'

The Imam scratches at his beard. 'It is not impossible that the Americans have arrested one of their own, in order to make him look guilty. They could always release him later and say they had to because of judicial problems.'

'You think it might be one of them?'

'I think nothing, Nabil. These are your men – it is you who must think. Think and act decisively. Does the holy book not tell us "fight the unbelievers around you, and let them find harshness in you?"'

'Yes, Imam, it does.'

'Then that is what you must do.'

Nabil feels relieved. He is going to be given a second chance. 'When I look into their faces, I will know who betrayed me.'

The Iman raises his arm and knocks twice on the wall behind him. The shadowy space he's sitting in is broken by yellow light from an opening door. A large, olive-skinned man enters, dressed in baggy white trousers and a white vest that showcases gym-pumped arms. His head has been shaved and his angular face is framed in a beard shadow as dark as his eyes.

'This is Aasif,' he explains. 'My most trusted enforcer. For now, he is your new recruit. He will help protect you and get to the truth.'

'Thank you.' Nabil bows his head in gratitude.

Aasif steps out of the shadows and stands intimidatingly close to his new colleague.

'I have a test for you and your men.' He looks up to the

giant at his side. 'Take him in the back room, Aasif and show him our "lie detector".'

Through the shadows, Nabil sees a glint of teeth, the hint of a rare smile.

'Go. It will help you determine who your traitor is – and teach the Americans a lesson into the bargain.'

32

GLASTONBURY, ENGLAND

Breakfast is served in the Gwyns' ornate Edwardian conservatory. The golden light of what is becoming a beautiful morning rests on white linen tables and sparkles on china plates and silver cutlery.

Owain is distracted. Myrddin's prophecies and the long conversation of last night are playing on his mind. That and Mardrid's mafia-like movements in the third world. Gradually, he becomes conscious of a white-coated waiter who's appeared at the table. 'Some Ceylon tea, fresh berries and a croissant, please.'

The young waiter looks to Lance Beaucoup, who is settling into a chair.

'Just coffee and a croissant. *Merci*.'

The waiter drifts off to his duties.

Lance nods to the third place set at the table. 'Is Lady Gwyn joining us?'

'No, she's already out. Apparently, while we were having our extra fencing session she decided to go and ride the new horse that threw her the other day.'

He looks concerned. 'Was she hurt?'

'Just her pride. It's a Welsh Cob stallion, a giant white that really doesn't want to be tamed.'

'That is part of the Welsh character, is it not?'

'It is.' He looks amused. 'I feel for the horse. Eventually, Jenny will win. She always does.'

'This is why I never married.' He laughs.

'I hope one day you'll feel differently.'

The waiter returns with breakfast on a large silver tray. He holds it while a young waitress in a dark uniform pours the tea and coffee and serves the food.

Owain waits until they've walked away before he strikes up a new conversation. 'Has the Knight's Cross been returned to the burial ground?'

'It has. Gawain and Danforth did it last night.'

'Good. I am still shocked and sickened that Angelo would commit such sacrilege. Robbing the grave of a fallen brother; it turns my stomach.'

'Grave-*s*. Remember he took *three* crosses.'

'Indeed. We have three fallen brothers who've been foully stripped of their honour. Is security now what it should be?'

'It is. And we are reviewing procedures in other countries as well.' Lance hesitates before voicing a more delicate question. 'Would you like me to ask George to review the British resting grounds, or would you rather tell him yourself? They and the French ones are after all the oldest and most significant.'

'You tell him.' He's pleased that Lance is pushing the boundaries of his authority, developing into a natural leader. 'I'm done here; I need to get to work.' He wipes his hands on his napkin and gets to his feet.

Lance follows suit. 'I will join you. If I stay here I will only fall asleep or drink too much coffee.'

They leave the conservatory and head into the main part of the house. A long corridor takes them to a set of stairs that drop another landing.

The two men use retinal and fingertip identification to pass into a short, wood-panelled cul-de-sac of three doors. The one to the left is filled by members of the Watch Team. To the right, Sir Owain's private office.

Straight ahead is the SSOA command centre. The heartbeat of their Order.

33

BRITISH EMBASSY, WASHINGTON DC

After security checks have been completed, Mitzi and Irish are left in a high-ceilinged, dusty waiting room full of echoes and framed photographs of generations of British monarchs.

Half an hour ticks by.

Mitzi's gossamer-thin patience is starting to shred when a blue-suited blond man strides in.

'Hello, I'm Richard Stevens – how might I help you?'

Irish badges him and spills several balled up tissues in the process. 'Lieutenant Fitzgerald from DC Police and this is Mitzi Fallon, from the FBI.' He pauses while she produces her credentials.

Stevens takes both IDs and examines them carefully before returning them. 'And you're here, why?'

'We're running a homicide investigation and need your help.' Irish gives a friendly shrug. 'Hell, I know there are all those procedural channels and policies, but I could sure do with cutting through the red tape and getting a jump on our killer. Can I ask you something?'

The young attaché says nothing.

'Take a look at these for me.' Irish opens a brown envelope and shows blow-up photos the lab rushed for him late last night. 'This Lincoln is registered to the British Embassy; we checked the plates.' He hands a print to Stevens. 'We need to know who was driving it last Friday night and where it is now?'

'Do you have a record book of that kind of thing?' asks Mitzi. 'A driver we can talk to?'

Stevens hands the photograph back to Irish. 'I'm sorry; you're going to have to go through those dreadful *channels*. Probably best to have your Chief of Police contact the State Department and let them deal with it appropriately.' He taps the face of his wristwatch. 'Now, I'm afraid I have other duties to attend to.'

Mitzi presses. 'If you don't have time, maybe your boss does?'

'That's not possible.' He looks amused. 'If you were better informed you would know that Sir Owain Gwyn's tenure is up. He returned to Britain yesterday along with his staff.' He pre-empts her next question. 'I have stayed on merely to help the new ambassador settle in. And he won't be here today, or the rest of this week for that matter.'

She steps into the attaché's personal space. 'Do I look like a barn wall?'

The consular agent looks confused. 'I beg your pardon?'

'I just wondered – what with all that whitewash you just slopped over me.'

His tone alters. 'I'm officially asking you to leave. If you don't, I will call security and have you forcibly removed.'

'We're going.' Mitzi pats him playfully on the cheek as she walks past. 'Love your accent, honey. God save the freakin' queen.'

34

NEW YORK

For the past three years, Halem Hussain has been a trusted member of Nabil Tabrizi's terror cell. Not for one moment has anyone within the group suspected he might be Antun

Bhatti, a devoted member of the SSOA, a secret organization known to only a few people in the world.

But today, things are different.

Given the raid by the Counter-Terrorist Unit, he knows Nabil must consider him, and everyone else left alive, as the possible source of a leak to the authorities.

He sits in a circle of hard chairs, in the damp basement of a safe house off Westchester Avenue, just a nervous spit from where the Cross Bronx Expressway hits Parkchester Metro and the Hugh J. Grant Circle. He's a stranger to the place. Brought here by Nabil, they made five different changes of transport and went to extraordinary lengths to make sure they weren't tailed.

He and Malek the bomber have been searched and electronically 'brushed' for bugs by a man Nabil simply introduced as Aasif.

The young cell commander looks strained and worried. He leans on his knees as he speaks. 'One of our colleagues is dead. Others have been captured by the Americans. Yet, *the two of you*, Malek and Halem, escaped unhurt. No bullet wounds. No scratches. No arrests. Tell me why did Allah look so favourably upon you?'

The small grey-haired bomb-maker, answers first. 'When the Americans blew open the door I was in the toilet. This saved me from the blast and the gunfire. I praise Allah and I pray for those who were not as lucky as me. My work will bring glory to the rest of our team, I swear it.'

Nabil studies the man by his side. 'And you, Halem?'

Antun doesn't rush his answer. He hangs his head in shame.

'Brother! I am waiting for your explanation.'

Finally, he looks up. His eyes are moist. 'I was frightened.' He lets the admission sink in. 'I was thrown to the floor when the Americans fired their explosives and I stayed there.' He drops his head again, before continuing. 'I was too scared to move and hoped they didn't kill me. Then part of the roof collapsed and I took the chance to run rather than fight.' He raises his eyes. 'Then I called and told you what had happened.'

Nabil remembers his horror at learning of the raid. Halem had indeed been the first to alert him and, had he not, maybe he would have been arrested or killed by the Americans. 'There is a traitor among us. Of that, I am sure. It may be one of you, or perhaps even Abbas or Samir. For the moment, I cannot be certain. But I will be.' He puts a hand on the man at his side. 'Aasif, show them how we will find out.'

The enforcer dips his hands into a black garbage bag that the imam has given him and lifts out a thick fold of light brown canvas. As he unrolls it, a tangle of coloured wires and deep pockets packed with explosives and shrapnel become visible.

'Tonight,' says Nabil, 'at the height of rush hour, one of our sisters will walk into Grand Central Station and turn a dull New York day into a truly historic one.'

35

GLASTONBURY, ENGLAND

The daily briefing paper that Lance places in Owain's hands is not dissimilar to one that will shortly be passed to the President of the United States.

But this missive hasn't been compiled by US or even British intelligence agencies. It's come from the Arthurians' Watch Team, a hand-picked group of security experts who gather information on the biggest threats to world security.

Today's dossier runs from A-U. From Afghanistan and Algeria to Uzbekistan. Down the alphabet of terrorism, Owain learns of changes in strength, new affiliations and successful and failed strikes. He picks up early intelligence on Cambodia's Khmer Rouge, the Zviadists in Georgia, the Japanese Aum Supreme Truth movement, Hamas, and the Harakat ul-Ansar in Pakistan. He reads and absorbs it all, then settles on the separate paper that is always prepared for him.

The one marked MARDRID.

The title is the name of a company in the Spanish capital that is a front for an arms supplier, delivering tanks to Syria, warplanes to Iran, missiles to North Korea without compunction. Its CEO is Josep Mardrid, entrepreneur and evil personified.

Owain reads each line carefully, knowing that somewhere in the world Mardrid is most probably perusing a detailed report about him and his various activities. If Myrddin's prophecies are right, they will meet again soon. Just as their ancestors did. Then there will be blood. Such a torrent of blood that it will sweep away some of the finest lives the world has ever known.

36

BRITISH EMBASSY, WASHINGTON DC

'You're going the wrong way.' Irish jabs a thumb towards the front gate as he fishes for the last of the clean tissues in his pocket. 'The car and the exit are over there.'

'I've never had a good sense of direction.' Mitzi saunters down the service road that snakes around the back of the embassy.

He sneezes then asks her, 'Where you going?'

'Garage will be down here. I figure we have less than five minutes before the Head of Ambassadorial Whitewash checks with security that we've gone.'

Irish struggles to keep up. 'Hey, we have no warrant and my captain doesn't even know that we're here. He'll kick my ass if you cause any problems.'

'Thought you said your ass was hard and kick-resistant?'

'I lied. I have a soft pussy of an ass, a real—'

'Enough, or I'll kick it myself.'

They follow the road as it winds through the cover of giant trees. In the clearing is a crop of old outbuildings and a spread of blacktop where embassy cars are parked.

Near the vehicles are a gas pump, oil drums, and a long single-storey garage with rolled up doors. Inside is a dark-brown Range Rover that looks several years old and alongside it, a black Jaguar, a supercharged XJL.

Mitzi's gaze skips over the roofs and hoods. Right at the back she sees a silver Lincoln MKZ, with a panoramic roof.

'Well looky look!' She runs her fingers down the wing. 'Don't this seem familiar?'

'This year's model.' Irish floats envious eyes over the badging and plump leather interior. 'Three-point-seven-litre V6 engine, with rich leather and wood trim. We're talking forty, maybe forty-five thousand dollars.'

'You wouldn't get change out of fifty.' The comment comes from a ginger-haired man in blue overalls. He wipes his fingers on a rag even dirtier than his hands. 'Can I help you with somethin'?'

'Lieutenant Fitzgerald, DC Police.' He flips his badge. 'Who are you?'

'Chas Dawkins. I'm the embassy's chief mechanic – what's wrong?'

'You got records, Chas? Can you tell me where these cars might have been and who's been driving them – like you, for example?' Irish raises an accusatory eyebrow.

'Me an' the rest of the boys don't do nothing but test

drives and most of that's on private roads.' He gestures to the garage. 'If the cars are taken out they have to be signed for. I've got logs.'

They walk into a darkness that smells of oil, petrol and spirit-based cleaners. Mitzi looks back for the security guards who will inevitably come.

Chas rifles through the drawers of a tatty wooden desk that has an ancient computer sat on top, along with a collection of dirty mugs that should have been washed yesterday. He produces an A3-sized hardback blue book and opens it. 'What day and car you interested in?'

'Friday last.' Irish feels his heart jump. 'Who had the Lincoln that night, say from eight onwards?'

The mechanic runs a finger down the columns until he finds a name and signature. 'Mr Dalton.'

'Who's he?' Mitzi watches a black Ford Expedition roll to a halt outside the garage.

'*George* Dalton. He's a consul.'

She sees guards slide from their vehicle, hitch up their pants, belts heavy with guns. 'How long did he have the car?'

Chas has his head in the book. 'Dropped it at the airport on Sunday morning. We pick—'

'Don't say anything else, Mr Dawkins.' The order comes from a guard in his mid-fifties. 'These people got no right to be here asking you questions.'

Mitzi winks at him. 'You did good, Chas. Whatever the Stasi here say, you've done the right thing.'

37

NEW YORK

'The thing is' – Nabil Tabrizi looks across at Halem and Malek as he speaks – 'none of us is going to leave this room. Not until long after the suicide vest has been collected and Grand Central Station is bathed in the blood of the infidels.' He studies their eyes for a sign of worry, a flash of recognition that one of them will be unable to contact his masters and prevent the attack.

Malek is the first to break a tense silence. 'May I see the vest?'

The cell leader regards him with suspicion. 'Why?'

'To check it will work. These garments are prone to malfunction.'

Aasif holds it up. 'Or is it because you want to sabotage it? Perhaps loosen a connection or two?'

The bomb-maker stays calm. 'I am a professional and I am acting professionally.' He turns his head towards the cell commander. 'Do you respect my opinion and my skills, or not?'

'Give it to him,' says Nabil curtly.

Aasif carefully passes it over.

The commander slips a Glock from his belt and inspects the magazine. It's a check done more out of boredom than anything else. 'You are very quiet, Halem. What is on your mind?' The rack of bullets makes a ratcheting click as it's shoved back into the gun.

Antun feels Nabil's eyes boring into him. 'I was wondering if any thought had been given to the scanners at the station and how to get past them? Or is the plan just to explode the device outside?'

'*Much* thought has gone into this plan,' says Nabil. 'The explosive is TATP and it will pass the scanners. Won't it, Malek?'

'It will. As you say, the maker has used triacetone triperoxide. It's a crude but sensitive charge made up mainly of acetone, hydrogen peroxide and a strong acid like hydrochloric or sulphuric acid.' He turns one of the vest pockets around to show the packed chemicals. 'Because most security scanners are really only nitrogen detectors, they won't pick this up. It is what we bomb-makers call "transparent".'

Antun, the man they all know as Halem, wipes sweat from his brow. His thoughts are on the station. It's not just the busiest stop in the New York City Subway system; it's one of the most hectic places on earth. GCS has more than a hundred tracks and covers almost fifty acres of land. On a quiet day three-quarters of a million people pass through it. A bomb will cause unbelievable loss of life.

He has to stop the attack.

Even if that means getting killed in the process.

38

WASHINGTON DC

Mitzi lowers the window of the Taurus as they head out to Sophie Hudson's apartment in North Bethesda. 'You sure you left the bodies at the morgue, and they ain't buried somewhere beneath your car trash?'

'Very funny.' Irish flips down the lid on the glove box. 'There's cologne in there; squirt it around and shut up.'

'What an offer.' Mitzi picks out a dubious green bottle of a scent she's never heard of and sprays it. 'Oh my God! I think I prefer the hidden corpse.' She puts the bottle back.

'Paid ten dollars for that.'

'You should have arrested them for robbery.'

He smiles. For someone like Mitzi Fallon, he could maybe buy sixty-dollar cologne and get his shit together. Shame she's just blowing through his life. Shame he has a life that just gets blown through. 'I think Sophie Hudson's holding back on me. I tell you that already?'

'You did. You told me at the airport.'

He jabs a finger against his temple. 'Got to the age when I can't remember half of what I've said. Better to say it twice than not at all.'

'Anything you can put your finger on?'

'No. That's the problem. It's just a hunch.' He drives lazily. Hands flopped together on the top of the wheel. 'I was thinking, maybe you should see her on your own. Could be that woman-to-woman you'll get something I wouldn't.'

Mitzi gives him the once-over. He's scruffy as hell and stinks of booze but beneath all that waste there's a bright cop trying to come up for air. 'I'll give it a shot.'

Ten minutes later, Irish pulls over and kills the engine. 'It's that brownstone. Eighth floor, apartment 802.' He slides his seat back and reclines it. 'I'm gonna grab a little rest. See if I can sleep off this flu.'

She opens the passenger side and steps out to the side-walk. 'Women get flu, they simply struggle on; men get it, they have to sleep it off. Healthiest thing you could do is clean up this dumpster.' She slams the door and looks around.

The street is clean and quiet. A few trees have grown mature around the old brownstone building, a patch of grass has got a path worn across the corner and there are a couple of benches where no doubt old folks sit during the day and kids congregate at night.

She takes the stairs, not the elevator and uses the time to run the details of the case through her head.

Sophie opens her apartment door on the first knock, but keeps it chained.

Mitzi shows her FBI badge. 'I'm working your boss's murder. Need to ask you some questions.'

'I already talked to Lieutenant Fitzgerald.'

'I know. Now you need to talk to me.' She puts a finger on the chain. 'Take it off, please?'

Sophie's eyes show resignation. The door closes and re-opens without the chain.

'Thanks.' As she walks in Mitzi asks, 'How you feeling? I'm told you're sick.'

'Getting better.' Sophie is in her old university hoodie with blue jeans, pink socks and no shoes. She motions reluctantly to the sofa. 'You want a drink or something?'

'No I'm good.' Mitzi sits and flips out a notebook. 'Let's do this quick.'

'Sure.' She settles opposite her. 'Like I said, I went through it all with Lieutenant Fitzgerald. I've told him everything I know.'

'I suspect not.' She studies the landscape of the girl's face, the tension in her cheeks, and the tightness around her mouth. 'You ever done word-association tests?'

She frowns. 'No.'

'Okay, it goes like this: I say something and you answer with the first thing that comes into your head. From your answer, I'll know whether you're a liar or just a sick kid whose door I shouldn't have knocked on.' Mitzi clicks the top on her pen. 'Here we go – word one: murder . . .'

The store assistant doesn't answer.

Mitzi repeats herself. '*Murder*, Sophie. *Murder* . . .'

'Mr Goldman?'

'Good.'

Mitzi lets her hang. She leans forward, challengingly. 'Hiding.'

Sophie's pupils dilate. Her skin glows pink. 'This is stupid. I'm not—'

'Don't!' Mitzi holds up a traffic cop palm. 'You don't want to know what I've done to people who lie to my face.'

The silence returns.

Mitzi puts the pen and paper down. 'Okay, game over. You got from *sick kid* to *lying little bitch* in two questions. Not a record, but still impressive.' She takes her shield out and places it next to her. 'The FBI didn't send me here to play games, honey – they want me to charge someone with your boss's murder. So, what happens now is I phone for a warrant, we toss this place and then charge you with suspicion—'

'All right.' Sophie rubs a hand nervously across her mouth and gets shakily to her feet. 'I need to bring something from the bedroom.'

Mitzi stands too. She's not in the business of sitting like an idiot while a suspect makes a run for it or, worse still, picks up something that happens to be loaded.

She follows her to the bedroom and as Sophie reaches for a drawer beneath a vanity mirror, she un-holsters her gun. 'Do that real slow, so I don't have a momentary lapse of judgement and blow your freakin' head off.'

The girl looks terrified. Her hands shake as she pulls a small USB stick from beneath a tangle of underwear and holds it out. 'This is all I was getting.'

Mitzi takes it and holsters the gun. She looks down at the tiny eight-gigabyte memory stick in the palm of her hand. 'What's on it and how did you get it?'

Sophie wanders back to the lounge. 'I couldn't make sense of it. Mr Goldman was given it by someone he was doing business with – I don't know who. He tried it in the work PC and it came out as a jumble of letters and numbers. He gave it to me to try to make sense of.'

'And what was wrong? Was it formatted for Mac or something?'

'No. It really was just letters and numbers.'

'Like what? A recipe for alphabet soup?'

'Just like a jumble. The only thing I could make out was writing on the side of the stick. Someone's scratched "CODE X".'

Mitzi holds the minuscule USB between thumb and forefinger. 'So why lie about this?'

She shrugs guiltily. 'I'm a store clerk – and an out-of-work one now. I figured it might bring me some money in the future.'

'How?'

'I thought I might sell it to a newspaper.'

'Classy gal. Make a buck on your dead boss. Anything else you took or you're forgetting to tell us?'

'No.' Sophie twists a strand of her hair to settle her nerves. 'You gonna charge me with something?'

'Not for now. Being scared of having no work ain't a misdemeanour, else we'd be jailing half the country. But wise up, honey: lying to cops is. You're lucky, you get a pass this time, but if I have to come back, then we'll be playing a different game with a different ending.'

39

NEW YORK

After six hours in the unventilated basement, Antun takes a bathroom break, shadowed by Aasif, who's been briefed to trust no one.

Antun watches the big man as he washes at the sink. It's clear that the enforcer's wide shoulders have been rounded from lifting titanic weights and working slow, repetitive curls in a gym. Thin white snakes crawl across his knuckles and jawbone, long scars from years of street brawls. Antun notes where they are. All are right-sided defence wounds except for the mark on the left of his face, no doubt delivered by a right-handed attacker with a knife. He suspects the assailant is no longer around to brag about the encounter.

Aasif rips a wad of green paper towels from a wall dispenser and holds them out in his fist. 'Here. Hurry up.'

Antun takes them and slowly wipes his hands. 'What's your rush? I thought *your kind* liked restrooms.'

'My *kind*? What's my *kind*?'

He smiles his way past him. 'You know what it is.'

Aasif grabs his shoulder. 'You say that again and I'll rip a new asshole in your face.'

'Sure you will.' He stands eyeball to eyeball. 'And we both know what you'd like to do with assholes.'

Aasif's fists ball in anger.

Antun laughs in his face. He's taken apart bigger and meaner creatures than Aasif. Most importantly he now knows where the ape's trigger is and how quickly it can be pulled.

The two of them return to their seats in the rancid basement and glare across at each other. Both know their time will come.

Three bangs on the floor above their heads prompt Nabil to break his silence. 'She's here.' He turns to Aasif. 'Bring the vest.'

40

GLASTONBURY, ENGLAND

As well as his diplomatic duties and stewardship of the SSOA, Sir Owain Gwyn is the owner and non-executive chairman of Caledfwlch Ethical Investments, a multi-billion-dollar global investment company, started by his family generations ago. He is also the patron of more than a dozen charities and as a result, much of his first full day back in the UK is spent contacting his various offices.

The knight takes a late lunch with his wife, then returns to the SSOA's underground control centre for a final briefing with Inner Circle secretary, Lance Beaucoup.

The room is dominated by a long wall of video screens and

several rows of staff manning terminals and monitors linked to data, surveillance and satellite systems.

The two men sit in one of four concave areas that contain large desks-cum-conference-tables buffered by slide-across soundproof screens.

'I'm afraid I have no news on Antun,' confesses the Frenchman. 'I just spoke to Gareth and he has been unable to contact him.'

Owain is worried. 'I thought we had him under surveillance?'

'We did. The team reported that they saw him meet Nabil, but we lost them both.'

'How?'

'We stayed with them for two changes of subway train, then they disappeared.'

'What about the electronic tracker?'

'Antun dropped it soon after the meet. Nabil must have gone to frisk him, so he had to.'

Owain is annoyed with himself. 'We should have pulled him out as soon as the Americans made their raid. If anything goes wrong I will never forgive myself.'

'Antun Bhatti is one of our best operatives; he can look after himself.'

'Sometimes being the best is not good enough. Over the centuries we have filled graves with the best of men.'

'I understand.' Lance passes over a stack of screen prints.

'What are these?'

'Latest satellite surveillance shots from Togo. Mardrid has

torched an entire village. Thirty deaths. Most of them burned alive. Fatalities include two coffee farmers shot in the head. I think they were the first to go.'

Owain throws the sheets onto his desk. 'Damn every bone in his body!' He rests his forehead on his hands and tries to control the rage. 'I want him dead, Lance. I don't care how. I want Mardrid lying beneath six feet of earth before he spreads any more of his cancer around the world.'

'We can never get near him. His security is better than a Saudi king's.'

'Then until you can, stop this!' He slaps a hand on the prints. 'We've got people in Ghana; move them over. Find the ring-leaders and give them to the locals to deal with.'

'We will need more than a handful of locals to contain Mardrid's thugs.'

'I know, but this at least will give them hope.' He takes a moment to think, then adds, 'I'll seek approval from the Inner Circle to raise crusaders and have the action ratified by an extraordinary meeting of the Blood Line.' Owain's mood darkens as he imagines what else Mardrid may have brewing. 'Any news on Marchetti? Is that viperous traitor already in the Spanish devil's nest?'

'He flew into Charles de Gaulle yesterday, but we haven't found out whether he caught a connecting flight or stayed in the city.'

'He'll have flown on. Find where Mardrid is and you'll find Marchetti.' Owain stands and straightens out the jacket of his navy-blue suit. 'I'm sorry; I really have to rush. Will you drive Jennifer to Caergwyn in the morning? I'll join you there when I can.'

'It will be my pleasure.'

'*Merci*.' Owain leaves to say goodbye to his wife.

He finds her stood by the front door in a short brown tweed skirt and an ochre-coloured jacket. The earthy colours complement her blonde hair and blue eyes.

'I'm sorry.' He stoops to kiss her. 'You have no idea how much I want to stay with you and be in your bed tonight.'

'I think I do.' And the look in her eyes confirms it. 'I've had your overnight bag with your dinner suit and change of clothes put in the aircraft.'

'Thank you.'

'Be careful.'

'I always am.'

He can still smell her perfume and feel the tingle of her lips as he boards the Bell.

The helicopter blades quickly build noise and speed. With a graceful lunge it leaves the ground, billowing dust and shaking trees.

Owain sees his wife wave and then drift back inside. He looks forward as the craft climbs into the pale evening cloud-base and banks east towards London and Buckingham Palace. In a short while, he'll take part in a meeting so secret he hasn't even told Jennifer about it.

41

NORTH BETHESDA, MARYLAND

It's gone three p.m. when Mitzi leaves Sophie Hudson's place.

Irish is asleep at the wheel, his seat laid out flat and the car sunk in a pool of shade beneath some elms.

She opens the passenger door quietly, gets in and slams it.

Irish sits up fast. 'Whadafuck!'

'Result,' she says mischievously.

He blinks and rubs blood into his face. 'What?'

She holds up the silver memory stick Sophie had given her. 'This is what your store girl was keeping from you.'

He cranks his seat back into an upright position and takes it. 'What's on here?'

'Remains to be seen. Scratch on the side says CODE X. Sophie Hudson said her boss got it as a kind of sample for some deal he was doing. Apparently, it contains only letters and numbers.'

'Sounds like a scam.'

'Run me to the hotel so I can dump my stuff, then we can look and maybe get something to eat and drink.'

He starts the engine. 'Good idea.'

'Coffee. That's the drink I have in mind.'

He lets the snipe slide as he swings the Taurus round and out towards Kensington. 'So the woman-to-woman trick worked, hey?' He looks pleased with himself. 'How d'you play it? Momsy or sisterly?'

'*Momsy?*' She shoots him a stare that could kill. 'You looking to spend the afternoon in hospital?'

'Okay.' He raises a hand to acknowledge his error.

'She needed a little jolt, that's all.' Mitzi glances out the window as they make their way down a long tree-lined avenue. 'It's pretty out here. We going far?'

'Too pretty for murder. We got about three miles to go.' He switches the radio on to pass the time. Country music crackles in cheap door speakers.

'Sign to your right says Rock Creek.' Mitzi points it out. 'That where the second body turned up?'

'Yeah. Rock Creek Trail. It's a twenty-mile woodland walk from Lake Needwood to just south of where the stiff was buried.'

'You got a name on him yet?'

'Not yet. I'm gonna call through to records when we get to your hotel. I'm sure his prints will bring up a hit somewhere.'

The Taurus bumps over the Knowles Avenue Bridge then glides along the asphalt to a T-junction. Irish takes them right down Connecticut into town and halts in front of a white two-storey building. 'Here you go, home from home.'

Mitzi gets out and heads to the trunk.

He gets there ahead of her. 'You check in; I'll bring your case.'

The gesture catches her by surprise. 'I'm fine. I can manage.'

He reaches around her and grabs the bag. 'I'd like to.'

She shrugs and walks past a board that says Silver Fall Lodge. A weed-free grit path cuts across a long green lawn fringed by overhanging oaks. The bag rumbles noisily on its hard plastic wheels a few feet behind her.

The small lobby is little more than a big square of white walls over a limed pine floor. A low-level desk supports a computer screen, keyboard and printer. Behind it is a row of brass keys on numbered hooks.

A young woman in a smart black jacket and pearl-coloured blouse checks Mitzi in to what she promises is 'the finest' of its six bedrooms.

Irish drops the bag. 'I'm going to the bar.' He catches Mitzi's disapproving look. '*For coffee.*'

The receptionist points his way. 'It's through to your left, sir.'

Mitzi takes the stairs, then a dusty red carpet down a narrow, dark landing to her room.

It's tiny. She's bought shoes in bigger boxes. The dull cream walls and dark wood floor crowd her. Brightest thing about the place is a mock-oriental jug of mixed flowers on a crappy bureau. Ruthy would know their species, but to her they're just big round reds and spiky yellows with sprigs of green.

Mitzi plugs in her FBI laptop and powers it up. While it's loading programs, she unpacks her bag and hangs clothes in a musty closet. Once the computer is up to speed, she inserts the memory stick that Sophie gave her and opens its directory.

There is nothing but nonsense.

Four lots of nonsense as far as she can make out.

There are big blocks of numbers and letters. Row after row of numbers and then row after row of letters. Never numbers and letters on a line together. Mitzi downloads the contents of the stick onto her hard drive, dials her office in San Francisco and traps the phone between an ear and shoulder.

The call's answered almost instantly. 'Vicky Cantrell.'

'Vicks, it's Mitzi Fallon. I'm in Kensington and I've got some data files I want to upload. Are you at your terminal?'

'Yeah, I am, Lieutenant. Give me a second to open the doc box and check the capture display.' Vicky's nimble fingers flick across the keyboard. 'Okay, send what you've got and I'll be able to check it comes in.'

Mitzi uses a secure FBI portal to upload the contents of the stick.

'Got it.' Vicky scans the file. 'Hang on. This is just lines of numbers and letters. Should it be like that?'

'That's all I saw when I plugged it in. Give it to techies and crypto to work out.'

'You got it.'

'The other thing I was calling about was the cross. Did you have any luck with your professors?'

'I did. Let me find my notes.' She opens her bottom drawer and they're in a newly created hang file entitled, 'Homicides – O.I.C. Lieutenant Fallon'. 'Here we go. I showed it around and the real expert on this kind of thing turned out to be a Professor Quinn at the Smithsonian. He said he'd never seen anything exactly like that in iron and the Smith had no records of any such design.'

'What's that mean?' asks Mitzi, a little confused. 'We got zip?'

'No, it's not that bad. Quinn says the fact that there are no records probably means it's Iron Age.'

'Which was when?'

'In Europe, somewhere between 1200 BC and 400 BC.'

Mitzi frowns. 'You mean to say that Europe has a different Iron Age time than everywhere else?'

'Egypt, Cyprus and the like have even older Iron Ages. Indian Iron Age is similar. Japanese and Chinese a bit later. Quinn thinks this was a Celtic burial cross, from the Irish Iron Age, which ended with the Romanization-Christianization of Britain.'

'Value?'

'He wasn't sure but he guessed not that much.'

'How much is not much?'

'He said a few hundred bucks, but then only to a keen collector. He's mailed some professor in Oxford for a second opinion on its origins and value.'

'When will the Brit get back to him?'

'I don't know. The UK is five hours ahead of DC, eight of San Francisco. Academics work at least twelve hours behind the rest of the world, so I guess tomorrow or the day after?'

'Not good enough. You've gotta be more on the ball, Vicks. Pester Quinn, get the number for the British guy and harass him directly. I don't do "waiting" and from now on neither do you.'

'Understood, Lieutenant.'

'Good. And thanks for your help. Can you put me through to Donovan. I guess I should check in with her.'

'She's out. I saw her leave with the director. You want me to ask her secretary for the AD's cell number?'

'No, thanks. But leave a message that I called and say she can contact me if she wants an update. Is Bronty there?'

'No. Eleonora is; you want to talk to her?'

She hesitates, 'Yeah, okay.'

'Hang on.'

There's a delay then the Italian picks up. 'M-itzi, how was your flight?'

'Two degrees of pain lower than a cervical smear. How you doing with your witch?'

'We've found the coven she worshipped at. It's a group that split away from the Church of Satan.'

'Glad you're making progress. Could you have Bronty call me when you see him? I want to ask him something.'

'*Si*. No problem. I have him call right away.'

'*Grazie.*'

'*Prego, Meetzee.*'

She hangs up and the phone immediately rings. It's a message from Fitzgerald. 'The coffee's crap. I'm over at the Phoenix Bar, a block east of your bunkhouse, on the corner. Join me when you're ready.'

She hangs up, grabs her laptop and hurries out.

Hurries because the last thing she wants is to babysit a drunk for the rest of the evening.

42

GLASTONBURY, ENGLAND

Lance Beaucoup makes his way out into the lawned gardens, near where he and Owain fenced. He follows several hundred yards of twisting, biscuit-coloured pathway that takes him past an ancient maze, a hilltop orchard and down to the south lake.

The Frenchman's feet clump on the teak decking as he approaches an elegant Victorian summerhouse that overhangs the fish-stocked water. Green painted rowing boats are moored beneath the decking and as he spots them he remembers how he and Owain caught salmon far out in the sparkling waters spread around the estate.

The curtains are closed and the summerhouse door is locked. He uses his key and enters the darkness.

She is here.

He knows she is. He smells her perfume. Her body. Her hair. Being so close and not seeing her makes his pulse race.

'Don't speak.'

The voice is followed by an elegant female hand, cold and soft, that covers the heat of his lips. 'I've been thinking all morning about what this was going to be like.'

Lance turns into her. Feels her soft body press against him.

She kisses his neck. His ear. Her hand stays across his mouth. 'Don't say anything. Not until you've finished making love to me.'

43

NEW YORK

Aasif rolls up the suicide vest and slips it back into the black garbage bag that it had come in.

Nabil steers the big man to the door and the wooden stairs leading to the room where 'the Chosen One' is waiting.

'Wait,' calls Antun.

They stop and turn.

'Let *me*.'

Nabil regards him with curiosity. 'What?'

'Let me wear the vest. It is why Allah saved me when the Americans came. My cowardice was meant to prepare me for this moment.'

'No,' says Malek, the bomb-maker. 'Do not do this.' He looks across at Nabil. 'He is too valuable to make this sacrifice.'

'Please,' says Antun, falling to his knees. 'Let me redeem myself by writing this page in our glorious history. Let me be the one.'

44

KENSINGTON, MARYLAND

To Mitzi's surprise, Irish is sat at a round table in the corner of the bar, with only a cup of black coffee in front of him.

No beer. No wine. No spirits.

Just coffee.

He's deep in thought and doesn't see her until she pushes back a stool opposite him. 'Hi, how ya doin'?'

'Good.'

'To be honest, you don't look good. In fact, you look so far from good I'm not sure Google Maps would be able to find you.'

'Thanks.' His eyes trip to the silver object in her hand. 'Anything on the stick?'

'Not that makes sense. I've copied it and uploaded it to my office to crawl all over.' She holds it out to him. 'You should keep the original.'

'Give it me later. I have a history of losing things in bars.'

'Like your reputation?'

He palms her off.

Mitzi slips the stick into her purse. 'From what I saw, it's like Sophie said: everything on it is in some batshit code.'

'That's an official type of cipher, is it? *Batshit*. Like Enigma and Caesar.'

'How do we get food and drink in here?'

'Old-fashioned way. I go to the bar and pay.' He points over her shoulder. 'There's a chalkboard behind you with what might be edible. While you're looking, can I get you a drink?' He reads her mind. 'Remember, you can have coffee, coffee or coffee.'

'Then I'll have coffee. I like mine big and black.'

He bites back a reply that would earn him a slap.

The bar is busy as hell and it takes an eternity for him to get her a drink and a refill for himself.

Irish's hands shake as he carries the coffee back to the table and he hopes she doesn't notice the spills as he puts the mugs down. 'Waitress will be over in a minute for our food. Anything on the cross?'

'Experts think it's Celtic but not worth a lot.'

'I thought it was ancient?'

'*Old* doesn't necessarily mean valuable.'

'Tell me about it.'

She laughs.

Irish thinks back to what the girl told him. 'Strange thing is, Sophie Hudson said Amir Goldman had been ready to pay thousands for it.' He sips his refill and wishes he'd left it to cool. 'How much exactly did your *expert* say it was worth?'

'A few hundred bucks.'

'So why would someone kill for something worth so little?' His phone rings and he glances at the display. 'The office.'

She watches him take the call and scribble in a dog-eared pad he's pulled from his crumpled brown jacket. He has all the hallmarks of someone who's fallen hard and is still crawling the sidewalk trying to get up.

Irish clicks off his phone. 'Vic in the woods was one James T. Sacconni. A twenty-six-year-old ex-con with a string of previous for aggravated assault with a knife.'

'Where's he from?'

'Originated New York. Has a juvenile rap sheet from there. Did two years in a Big House in Chicago.'

'Mob connection?'

Irish is impressed. 'Were you listening in?'

'Italian-sounding name plus Big Apple and Windy City usually equals mob or gangs.'

'Maybe both. He's a known associate of Kyle and Jordan Coll, two brothers who head MS-13 – that's the Mara Salvatrucha mob. It started independent but is now mafia-run.'

'I've heard of it. They tangled with the Bloods back in Compton.' Mitzi picks up her coffee. 'You get a look at the plate on the SUV he was in before he got whacked?'

'Yeah. We ran that. Came up cloned. Some whiter-than-white businessman out in Annandale owns the original and an Escalade that's never seen anything dirtier than the paws of his Labrador.'

'So let's summarize what we've got. A missing Escalade that's probably in the Potomac. Two dead guys – one an old antiques dealer, the other a known mob affiliate.'

Irish chips in. 'A religious cross of indeterminate value and a memory stick full of "batshit code", if I remember your words correctly.'

'The code's the clue,' says Mitzi. 'No point using batshit unless you want to hide something. And you only hide what's valuable.'

'Then we have the Lincoln, driven by a British consular official who follows our mobster's SUV and the next day flies out of the country.'

Mitzi puts it together. 'So, we need to talk to this George whatever-he-was-called.'

'Dalton,' says Irish. 'But he's back in London and will have diplomatic immunity.'

'He's key, though. Question is – do we make the approach through your boss or mine?'

Irish drops his head in his hands. He knows what the answer is. It's his case. It has to come through his boss. And his captain is gonna love him for it.

45

NEW YORK

Outside the building, the young woman breaks down and sobs.

Not out of disappointment that she can no longer be a martyr, but because by some incredible twist of fate she's been saved.

She falls to her knees and kisses the ground.

Unbeknown to her, the man she will forever thank in her prayers is standing nervously in a 'clean room' above the basement.

After washing, Antun and the three others roll out prayer mats. They face Makkah and perform Salat al-'Asr, the afternoon dedication that is fourteen hundred years old.

Nabil leads the prayers by raising his hands to his ears and praising God. '*Allahu Akbar.*'

The others respond and follow him as he runs through Takbir, Qiyaam, Ruku, Sujud, and Tashahhud. Each stage is marked with readings, prayers and exhortations.

As they near the end, they turn their faces, first to the right and then to the left. Each movement sees them address the angels that follow all Muslims and record both their good and bad actions with the exhortation, 'Peace be upon you, and the mercy and blessings of Allah.'

The mats are rolled away. It is time to fit the suicide vest.

Antun strips to the waist. The packs of explosives feel cold against his skin. The canvas of the garment is rough. Hard wires press his flesh.

In the midst of these final preparations, he has to remind himself who he is, what he stands for and where he came from. He is Antun Bhatti, a proud member of the SSOA, the Sacred and Secret Order of Arthurians. Put simply, he's a Christian soldier, prepared to lay down his own life to save others.

This vest is his crucifix. It is the holy instrument of death that he must carry to the end of his mortal road.

He remembers being a child in India. Eight years old, an orphan in the slums of the Punjab, running barefoot towards a squalid block of concrete that is his church. A giant wooden cross stands out at the end of a track covered in dusty black sewage, multi-coloured trash and fried grass. Muslim children throw rubble and stones as he races towards the sanctuary. He hears the missiles whizz in the air and clunk on the ground alongside him, feels the sting of those that connect with his flesh and bones.

Inside the cool of the church, young Antun sits on one of the old dark wooden pews, his feet not touching the floor, and counts the cuts and bruises on his bare legs and arms. Fourteen this month. The same number as the Stations of the Cross.

He puts a finger in the blood of a fresh cut on his knee and licks it. It tastes of iron and reminds him of the metal cross the priest put to his mouth at his confirmation.

The memory is vivid. As though it happened only yesterday.

Not a whole lifetime ago.

'It is done.' Nabil's voice bridges past and present. He looks earnestly at Antun. 'My brother, the Garden of Allah awaits you.'

46

KENSINGTON, MARYLAND

Irish calls his boss and says he needs to see him.

Only when Zach Fulo hears the words 'British Embassy' does he tell his least popular cop that he's got a slot at five-thirty p.m. and bad traffic or no bad traffic he'd better be on time and bring the Fed with him.

Before they head to Washington, Irish and Mitzi order the house special of deluxe quarter pounders, fries and onion rings.

The cuisine is more ballast than food and once the warm orgy of salt, carbs, fat and protein is over, they both wish they'd had the chicken salad.

He gets the check, while she takes a walk outside and calls her daughters. To be precise, she calls Jade, knowing that Amber won't be far away and Jade will be annoyed if she doesn't get called first, while Amber never thinks of such things.

'Hi there – how are ya, honey?'

Jade is half-reading a magazine and answers in a bored and distracted voice. 'All right.'

Mitzi tries not to be dispirited. 'What've ya been doin'?'

'Nothing much. Just hanging at Aunt Ruth's.'

She really wishes her daughter wasn't such hard work. 'Everything okay?'

'Don't know. Uncle Jack's gone to stay at a friend's. I heard him and Aunt Ruth arguing this morning.'

'About what?' Her heart thumps.

Jade finally abandons the article on teen sex entitled 'Should She, Shouldn't She?' and concentrates a little. 'It was something about you. Uncle Jack said you're a fucking bitch and then Aunt Ruth slapped him and told him to get the fuck out of the house.'

Mitzi takes a deep breath. 'Wow. I wonder what I did to piss *him* off.'

'Maybe the same thing you did to piss Dad off?' She knows she's now on borrowed time before she gets an earful. 'Amber! Mom's on the phone; she wants to talk to you.' She drops the handset on a table.

Mitzi's left seething.

Her other daughter picks up the phone, 'Mom?'

She swallows the anger. 'Hi, baby. How are you?'

'I'm okay. When you coming home?' She corrects herself. 'I mean back to Aunt Ruth's.'

'Maybe tomorrow. Latest the day after. Are you having fun there?'

'Yeah, we are. Well, me and Aunt Ruth are. Jade's being – well, you know, Jade's being Jade. We're making cupcakes. Aunt Ruth's baked a giant one. Wait 'til you see it, Mom. It's bigger than the top off a trash can.'

'Sounds great. What flavour?'

'Chocolate. I mean – could it be anything other than chocolate?'

She laughs. 'No, I guess not. Chocolate's good and giant chocolate is super-good.'

'Right! Do you want to talk to Aunt Ruth? I can go get her.'

Mitzi hesitates. 'No. I'm okay. Don't interrupt her if she's busy in the kitchen. Just send her my love. Love you too, baby.'

'Love you as well, Mom.'

'Amber, give your sister a hug and kiss from me, and tell her not to be such a sourpuss.'

She laughs. 'I will. Love you, Mom.'

Mitzi hears her shouting 'sourpuss' across the room as she hangs up.

Irish is stood by the Taurus, hands on the hood, looking as though he's going to throw up.

She's not ready to walk over to him. Her mind's still on her kids and how Jade blames her for the break-up with her father. And it's on Ruth and how she might well be blaming her for her break-up with Jack.

47

LONDON

The armour-plated Bell is cleared to enter the secure airspace around Buckingham Palace and land on the royal helipad.

Visual security checks are conducted by armed protection staff before Owain is even allowed to step outside the craft.

Once he's been cleared, he's whisked inside by what seems a battalion of guards and footmen.

As he enters the Grand Hall, he remembers that it's fifteen years since he was here for his investiture and how back then he'd realized his own family had frequented the building when it was no more than a town home for the Duke of Buckingham.

Such familiarity doesn't stop him admiring the priceless works of art hung on the walls. Paintings by Rembrandt, Vermeer, Van Dyck and Rubens that form part of the Royal Collection.

He passes the Throne Room, its proscenium arch supported by a pair of winged figures of Victory holding garlands above the chair of state. Then the giant ballroom along the East Gallery, the site of state banquets and diplomatic receptions.

The security escorts leave Owain to wait in the White Drawing Room, a name that amuses him because it is so non-white. The ceiling-to-floor drapes and pelmets, the chairs and sofas, cushions and footstools, fire screens and even the surrounds of the giant ornate mirrors that amplify every expansive wall are either a rich yellow or glistening gold.

The Prince of Wales enters.

He's in a slimly tailored, light-grey suit with a white shirt and pink and gold silk tie, looped of course in a Windsor knot.

'I hope you don't mind us meeting here instead of Clarence House.' He holds out a hand to the knight.

Owain bows as he shakes it. 'Of course not, Your Royal Highness.'

'Please, not so official when we are alone.' The prince motions towards two three-seater sofas arranged opposite each other. 'I know my father wants to say hello, so don't be surprised if he bursts in on us.'

'I won't. It would be delightful to see him again.'

'Have you been asked if you would like tea?'

'I have, and I don't but thank you.'

'Owain, I asked you here to discuss your new position, that of ambassador-at-large, with responsibilities for defence and counter-terrorism.'

'I'm honoured to serve and highly delighted to do so from British soil.'

'I know. One can only exist in America for so long without going slightly crazy. It's like holding your breath under very pleasant tropical water. You still have to come up for air.' He unfastens his suit jacket and cuts to the chase. 'I'd like to speak bluntly.'

'Please do. I'm keen to know what flow of information you'd like and how often you'd like it. Being kept in the loop is one thing – getting strangled by it is quite another.'

'Indeed. And this is where I have a problem.' He tries to choose his words carefully. 'It's that I know so little of the inner workings of the SSOA.'

'It is perhaps best that way.'

'Perhaps, but please credit me with the intelligence to decide that for myself.'

Owain doesn't respond. He knows there is more to come.

'I wish to join your Order.'

'With respect, I think it best that we operate at arm's length from your good self.'

'And I think it best you don't.'

The gold-cased antique clock on the marble fireplace beside them ticks three times before the prince adds, 'You know my military background, Owain, so please don't give me some guff about any refusal being a way to protect me. I have spent most of my life on the hit list of some terrorist group or other and I've been in more than my fair share of trouble spots.'

'It isn't that.'

'Then what *exactly* is it?'

'Unless there is a genetic link to an original knight, the Blood Line is closed to you. And membership of the Inner Circle is not mine alone to grant. It has to be sanctioned by others.'

'Then have them sanction it; I'm sure you have the influence.'

'I do. But even then, it is only possible to become a member if you pass the initiation.' He lets the word sink in, then adds, 'There have never been any exceptions and can never be.'

'I seek none.' The prince looks pleased to have made some progress. 'What exactly do these initiations involve?' He smiles like a child anticipating a dare. 'I still have some scars from the rites I endured during my military days.'

'Blood, Your Royal Highness. The ritual spilling of yours and the fatal spilling of our enemy's.'

48

NEW YORK

Any hope Antun harboured of simply slipping off the vest and defusing it is being crushed.

Aasif fixes handcuffs behind his back and leads him to a green parcel-delivery van, parked around the corner from the basement hideaway. The enforcer bundles him in to the passenger seat and fastens the safety buckle.

They drive out to the Cross Bronx Expressway, then south-west towards Port Morris, East Harlem and ultimately Midtown East.

The big man dips his hand into his pocket and produces what looks like a metal cigar with a red button on the top. 'This will help things go smoothly. Just in case you have second thoughts about your redemption and turn into a coward again.' He gives a yellow-toothed grin as he slips the remote trigger back into his pocket.

The young SSOA operative watches the world rush up and hit the windshield. Sights he may never see again, sounds he'll never hear.

The journey to Grand Central's likely to take close to an

hour. Best-case scenario is that he's got sixty minutes in which to get himself out of the biggest jam of his life, or end up scattered in pieces, along with hundreds, maybe thousands of people.

He remembers this isn't the first time the station has been hit by a bomb. Exactly twenty-five years to the day before 9/11 a group of Croatian nationalists planted one in a coin locker and at the same time hijacked a plane.

Back then, the terrorists had a change of heart. After stating their political demands, they revealed the location of the explosives.

Antun knows that today there will be no change of heart.

Al-Qaeda has no heart.

Only as they join the toll road at Robert F. Kennedy Bridge, about five miles from their destination, does Aasif have all fingers and thumbs on the steering wheel.

Antun sneaks a cuffed hand down to the seatbelt clasp and starts to unlock it.

A coach full of young children pulls alongside the van. Excited faces are pressed to the glass.

He hesitates.

Aasif puts his hand back into the detonator pocket and pulls away from the toll.

The moment has gone.

The next four miles roll by in silence. They come off at exit eleven and join crawling traffic onto East 53rd, then hit gridlock as they reach Second Avenue.

Antun feels his heart belt his chest. They're less than a mile away but surrounded by cars. An explosion here would be as bad as inside the station.

Aasif sees the anxiety on his face. 'Be patient. We are nearly there. I suggest you cleanse your mind and prepare yourself for the greatest moment of your miserable life.'

Traffic moves. Cars creep forward. They turn right onto 42nd. Antun sees the outline of the station at the bottom of the street. Time speeds up. The last frames of his life play double-speed.

Aasif insists on running through the plan once more. 'I will stop just past the Grand Hyatt, then we will get out and walk to the main entrance. You will enter and keep walking. Count to twenty and then detonate. I will be going in the opposite direction but I'll also be counting. If after twenty seconds I have not heard anything, then I will press my detonator. Do you understand?'

Antun nods.

They join a crush of cars and yellow cabs heading to the Hyatt and the other side of the station.

Aasif stops the car, pulls on the handbrake and takes out the ignition keys. He turns the ring around until he finds the one for the handcuffs and unlocks them.

Antun rubs his wrists. He pops the safety belt free and gets out. There are crowds all around him. The noises, smells and light of early evening seem more vibrant and meaningful than he's ever known.

He sucks in what might be his last air as he waits for Aasif to lock the van.

The big man walks alongside him. They head slowly to the station entrance. The terrorist puts his hand on Antun's shoulder and stops. 'This is where I leave you, my brother.' He shows him the detonator gripped tightly in his hand as he spreads his arms to embrace him.

Antun makes his move.

49

POLICE HQ, WASHINGTON DC

Captain Zach Fulo, rests his elbows on his paper-strewn desk and listens patiently as Irish summarizes the case.

Occasionally, he glances at the FBI woman to see if her face shows any disagreement with his lieutenant's account.

It doesn't.

Far as he can make out, she's the serious type. Not a drinker. Certainly not a sleep-around, screw-your-way-to-the-top kind of girl. Ten years ago though, he imagines she would have been quite a looker. She's got eyes that have seen life and the lack of a wedding ring on her finger probably means life has seen a lot of her as well.

Irish finishes with a plea to interview the British Consul George Dalton about his movements on the night of Amir Goldman's murder. 'Even if he ends up claiming diplomatic immunity, we owe it to the victim to pursue this line of enquiry and find the killer.'

'Do you go along with all this?' Fulo asks Mitzi. 'You think *we* – and by that I mean the august bodies of the FBI and DC police – should go shouting through diplomatic doors and demanding ambassadors and attachés turn out their pockets and account for their actions?'

'I do, sir. I don't think anyone should be treated any different than anyone else. Regardless of their job, title, sex, age, religion, race or nationality. Equality for all perps; that's my motto.'

He corrects her. 'Suspected perps.'

She can see she's winning him over. 'Speaking plainly, Captain, if this guy Dalton wasn't out of the country and wasn't a member of the British diplomatic corps, we'd already have his evasive ass polishing a seat in one of our interview rooms.'

Fulo rocks on his chair. 'Amazingly, Irish, I find myself agreeing with you and the lady here. I'm not one for people hiding behind position or privilege. Bad is bad, even if it's dressed up in a diplomat's thousand-dollar suit.' He sits up straight and clicks open the log on his computer. 'I take due note that you've referred this to me, so feel free to ask whatever questions you need, in whatever quarters you have to. Hell, go to England and shout them through the gates of Buckingham Castle if that's what it takes to solve this case.'

'Palace,' says Mitzi. 'It's a palace, not a castle.'

He gives her a famous Zach Fulo stare then eyeballs Irish.

'Wherever it is – and wherever you go, just make damned sure you take your manners with you. Do things politely, quickly and as economically as you can.'

'Yes, sir.'

Fulo adds a final remark. 'Don't screw this up, Fitzgerald or so help me God you'll need a castle to keep me off your ass.'

50

GRAND CENTRAL STATION, NEW YORK

Antun smashes his forehead into the middle of Aasif 's face.

The terrorist grunts and snorts blood.

Antun twists his left wrist and breaks it. He rams the busted bone up the giant's back and feels the shoulder dislocate.

Aasif doesn't want to die. He knows he's got to overcome Antun and then get away from him before he detonates the vest. He also knows he's being beaten. He focuses past the pain and kicks out wildly.

Antun sidesteps the sweep. He hooks his heel around the hulk's shin and clatters him onto the hard ground.

Aasif rolls over on his good arm and gets to his feet. He's pumped with adrenaline and delivers a nerve-numbing kick to Antun's thigh.

Antun takes it and doesn't fall. He retaliates with a punch that a heavyweight would be proud of. While the big guy sways from the shock, he spins and dropkicks him in the abdomen.

The enforcer hits the ground like a felled oak.

Antun drops on top of him and jams two knuckles over his windpipe.

Aasif senses death. He punches with his one good arm and connects with Antun's lower jaw.

Antun channels his weight into his fingers and the softness of the throat beneath them.

People gather round. They shout for the cops. Someone tries to drag Antun off, but he doesn't loosen his hold. The body below him goes into spasm. Legs kick. Heels bang on the sidewalk.

A final downward thrust of knuckle.

It's over.

Antun falls back and catches his breath.

Someone shouts, 'Jesus!' Screams break out. Enough yells to stop every beat cop for a mile.

Antun stands. Sweat drips from his face. He turns to the freaked-out crowd, 'Stand back! All of you, get right back.' He opens the black, baggy jacket he's wearing. Shows the vest. 'I've got a bomb. They've made me wear a bomb.'

Bedlam breaks out.

To his left, uniformed cops stand frozen in their tracks. One of them mutters into a radio. Another sneaks his fingers towards a gun. To his right, fifty yards away, Antun sees a face he recognizes.

Nabil.

The cell commander turns and walks away.

Antun knows what's about to happen. He closes his eyes just before the remotely detonated explosion blows his body into a thousand pieces.

51

WASHINGTON DC

Mitzi and Irish are on the way out of police HQ when the newsflash comes in.

'Bomb blast at Grand Central!' The shout comes from an old timer working the front desk. 'Hell of a fucking mess.'

The two cops drift back his way.

'More than a hundred dead.' He reads the graphics bar crawling across the TV on a shelf to his right. 'Maybe as many again injured. Reporter said the bomb could be heard more than a mile away.'

Mitzi swears.

Irish leans on the counter to see the screen. 'They say who's responsible?'

'Not yet.' The uniform guesses the story is so important it's okay for him to crank up the sound.

A journalist is doing her best to report live from the scene. The constant wail of ambulances and fire trucks fights with her piece to camera. 'The blast happened a little before six p.m. at the height of rush-hour traffic here in the centre of New York. At that time, this station, the sixth most visited tourist spot in the world, was at its busiest. Early reports say the explosion was caused by a male suicide bomber. Eyewitnesses describe him as being in his late twenties and of average height and build. Police are investigating reports that he got into a fight with another man on the sidewalk before revealing his suicide vest to onlookers and then detonating it.'

A caption rolls across screen with a number for people to call if they're worried that a loved one, relative or friend might have been at the station.

Mitzi's seen and heard enough. Everything beyond this point is just news people doing their business and depressing everyone else in the process.

She wanders outside and thinks of Jade and Amber, Ruthy and Groping Hands Jack and even her bum of an ex. She thanks God that they're safe in boring old California rather than NYC, the new bomb capital of the world.

After a few minutes, Irish emerges scratching a muss of hair that feels like it's turning into a bald patch. He glances at the news footage on the screen. 'Kind of takes the shine off the good news the captain gave us.'

She's not really listening. 'D'you mind if I head back to the hotel and see if I can fix a flight out of here in the morning? I reckon I can be as much use to you on the phone from San Francisco as I can from here.'

He wishes she was staying but understands her desire to go. 'Sure. Give me a minute and I'll drive you back.'

'No need. You look like you're ready to crash out. I can get a cab.'

'I'd *like* to drive you. That's if you don't mind sitting in the trash one last time.'

She appreciates the gesture. 'I guess my tetanus and cholera jabs are good for a final ride in your crapmobile.'

52

BUCKINGHAM PALACE, LONDON

The encrypted phone vibrates inside the pocket of Owain's black dinner suit. 'I'm very sorry,' he says to the Canadian ambassador, 'I'm afraid there's an urgent call and I really have to take it.'

He doesn't wait to hear the diplomat's answer and presses the answer button as soon as he reaches the refuge of a corridor. 'Hello, Gareth.'

'Antun is dead.'

'Dear God.'

'A bomb has gone off at Grand Central in New York and he was at the centre of it.'

Owain feels sick. Sick and angry. He tries to keep a soldierly focus. 'This presumably is the work of the cell he'd infiltrated and Nabil.'

'It is. We have eyes back on Nabil.'

Owain wants to kill him. Have him shot within the hour. But he knows it's not the answer. 'Tabrizi is a commander but he's not the main man. In fact, he's probably their weak link.'

'I agree. That's what Antun told us. It's why he wanted to stay within the cell and try to work his way up the chain of command.'

'Then we must respect his bravery and not shoot this animal on sight. How many dead at the station, Gareth?'

'Latest count is a hundred and eleven. Close to two hundred injured by debris.' He's almost reluctant to add the information he's just learned. 'It seems Antun was made to wear a suicide vest.'

Owain grimaces. 'Then either he volunteered, hoping he could do it, or his cover was blown. Do you have an idea which?'

Gareth Madoc has been trying to piece together the same puzzle. 'The police say he fought with another man on the sidewalk and killed him before detonating the vest.'

'They have their facts wrong, someone else will have detonated it.'

'It could have been Nabil. We only got eyes back on him post-explosion as he returned to a safe house.'

Owain watches guests heading in to the dining room to take their places at tables. 'I have to go. I'll call you later. For God's sake, make sure we don't lose Nabil. He's young enough to make mistakes. We're old enough to capitalize on them.'

'I'll look after it personally.'

'Thanks. I want you back here unhurt. We've lost too many good men in too many bad situations and I fear this wave of attacks is far from over.'

53

WASHINGTON DC

Mitzi and Irish listen to the news on the car radio as they drive to her hotel in Kensington.

She notices he's pale and sweating. He's gripping the wheel and seems pained by a migraine or more likely the mother of all hangovers. 'You got any help on this case? Maybe you do need to lie up for a day or two.'

'Some borrowed hands from other investigations, that's all.'

'A double homicide doesn't get you your own team?'

'*Team?* Child murder will get you a *team*. That's about all that does these days.'

'Times get tough, criminals get tougher. It's the way of the world.'

'Sure is. There's a bright kid called Kirstin Collins doing some leg work for me. She'll be a good cop one day. If the system lets her.'

'Or she doesn't get pushed upstairs to drive a desk.'

He thinks about asking her some personal stuff. About her career. Her colleagues. Her life. Men. Relationships. Only a wave of sickness washes over him.

'You okay?'

Irish coughs. Blood spatters the wheel.

He splutters red all over his hands and collapses.

'Christ.' Mitzi grabs the wheel.

His foot is jammed on the gas.

The Ford surges forward.

Sixty.

Mitzi swings the Ford wide of an SUV. Horns honk all around her.

Sixty-five.

Her heart hammers as she struggles to push Irish off the wheel.

Seventy.

A monumental shove sends his unconscious body crashing into the drivers' door but his foot stays heavy on the accelerator.

Mitzi can't move him any more.

Seventy-five.

Traffic brakes hard in front. She jerks the wheel. It twitches and skids from the outside lane to the middle one.

Eighty.

There's a truck ahead. Red brake-lights flare. Mitzi squeals the Ford through to the inside lane. Crashing is now inevitable. It's only a question of where.

The Taurus mounts a grass verge. A wing mirror clips a

tree. The back of the car fishtails. Mitzi sees a clump of oaks rushing up fast. She spins the steering wheel.

The car flips. Slides on its side. Rolls on its roof. Metal crunches. Glass shatters.

There's a deafening thump. She feels a vicious stab of pain in the middle of her face.

Then there's blackness.

PART TWO

54

LONDON

Angelo Marchetti feels like someone clubbed him with a baseball bat. He puts a hand to the pain in his forehead. Opening his eyes is like winding up rusty metal shutters and squinting into the blaze of a scorching summer's day.

He's in bed. That much he can work out. The lights are on, the curtains open. But it's black outside. The digital clock next to him says 0447. No time to be awake.

But this is not his own room. It's a hotel. Not in America. Abroad.

There's a noise. The stirring of a body. He pulls the duvet back.

A naked woman is asleep alongside him. No one he recognizes. Which isn't so strange. Women he had *relationships* with bailed on him a long time ago.

Angelo pulls himself upright and looks at her. She's olive-skinned, Latin, maybe Hispanic. Hair even longer and blacker than his. Small-breasted and full-hipped. A tattoo of a serpent hugs her waist like a belt. Its diamond-shaped head rests upon her shaved pubic area and its long, thin tongue disappears between her legs.

Insects are buzzing. Not in the room but in his head. Swarms of crickets, wasps and bees are angry at being woken and are stinging the soft grey honeycomb of his brain.

Marchetti gets up and wanders around. There is white powder on a low table. Needles. Mirrors. Antiseptic wipes and empty plastic bags. Speedballs.

Now he remembers. He'd sat in here with the hooker. Gisela – her name had been Gisela. Spanish and wild. They'd done enough coke to kill a rock band.

The floor ahead of him is covered with torn-off clothes. Empty bottles of water. Money.

Stacks and stacks of pound notes.

It all comes back to him. He's in London. And last night he got lucky. Very lucky.

55

POLICE HQ, WASHINGTON DC

Sharp morning light bursts through a beat-up shade in Fulo's office and makes Mitzi squint painfully.

An airbag in Irish's car broke her nose and left her with

multiple bruises, including two black eyes and lips that look like she's just done Botox.

Mitzi shifts her chair into a patch of shade while the captain reads a note on his computer.

'The latest from Memorial Hospital is that he's stable but still critical.'

'He's lucky to be alive.' Mitzi tentatively puts fingers to the painful throb in the middle of her nose.

'Not *so* lucky.' Fulo reads the rest of the note. 'He has broken ribs, left collarbone, and right wrist. He's dislocated his right kneecap, sprained his left ankle and' – he dries up.

'And what, Captain?'

Fulo continues in an even more sombre tone. 'His liver's failing. It's totally screwed. That's what caused the blood you say he coughed up just before the blackout.'

'Liquor?'

'Years of it.' His face contorts with anger. 'Fuck, he was a good cop. Once. Before the freezer case.'

'The what?'

'Domestic over in Brookland. Young woman staggered into the precinct looking like she hadn't eaten in a year.' He points at Mitzi, 'She had panda eyes – like yours. Kid was black and blue. Scars all over her flesh and she couldn't speak.'

'Shock?'

'Doctors said some years back her tongue had been stapled to her lip with a carpet-fitter's gun. When it turned gangrenous, her captor sliced off the end. Kid was left with a stump. But she could write. Wrote down stuff you'd never want to read. Fitzgerald was lead on the case. He went back to the shack she picked out as the one she'd been kept in and abused. Unsub had long gone. Searched the place and he found a freezer in the garage.'

'I think I can guess what was in it.'

'I don't think you can. Fitzgerald found corpses of newborns.'

Mitzi hangs her head.

'Four of them. Laid out in a line. The psychopathic son-of-a-bitch had abducted the woman when she was thirteen, and got her pregnant four times.'

She grasps at a straw of hope. 'The kids were stillbirths?'

'No. He'd delivered them, cut the umbilical cords and put them in the freezer to die.'

'Why? Why did he keep them? Why not bury them?'

'Trophies. He told the woman they were proof of his virility.'

'Jesus. Please tell me this psychopath is on Death Row so I can go cheer when the big day comes.'

'Better than that. He turned up dead in a motel in New York. Someone tied him to a chair, stuffed part of a bed sheet in his mouth and shot him in the testicles. According to the ME, the killer waited at least an hour before he pulled the sheet out of his mouth and put the gun between his teeth and fired the second bullet.'

'Nice job.'

'You're not alone in thinking that. No one dug too deep

to find the triggerman. Least of all, Fitzgerald. He barely seemed surprised. If you follow my drift.'

She nods. 'I hope the hospital manage to fix him up. Get him a liver transplant, or whatever it takes.'

'We'll pull some strings. See what we can do to hike him up a donor list.' He searches the layer of papers on his desk and pulls up a sheet. 'This is for you.'

She takes it and stares at a list of names.

'They're private numbers for all the main British Embassy staff here and in London.'

'Thanks. I'll trawl them when I get back to California.' She notices a half-smile. It's the kind bosses always have when they know something you don't. 'What'd I miss?'

'I spoke to your supervisor, Miss Donovan. She's happy for you to be seconded to run this case from Washington, least 'til we see whether it's got road to run or is just a dead end.'

'She never mentioned this when I updated her last night.'

'I spoke to her an hour ago. She expects you to call her after this meeting.'

'Captain, I'd really like to see my daughters. I'm sure you can understand that.'

'Then clear this up quickly, Lieutenant. And let's not kid ourselves, both you and I know that someone's going to have to go to England, and that sure as hell isn't going to be me or Lieutenant Fitzgerald.'

56

SOHO, LONDON

Angelo Marchetti wakes Gisela the hooker.

He pays her off and bundles her out. Now he needs to shower, dress and get ready for his breakfast meeting.

The upcoming face-to-face is, after all, why he flew here some thirty hours ago.

He's acutely aware that the man he's meeting also owns the room he's staying in and the illegal casino downstairs where last night he won several thousand pounds. No big deal, considering the business he's about to conclude will net him millions. Millions and a new start. One far away from Owain Gwyn and his army of do-gooders.

Marchetti fastens the slim-cut white shirt that hangs loose over blue jeans. In the mirror, the thirty-four-year-old studies flecks of grey in his jet black locks and designer beard. His youth has gone and the signs of ageing make him nostalgic. As a teenager he played soccer for Napoli. Three short years during which he earned millions and spent much of it helping the poor in Campania.

Then came his blackest day.

A leg-breaking tackle that robbed him of his first international cap. The type of injury that would lead to years of rehab, painkillers and failed comebacks. At first, he fell back on his investments and continued to be a dedicated young philanthropist, building projects and hope for street kids in Scampia and Secondigliano. It was these acts that attracted the Arthurians to him and for a time gave him a reason to live. He worked hard at keeping young Italians out of the grasp of the Camorra and the Mafia.

Then had come the second blow.

Both he and his wife were having secret affairs. She with a former teammate. He with drink and drugs.

At first, the addiction was purely painkillers. They tamped the physical and mental hurt. Then as loneliness bit he befriended cocaine and heroin.

He moved to America to be out of the reach of the mob-owned dealers he owed money to, but as his debts grew so too did his addictions. He added gambling to his opiates in a bid to raise enough cash to pay everyone off and start again. Only he lost ten times more than he won.

The rap on the door shakes him from his thoughts.

He peeps through the spyhole.

Three figures fill his view – two large men, both armed.

And *him*.

The man Gwyn had spoken so much of.

The one the SSOA fear and hate the most.

57

POLICE HQ, WASHINGTON DC

Mitzi all but slams the phone down on Donovan.

The last thing she wanted was to stay in DC.

Ruthy, Jade and Amber are going to give her hell when she tells them that the couple of days she promised to be away is going to be more like a couple of weeks.

Now she needs more clothes. Unless she wants to end up smelling worse than Irish or his car. What's left of it. What's left of him, for that matter. She makes a mental note to call the hospital – right after she's worked her way through the list of names Fulo gave her.

A vending machine coughs out something close to coffee and she takes it to Irish's desk in the Homicide Squad Room. The whole square yard of space smells of him. Booze, fast food and dust have seeped into the cloth and wood where he's done all his hours. Or not done it, judging by the piles of stuff stacked up.

She clears junk and gets down to the job of calling around. Systematically, she works her way through the private office and cell phone numbers of Britain's entire senior diplomatic staff in the USA, both present and past.

No one picks up.

Unperturbed, she leaves messages for them to get back to her but doubts that they will.

Mitzi's about to call her sister when a woman with spiky black hair and a pale, androgynous face appears at the edge of the desk and catches her by surprise. 'Hey! Don't go creeping up on people like that.' She puts her hand to her chest. 'You nearly gave me a heart attack.'

'Sorry. Are you the lieutenant sent from the FBI?'

Mitzi looks over the dyed locks, black top and matching skinny jeans and boots. 'Not if you're the Grim Reaper. What's with the look?'

'I'm Kirstin Collins.' She gestures to her clothes. 'I'm working drugs, undercover at a club, but I was helping Irish out as well. Do you know how he is?'

'Lieutenant Fallon.' She stretches out a hand. 'From what I heard, he's in a bad way.'

'Looks like you took a whack yourself.'

'Yeah, that's just because I can't put make-up on. I always look this bad, even without the bruises.'

Kirstin laughs.

'I'm going to call the hospital in a minute and check on him. Take a seat.' Mitzi points at a chair. 'Irish spoke highly of you. Said you'd make a good cop one day.'

'*One day*?' She laughs. 'He's got a cheek. Fulo says you're running his case, that right?'

'I guess so. Why? Have you got something?'

She tries not to stare too much at the black eyes and plastered nose. 'You know Irish got a lead on the SUV and the Lincoln from Traffic?'

'Yeah, I'm up to speed.'

'Well, I looked on the map for all-night food joints near the exit where the vehicles came off. There were only a few. None had surveillance on their parking lots.'

'That's the way the cookie *usually* crumbles, Kirstin.'

'I know. But I did talk to the overnight managers about whether they saw anything suspicious.'

'I'm guessing one of them did, or else you wouldn't be recounting this tale.'

'Right. Guy called Ludo working ANAR, the All Night All Right franchise out near Stead Park, noticed a Lincoln leaving his lot. Minutes later a tow-truck appeared, hooked up the SUV and hauled it away.'

'This Ludo get the name of the garage?'

'No. But that wasn't what stuck in his mind.'

'What did?'

The SUV driver had eaten in the diner, but the Lincoln owner hadn't. Soon after the paying customer left, Mr Lincoln owner came in and used the washroom. Then he reappeared and went straight back out again. This got the supervisor pissed, because they hate people just using the john and not ordering anything, so he went outside to shout at him. Only he didn't holler because he saw the guy was at his car and looked like he was in pain. Ludo said he was struggling to get into the seat, holding a stack of paper towels to his arm. Then, as the Lincoln drove past him he saw the plates. He asked himself why a diplomat wanted to use his bathroom so urgently and why he needed a stack of towels for his arm.'

'And?'

'He went back to the restroom and found spots of blood on the floor.'

'I'm going to ask a stupid question. By any chance did he mop up and keep the rags or sponge?'

'No.'

'I thought not, but deep inside me lives a young pixie called Hope and sometimes she just won't shut the fuck up.'

Kirstin laughs. 'Well, your pixie might be in luck because Ludo did notice something strange. Despite the spatter on the floor, there were no stained towels in the bin. No mess. Just the drips.'

'So he came over all Dexter and did some blood analysis?'

'Kind of. He thought maybe Mr SUV had been caught banging Mr Lincoln's wife and been chased down to the diner where it all kicked off. He went outside to check everything was okay and saw the SUV being trucked away.'

Mitzi curses a lost opportunity. 'Shame about the blood.'

'Not really. My boyfriend's a CSI. He went round and swabbed the floor for me. Even though it had been cleaned, he got traces from the mortar between the tiles. They've been processed in the labs and we have two good DNA profiles.'

'Two? As in killer and victim?'

'I guess that's your pixie mouthing off again, Lieutenant. I really don't know what he got. I'm just about to run the profiles through Records. You want to join me?'

58

SOHO, LONDON

The two bodyguards are not as tall as Marchetti but they're more muscular and much younger.

In contrast, their employer is a small, slender man in his mid-forties. The Italian can hardly believe this unassuming figure is the notorious Josep Mardrid. He walks them through to the lounge area of the suite.

Mardrid sits on a cotton sofa, while the muscle stand around him like bookends. 'Are you disappointed, Marchetti?' He unbuttons his jacket. 'Did you expect me to come wearing a black cape and have the horns and tail of a devil?'

'I didn't expect anything. Your intermediary gave you one of the burial crosses. Do you want to do business or not?'

'What do you have for me?'

Marchetti slips a hand onto the shelf beneath the table and produces a Celtic cross.

Mardrid takes it and turns it in his palm. 'You promised me valuable artefacts and secret information, Mr Marchetti. All I see there is a lump of old iron.'

'It's more than that. It's an Arthurian burial cross.'

There's a flicker of interest in his eyes. 'Tell me more.'

'When one of their knights is killed, he is buried with a cross placed on his chest. It is said they are forged from the same ore as Excalibur.'

'A quaint story. How is this any use to me?'

'It's more than quaint, it's true. Thousands of these men have been buried for centuries on land owned by Gwyn. They are laid in what the Order knows as Knight's Graveyards. Sacred plots in secret places, all over the world. I imagine that if I were to give you their locations, and you were to make them public, then as the police and press began their enquiries, it would be advantageous to you to see Sir Owain exposed in such a way.'

'Go on.'

'I can do that.' He picks up the cross. 'This circle in the middle of the crucifix isn't Celtic; it symbolizes the Arthurian round table. You can expose Gwyn as a fantasist, or whatever you like.'

'I may have misjudged you, Mr Marchetti. If this cross is all you say it is, why did one of your men try to sell it, or one like it, to a Jew dealer in America and then have him killed?'

'A mistake. Some idiots I employed acted out of turn. It was a question of money.'

'Idiots do that kind of thing.' He turns the cross over in his hands. 'I would like to do what you said. It would be pleasing to see Gwyn's warriors dug from the earth, and amusing watching him cope with the press fervour.' He stretches out a hand. 'Give me the details of these burial grounds.'

Marchetti laughs. 'I may have employed idiots, but I am not foolish enough to have such details here with me. They are safe and tradable.'

'Then let's trade. What do you want for them?'

'Ten million dollars for every graveyard.'

Mardrid smiles. 'A ridiculous price. But not unreasonable for the ruin of Owain Gwyn.' He gets to his feet and straightens out his suit. 'Mr Marchetti, know this: there is now no going back on this deal.' He wags the cross at him. 'If you do not deliver as promised, I will have my men dig you a grave and bury you alive with your cross. Good day.'

59

POLICE HQ, WASHINGTON DC

Mitzi tips the water cooler and drains the last drops into a blue plastic cup. It's enough to swill down another dose of painkillers.

Kirstin Collins stares at a monitor. She's waiting for the national lottery of databases to play out and tell her if she's struck lucky with matches to the two DNA profiles created from blood found at the diner near Dupont Circle.

'How we doing?' Mitzi drags a chair next to her.

'Still searching. I like how on TV cop shows it's all done in a single click.'

'Yeah, and the guys in the squad are so handsome and have hearts of gold.'

The screen pings up the first result.

'Profile One is not a winning ticket,' says Kirstin. 'No matches to any known offender.'

There's an agonizing pause before the second profile result is revealed.

'We have ourselves a hit! Bradley John Deagan. Forty-two years of age. One previous conviction for fraud.'

'What kinda fraud?'

Kirstin scrolls down. 'Something to do with a painting.' She reads on, 'Looks like he tried to sell one that never existed.'

'What?'

'Hold on. Let me click through to find the rest.' Kirstin follows a link to supporting documentation. 'Okay, here we go – the artwork was done by a guy named Eyck. It's called *The Ghent Altarpiece* and was made up of different paintings – what they call panels. One of these was stolen and never found. Deagan tried to con a man called Christie by saying he had it and wanted to sell it.'

'I think you mean Christie's – it's an auction house, not a person. They specialize in art and antiques.'

'My bad for not knowing. I don't buy a lot of art. Not unless you count my Chippendale poster.'

'I don't.'

'If you saw it, you'd change your mind.'

'I'm sure I would. Does the report say anything more about the piece he tried to sell?'

Kirstin scans the text. 'Not much. Says part of the altarpiece shows four groups of people gathering in a meadow to worship the Lamb of God and Deagan claimed his painting showed a fifth group, one that had never previously been identified.'

'Any values on there? Either for the real painting or what Deagan wanted for his fake?'

She reads as she scrolls. 'The altarpiece was fifteenth-century – and wow was it big – eleven feet by fifteen.' Kirstin spots a dollar sign. 'Ten million. Deagan wanted a minimum of ten million bucks for his fake. Man, it must have been good.'

Mitzi mentally lists her catalogue of clues:

The panels of *The Ghent Altarpiece*.

A Celtic cross.

A memory stick full of code.

A murdered antiques dealer.

A dead crook.

A missing art fraudster linked to a British diplomat who's left the country.

A man's voice breaks her concentration. 'Listen up.'

'Hang on,' she says to Kirstin. She looks around and sees Captain Fulo in the doorway.

He lifts his pitch, so the cops and clerks at the back of the room can hear him, 'People, give me your attention. I just got a call from the hospital. Lieutenant Patrick Fitzgerald died ten minutes ago.'

There are gasps and he waits a respectful second or two.

'Anyone want to talk privately, I'm in my office.'

60

SOHO, LONDON

There are things that Angelo Marchetti had forgotten to tell Josep Mardrid. Things that could now get him killed.

Sat in a run-down pub, next to a seedy strip joint, he throws back his third shot of vodka and tries not to think of the mess he's in.

He lied when he said he had the details of all the Knights' Graveyards. He hasn't. Truth is, they were on a digital file that he made on an SSOA memory stick when he was based at Caergwyn Castle in Wales. He copied them from the master computer along with scans of sacred books kept in the Arthurian Library.

The plan was to demand money from Gwyn in return for the stick. But he lost his nerve and looked for another way of making cash without directly exposing himself to the wrath of the Order.

His chance came when he returned to America.

He was put in charge of the burial of a young knight killed by arms traffickers. The internment was close to Glastonbury inside the Meshomasic State Forest in Connecticut.

After the ritual he sent his men away, telling them he needed time alone with his fallen brother. Only instead of paying his respects, he stole the man's burial cross and those of his father and grandfather, who had been laid to rest in the same tomb.

Marchetti had connections who could sell them for him. Men who supplied him with drugs. Gang bosses who were likely to kill him if he didn't settle his debts soon.

Out of financial desperation, he ended up giving one of the crosses and the original SSOA memory stick to Kyle Coll, the head of the Mara Salvatrucha family. He'd separately transcribed parts of the books on to a sheet of paper, so a dealer would be interested in the extracts, but he'd kept back the key to the code.

What he hadn't realized, until he checked the copy he'd made for himself, was that whenever the data was copied to non-SSOA software or hardware it corrupted. The copy he'd kept for himself became worthless.

Despite that setback, for a short while, it looked like things were still going to work out. The gang found Goldman, who specialized in religious artefacts. He came up with a deposit and was keen on buying all three crosses. When they threw in the extracts of the books he saw big dollar signs.

Then the old man did something stupid. He chipped his offer price at the last minute and threatened to expose them to the cops if they didn't accept it. The bluff cost him his life.

Things lurched from bad to worse.

Angelo had arranged to meet Brad Deagan at the Dupont diner, but he got wasted on crack and arrived late. So late, that all he saw was George Dalton leaving the parking lot. He watched the Lincoln go, then the tow truck come for Deagan's SUV. It was then that he knew the game was up and he had to flee the country before the Order got to him.

Now he has another chance.

A final one.

He finishes his drink and prays he doesn't blow it.

61

POLICE HQ, WASHINGTON DC

There's no way Mitzi can sit at Irish's desk. It wouldn't be right. Neither would hanging around while colleagues bad-mouth him.

She grabs a cab and gets to thinking she could have developed a soft spot for Irish. Bad boys and broken-downs have always been her type. And he was certainly a renovation job.

Back in her room at Silver Fall Lodge, she flips open the minibar, finds a bottle of the hard stuff and unscrews the top. 'Here's to you, Lieutenant Fitzgerald. I hope heaven has a free bar and a good woman to love you.' She jolts back enough brandy to burn her throat, then grabs a dose of painkillers and lies down for a five-minute rest.

Two hours later, she's woken by the jangle of her phone.

Her heart hammers as she grabs it from the bedside table. 'Hello.'

There's a pause before a man answers, 'Is that *Lieutenant* Fallon?'

She struggles to sit up. Pain drives a stake through the middle of her face. 'Yeah, it is.' She sees the number is withheld. 'Look, if you're another cold-calling asshole trying to sell me insurance or a car loan, then I warn you buddy, now is NOT the time.'

'This is Sir Owain Gwyn, former UK ambassador to America.'

She closes her eyes and begs for the floor to open up and swallow her.

'You called me and several of my colleagues saying you needed help with regard to a homicide investigation. How can we assist you?'

Mitzi is *so* not ready for this. The sleep and painkillers have left her mind all fugged. 'My apologies. The case I'm working involves the death of two people and there's a link to one of your staff, a Mr George Dalton. I'd like to ask him a few questions.'

'What questions, Lieutenant?'

'Where he was at certain times, who he was with and what he was doing. The *usual* kind of questions.'

'He was most probably with me. He's a senior member of my staff and I'm afraid I work him very hard. How about I have my secretary call you and you submit a list of questions for Mr Dalton? I will see that he answers them for you.'

'How about I talk to him directly?'

'I don't think that's preferable or convenient for us. There are certain protocols we have to follow.'

Mitzi senses she's being shut down. 'Your consul and my

homicides are linked to a religious relic, a Celtic cross; would that mean anything to you, ambassador?'

'Not particularly.'

'What about Code X?'

He pauses. 'I'm sorry; someone distracted me with a message. Can you repeat what you said, please?'

Mitzi knows she's struck a nerve. 'Code X. Does that mean something to you?'

'It does, Lieutenant, but I can't speak about this on the telephone. It is somewhat complicated, and delicate. Is there a way we can talk face to face?'

She lets out a long sigh and faces up to the inevitability of a painful flight to the UK. 'I can be on a plane tomorrow.'

'Good. My secretary will call you to make arrangements. I'll have a driver meet you at the airport.'

The phone goes dead.

She slaps it down on the table and collapses on the bed. 'Shit. Shit. Shittety-shit.'

It rings again.

She gives it a sideways look that could melt iron then takes the call. 'Hello.'

'Mom, it's Amber.'

'Oh, hiya, honey. How are you?'

'I'm sick. Aunt Ruth says I have gastro-something.'

'Gastroenteritis?'

'Yeah, that. I'm just living in the bathroom and Jade's driving me crazy. When are you coming home? I really need you, Mom.'

62

MARYLAND

It takes Mitzi twenty minutes and a whole lot of bribery to persuade Amber that she isn't the mother from hell. It takes twice as long to do the same with Jade.

Ruth is predictably cold when she's told that the overnight stay in Washington is going to be stretched into a transatlantic trip that most likely will last another week.

Years of being a cop tells Mitzi her younger sister is more than just pissed about being put on. She sounds depressed, angry and confused and Mitzi wishes she were there to help her work through the mess with Jack.

Once the call's done, she sinks another brandy miniature and bins the bottle. A mirror on the wall of her tiny hotel room throws back an almost unrecognizable woman with black eyes, a fire-truck-red nose and unattractive strap of white plaster. The only consolation is they straightened a crooked break delivered by her ex's fist half a decade ago.

Mitzi thumbs through a room-service menu and intends to order only a chicken salad and milk but somehow a side of fries and a slice of pecan pie get added.

While waiting for the food, she calls Donovan and updates her on everything from Irish's death to her conversation with Gwyn and the need to go to London.

'Your timing's good,' says her boss. 'Eleonora got a break

on the satanic killing. She's with the cops and they'll be bringing charges within the hour.'

'Lucky her. Who was it down to?'

'Brother of the husband. You weren't far off with your initial guesswork. She'll tell you the story when you're back. Point is, Bronty can be freed up, if you think he'd be of help to you.'

'Given all the religious connections, I'm sure he would be.'

'Thought so. You want him here, or do I send him UPS to London?'

'London would be better. Is he going to be okay with making a trip like that with so little notice?'

'About as okay as you were.' Donovan waits a beat. There's something she needs to make her lieutenant aware of. 'You know that we're going to draw heat on this. British diplomats have friends who are American diplomats who have friends in the justice system who pull strings in every puppet theatre from the grubbiest station house to the Oval Office.'

'Yeah, I can imagine how it might play out.'

'Good, then you know that I need you to be smart. I'll keep them off your back as long as possible, but if I tell you we have to pull out, you pull out. No tantrums. No shit storms. Agreed?'

She's too tired to fight. 'Agreed.'

'Remember you said that, because if you leave me hanging on this one, that car crash you've been in will feel like a day at the spa when I'm done with you.'

63

WASHINGTON DULLES AIRPORT

Mitzi eases her physical and emotional pain with some retail therapy.

By the time she settles on the Airbus to the UK, she's assuaged herself with the purchase of several packs of Calvin underwear, a red button-up long-sleeved top and a navy-and-white striped shirt to go with a long milled wool skirt in the same colour, a pale-blue V-neck lambs' wool jumper and a matching T-shirt to wear beneath it.

It's been a long time since she's bought wool but she has no intention of freezing in those crazy British temperatures. Given the option, she'd never even visit a country that thinks seventy degrees is a good summer's day.

The transatlantic trip turns out to be more bearable than the internal flight was from San Francisco to Washington. No screaming kids around her. No warring families dug into the trenches of coach-class seating. By the time she's had a deep Ibuprofen-induced sleep and watched several weepy movies, the plane is hitting the blacktop at Heathrow, or Hell Row as she heard the cabin crew calling it.

It's gone midnight when she clears customs and finds her way to the airport Hilton. No sooner does she set the digital clock by her bed and crash out than it's buzzing and flashing with all the urgency of a nuclear alarm.

It's seven a.m.

Mitzi can't believe six hours vanished in a blink.

Her shoulders and neck have stiffened post-car-crash, especially on the side where the safety belt jerked tight on impact and prevented her being thrown around the tumbling vehicle like a rag doll in a washing machine.

She puts on the new skirt and striped shirt and finds it doesn't really go with the lamb's wool jumper like she hoped. Worse than that, the black rings around her eyes are now so dense and circular they look like some joker painted them on her face while she was asleep. Her nose has also swollen more and turned black across the fracture. She uses a bathroom mirror to fix a new dressing and tells herself, 'Mitz, you're gonna have to give up that dream of pulling a royal husband while you're here.'

Around eight she heads downstairs to breakfast. She has an hour in which to meet up with Bronty, brief him, check out and be in reception to meet the ambassador's driver to take them to their meeting.

A young woman stood by the restaurant door takes note of her room number and shows her to a table for two, which by no accident is in the far corner where she can't frighten other guests.

Bronty turns up soon after a young Polish waiter has left her with a pot of black coffee and a sympathetic look. The FBI man's dressed in caramel-coloured cords and a pink Lacoste polo shirt. He has a cable-knit brown sweater draped over his shoulders.

'Sweet Mother of God,' says the ex-priest as he settles at the table. 'What happened to you?'

Mitzi puts her cup down. 'That's your one free cheap shot. Now, do you want coffee? Or do you want to push your luck with more questions about the face?'

64

GLASTONBURY, ENGLAND

The tinted windows of the armour-plated Range Rover give Lance Beaucoup and Jennifer Gwyn the sinful luxury of holding hands without worrying whether bodyguards in the following car might see them.

They travel north along coastal roads, past Avonmouth, then west over the Second Severn Crossing, skirting Newport and into the six hundred square miles of wilderness that is the Brecon Beacons.

The four-by-four rumbles into a rugged landscape of forests, fields, lakes and mountains. It's a stretch of countryside that is the among the most guarded in Britain.

Jennifer runs a finger gently over the ridges of Lance's scarred knuckles as he grips the steering wheel. 'What are these? Evidence of a misspent youth?'

'Fights won and lost. Childhood scuffles and adult battles. I remember each and every wound.'

She puts him to the test. 'This?'

He glances at a shiny white bridge spanning the first and second knuckles of his left hand. 'A brawl in a Parisian bar. My best friend's twenty-first birthday.'

'And this?'

He looks at a sliver crease the length of his little finger. 'Ah, that was a fall from my girlfriend's Vespa.' There's a hint of nostalgia in his voice. 'I was seventeen and she nineteen.'

'And pretty?'

'*Very.* We hit a patch of oil and I came down hard on my hand. Fractured my collarbone as well. It hurt a lot, but not as much as when she left me for a married man.'

'*C'est la vie,*' says Jennifer. 'Love sometimes ends in people being hurt.'

He takes a beat, looks at the road ahead and then asks, 'Will you hurt me one day?'

She grips his hand tightly and smiles sadly. 'You know I will. Ours is a love that will break both our hearts.'

65

LONDON

Bronty excitedly tugs Mitzi's arm as she checks them out at the reception desk. 'They've sent a Rolls-Royce for us.' He virtually scampers out of the hotel towards the waiting vehicle.

She gets her credit card receipt and follows him outside. 'Looks older than Joan Rivers,' she says eyeing the vintage vehicle.

'It is,' says the driver, a former soldier called Harold, now in his fifties. 'Considerably older. This is a Phantom IV, ma'am. Hand-crafted by the same team that created the first Rolls for the queen.' He opens the rear door for them. 'If you please.'

Mitzi slips inside, followed awkwardly by Bronty, who is pulling an antiseptic wipe from a travel-pack he's clutching.

The door shuts without a sound and the driver continues his story as he settles into the front seat and glides the car away from the hotel. 'You are sitting in the most exclusive Rolls-Royce ever made.' He eyes Bronty wiping the armrests. 'It is also valeted every day, sir.'

The FBI man embarrassingly balls his tissue and slips it into a pocket.

'This model is one of eighteen built in the early fifties and they were only made for royalty and heads of state.'

Mitzi looks at him in the rear-view as she responds, 'So, did Sir Owain buy it from a royal or a state official?'

'I have no idea, ma'am. You'll have to ask him yourself.'

Bronty notices the traditional flying lady statue over the front grille has been replaced by a different symbol. 'What's that figure on the hood, the one where the usual Rolls statue goes?'

Harold takes delight in explaining. 'Ah, well, sir, just as the queen's original Rolls had a special mascot of St George slaying a dragon, Sir Owain's has an individual sculpture on the bonnet. We call them bonnets, not hoods, sir. The statue is of an unknown knight, atop the crest of a hill where a famous battle was fought. It's part of the family's heraldic crest. Honour in Anonymity.'

'That's a motto that wouldn't work in Hollywood,' says Mitzi. She accidently presses a button on her armrest and a glass screen slides up behind the driver.

His voice crackles from recessed speakers. 'That's for privacy, ma'am. Should you wish to speak to me, there's a microphone button next to the one you just pressed. When the green light is on I can both hear you and speak to you. Otherwise, I will leave you in peace for the rest of our journey, which will take approximately fifty minutes.'

Mitzi says, 'Thanks,' but she's not sure if he's heard her or not. She turns to Bronty. 'Did you get a message from Vicks to call me about the cross?'

He covers his face with his hands. 'Sorry, I forgot. Eleonora had me working so hard on her case, I just didn't get round to it.'

'Great. At least I know where I stand in the food chain.'

'You're now at the very front.' He smiles as genuinely as he can manage. 'What do you want to know?'

'Whatever you can tell me. Why is the Celtic cross unlike normal crucifixes, and what does the circle signify?'

'Well, it's popularly believed that when foreign missionaries started to try to convert Druids to Christianity, St Patrick came upon a stone carved with the circle for the moon and he insisted a Latin crucifix was carved over it. He blessed the new symbol of crucifix and moon united and the first Celtic cross was born.'

'Neat. You think it's true?'

'There's as much to prove it as disprove it. Another theory has it that the circle is a Eucharistic emblem, the holy wafer of Christ, which is always round. Others believe it represents the halo of the Holy Ghost. These days everyone from the Church of Wales to any tourist company with a connection to Ireland, Scotland or Wales seems to use it. Plus online mystics, astrologers, shops selling fortune-telling crystals and any Irish folk group that's ever played in public.'

'All bullshit, then?'

'One man's bullshit is another man's faith. And as we both know, faith can move mountains.'

'And make lots of money.'

'Of course. Nothing ever works without money – not even the church.' Bronty remembers a story from his days as a priest. 'Crazy old father in my seminary insisted the circle on the cross was nothing to do with the Eucharist or St Patrick. He said it was Christian recognition of an alliance with the Round Table Knights of King Arthur.'

'Hard to imagine Jesus and Merlin in the same breath.'

'Any harder than envisaging St George slaying a dragon, water being turned into wine or a virgin birth?'

'Suppose not.'

'Anyway, the old priest was a great storyteller. He used to entertain us with tales about how holy crosses for the knights were cast from metal dug from Jesus's tomb by the Apostles. He said they were half dagger, half cross and would also be used to sink into the hearts of heathen warriors to save their souls.'

'That's a nice Christian act. Have you seen the sketch made by the store girl in Maryland?'

He looks guilty. 'I'm sorry, I haven't.'

She digs in her purse and takes out a folded copy.

He takes it off her and looks. 'It's hard to tell from this, as I guess the scale and dimensions are all wrong, but it looks part dagger, part crucifix.' He hands it back with a smile. 'That said, the pointed end was probably so the cross could be stuck in the earth and Mass held on a hillside or suchlike.'

She folds the paper up and returns it to her purse. 'You think we should call your old priest and show him this?'

Bronty laughs. 'Mitzi, Father Ryan was very fond of the altar wine. It aided the colour of his storytelling, if you get my drift.'

'Okay, but if he believed this King Arthur and holy cross stuff maybe other people do. That would explain why it was valuable and why people killed for it. You know, like the Holy Grail and fragments from the True Cross?'

'King Arthur didn't even exist,' he says dismissively. 'Anyway, I thought you said Vicky had shown the sketch to someone at the Smithsonian?'

'She has and they said Iron Age, remember?'

'I do,' he answers snappily. 'And they're much more likely to be right than Father Ryan.'

'Still no harm in checking. Experts almost always disagree with each other.'

He shakes his head at her stubbornness. 'Then you'll need to do it through prayer and divine intervention – he died six or seven years ago.'

Mitzi falls quiet and mulls over the cross as she stares out of the car window. The landscape is rapidly changing as the city starts to rise up and wrap its arms of bricks and glass around them.

She takes out her smartphone, clicks on the camera function, leans close to Bronty and demands, 'Smile!'

He forces a grin.

She takes the shot, and holds the camera so they can both see the result. 'It's for when I get back. I want to show the girls that I was in a Rolls. It might distract them from wanting to kill me for staying away so long.'

66

CAERGWYN CASTLE, WALES

Caergwyn Castle blushes pink in the afternoon sun. Its four corner towers and a sturdy central keep stand rudely exposed against the soft greens of fields and forests.

Jennifer Gwyn steps from the Range Rover. She's wearing a light boat-neck sweater and blue Jacquard trousers, having chosen comfort over glamour for the two-hour road trip. The air is refreshingly crisp, with a hint of flint and iron and she enjoys the feel of a gentle wind in her hair as she looks up at the battlements.

She knows he is there. Behind the stone at the top of the tower, watching. Looking down through glassed slits that once concealed the deadly arrows of the country's finest bowmen.

Myrddin.

He has known her all her life. At times, understood her better than she could herself.

The old man has had much to say while she's been away in America. Once she's face-to-face with him, he's bound to peel open her thoughts.

The burly bodyguards spill from their vehicles and begin to relax. The SAS and Marines constantly train in outer sections of the fortified grounds. Arthurian 'soldiers' are drilled and barracked closer to the castle walls. Those two rings of deadly steel are supplemented by an armed security team that only operates inside the ancient building.

A moon-faced butler in black suit and white shirt approaches, followed by two young footmen in red jackets. 'Welcome back, Lady Gwyn.'

'Thank you, Alwyn. How is everybody?'

He walks with her to the door, as the footmen take cases from the Range Rover and instructions from Lance. 'I am pleased to say that all are well, m'lady. Mrs Stokes is off as you know, due to have her first child next week, so Nerys is filling in as head chef.'

'She's up to that?'

'Most certainly. Don't tell Mrs Stokes this, but Nerys's lamb cawl is the finest since my mother made it.'

Jennifer laughs and gives a traditional Welsh response: *'Cystal yfed o'r cawl a bwyta'r cig'* – 'It is as good to drink the broth as eat the meat.'

He's pleased to hear her use the old language. 'Will you and Mr Beaucoup be dining alone tonight? Only—'

She anticipates his comment. 'No. We will eat with Myrddin. He will curse me into my next lifetime if we do not join him.'

'A wise decision, your ladyship.'

Alwyn leaves her in the grand entrance. It is a cavernous space of dark wooden floors and walls, coats of armour, heraldic crests and mounted animal heads.

The young footmen smile as they pass her and haul cases up a grand staircase that splits at the top into two galleys.

Lance appears. Apprehension shows in his eyes. There is no escaping Owain's presence in here. The castle is steeped in his heritage. His spirit runs like electricity through every room.

Jennifer sees his fear. 'You feel him, don't you?'

He tilts his head in resignation. 'It is impossible not to.'

She takes him lightly by the hand and walks him into a corridor. 'Come, let's take tea in the southern drawing room. Afterwards, you can do your work and then we'll meet again for dinner.'

'With Myrddin?'

'Yes, with Myrddin.' She sees his worry. 'I will see him first. Make sure that I soften the blows.'

67

LONDON

The street names flashing past the windshield of the vintage Rolls are places Mitzi's only ever heard about. Piccadilly Circus. Oxford Street. Covent Garden. Leicester Square. The Strand.

Traffic slows as they approach a giant building of blasted white stone, tall arched windows, heavy black gates and soaring spires. It looks like a wing of Hogwarts. An impression compounded by an isolated stone plinth and grotesque sculpture of some kind of bird. She presses the button that Harold the chauffeur said would get his attention.

'Excuse me. Can you tell me where the hell we are and what all these buildings and freaky statues are about?'

The driver glances back as he answers. 'We're on Fleet Street, ma'am. That's the Royal Courts of Justice alongside us. Sir Owain's office is just around the corner.' He glances at the priceless Charles Bell Birch sculpture standing proudly on its column and tries to prevent a tone of cultural superiority from creeping into his voice. 'This is the Temple Bar monument; it used to denote the edge of the city. The statue you mentioned is a heraldic dragon. You will find there are two on the crest of the City of London, along with the cross of St George.'

Bronty is listening with interest. 'You said Temple – is that connected to the Knights Templar?'

'Yes, sir. Its name comes from the Temple Church and the Temple area. They were once in the ownership of the knights but are now home to the legal profession.'

'Saints and sinners,' adds Mitzi, sarcastically. 'A modern-day lawyer is about as far as you can get from a chivalrous and honourable knight of old.'

'You might well be right about that, ma'am.' The traffic starts to move a little faster and Harold manages to get into second gear. 'It may interest you to know that each year the monarch customarily stops at Temple Bar before entering the City of London, so that the Lord Mayor may offer up the City's pearl-encrusted Sword of State as a token of loyalty.'

'I confess to being completely uninterested,' replies Mitzi, 'until the point you mentioned pearls. Then you got me. Next life, I'm sure as hell coming back as a British queen.'

'I wish you luck, ma'am.' He glides the car silently around a corner then noisily over a cobbled backstreet that ends at a gated archway. The Rolls stops until the metal slides back, then it effortlessly slips into a long passage.

Mitzi watches the gates close and the sunlight disappear. The narrow passage gradually becomes a spiralling underground ramp that makes tight twists and turns into a vast underground parking lot where it stops.

The chauffeur gets out and opens the door for them. 'Please follow me.'

He leads the way into a smart reception area of glass and steel, and an elevator guarded by two blue-suited men. Words are quickly and pleasantly exchanged then Harold swipes a finger over a print scanner near the elevator's call button.

'This will take you to reception. I or one of my colleagues will be here for you when your business is finished.' He nods courteously and steps aside as big steel doors slide open.

The door closes automatically once Mitzi and Bronty are inside and the lift rises without any sensation of movement.

When it stops and opens, they're facing a large picture window with a panoramic view of London.

'Wow,' says Bronty as they step out. 'We must be what, two or three hundred feet above ground.'

'Three hundred and sixty,' says a slim brunette in a business suit. 'Welcome to CEI. I'm Melissa Sachs, Sir Owain's personal secretary.' A gold bracelet shimmers on the bronzed skin of her elegant wrist as she extends her hand to greet them. 'He's waiting for you.'

68

CAERGWYN CASTLE, WALES

Lady Gwyn crosses the cobbled courtyard to the south-eastern wing and what's always been known as the Augur's Tower. Generations of servants have assumed the name comes from an old wives' tale that if you stood at the top you'd be so high you could see into the future.

Despite the modern security cameras and armed guards around her, the walk always takes Jennifer back in time. It's easy to picture the battlements filled with archers and the thick walls running red with the blood of her ancestor's enemies.

She takes a calming breath as she pushes the old oak door that has been left open for her and enters the cold, sparsely furnished space that constitutes Myrddin's living quarters.

The old man is sat in a seven-foot-high wooden throne. A large heraldic coat of arms hovers over his head. It depicts two fiery dragons back to back, divided by a broadsword. His green eyes shine from beneath wrinkled hoods of flesh and his liver-spotted, bony hands hang over the ends of the arched armrests.

'I expected you earlier.' His tone isn't critical. It has no trace of disappointment or judgement in it.

Jennifer understands it well. She's listened to it all her life, learned how to decipher every decibel of speech. 'I had to settle my lover.'

It is no shock to him. He'd had visions of the affair long before she tilted her head at the young man and he's sure she realizes that. 'Have you no warm embrace to raise the cold spirit of your old confidant?'

She smiles and goes to him.

Myrddin folds her into his musty robes. For a moment, they hold each other tightly, then she takes his icy fingers in her warm palms and opens up to him. 'I am frightened. Afraid of the changes that I know you and Owain sense are coming.'

'My child, you and your family have been through such things so many times before. The seasons change. Winter kills and spring gives life.' He drops his gaze pointedly to her stomach. 'Have you told him yet?'

'You know I haven't.'

'Then you must.'

'And how will he react? With joy or sorrow?'

'With understanding. I have told him I have seen the child. He knows the vision points to his own mortality. Remember, in the birth of the new, the spirit of the dead is born again and grows stronger.'

'I wish this wasn't our way.'

'But it is and always will be.'

She steels herself to ask the most awful of questions. 'How will it come?'

'I have not yet seen.' He looks kindly on her. 'It will be honourable and brave; of that alone you can be certain.'

Jennifer closes her eyes to stop the flow of tears. It is too soon to feel sad.

He sees her fighting her emotions and bends to comfort her. 'There, there, my child. A love like yours and Owain's never dies. That is the point of the Arthurian Cycle. Your children perpetually recreate the spirit and goodness that is needed to project the old Order into the new world.'

'I know. But it does not stop my heart and soul from hurting.'

'Then let us hope that the other man you share your bed with is as good at drying tears as he is at coaxing sighs.'

She blushes. 'I trust tonight you will not be as shocking with him as you are with me.'

'Only if you promise to come and see me every day that you are here.'

'Then I promise.' She leans forward and kisses him. 'Now be sure to keep your side of the bargain.'

He smiles as she starts to leave. 'Soon, Jennifer. Tell Owain sooner rather than later. Time is not feeling kindly towards us.'

69

CALEDFWLCH ETHICAL INVESTMENTS, LONDON

At the end of the top floor, Melissa Sachs stops in front of a set of double oak doors, pushes one open and steps aside to let the visitors through.

The room they enter is breathtaking. It is a giant dome of glass that overhangs the edge of the building. Reinforced panes and floor panels give the impression of walking on air.

Mitzi and Bronty move apprehensively towards the centre.

'Please come all the way in – it's perfectly safe.' The amused reassurance is from an exceptionally tall and broad man in a bottle-green suit and waistcoat. 'I'm Owain Gwyn and this is my colleague, George Dalton.'

'Mitzi Fallon.' She stares nervously through the floor onto

the sidewalk hundreds of feet below. 'This is my colleague, Jon Bronty.'

Owain shakes hands then leads Mitzi to two leather settees where there is a stretch of solid floor around her. 'Please, sit here. I know some people find the room a little daunting.'

She lowers herself onto a seat. 'Thanks. I get a little vertigo. Especially when there's nothing between me and a splat, save an inch or two of glass.'

He smiles. 'It looks like you've already had some kind of *splat*.'

'I have. A car accident back in the States.'

Bronty and Dalton join them on the sofas.

'Help yourselves to drinks.' Owain gestures to bottles of juice, soda and water laid out on a small table between them.

'Thanks.' Mitzi pops the cap on a squat bottle of water and takes a swig.

He waits for her to put it down before he continues. 'Lieutenant, both George and I wish to be as helpful as *possible*. I stress the word *possible* because there may be matters of national security that prevent us giving you complete disclosure and I wouldn't want you to misunderstand the reasons for that.' He angles his body towards Bronty, who's just produced a notebook and is digging around for a pen. 'I must also stress that this conversation is purely "off the record". We are seeing you without the presence of embassy lawyers and without reminding you of the rigorous defence that can be presented by diplomatic immunity.'

'Except of course you just did.' Mitzi smiles politely. 'I get the picture. You're both going to clam up; it's just a question of when.' Without hurrying, she takes out a deck of photographs from a file she's brought. Like a Vegas croupier, she places them face down on the table, alongside the bottles.

As she looks up, she notices a stark contrast in the two men opposite her.

Owain Gwyn is relaxed and attentive. George Dalton, who is still to utter a word, looks as nervous as a kitten on a lake of ice.

Bronty is studying them as well. As a priest, he developed a strong intuition about character, almost as though he could tell who was struggling with the weight of sin and who wasn't. Neither of them seems to be carrying heavy loads, but there is something unusual about Gwyn.

More than charisma.

He seems to radiate peace and gentleness. It's the kind of intensity Bronty felt around missionaries in Africa, only more so. *Considerably* more so.

'This is Amir Goldman.' Mitzi plays her first card. Face up. A post-mortem shot of the old man. Naked. White. A clear view of the wounded stomach. 'Knifed to death in his antiques store in Maryland last Friday night.'

She turns over the second. Another PM shot. Taken in the woods just as the body had been pulled from worm-infested earth. 'This gentleman is James Tiago Sacconni, an ex-con with previous for knife attacks. He was seen coming out of Goldman's on the night the store owner was murdered. He got into a brown SUV, an Escalade hybrid and was killed minutes later. His body was buried in nearby woods.'

Mitzi notes that neither diplomat flinches when shown the pictures. She dips into her folder and pulls out a printed Google map. 'Please look at this for me, Mr Dalton. On there, you'll see the antiques store. It's marked "A". The woods where Sacconni was found are marked "B". You'll notice there's a "C". This is Massachusetts Avenue in Washington, where the British Embassy is.'

She watches the younger man fixate on the map. Spots how he crosses his ankles to stop his foot tapping. Doesn't miss the way he pushes his lips together to wet them as discreetly as possible. She slides her gaze over to Gwyn and finds he's not at all interested in the map, only in his colleague and how he's holding up.

Mitzi sits back and relaxes.

There are still cards to play but now it's time to bluff a little and raise the stakes.

She waits until the consul lifts his head and catches her penetrating stare. 'My question, Mr Dalton, is this – where were you between nine-thirty p.m. Friday last and daybreak Saturday?'

The lips are licked again. 'I'm not sure. So much happened just before I left Washington to return to the UK.' He looks towards the ambassador. 'I think I was collecting something for Sir Owain. Something confidential.'

The knight gives a confirmatory nod.

The collective evasiveness encourages Mitzi not to rush things. 'What vehicle were you in?'

'The embassy Lincoln.'

'That's a silver MKZ with a panoramic roof?'

'Yes.'

'What would you say if I told you that an eyewitness saw *that* Lincoln follow a brown Escalade, driven by Mr Sacconni, away from Goldman's store just after he was murdered?'

'I'd say your witness might be confusing my car being on the same road at the same time as the other vehicle, with the notion of me deliberately following it.'

'I don't think so.' Mitzi plays her next cards. She flips over the third, fourth and fifth photographs. 'This is a sequence of shots taken of the Lincoln, with you at the wheel, heading south from the Beltway intersection. For some reason, you are always a quarter mile behind the SUV.' She taps the last photograph. 'And when it comes off at Dupont, so do you.'

The consul shrugs dismissively. 'I can see half a dozen cars in your shots there. You could say any one of them was following that target vehicle. And I'm absolutely sure I wasn't the only person to exit at Dupont.'

Mitzi makes mental notes. He just gave her two valuable insights. But she's not going to mention them. Not now. Not until the time is right and the advantage high. 'It's a nine-mile stretch from Kensington to the diner. You were the only driver that joined the road within sixty seconds of the Escalade and you didn't overtake it during that short journey south. A little strange, don't you think?'

Again the shrug. And another confident answer. 'I'm a safe driver. I represent the British Government and I'm conscious of that honour, so I stick to the speed limit.'

The door opens and Melissa Sachs appears and looks pointedly towards her boss.

'Excuse me.' Sir Owain gets up and walks to her.

They talk briefly.

The ambassador returns to his guests. 'I'm afraid you'll have to carry on without me for a moment. I have an urgent call I need to step out and take.'

Mitzi turns back to Dalton. Time to play her trump card. She flips over a grainy photograph of the All Night All Right Diner that she had Kirstin take and make look as though it had come from a security camera. 'This is a fast food joint off Connecticut Avenue, out from Dupont, down seventeenth near Stead Park. Not the kind of place I'd imagine a person like you would visit. But you did.'

His eyes flick from it to the two remaining face-down photographs on the table and guesses that they show him both inside and outside the diner.

'What were you doing there, Mr Dalton?'

He shifts awkwardly in his seat. 'It was a call of nature. I used their washroom.' He picks up a bottle of water and casually drinks, then adds, 'We Brits are a bit old-fashioned. We can't just go urinating in the wild.'

'Hell, no!' says Mitzi. 'What would the world come to?' She opens her own bottle and mirrors his actions. 'How did things go in the men's room?'

'What do you mean? I went to the toilet. How do you think it went?'

She notes his touchiness and puts her bottle down next to his. 'Talk me through it. Tell me.'

His face flushes with anger. 'I went in. Used the urinal. Went out and drove home.' He sits back and glares at her. 'Did you really come all the way from the States to ask about my toilet habits?'

'You'd better believe it, buddy.' The guy's as guilty as hell. If she gives him a little more rope sure as night follows day he's going to hang himself.

The office door opens.

Sir Owain enters. There's purposefulness in his stance. 'I'm very sorry; I'm going to have to ask you to leave. Something of extreme importance and urgency has happened.'

Mitzi collects the photographs, drops them in her folder and grabs her bottle of water. She's as mad as hell and struggles to hide it. Sir La-de-da was probably watching on a hidden camera and didn't like the fact his boy was in trouble. She gets to her feet and walks over to him. 'Is whatever just happened *really* more important than the Code X files, ambassador? I was *so* looking forward to discussing them with you.'

'It is, Lieutenant.' His eyes narrow. 'You will learn soon enough what detained me and why this meeting had to be curtailed. I only hope that when you do, you will apologize for that remark and then it may be possible for us to meet again.'

70

CAERGWYN CASTLE, WALES

From the rain-puddled roof of the Augur's Tower, Myrddin gazes nostalgically across the shimmering estate's vast lake into the distant forests where the red deer run.

It seems only a couple of springs since he hunted and fished there as a young man, his head full of plans and his heart swollen with love. In those days, he lived on whatever he caught. Venison, rabbit and salmon, when he was lucky. Rat and squirrel when he wasn't. Every day brought fresh adventures. His craft needed to be learned. Secrets had to be discovered. The magic of life was still to be learned.

As he descends to his solar, he can't help but think that the years have flown faster than the falcons he used to train. Nowadays, he feels he has become a slave to the very crafts he strove so hard to master. Knowledge has tired him. The sheer weight of it has fixed leaden boots to his weary feet.

He is sinking.

And Owain Gwyn is the reason why.

He guided him from boy to man. Made him his charge. His protégé. The manifestation of all his hopes and loves. It became his life's work to empower him, to help him achieve his greatness – and goodness. To make Owain a king among men.

The small cot of a bed creaks and his old spine cracks as he stretches out on the hard boards and worn-out mattress. He's never afforded himself luxuries – except for his imagination. Inside his mind, he has indulged himself in pleasures mere mortals would never comprehend.

Sleep comes quickly.

And visions, too. Mixed and confused. Like multiple movies spliced together.

There is water. Vast stretches of it. Bigger than a lake. Smaller than a sea. People speaking in foreign tongues. Loved ones separated by geography, united in grief.

Then there are bodies. Burning bodies. Buried bodies. Decomposing bodies that stir in the soil and rise from their wormeries. Living bodies, still bleeding, rattling with death but not yet surrendered.

And women.

There is a young woman and an old one. Together but strangers. Women from different lands. One he recognizes; one he doesn't. The older one is terribly powerful. A threat to everything and everyone he holds close.

But there is goodness about her as well. And vulnerability.

Out in the unmarked fields, in plots known only to the Arthurians, bones that once bent and broke for the betterment of mankind shake off their blankets of soil and once more feel the kiss of the sun.

But this is no resurrection. No Day of Judgement. No moment of divine redemption. This is exposure. Destruction of the Order. The end of secrecy.

Myrddin's closed eyes are blinded by the bright lights of his vision. Blues and reds and oranges and whites. His ears ache from the shouts of voices, male and female, adult and child. They are crying. Begging for the pain to stop. Their screams overlap. Fight to be heard above each other.

And there is Owain. At the centre of the pain. Desperately trying to soak it all up.

Unable to stop it.

71

CALEDFWLCH ETHICAL INVESTMENTS, LONDON

Melissa Sachs shows the Americans out and returns to Sir Owain's office. 'Are you ready for your call with the Home Secretary, sir?'

'I am. Thank you, Melissa.'

George Dalton rises from the sofa. 'Would you like me to leave?'

'No. Stay. We need to talk as soon as I've dealt with this call.' A light on his phone flashes. He picks it up and answers. 'Hello, Charles. How are you all coping?'

'Best we can. How much do you know?' Charles Hatfield suspects it's at least as much as he does.

'Only the briefest details. Bomb on the Eurostar. Explosion at the British end. Something like fifty dead.'

'Might be more. We won't know until the emergency services report back. The device went off south of Ashford, five minutes from the station. A pensioner saw a man doing something with wires inside a rucksack and she alerted train staff. When the guard questioned the suspect, he made a run for the toilet, locked himself inside and exploded the bloody thing.'

A live video feed from a helicopter is already up on the monitor in front of the ambassador. It shows the splayed track, smoke and flames rising from the concertinaed carriages, corpses on the rails and the blinking lights of fire engines and ambulances. 'I'm finishing up a meeting here and then I'll come into Whitehall. I assume you'll be putting together a Cabinet Office briefing?'

'Research team is already working on it. When can you join us?'

'Within the hour.'

'Good.' Hatfield checks fresh data on his computer as he speaks. 'I know this is of no comfort to those victims or their blessed families, but thank God the bomb didn't go off in the tunnel. A blast mid-channel would have been an even bigger tragedy.'

'That must have been the intention.' Gwyn watches the helicopter on his screen come to a stationary hover directly over the cratered track. 'Anyone claimed responsibility yet?'

'Not yet. But it'll be al-Qaeda.'

Gwyn puts the phone down and returns to Dalton. He can tell his colleague is worried. 'What is it, George?'

'I've been thinking about the interview with the Americans. I fear I may have messed things up.'

'Why?'

'In retrospect, I don't think that lieutenant knew I was at the diner near Dupont, and now I've confirmed I was.'

'The fact she raised it with you meant she had good reason to believe you were there. The big mistake was taking the Lincoln.'

'I had no choice. I was in the Lincoln when I got the message that Marchetti's men were heading out to Kensington. Had I swapped cars, I would never have got there in time.'

'I need to get directly involved in this Eurostar blast, so you must take care of the Americans. Have someone find out where they're staying. I want their room turned over and electronic or human surveillance on them all the time, until I say otherwise. Let's see if we can stop this investigation before it stops us.'

72

LONDON

News of the train bombing plays on the radio in the Rolls.

Once the bulletin finishes, Mitzi calls Sir Owain's office and leaves a message with Melissa. The ambassador had been right, there was good reason for her to apologize.

The journey to their new hotel is a long and muted one. Despite the privacy glass, neither she nor Bronty feel comfortable discussing their interview.

They book into The Dean, a new hotel in Soho, close to famous media haunts like the Groucho Club and Ivy and debrief over room-service club sandwiches, fries and two large pots of coffee.

'So what did you make of our friend the British Consul?' He slaps the bottom of a ketchup bottle to release a blat of sauce.

'Dalton's up to his neck in the whole thing.' She opens her sandwich like a book. 'Why is this bacon so much better than the stuff I have back home?'

'The Brits do good bacon. How d'you know he's implicated?'

'First slip he made was to admit the Lincoln had been outside Amir Goldman's store. No surveillance footage put him there. Then he got nervous and referred to the brown SUV as "the target car".'

'Maybe he's an ex-soldier, or policeman.'

'He's not. I checked before we flew out. But he might be a former spook, MI5 or 6.'

'It'd explain the manner in which he followed the Escalade.'

'Yeah. But not *why* he followed it. Or what he was doing when the SUV stopped in the woods and Sacconni got whacked.'

'You think Dalton killed him?'

'No. I think Sacconni was killed by his partner-in-crime, Bradley Deagan. But I think Dalton may have killed Deagan at the Dupont diner.' She reaches into her purse and produces a small plastic bottle of water. 'Which is why this little baby might help us.'

'Your drink from Gwyn's office?'

She smiles, 'No, not mine. Dalton's. And I'm willing to bet the DNA on this matches the profile we lifted from blood in the diner's bathroom – blood mingled with Deagan's.'

'Who exactly is Deagan?'

'A fraudster who tried to pull a con on an auction house with a painting called *The Ghent Altarpiece*.'

His eyes widen. 'Also known as *The Adoration of the Mystic Lamb.* One of the greatest and most stolen pieces of art ever created.' He points to her laptop. 'Mind if I use that for a second?'

'Be my guest.'

He opens a search engine and types in 'Ghent Altarpiece'. 'Here, look at this.'

He paraphrases text below the paragraph. 'It was commissioned in the fifteenth century for an altar in a private chapel in Belgium. The twenty-four panels form one overall picture when opened up and then a completely different one when closed.'

'I only see twelve.'

'Twelve front, twelve back.'

Now she sees it. 'Stupid me.'

'It's been the object of thirteen crimes over six centuries, including six separate thefts and a ransom demand.'

She pours fresh coffee for them both. 'Come on then, more detail: tell me the juicy stuff.'

'In the early nineteenth century some panels were pawned by the Ghent Diocese and ended up in England. They were bought by the King of Prussia and exhibited in Berlin. After the First World War, they were confiscated from the Germans as part of reparations. When the Second World War broke out the Belgians sent the paintings to the Vatican for safekeeping. At least that was the plan. Hitler's troops intercepted them, brought them to Bavaria and locked them in a castle. When Allied attacks intensified, he moved them into salt mines. Then when we beat the Nazis, our troops returned them to the Belgians.'

'And the ransom?'

He takes a second. 'Let me get this right. Back in the thirties, two panels, a front and back, were stolen from St Bavo Cathedral in Ghent. Often it's reported as one, but actually there were two. One called 'The Just Judges' and the other

John the Baptist. A lot of ransom letters were sent. They demanded more than a million Belgian Francs and warned that unless it was paid the paintings would be destroyed.'

'What happened?'

'The bishop never paid the money. There were some negotiations and the John the Baptist painting *was* recovered, but 'The Just Judges' was never found. Another painter was hired to fill in the blank on the altarpiece, but by all accounts there are errors in the scene.'

'Okay, enough history,' says Mitzi. 'My head's exploding and to be honest the last thing I want is a missing painting to add to a homicide that already has religious relics and secret codes.'

'Have the cryptologists got anywhere with that?'

'I have to call Vicks and check. It would be great if this Code X stick gave us all the answers.'

'Did you say "Code X", as in the letter X?'

'Yeah. Why do you ask?'

'Have you got the stick?'

'Sure.' She digs it out of her purse and passes it to him.

Bronty reads 'C-O-D-E-X' and smiles.

'What?'

'It's "Codex" not "Code X". One word, Latin by origin, as in ancient bibles and manuscripts. So your secret code is no new thing. It's hiding something that's probably been hidden for centuries. Something people are probably prepared to kill to keep hidden.'

73

WHITEHALL, LONDON

Cabinet Office Briefing Room 'A' is said to be the venue from which the press originated the acronym COBRA. Around its famous conference table are Defence Secretary Sir Wesley Piggott-Smith, Home Secretary Charles Hatfield, Deputy Prime Minister Norman Batherson and the ACPO chief, Milton Coleman.

Ambassador Gwyn is shown into the cool, darkened room by a Whitehall aide and takes a seat next to the deputy PM.

The Home Secretary acknowledges his appearance, 'Good afternoon, Sir Owain. I had only just started.' He stands in front of a giant screen playing mute video footage from the blast scene. 'The latest figures we have are fifty-four dead and forty injured. The prime minister is in Scotland but in the next half hour will helicopter down to Ashford and hold a press conference at the scene. The bomb squad is checking the remains of the train for secondary devices and, of course, the track is being inspected as well. The railway operator has contingencies to bus people around the derailment, but they've been told there's no chance of trains running through the tunnel for at least the next twelve hours.'

The police chief, a tall, thin man in his late fifties, throws a question across the table. 'Have we got confirmation it's al-Qaeda behind all this?'

'They plan to post a video,' answers Owain. 'It will be uploaded to an Al Jazeera server in the next few minutes. It will warn travellers in the West to expect more bombs and deaths.'

No one asks how the ambassador knows this. He does, after all, have special responsibilities for counter-terrorism and everyone in the room has been present at other meetings where he's been more reliably informed than they were.

'What are we facing, Owain?' asks the Deputy PM. 'A specific campaign of terror aimed at the UK? Or is this a wider strategy linked to the US bomb?'

'It's wider. And not just America. I expect there to be further attacks, and on soil less used to bloodshed than ours.'

The Defence Secretary knows what he's alluding to. 'Italy?'

'Exactly.'

Sir Wesley explains to the rest of the group. 'We've been hearing the same thing. Possibilities of attacks on Rome as a response to the Pope's condemnation of what he called 'maliciously misguided Muslim fundamentalists.'

Owain adds a little more depth to the comment. 'Al-Qaeda is thought to have a new, three-pronged strategy – firstly, business as usual; that means bombing the hell out of Britain and America. Secondly, as Sir Wesley just said, attacking soft Christian targets, such as Rome. This hasn't been done before and has the Spaniards just as worried as the Italians. We also believe they intend to use a new generation of highly trained assassins to kill high-profile VIPs.'

The door swings open and a young civil servant steps in and whispers discreetly to the home secretary, then leaves.

Charles Hatfield fingers the remote control and points it at a screen. 'Al Jazeera just ran this. It's exactly as Sir Owain said.'

The man who appears on screen doesn't fit the traditional stereotype of the Muslim terrorist. There's no straggly beard. No loose white robes. No Koran in hand. For once the video doesn't look like it's been shot in a school hall, with a dark curtain behind. There are no masked soldiers in the background with rifles across their chests. Instead, a calm young man in his late twenties, with neat hair and beard looks straight into camera. He is dressed in a charcoal-grey suit and, despite the rugged sandy backdrop of an Afghan hillside, he looks as calm as a foreign correspondent.

'Citizens of the west,' says a steady voice in excellent English. 'When you see this, it will be because I have killed and injured many people. Many innocents who did not deserve for such a thing to happen to them.' His tone is flat and without a trace of rage. 'I regret their deaths and injuries. But most of all, I regret that their governments made it necessary for them to die. As you watch, listen and read of the deaths, ask yourself this: what does al-Qaeda want? Why are they doing these things? Why are they killing so many people?' He takes a pause and lets the seeds of the questions he scattered germinate in the fertile minds of those who might listen.

'There has to be a good reason, doesn't there? Such as the

belief that your own country should be free of your enemies. That every person should have their own home, their patch of land, their personal *base* in life – because that's what the words al-Qaeda mean – "the base". Ask yourselves this, if foreigners tried to occupy *your* country, change *your* government and kill *your* friends, family and parents, what would you do?' His soft dark eyes hold the camera before he continues, 'I think I know. You would fight. You would fight to the death. As you count the bodies of today and the bodies of tomorrow, think beyond the rhetoric of your leaders, think about my words. When would you surrender?' Now the gentle eyes narrow and the camera shot tightens. 'Never. You would never surrender. Nor will we.'

The video stops on a freeze frame.

Owain Gwyn points at the screen. 'This is a new breed of terrorist. And the start of a new campaign of terror. Fought by new leaders in new ways.'

'I think you're wrong,' says the Defence Secretary. 'New *faces* perhaps, but it's the same old game. They bomb. They run. They hide. They have limited resources and limited support. We'll find them soon enough and this time we'll wipe every one of them from the face of the earth.'

Owain bites his tongue. Sir Wesley couldn't be more wrong. A storm is coming. One unlike any seen before.

74

NORTH BETHESDA, MARYLAND

A soft summer shower falls as the handsome delivery driver juggles the cardboard box in his arms and struggles to lock the back doors of his van. The neighbourhood he's in looks decent, but you can never be sure. Leave the vehicle unlocked and you're as good as asking for some scumbag to climb in and steal stuff. Maybe even the van itself.

As far as he's concerned, they're welcome to it. It's a piece of shit. The engine's slower than a constipated snail and it stinks of sweat and cigarettes. Still, he'll be shot of it soon.

He checks the name and address on the package, then climbs the short stack of steps to the apartment block. Dark marks appear on top of the box where raindrops hit and get blotted by the cardboard.

He knocks on a tatty door and waits.

There's a noise on the other side. The sound of someone pressing against the door. He sees a little fisheye lens in the middle of the wood and guesses the occupant is on the other side peering through at him.

'Who is it?' The voice is female and hesitant.

'Amazon. I've got a package to be signed for.'

The door opens a chink and a chain pulls tight. He pushes the box forward so she can see the smiley river logo.

It closes again and opens fully.

He extends the parcel in his hands. 'Careful with this; it's a little heavy.'

The woman takes it from him.

He lunges forward and pushes her so she staggers back and falls. The heavy parcel bangs painfully against her chest as she hits the floor and cracks her head.

The delivery man kicks the door shut and stands over her. He leans down and pushes the end of a silenced handgun into her mouth. 'You really should have asked for some ID, cupcakes.'

75

AMERICAN EMBASSY, LONDON

Less than two miles from the Cabinet briefing in Whitehall, Mitzi Fallon and Jon Bronty set up base in an FBI office inside the American Embassy in Grosvenor Square.

Intelligence officers have been working from here since the days when the country's second president, John Adams, had a home in the picturesque square.

Two doors away, field officers are getting up to speed on the Eurostar bomb blast and working out how it fits with the attack on Grand Central in New York.

Mitzi watches bigwigs come and go as she passes over the water bottle she took from Gwyn's office. She completes all the necessary chain-of-evidence paperwork and asks how long she'll have to wait to get the DNA profile.

The answer comes from a young clerk being run ragged by all the sudden activity. She's mid-twenties, with frizzy brown hair and hard black spectacles that sit on an aquiline nose amid a pale, freckled face. 'Within the week. Maybe sooner if the labs are at full strength.'

'How about tomorrow?' There's a hint of annoyance in her tone. 'I'm only here for a couple of days and this is linked to a homicide back in the US.'

'Homicides aren't priority.' She pushes the bagged evidence into her tray and starts fresh work on her computer.

Mitzi takes it back out and drops it in front of her. 'Then what is?'

The young Chicagoan gives her a scornful upward glance. 'If you don't know don't ask, ma'am.'

Mitzi bends low over the computer and lifts the nametag on the lapel of the clerk's black jacket. 'Please don't screw with me, Annie Linklatter. As you see from my currently less than pretty face I'm in a bad place at the moment and people in bad places do bad things. So how about you cut me a break and save us both a lot of pain?'

The girl's face reddens. 'I'll try for tomorrow – or the day after.'

'Tomorrow would be real good.' She wanders away. 'I'll be by first thing.'

Bronty is on the phone when she gets back to their temporary office. 'I've got Vicks on the line,' he says.

'Put her on speakerphone.'

Bronty obliges. 'Vicks, Mitzi has just walked in – you're on speaker.'

'Hi, Lieutenant! I've got some good and bad news for you. Which would you like first?'

'I only do good news, Vicks. Keep the bad to yourself and go fix it. What you got?'

'Okay. I've done the extra digging you asked for on Owain Gwyn. I'm just mailing it to you.'

'Great. I'll log on while we're speaking.' She flips open her computer and powers up.

'And the cryptologists have made progress on the data you sent over. It's really weird. Seems to be a story about King Arthur and his knights.'

'Codex,' whispers Bronty to Mitzi in a triumphant told-you-so tone.

Vicky continues her update, 'The file directory they decrypted is entitled "The Camelot Code" and it contains four parts – *The Fallen*, *Avalon*, *Modern Prophecies* and *The Arthurian Cycle*.'

Mitzi writes the names down on a pad next to the computer, which is still running start-up security programs. 'So, what is this, a kind of Arthurian *Twilight Saga*?'

'They've only transcribed the first page – apparently the code is problematic.'

'They say what kinda code it is?' asked Bronty.

'Yeah, they call it Random Revolver. Every letter of the alphabet is represented by a number – that's the simple part, like a kid's cypher – but then the numbers and the letters related to them don't stay the same, they keep changing. So for example, say the letter A is represented by 1, N by 2 and D by 3. The word AND would be coded 123. You get that?'

'Yeah, that's easy to follow.'

'Right, but in the next sentence, the letter A is represented by 2, N by 3 and D by 4, so AND now becomes 234.'

Mitzi gets it, 'So everything just moves down a number.'

'No, sometimes letters and numbers are randomly matched. Hence the name. The cryptologist I spoke to said the only way they cracked it was to create two virtual circles – the outer one had twenty-six letters on it, the inner one had twenty-six corresponding numbers. The letters got a new number every sentence. But this didn't make sense when they hit the seventh, fourteenth, twenty-first and twenty-eighth lines. At those points, the whole sequence reset and sometimes would go backwards or start skipping odd or even numbers.'

'Days of the week,' observes Bronty. 'It reset because there are seven days in a week. Monks used to write what were called Calendar Codes, where every week or every month they changed the key to the code they wrote secret messages in.'

'Enough,' says Mitzi. 'You two are making my head pound. Vicks, just tell me what this damned Camelot Code said.'

The young researcher gets excited. 'It's wonderful, weird gothic stuff. You have to read it to make sense of it. I'm sending a transcript of what they've cracked so far. It's from a section called *The Fallen*.'

'Can't wait to read it,' says Mitzi sarcastically. 'Anything else to brighten my day?'

'That's it.'

'You said there was bad news.'

'I did, and you told me to keep it to myself.'

'I know, but as well as being a lying bitch, I'm nosy as hell. So tell me.'

Vicky braces herself for a verbal backlash. 'The data you sent to me – it started to self-corrupt as soon as I opened it. I lost a lot of the files and—'

'What?'

'*Please* – before you holler – the cryptologists say it wasn't my fault. They say it was primed with a suicide bug.'

'What's that?'

'It means that when copies are made on software or hardware that doesn't belong to the originator the code corrupts. You must have the original authorized copy.'

'So how come it didn't corrupt instantly when I sent it to you?'

'It would have done on any other system but ours. The FBI computers locked the first digits, that's all. Everything else died within that split-second. The techies say the coding and technology behind all this is super smart – as in intelligence agency smart.'

Mitzi glances at the small memory stick lying free in her purse. 'Good job I took high security measures to protect the original, then.'

'Absolutely,' says Vicky, unaware of the irony.

There's a ping on Mitzi's computer. She glances at the screen. 'Just got your stuff. I'll go check it with Bronty and one of us will get back to you. Thanks, Vicks.'

She kills the call and Bronty comes round behind her to look over her shoulder.

Mitzi opens her mailbox and clicks on a document marked *The Fallen.*

> It has been decreed that in each kingdom the knight's place of rest must be sited no more than a day's strides on a beast from water and no deeper than the height of the tallest man. The ground that holds the sacred bones of the fallen must forever be in the protection of his brothers and the soil that covers his blessed skin must be touched in equal measure by the sun and the moon.
>
> Once every turn of harvest, those who live and serve will visit and tend the land of those who fell. They will light great fires and speak richly of the deeds of those who have passed. In the Ritual of the Eternal Flame, they will reignite the Spirit of Goodness that forged the great sword and served the only king.
>
> And it is hereby decreed that in the homeland the place of rest will forever be where the great Celts cross and where the bards stand alone to deliver their eulogies.

The two investigators exchange glances of bewilderment.

Mitzi shrinks the mail and looks for the other document that

Vicky promised. 'Let's read what she found out about Owain Gwyn before we start trying to work out what all this means.'

The next attachment is a series of factual points. It lacks the lyrical narrative of the decoded transcript but the contents are every bit as dramatic.

FULL NAME: Owain Richard Arthur Gwyn

AGE: 42

NATIONALITY: British.

PLACE OF BIRTH: Wales.

CURRENT POSITION: Ambassador-at-large, with responsibilities for defence and counter-terrorism.

PREVIOUS POSITIONS: British Ambassador to USA. British Ambassador to Germany. British Ambassador to France. Special Adviser to HRH Prince of Wales.

EDUCATED: New College Oxford. BA, History.

MILITARY SERVICE: Commissioned officer in the Welsh Guards (*Gwarchodlu Cymreig*). This is an elite infantry regiment in the British army, of which HRH the Prince of Wales is the regimental colonel. Gwyn served in Afghanistan as lieutenant and captain. Awarded CGC – Conspicuous Gallantry Cross for bravery in battle and the Victoria Cross for inspirational leadership on the battlefield (this is the UK's premier award for gallantry).

FAMILY STATUS: Married 18 years. Wife: Lady Jennifer Gwyn (née Degrance). No children.

HONORS: UK – Knight of the British Empire. Knight of the Most Noble Order of the Garter (*). Knight Commander of the Order of St Michael and St George (**).

USA – Medal of the Legion of Merit for exceptionally meritorious conduct in the performance of outstanding services and achievements.

* *Membership of the Garter is limited to the sovereign, the Prince of Wales and no more than twenty-four members.*

** *The Order of St Michael and St George stretches back to 1818 when the prince regent set it up in the name of the great military saints to honor men and women who render extraordinary non-military service in a foreign country.*

BUSINESS INTERESTS: Gwyn owns eighty per cent of the stock and acts as non-executive chairman of Caledfwlch Ethical Investments. The firm acts as an 'angel' for emerging companies across the globe and will only bankroll businesses that meet its stringent ethical standards. CEI last year turned over £2.48 bn ($4 bn) and has 32 offices in 27 countries. It recorded net profits of £200 m ($322 m) and made charitable donations in 21 countries totalling £150 m ($241 m). CEI is a family-owned company dating back more than 300 years and is believed to have been one of the original investors in Lloyds of London.

Mitzi finishes Gwyn's biog and types a note to Vicky asking

her to dig deeper into the history of the ambassador, his family and his business. She hits SEND, pushes her chair back on its wheels and turns to Bronty. 'Why, oh why, did I never find a guy like Owain Gwyn? On paper, he's everything a girl could ask for. A man with almost as many medals as millions.'

Bronty is unimpressed. 'He's not all he seems, Mitzi, trust me on that. He has amazing charisma, I'll grant you, but there's a dark side to him as well.' He leans across the laptop and taps the screen with his finger. 'Look at this: the Conspicuous Gallantry Cross for bravery in battle and the Victoria Cross for inspirational leadership on the battlefield. What do those medals mean to you?'

She answers with one word, 'Hero.'

'It means he's a killer. A trained and ruthless life-taker. One so good at it, his government and Queen have awarded him their top prizes for doing so. People like Owain Gwyn redefine the word dangerous. We have to be careful – very careful – in how we deal with this man.'

76

SOHO, LONDON

Angelo Marchetti is buzzing from the line of coke he's snorted in the washroom of a dingy café behind Tottenham Court Road Tube station.

The full rush hits him as he steps into the street and gets swallowed up in the fast, noisy tide of people. His senses are super-sharp. He can smell the rich, roasted coffees they carry in their hands, the sweet dope some of them are smoking, the colognes and perfumes on their cheeks.

His iPhone pulses and he slaps several pockets until he finds it. There's no number on the caller display but he knows who it's from. Right now, no one in the world is more important than the man at the other end of the line.

He hits the green answer button, 'Tell me all my troubles are over.'

The noise on the street disappears as he listens. It seems for a moment the whole world has stopped. Marchetti's drug-induced high has just been depressingly blown away. 'You're sure? You're absolutely sure.'

The caller is certain. He insists there is no way he could be wrong.

Marchetti looks around the street. The energy has gone. People are only ghosts to him now. He's lost all connection and feeling for the world around him.

He's a dead man walking.

Unless he can think of something new, it's only a matter of time before either Mardrid or Gwyn end his sorry life.

The caller is still on the phone. He wants a decision. In light of what's happened, he wants to know what needs to be done.

'Okay,' says Marchetti. 'Do what you have to. But do it quickly and never call me again.'

77

CALEDFWLCH ETHICAL INVESTMENTS, LONDON

It's late evening by the time Owain Gwyn gets back to his company desk.

Melissa Sachs sticks her head around her boss's door. 'Do you need me to stay longer?'

He glances at the clock: 21.15.

'No, I'm sorry. I had no idea it was that late.'

She smiles understandingly. It's always that late and he never seems to notice.

'I'm fine, Melissa. Thanks for hanging on.'

'You're welcome.' She starts to leave, then has an afterthought. 'Would you like me to order you any food?'

'No thanks. It'll do my waistline good to miss a meal.' He playfully waves her away.

Once she's gone, he presses a button that locks the door and another that slides back a wooden panel in the opposite wall and reveals an eighty-inch LED monitor. He uses his desk computer to pull up live satellite feeds of the carnage near Ashford and at the same time a video link to the SSOA offices in America.

Gareth Madoc slips into a seat thousands of miles away and activates the conferencing facility. 'Hello? Can you hear me?'

Owain takes off the mute control at his end. 'Loud and clear. How are you?'

'Holding up. Nothing that a night's sleep wouldn't solve.'

'All in good time. Tell me about our friend Nabil Tabrizi.'

'We've had eyes and ears on him and Malek the bomb-maker since the blast. There's been no movement from either of them and no contact between them.'

Owain grimaces. 'I'd hoped Nabil would be careless.'

'He hasn't been. Not yet. I think Malek still being around is significant.'

'Why?'

'It confirms that the suicide vest wasn't his handiwork. If it had been, they'd have moved him out of the area for fear of any connection.'

'Meaning they still want him in NYC to do something else.'

'I think so.'

'Then we have to find out who the other bomb-maker is. Do the Americans have any idea?'

'The CIA is all over the two terrorists seized in the raid on the body shop. They've introduced them to a whole new world of pain but neither have given anything up.'

'They will,' says Owain. 'Providing of course that they have anything to give up and the CIA don't kill them in the process.'

'We have one lead that might prove fruitful, but I don't want to raise your hopes prematurely.'

'They need raising, even if it is only temporary.'

He gives it his best shot. 'Antun's death was caught on CCTV cameras at the station. We were able to work backwards, block-by-block following him on street surveillance systems. He came to Grand Central in a white van that had been parked at the back of a group of old row houses down Westchester Avenue. There's a shot of Antun and the man he fought with and killed getting into it.'

Owain had to cast his mind back 'Hadn't we been watching one of Nabil's safe houses near there?'

'Yes, but it's not where he is now. We do however have footage from there showing a young Muslim woman going in, looking terrified.'

Poor kid.'

'*Lucky* kid, more like. When she comes out, she's on her knees, kissing the ground. Praising Allah for something.'

'Her life.'

'That's what I thought. My guess is she was the original candidate for the suicide vest, then Antun volunteered to take her place.'

'Let's hope she stayed lucky.'

'She has so far. I've got a crew monitoring her. If we can offer her a new start somewhere far away then she might be turnable.'

'Does the CIA know about her?'

'Not yet. But they'll be doing the same surveillance backtrace that we did, only with more primitive equipment.'

Gwyn drums his fingers on the big table. 'I'm hesitant because I'm trying to see the bigger picture. Lance has intelligence pointing at an al-Qaeda strike in Rome and I'm trying to reconcile the two locations.'

'Surely it's an either or?'

Owain grimaces. 'Maybe not. Mardrid is pumping money into AQ like never before. For some time, he's been riding the coat tails of the Muslim Brotherhood, helping them build powerbases in Egypt, Syria, Algeria and Libya. If you couple that with his activities in Africa, you can see an ambitious plan of destabilization.'

'Good old-fashioned monetary warfare.'

'War always is, Gareth, and for centuries the Mardrids have funded the most brutal of them. I've told Lance I want Josep Mardrid dead, and I mean it. We have to cut the head off the serpent. If we don't, many innocent lives will be lost.'

78

CAERGWYN CASTLE, WALES

A simple meal of roasted lamb, new potatoes and summer vegetables is served in a wainscoted room decorated with a hundred and fifty medieval shields. Each one comes from a Blood Line knight, a founding member of the secret Arthurian Order.

The room is wide and tall, with heavy crimson drapes and leaded ceiling-to-floor windows to three walls. In winter, a raging fire would roar in the massive inglenook hearth that dominates the fourth wall.

Lady Gwyn, Lance Beaucoup and Myrddin sit at a long table made from a giant oak that grew for centuries in the castle's grounds. Down the length of its noble grain stand ten silver candelabras, all dripping candle wax.

Myrddin puts down a silver jewelled wine goblet that he's owned all his life and blots red wine from his lips with a white cotton napkin. His green eyes settle on Lance as though reading his thoughts. 'I believe it was February of last year.'

'What was?' The Frenchman puts down his knife and fork.

'This was the first time that you were bold enough to declare your affections to the good lady.'

Lance picks up his wine and drinks nervously.

'Since then, you have thought of her every morning and every night. You are so hopelessly in love you would die for her. You'd give up your own life in a heartbeat. Wouldn't you?'

He knows there is no point denying it. 'I would.'

'It is good to know there is honour in dishonour, because one day you most probably will have to lay down your life for her. I believe it is something Owain knows as well.'

Lance looks alarmed, 'Does he—'

Myrddin cuts him off with a mocking smile. 'You insult both him and me with your question. What is important is that he thinks much of you. He sees you as brave and . . . *gallant*.'

The comment angers him. 'In days of old such *gallantry* would deserve more than ridicule from an old man.'

Myrddin runs a finger across his throat. 'In days of old cold steel may have been drawn across warm flesh in response to indiscretion such as yours.'

Lance looks to Jennifer. 'Was this why you arranged tonight's dinner? To have me lectured and embarrassed in this way?'

Myrddin prevents her answering. 'No, it is for me to remind you that discretion is the better part of valour. Some things in the great Cycle are inevitable and it behoves me to instruct those central to its motion to behave in a manner that does not cause concern among the circles. Do you understand, my young and *gallant* knight?'

'Enough, *monsieur*. I am done with this.' Lance drops his napkin on the table and pushes back his chair. 'It is better I go and swallow my words, than stay and spit out poison that sickens our future relationship.'

'As you wish.'

Lance nods at Jennifer and leaves.

Myrddin stretches out his hand and takes hers. 'He has made a wise decision. In the mathematics of the heart, love and goodness are multiplied by sacrifice and so far your lover has made but a small contribution.'

'Don't chide him so.'

'My child, soon you will be called upon to make the greatest of sacrifices and I need to ensure your account is not empty of love when life withdraws all that matters to you.'

She squeezes tight. Holds on like she did when she was a child and ran to him, frightened. 'How long has Owain known?'

'Long enough to prepare and not so long to be immune to hurt. The blackest of times is coming and both your husband and I believe your fiery French friend is best suited to guide you to the light.'

79

SOHO, LONDON

At the end of what seems a long day Mitzi and Bronty eat in the hotel restaurant. Soup. Steaks and fries. Nothing fancy. No dessert but one too many glasses of wine. Bloated and sleepy, they crash out as soon as they're finished.

Mitzi climbs into bed and calls her sister.

Ruth still sounds angry with her. 'I was wondering if you were going to bother to call.'

She fights back a curt reply. 'Busy day, Ruthy. You may have noticed there's been a bombing in the UK. On top of that, I'm still working a double homicide.'

'I wasn't criticizing.'

'Sounded like you were warming up to it. How's Amber?'

'A little better.' Her tone softens. 'She's not eating yet but we got her a prescription and she's moved from the bathroom to her bed. She's on the mend.'

Mitzi tries to build bridges. 'Thanks for looking after her. I'm really sorry I'm not there.'

'Yeah. I wish you were here too. I know what happened with Jack wasn't your fault.' There's an awkward lull before she adds, 'I just needed someone to blame. Other than me.'

'Then blame him. Not you.'

'I know. Hey, what I said about you finding another place. There's no rush. You're welcome to stay here as long as you want.'

'I'll find somewhere soon. Promise.'

'Not too soon. I'm gonna miss having people round.'

'Oh, we'll still be around – just not under your feet. Do either of my daughters want to talk to me?'

'I think Amber's asleep, but I'll put Jade on.' She holds the phone and shouts across the open-plan room. 'It's your mom; she wants to talk to you.'

Mitzi hears the sound of the dishwasher being emptied and her daughter's voice in the background: 'I don't want to talk to her. If she can't be bothered to be here, then I can't be bothered either.'

'Jade!'

There's a pause before Ruth comes back on the phone. 'Sorry, she's doing stuff.'

'Yeah, it sounded like it. I heard her, Ruthy. She's clearly still mad at me.'

'She's a teenager; she's mad at most things. I'll try to get her to call you later.'

'Thanks.' Mitzi doesn't want to hang up without acknowledging her sister's wish to put things right between them.

'And thanks for not being mad with me any more. I hate it when we row.'

'Me too.'

'Then we won't. Not any longer. Tell the girls I love them and I can't wait to see them.'

'Will do.'

She hangs up and feels horribly sad and lonely. Maybe taking this job was the wrong thing. It's provided the new start she needed but now it's torturing her with guilt about not being with the kids.

Her cell phone rings. She looks at the number and sees it's a Washington area code. 'Fallon.'

'Lieutenant, it's Kirstin Collins. I hope I haven't woken you?'

'No. But me and my beaten-up face are about to turn in for the night.'

'Then I'll try not to keep you. Sophie Hudson, the assistant at Goldman's, has been found dead in her apartment. Her neck's broken and her home has been trashed.'

80

LONDON

It's gone two in the morning when Angelo Marchetti staggers out of Experientia, a basement club regarded as the West End's coolest.

He's more wasted than he's been for years and is uncertain he can find a cab, let alone his hotel.

Today's been a shitter. A Grade One crap-a-doodle-dandy of badness.

And even now, out of his brain on poorly cut coke, he can't bury the thought that he had a young girl killed and still hasn't recovered the digital data that would have been his passport to an unworried life of plenty.

He staggers down a narrow, dark side street and heads towards the haze of lights at the far end.

He hears the click, a second before a voice demands, 'Give me your fucking money.'

Marchetti doesn't answer.

'Your money, phone 'n' watch, or I'll fuckin' shoot you.'

He doesn't speak because he's wondering if it would be a good thing to get shot. To put an end to all the crap he's in. If the stick-up guy is any good, it'll be over real quick. 'Go fuck yourself.'

'I mean it, man.' The voice gets closer. 'Empty your fuckin' pockets, or I'll waste you.'

Marchetti's SSOA training kicks in. He sobers up fast. The loudmouth is a punk but he's not alone. There are two, maybe three others shuffling in the shadows. In a second, someone will grab him. They'll throw punches and kicks and pile in on him and have their fun.

'Okay. Okay!' He holds up his hands. 'I'm doing the watch. I'm taking it off.' He steps forward placidly and then snaps a full-blooded punch into one of the hazy outlines.

'Fuuuck!' A shadow reels back holding a broken jaw.

Marchetti drops to the floor and grabs an ankle. He tugs hard and the body goes down. He keeps hold of the foot and twists until the ankle breaks.

There's a roar of gunfire.

Stick-up boy has finally found the balls to pull the trigger. But it's only a warning shot. And that's his big mistake. He's given away his position.

Before the goon recovers from the recoil, Marchetti is at him. He smacks the weapon away with his right hand and smashes his skull into the shooter's face.

Someone punches Marchetti in the side. A dull pain registers. He drives an elbow into the attacker's head and sends him crashing into a wall.

It's getting messy now and he knows that, even sober, three against one is eventually going to turn bad unless he wants to start killing people.

The blow in his side is achingly painful. He puts a hand down and realizes he's been knifed not punched.

Marchetti goes after the stick-up guy while he still has the strength. He throws a disciplined right-hander that cracks the gunman's ribs. The punk gasps for air. Marchetti plucks the gun from his helpless fingers and shoots him in the leg.

The muzzle flash shows the whereabouts of the other two men. He swings and fires low. Leg shots, aimed to cripple, not kill.

The air fills with the smell of cordite and screams of wounded men.

Marchetti jams the gun in his belt and hobbles out of the alley. None of them is going to be rushing after him. Not now. Not ever.

PART THREE

81

CAERGWYN CASTLE, WALES

It is the middle of the night when Myrddin hears Sir Owain's helicopter land in a distant part of the grounds.

He eases his tired bones from the straw-packed mattress, stands by the window slit and watches blinking lights illuminate the dark sky. He doesn't have to look at a clock to know it's an hour before dawn. He's spent countless decades telling the time by the stars, the moon and the sun.

Myrddin wraps himself up and shuffles down the spiral staircase to his rooms.

Owain always comes here first.

Even though it's summer, the stone chambers are chilly so he stoops before the great hearth and sets light to paper, straw and kindling. He sits and watches red and orange tongues hungrily lick the dry vanilla-coloured wood logs.

There's a polite thump on the door.

'Come in.'

Metal locks clunk. Oak creaks. A dishevelled Sir Owain enters, a bag in each hand, his hair blown wild by the helicopter's rotors. 'I hoped you would be up.' He smiles appreciatively.

'As if it would be otherwise. Put those down and come sit by the fire with me.'

'Do you have any water?' He takes off his jacket and heads to one of two hard chairs set either side of the blaze.

'I drew some from the well, last night.' Myrddin reaches to a rough wood side table and tips a terracotta jug until crystal clear liquid fills a matching beaker.

Owain takes it and remembers he's been drinking sweet fresh water from this ancient spring since he was a child.

Myrddin waits for him to finish. 'Has Jennifer spoken to you of matters of the Cycle?'

'No. She cannot bring herself to do so. But she carries the secret in her eyes. I saw it in Glastonbury and felt her pain in trying to hide it.'

'These are tough times.' He looks to the roaring flames. 'The most vicious of fires forges the strongest steel.'

'Vicious is a good description of my dilemma. My wife is pregnant with our first child, and instead of preparing for the birth of my son I must prepare for my death. And, to add insult to such fatal injury, in the white heat of this pain I must hammer out a new love for her.'

'Such is the way of the Cycle.'

'Then forgive me, but I wish it were not this way.' He laughs sadly. 'Have we picked well, Myrddin? Is Lance truly the man I hope he is, one who can protect her and my son?'

'He will become that man. Fate decrees it and I will ensure it.'

'Thank you.' Owain looks at the grey light pressing the windows. 'Enough of this now. I am stuffed to bursting with pains of the heart.' He picks up a gnarled log and throws it on the fire then settles back in the chair. 'Talk to me about other things. Of life and memories. Anything but our never-ending duties and what is expected of us. I shall spend the rest of the night here with you and will return to the house when a new day has broken and prepare for the meeting with the Blood Line.'

82

SOHO, LONDON

Jet-lagged and hungry, Mitzi sips coffee and watches dawn break, not in all its glory, but in shabby shades of nicotine and burned orange.

She's come out on the roof garden of the hotel for fresh air, her eyes fixed south towards the Thames but her mind on events thousands of miles away. Her children: one sick and needing her, the other angry and not wanting her. Her sister: lonely and confused because her heart's been broken. Her ex: violent and troublesome, but still the only man she ever loved.

Irish: a good soul, ground down by the job, now just bones and skin waiting to be buried. Life seems to go so fast and to do such damage with its speed.

Mitzi returns to her room, makes instant coffee and tries to work out why Sophie Hudson got killed. She has a very good idea what the motive was, but needs to know all the facts before she draws conclusions.

Once her computer's powered up she reads the full report from Kirstin, then examines JPEGs of the crime scene. Digital shots of turned-out drawers, smashed vases, and emptied containers. Coffee, sugar, chocolate, rice and cereals are spread all over the floors. Sophie's clothes have been torn to shreds. Including those she was wearing.

Mitzi checks the ME's report. The girl was badly beaten. Punched both sides of the face. Hit in the stomach and breasts. There are signs of bruising to oral, vaginal and anal cavities.

A rookie might write off the scene as a rape robbery. It looks for all the world like a cokehead came looking for cash and lost sexual control when he found a pretty girl home alone.

But Mitzi knows better.

Whatever swabs have been sent to the labs will come back to show nil semen and nil DNA. She hadn't been raped, she'd been cavity searched. The bruise patterns around Sophie's wrists and cotton traces in her mouth indicate she'd been bound, gagged and interrogated by someone ruthlessly looking for something.

Mitzi opens her laptop case and takes out the memory stick.

It has to be this.

Having seen the autopsy pictures she was in no doubt that Sophie had told her torturer that she'd given the stick to the FBI woman. She'd have spat out that particular fact soon after the first punch in the face, but the murderer would have tortured her just to check it right up to her dying breath.

Now he'll be coming after her.

Either him, or the men who are paying him for his brutal and homicidal skills.

83

LONDON

Angelo Marchetti wakes in pain.

It had been nearly four a.m. by the time nurses at St Thomas's finished stitching him up. There'd been a couple of awkward moments. One when he'd needed to drop the triage nurse a fifty-pound note and a story about a jealous husband coming home early to stop her calling the cops. And another when he was leaving and saw an ambulance unloading two of the guys he shot.

Aside from that, he counted his blessings. The wound was only two inches deep and hadn't hit anything except fat on his hips.

He fumbles in the little white bag the hospital pharmacist

gave him and takes two painkillers with the last of the water he'd put on the bedside cabinet. For the next hour, he sleeps. Submerges himself in a soft and healing slumber, glad to be unconscious.

It's eight o'clock when he comes round and stares at the digital clock that's also charging his iPhone. He makes it three in the morning in DC, the place where there is one less store assistant sleeping soundly because he paid for her to be murdered.

He swings his legs out of bed and blood rushes to his head. He can almost feel the guilt too, growing inside his cranium like a tumour. He knows he mustn't think about it. He can't afford to let it eat away at him.

The girl's a casualty. Collateral damage. Nothing else.

But the harder Marchetti tries to blot her out, the more her ghost haunts him.

He staggers to the bathroom and looks at the blood-soaked patch around his hip. He wishes he'd been killed last night. Wishes those punks had got their shit together and put him out of his misery.

He runs the shower and tries to face up to what he has to do.

Today is the start of another day. Another series of bold steps in the quicksand of sin. And unless he gets what he needs, at least another murder to blacken his soul.

84

SOHO, LONDON

Bronty knuckle-raps Mitzi's door to walk her to breakfast.

She ushers him in with the overnight news: 'Sophie Hudson, Goldman's assistant, got killed in her apartment.'

'When?' He shuts the door behind him.

'Yesterday. I got a call from DC Police just before I went to sleep. Tortured and neck broken. Pro job by the look of the autopsy shots. Twist and snap, it's much harder to do than they show on TV.'

He flinches. 'Too graphic, Mitzi. I don't do death this side of coffee and carbs.'

'I figure someone's after the stick she gave me.' She hands him two sheets of paper that she ran off in the business lounge more than an hour ago. 'Top page is a copy of the transcript Vicks sent us last night. Underneath is a new fragment she just mailed through from the cryptologists.'

Extract from directory headed 'The Arthurian Cycle':

Beware you who boldly turn this page and bend inquisitive head to look upon these weighted words.

Be sure your soul is strong enough to support their meaning and you are naught but noble and chivalrous.

Be certain you have only fullness of courage and surfeit of kindness in your mind and heart.

Be absolute that you are virtuous and incorruptible, for this text is written in holy blood and is by divine right a mirror held to your soul.

Should you be found wanting then your search for the secrets of 'the ruler known by many names' will not only be the death of you, it will be the ruination of your afterlife. Be warned – if Darkness finds a home in you, then you in turn will find no home in the Promised Land and you will curse your family with your sins.

Take not my words lightly, for I am the sorcerer who made the true king, the one who was, who is and who will always be.

It is I, who forged his righteousness in the image of man and doused his soul in human mortality, I who curdled fact and fiction to create the clouds that cover centuries of history.

Know that knowledge is never absolute. Learn this, or you will never understand the Arthurian Cycle and how it turns with the planets and shapes the history of the earth.

Every man has a birth. All belief has a beginning. Every circle has a start.

But what if the strongest of circles were cast whole? If, like molten iron, they were poured into a seamless mould. Would the beginning of such a circle be said to come at the moment the hot metal touched the cold? Or would the start lie in the creation of the mould? Or in the hand of he who created the mould? Or in the bodies of those who created the man who created the mould? Or in the mind and heart of the one who imagined it all? See how ill-equipped we are to speak of beginnings and endings, of time and place and our positions within them.

To separate great men from the great myths that surround them, you must understand the forging of the Circle of Iron. For the King of Kings is a Man of Iron. Belief is the mould and generation by generation a new man is poured into it. Century by century, those who stand around him point him out and say he was the one, is the one, will be the one.

And, so it is, that to those who chronicle such feats, it seems at times that there are either many of him, that he lived for ever, or that he never lived at all.

Be careful in your quest for knowledge.

The road is long and journey perilous.

I know for I have fallen a thousand times in its rocky ditches and sunk ten thousand times in its sulphurous lakes.

Better to live happily with Ignorance than suffer the unrequited love of Knowledge. Remember, Ignorance is the father of Peace and Peace has no prejudice. Both Ignorance and Peace can sow as bountifully in the soils of Deceit as they can in the earths of Honesty.

Bronty lowers the paper and sees Mitzi waiting for his opinion. 'Without seeing much text it's difficult to know what to make of this. I could easily jump to foolish assumptions and—'

'Oh, for God's sake, Bronty! People got killed for this. Just tell me what you think without all the lawyery cop-out crap.'

'Okay.' He holds the paper so she can see it and slides his finger over a line. 'Here the writer claims to be a sorcerer.' He stabs another paragraph. 'And here he expounds *The Arthurian Cycle and its role in the universe*. The author goes on to claim he is the sorcerer who made "the true king". He says he cast him in the image of man. Created him like a circle of iron that has no beginning and no end.' He pauses to see if she's making the connections on her own. 'Does any of this sound familiar to you?'

'Yeah, I'm thinking about superheroes, Iron Man in particular and how cute Robert Downey Junior is.'

'Think God instead of Hollywood.'

'You're going to have to explain that to me.'

'Forget King Arthur for a minute, this is a tale of God the Father – he is the sorcerer, and Jesus Christ the true king. It is about how Jesus was created by a divine power, how he died but never died, how he rose and is still among us. How some people believe in him and others think he's just the stuff of legend, myth and fairy tale.'

'Shit. Really?' Mitzi takes the paper from him. 'You *really* see that?'

'Was Christ not the King of Kings, the one true King?'

She plays devil's advocate. 'Not to everyone.'

'But you get my drift?'

'Drift a little more, so I'm certain.'

'Well, perhaps what's on that memory stick isn't a stack of

stories about some old king and his knights. It could be that Arthur was just another name for Jesus and what you have here, concealed in centuries of code, is an extract from an unknown gospel. Now, think how precious *that* would be.'

85

CAERGWYN CASTLE, WALES

Blossom blows across the courtyard as Owain makes his way from Myrddin's quarters to the main part of the castle.

Ahead of him, lost in thought, is Lance Beaucoup. His head down as he walks, Owain is sure his mind is on Jennifer and what kind of future lies ahead for them.

'*Bonjour*,' he says when only a yard away.

Lance turns in shock. His eyes glisten with guilt. He quickly tries to recover his composure. 'I'm sorry, I didn't see you there. Good morning, when did you get back from London?'

'Just in,' Owain lies. 'I wanted to make an early start because we have the Blood Line meeting this afternoon.'

Lance glances at his watch. 'Some of the older members arrived yesterday evening. I heard them talk of going to watch the new recruits training, then a walk down to the lake.'

Owain smiles. 'It brings back memories for them. As it will for you one day.'

He laughs and relaxes a little. 'I want to forget my training.

All those weeks out in the wild with nothing to eat or drink.' He pulls a face. 'Give me a five-star hotel and fine dining any day.'

'I agree. Though I now have to take care I don't turn too soft in my older years.'

They walk together along the foot of the castle wall and Lance makes small talk. 'How were things in London? As chaotic as I imagine?'

'Almost. The Cabinet is next to useless and the Prince of Wales wanted to see me twice a day for updates on the Eurostar bombing.'

Lance opens a door from the courtyard to the southern wing. 'An over-interested patron is not always the best thing.'

Owain walks inside. '*Interest*, no matter how intense, is always better than a lack of interest.'

'*Je comprends*.'

'HRH also wants to join our Inner Circle.'

'Figuratively?'

'No. He really wants to take part, to get involved.'

Lance stops walking. 'What did you tell him?'

Owain halts as well. 'That I would put it forward for consideration.'

'And are you in favour?'

'I'm still deciding.' He starts them walking again. 'As well as his considerable wealth, which as you know is an important weapon in any war, the prince has enormous domestic and international influence.'

'Today's influence turns into tomorrow's interference.'

'You may be right.' Owain changes the subject. 'Were you with Jennifer last night?' He lets the question hang until he sees his colleague tense up. 'Only I called her mobile and she didn't answer, and I couldn't get through on the landline.'

Lance has to hide his anxiety. 'Yes. I saw her for dinner. We were with Myrddin. I didn't hear any phone call.'

'How strange.' He changes his tone. 'You know that when I am not here, I really count on you looking after her. You realize that, don't you, Lance?'

His heart thumps hard. 'I do.'

Owain gives him a hearty shoulder punch. 'Good man. I knew I could trust you.'

86

SOHO, LONDON

The hotel receptionist finishes dealing with an elderly Chinese couple, and then manages a welcoming smile for the smart-suited executive next in line. 'Hello, can I help you?'

The dark-haired visitor looks at her name badge as he produces his ID. 'I hope you can, Kata. I'm DCI Mark Warman from the Metropolitan Police. Can I see your manager, please?'

The young Hungarian presses a button beneath the desk. 'I get him for you.'

'Thanks.' He senses a personal nervousness beyond any that his request should have prompted. Fortunately for her, he's not interested in checking her immigration papers.

A portly man appears, dressed in a brown wool suit that looks at least a size too small. He straightens his tie and introduces himself. 'Jonathan Dunbar, hotel manager. You asked to see me?'

'Yes, sir.' He edges away from queuing guests and is joined by a young woman in her thirties who's been hanging back. He shows his credentials again. 'DCI Warman. DS Jackson and I are from SO15, the counter-terrorism unit. We have an interest in two of your guests.'

Dunbar's face turns pale.

'Americans,' adds Jackson. She produces two photographs from inside her lightweight red blazer. 'The woman is Mitzi Fallon, a brunette in her late thirties. Her colleague is Jon Bronty, a thin man, with chestnut hair.'

'I've seen them,' he says nervously. 'They checked in yesterday. They had FBI credentials.'

She smiles understandingly. 'Credentials aren't always genuine. Are they here now?'

'I really don't know. I'll have to find out.'

Warman's eyes grow intense. 'Don't tell them we're here. We don't want things to get . . . how shall we say . . . *complicated.*' He opens his jacket slightly, lets Dunbar see the Met-issue pistol in its holster.

The manager scurries back behind the front desk. He talks to the receptionist, checks a computer then returns. 'They've just left. No more than ten minutes ago.'

Warman looks relieved. 'Can you take us to their rooms?'

Dunbar seems surprised. 'Certainly.' Then his left eye twitches nervously. 'You don't think there are explosives in there, do you?'

'Highly unlikely. If we did, we'd have the bomb squad with us.'

'Right.' He stands frozen to the spot.

'Now can you take us, please?'

'Yes, yes, of course.' He jumps into action. 'I have a master key. Follow me.'

They ride the elevator to the top floor and Dunbar strides down the carpeted corridor ahead of them. 'Rooms 602 and 604 are theirs.' He slips a key card into both slots and pushes the doors open. 'Do you need me to come in with you?'

'No, that's not necessary, sir,' says Warman. 'Not unless you wish to?'

'Er, no. No thank you. I'll be downstairs if you need me.' He smiles and walks away.

Warman pulls his pistol and checks it. 'Ten minutes, then we have to be out of here.'

Jackson nods.

'We don't want to give that dope long enough to think about actually calling the Yard and checking our credentials.'

87

AMERICAN EMBASSY, LONDON

To Mitzi's dismay, there's still no DNA profile from the water bottle she stole from George Dalton at Gwyn's office.

There's more than a hint of fear in Annie Linklatter's voice as she promises, 'I'll have it by the end of the day.'

Mitzi gives her a parting glower and returns to the small office she and Bronty have commandeered.

The ex-priest looks up from his spread of papers and maps. 'Any luck?'

'Don't freakin' well ask. The Brits move at a pace that predates modern civilization.'

He laughs at her. 'She's *American*.'

'No matter. It's being over here that's made her slow. What are you doing?'

'Come and see.' He flattens out a large Ordnance Survey map and places a page of A4 paper next to it. 'I've been thinking about this passage of text in *The Fallen*: *It is hereby decreed that in the homeland the place of rest will for ever be where the great Celts cross and where the bards stand alone to deliver their eulogies.*'

She reads it and then confesses, 'Aside from the Celtic cross, it means nothing to me.'

'I don't think it means cross as in crucifix. I think it refers to a point where Celtic clans or borders crossed, the Irish and the Welsh cross.'

'A physical place.'

He taps the map. 'Here. It's a place that the Knights Templar once owned.'

She stares at a fingernail of an island off the west coast of Britain. 'Lundy? I've never heard of it.'

Bronty looks animated. 'This might well be where holy knights were buried. It's the spot where the Celtic Sea hits the Bristol Channel.'

Mitzi studies the map. 'The place looks tiny. It can't be more than five miles long and maybe a mile wide?'

'Less than that. The text refers to " . . . . *where the bards stand alone to deliver their eulogies* . . . .", well there's a cemetery out there and I can't imagine a more isolated place in Europe to say kind words over the body of a fallen brother.' He moves to the computer. 'Now look at what I found.' He pulls up a web page featuring the island. 'Lundy is owned by the National Trust and leased to the Landmark Trust, to protect it from being built on or exploited.'

'So?'

'Look at the bottom.'

Mitzi reads aloud, '"British diplomat Sir Owain Gwyn is a leading contributor to both Trusts and a patron of numerous Lundy support groups."'

'So, if there are secrets out there,' says Bronty, 'then Gwyn is well positioned to protect them.'

'You need go snoop. How far away is it from here?'

'I feared you'd say that. It's a good two hundred miles and a ferry boat ride.'

Mitzi smiles. 'You better get booking your trip, then.'

88

CAERGWYN CASTLE, WALES

Members of the Blood Line have come from all over Britain, France and Belgium, the old countries that produced the original knights and centuries-long allegiances that constituted the Round Table.

Each of the honoured warriors shows no documentation at the armed checkpoints. Instead, their fingers are pricked by SSOA guards at the lodge gates and blood matched on special DNA passes that both they and the security teams hold. Once ID'd by haematology, Knights of the Blood Line are given complete freedom of the castle and its grounds.

A small group winds its way to the woods, where newly recruited knights are trained in hand-to-hand combat by former SAS commanders. Nearby, bursts of gunfire crackle inside a single-storey row of outbuildings. Every member of the Blood Line has done his or her time inside the dense labyrinth of darkened rooms where simulated hostage recovery operations are staged.

Back at the castle, Owain Gwyn enters Keep Hall and settles at the middle of one of four exceptionally long tables butted together to form not a circle but a perfect square. A hundred and fifty high-back thrones are arranged symmetrically. Each bears the individual family crest of a member.

The one behind Owain's head shows a white shield and on

it a red cross, identical in shape to crosses laid on the bodies of fallen knights. In the top left quadrant is an open-mouthed red dragon. In the bottom right, a large brown bear. The other two are filled with three golden crowns and a round wooden table.

Owain looks up from the centuries-old, wooden-bound book that is spread open before him. Old timers are filtering in for the meeting. They're always the first. The new Bloods will predictably breeze in, ruddy-cheeked, just in the nick of time.

The head of the SSOA leaves his seat and shakes the hands of Terry Lyons, descendant of Tristram de Lyones and Gerry Erbin, descendant of Sir Geraint. Others form an orderly queue behind them and Owain spends the next fifteen minutes personally welcoming every member of the Blood Line.

Finally, Myrddin enters, and as is his custom and right, he locks the great doors of the hall by jamming a broadsword through the hoops of two iron handles and takes his seat by the door.

Owain Gwyn looks across the vast tables to the faces of the great and the good. A hundred and fifty men and women whose ancestors lived and died for their common belief in freedom and fairness.

'Great members of the Blood Line, I thank you for travelling long and far to come here to our home at such short notice. My dear friends and colleagues, you know I wouldn't ask for this assembly if it wasn't to discuss matters of a most extraordinary nature.' He watches seriousness creep across faces, notes the tension in tightly folded arms and fidgeting hands. 'You know from the Watch Team bulletins the growing threats our countries face. And you know, too, of how our operational knights are fighting the old enemy Mardrid as he pays organizations like al-Qaeda to sow the seeds of discontent so he may reap the rewards of a bloody harvest. As this man increases his power base in the developed world, so too does he exploit the poorest nations, where he is using thuggery to rob generations of their future.'

Mutters break out among the venerable members, many of whom are old enough to remember the atrocities Mardrid's father and grandfather carried out in Ethiopia, Uganda and Rhodesia.

Owain waits until they grow quiet, then continues. 'The Inner Circle asks for you to ratify their decision to send crusaders to Africa to ensure no free man, woman or child falls victim to Mardrid, his men or machinations. Two hundred of our knights are on standby to enter Togo, the scene of Mardrid-initiated rape, murder, torture and arson. A thousand more are being mustered as we speak.'

Percy del Graal, descendant of Sir Percivale, raises his hand. 'Has NATO been informed, Sir Owain?'

'They have been appraised. None of the treaty members is stirred enough to send its own troops. Country defence budgets are cut to the bone. We have the tacit approval of the General Secretary.' He looks around the tables. 'Any more questions?'

Heads shake.

'Then, great members of the Blood Line, I respectfully ask you to favour the Inner Circle's decree in the form of the crusade I proposed. Do I have your support?'

All one hundred and fifty members clench their fists and put hands to their hearts.

'I thank you one and all.' Owain dips a quill into an inkpot and records the vote in the great ledger laid before him and adds the date, his name and his own seal. He carefully blots the entry, downs the ancient pen and returns his gaze to the assembled members.

'Dear friends, there is one other reason why I asked you here today.' Unexpectedly, he feels emotional. He catches his heart thump and his throat dry. He looks to Myrddin and sees the old man wiping an eye. Across the tables, others are already discreetly touching their faces. Owain forces a brave smile and soldiers on. 'I see some of you have guessed what I am about to say. The gates of Avalon are opening for me and I am readying myself for that great journey.' There are gasps but he daren't look up to put faces to sounds. 'Today may be the last time I stand here with you, the last chance I have to thank you for your friendship—'

Someone shouts, 'No! It is too soon.'

He halts the emotion with a raised hand. 'I wish that were the case. I am afraid, the hour is always later than we think. May God bless you and protect you and your families, and may your blood lines run rich and run long.'

89

NEW YORK

Twenty-one-year-old Zachra Korshidi hears them laughing at her as she struggles out of the grocery store.

'Excuse me, miss. May I speak with you?'

She ignores the smartly dressed man and walks on. All she can think about is how much she hates the burqa and niqab that her parents make her wear. The long sexless cloak and veil are swelteringly hot as she carries the heavy plastic bags along the sidewalk.

'Just one minute, miss.' The man walks behind her.

She remembers a time when they let her wear jeans and a T-shirt. When she could cover her hair with a multi-coloured scarf, a nice *roosari* – but all that's changed since 'the boy'.

That's what her parents called him. Not Javid, or her boyfriend.

The boy.

They said the words like he was a demon. All because they didn't choose him. Because he was an orphan, with no traditional family, raised in America and full of all the modern values and opinions that they hate.

It's little wonder she adored him. Loved him with all of her mind, soul and body. And wasn't afraid to admit it. Privately or publicly.

That was the problem – the final straw.

Admitting to having sex before marriage won't draw a second glance in New York, but back in Iran, it gets you publicly flogged and possibly executed. And these days, her parents spend most of the time behaving as though they are back in the old country.

She'd have left home and run away with Javid if his younger brother Sadeq hadn't been in the final stages of leukaemia. Instead, she stayed and her father beat her so badly that for days she was unable to walk.

It was at the same time that Javid disappeared.

He didn't call or text. He just vanished. He'd either been scared to death or put to death. Either way, she hadn't heard from him again.

Not seeing him was like the end of her life. She overdosed on her mother's sleeping pills. After having her stomach pumped at hospital and being told she'd brought even more shame on her family, she was brought home and locked in her bedroom.

Imprisoned.

Then came the chance to redeem herself. To make amends and bring honour back to her family and herself. A glorious suicide instead of a pointless one. That's how her father put it.

Not surprisingly, when the day came she was frightened. Sick with fear, remorse, regret and rage. Disgusted with the fact that innocent people were going to die along with her. People she had more in common with than her own flesh and blood.

It was a miracle someone else had volunteered.

'Miss!'

The insistent man is in front of her now. Blocking her way.

He peers into her dark eyes. 'I'm a friend of the man who saved your life. The man who wore the vest.'

She feels her pulse race and pushes past him.

'How long will it be, Zachra? How long before they come to you and ask you again? How long, Zachra?'

90

HRU CRIMES UNIT, SAN FRANCISCO

The email on Vicky Cantrell's computer is from Professor Quinn at the Smithsonian.

Dear Miss Cantrell,

I have now discussed the sketch of your relic with Professor Wilson at Oxford and he concurs with my view that it is Irish Iron Age. He does however think that the shaped endings of the cruciform make it unusual for the time and he believes the hole in the centre of the cross may have been of ceremonial significance.

Professor Wilson told me that he thought it possible that the cross was planted on high ground for prayer in such a way that sunlight might be seen through it. He also mentioned that Celtic legends have great warriors being buried with objects like this that not only showed their faith to mortals coming upon their graves, but also equipped the dead with a holy weapon to fight evil spirits in the afterlife.

I hope this proves to be of value to you.

Yours truly,

Simon Quinn.

Vicky prepares an email for Mitzi and attaches Quinn's findings. Eleonora Fracci is downtown with the cops on the witchcraft case, so she's got time to do a bit more digging into the history of Owain Gwyn, his family and company.

She starts with Caledfwlch Ethical Investments and finds the company pre-dates the start of official public records. It's a generous contributor to more than a dozen British charities, including Natural England, a group that helps the British government manage nature reserves and areas designated as being of special scientific interest.

There are also a number of intriguing connections to the Arthurian legend. Caledfwlch, the company name, turns out to be Welsh for Excalibur and the Gwyn family has large ancestral homes in Wales and Glastonbury, one of the spots where King Arthur and his wife Guinevere were allegedly laid to rest. Glastonbury is the place that Joseph of Arimathea, a central figure in the stories of the Holy Grail, was reputed to have fled to after Jesus had risen from the dead.

Owain's home in Wales, Caergwyn Castle, is close to the Preseli Mountains and a landmark called *Cerrig Marchogion* – The Knight's Stones – another location named as the final resting place of Arthur. The mountains are known for their geology, especially a distinctive bluestone that, according to legend, Arthur's magician Merlin used to create Stonehenge. Additionally, the ambassador has an extensive personal property portfolio that includes numerous cottages in Tintagel, a south-western town where Arthur is alleged to have been born.

From financial records, Vicky learns that Gwyn has been purchasing sizeable amounts of property and land in Cadbury in Somerset. All the acquisitions are close to the ruins of an ancient Iron Age fort, a place widely reputed to have been the site of Camelot.

Further digging into CEI reveals a span of subsidiaries, including one called 'CEIDP', which is run solely by Jennifer Gwyn. At first the researcher believes it's purely a shell company, but then finds it also has extensive property, land and rights, including 'water access, research and usage' at Dozmary Pool in Cornwall. Back in the fifties, the area was declared a site of special scientific interest and access became limited. CEIDP records show it funded extensive research into fish projects and explorations of the pool's Stone Age history.

Out of curiosity, Vicky searches for legends associated with Dozmary. She finds two. The first is that of Jan Tregeagle, a local lawyer/magistrate who gained money and power by making a pact with the Devil. Inevitably, the Prince of Darkness took his soul and cast his body to the bottom of the lake, from which it came back to haunt villagers.

The second legend is more interesting. Dozmary Pool is claimed to be the home of the Lady of the Lake, the place where King Arthur rowed out and received Excalibur. It's also the spot where the knight Bedivere returned the sword, after the battle of Camlann where Arthur lay dying.

Head spinning with history and legends, she takes a break and heads to the canteen for lunch. She's also hoping a certain young man called James Watkins will happen to be there.

A little older than her and built like a linebacker, he's new to the bureau and drives a desk in IT. Yesterday, they ate side by side and she got goose bumps and hot flushes all at the same time.

She orders tuna salad and takes an eternity eating it, hoping with every mouthful that he might show.

He doesn't.

After another soda, she's still sat alone. Dejectedly, she packs her tray in the rack by the door and returns to her work.

Her mood brightens as she searches the background of Lady Gwyn. Boy, does the woman know how to look good. Vicky savours the shots of her in sumptuous ball gowns at charity dinners, sparkling cocktail dresses at VIP parties and even in waterproofs and life vest on a racing yacht.

Her ladyship seems quite the fashionista. A celebrity in her own right. Daughter of Leo Degrance, a rich and influential business tycoon, she went to all the right public schools, became part of the British Equestrian Team, a medal-winning horsewoman and patron of almost a dozen charities.

For fun, Vicky Googles the name Jennifer and is amused to find that it has Cornish and Welsh connections – Jenny the Fair, Gwenhwyfar and Guinevere.

She does the same with the name Owain and, given that's another roll of the dice in the game of coincidences that she's playing, expects it to come up as Arthur or King.

It doesn't.

But in Welsh, the name Owain does mean Young Warrior, which is rewarding enough for her to continue tapping in his name and trawling the net.

Her perseverance is rewarded with a couple of news reports and legal articles that disclose that the British Knight is highly litigious and has taken legal action against innumerable companies and individuals who in his mind have threatened his privacy.

Top of the list is a notoriously eccentric Welsh historian called Rhys Mallory, who had written an unauthorized biography about him. Gwyn also obtained a series of injunctions to prevent Mallory from '*. . . in any way conveying any information about the Gwyn family that is not already in the public domain to any individual, group of individuals or data distribution system that can be privately or publicly read, seen, heard or in the instance of braille, felt.*'

While Vicky is no detective, she's smart enough to realize

the historian has some sensitive story to tell that the ambassador *really* doesn't want anyone to hear. She finds contact details and adds them to the summary paper that she types up and sends to Mitzi and Bronty.

Job done, she decides her hard work is worth a small bar of peppermint cream chocolate. She's just about to claim her prize when her desk phone rings. 'Cantrell.'

'Vicky?' The voice is the linebacker's.

Her heart misses a beat. 'Hello.'

'Hi, it's James. How you doing?'

She thinks of his easy smile and soft brown eyes and instantly makes herself nervous. 'I'm . . . I'm . . . good.'

'Listen, I'm sorry I missed lunch. I'm out in the field, helping rig a computer surveillance system. How are you fixed for dinner tonight?'

'Dinner?' She really hadn't been expecting this. 'You mean as in dinner date dinner, or just dinner as in food?' She can't believe she said all that. 'Oh God, I sound stupid now, don't I?'

'No, you don't. Yes, I mean dinner as in dinner date dinner.'

'Then yes. I like you very much – I mean, I'd like *to* very much.'

He laughs. 'That's good, because I like you very much too. Say eight?'

91

NEW YORK

Behind the privacy of the limo's tinted windows, Zachra Korshidi removes the niqab from her face. She straightens her hair and stares at the driver and the man she's sat in the back with. 'Who are you? Police? CIA?'

'Neither,' replies Gareth Madoc. 'Though I can get both here within minutes if you'd prefer to talk to them?'

'No.' Her voice is sharp with tension. She's taken enormous risks getting into the vehicle. Her father has friends everywhere in the neighbourhood. 'Who, then?'

'Let's say I work for a philanthropically minded organization that would like to help you.'

She looks at him cynically. 'Why?'

'Because in stopping young women like you becoming suicide bombers it saves American lives.'

Now she feels so ashamed that she can't look at him. 'You said you could help me.'

'Yes.'

'Does that mean if I wanted to get far away from here and never be found, you could do that?'

'If you cooperate with me, I can fix for you to live anywhere you like, with a new identity, a little money, maybe a job and somewhere to live.'

She stares at the black robe on her lap and knows all

it stands for. But what the man with the English accent wants is for her to betray her family and everything they stand for.

Gareth dips inside the jacket of his blue suit and pulls out a pack of small photographs. 'You need to see these. They're not pleasant, but you should look.'

Hesitantly, she takes them from him. The first picture is a wide shot of a big, round dumpster on thick, black roller wheels. It's at the back of a fried-chicken joint and the kitchen door is open, a fryer and long grill are visible. The second is of a pile of semi-tied, semi-ripped black garbage bags dumped in the yard. In the third, the bags are being opened by uniformed cops. The fourth shows the contents. Severed limbs. Hands. Feet. Arms.

Zachra's heart makes the connection before she sees the fifth.

Javid's head.

The face of her lover stares up at her. His skull has been severed from his body and his eyes are milky-white and pitted with flies. The hair she once loved to hold as she kissed him is matted in blood and food slops.

It takes almost a minute for her to get her breath back. For her to survive a hurricane of emotions. Finally, she finds her voice. And the words that she knows will change her life. 'I can help you. There are things that I know.'

92

POLICE HQ, WASHINGTON DC

Kirstin Collins runs nail-bitten fingers through her spiky hair and stares at the painting in front of her.

The small, crappy old oil was recovered from Bradley Deagan's small, crappy old apartment. She's really not sure it's going to be of any interest to Mitzi but she promised to keep her up to speed on developments, so that's what she's doing.

The young detective puts it face down on the big scanner in the squad room, makes a JPEG, attaches it to an email and calls Mitzi's number.

'Fallon.'

'Lieutenant, it's Kirstin Collins. You near a computer?'

'Too near. I'm going stir-crazy in an office smaller than my kids' bathroom. What've you got?'

She hits send. 'I just mailed you a copy of a painting uniforms recovered from Deagan's apartment. It was wrapped in cloth and hidden beneath boards.'

Mitzi checks her mailbox. 'Not here yet. Any sign of Deagan – dead or alive?'

'Nope. He and his vehicle have just vanished. Mail was stacked up at his place. No one has seen or heard of him since he was at the Dupont diner.'

'This painting, is it the one he tried to stage the con with?'

Kirstin stares as it. 'I don't know. I've not had time to check. There was no picture on the case papers.'

'Does it look religious?'

'Not really. But it's very old and seems the right shape and size. Way I figure it, if it was a fraud the court would have let him keep it, right?'

'Sure. It'd be his property. Your mail's just come. Hang on while I open it.'

Kirstin doodles and waits. She draws flowers. Big sprays of them. It's the only thing she can sketch.

Mitzi watches the image shutter its way from top to bottom of the frame. 'How're things, Kirstin? How you holding up?'

She finishes the head of a rose. '*Okay,* I miss Irish and can't believe he's not about to walk through the door. The funeral's in a couple of days. Probably won't be many people there. Hell, it might just be me and the priest. Will you come?'

Mitzi squirms. 'Like to, but to be honest, I can't afford the flights or the time. I've got two kids waiting for me back in California, my sister's breaking up with her husband and my ass is stuck in London. I'm sorry. Why don't you mail me the details and I'll send flowers.'

Kirstin scrubs over the roses she's drawn. 'You know what – he's got no use for flowers. Send me a bottle of whisky and I'll drink it in his memory and have one for you too.'

'You got it.' The full painting is now on her screen. 'Download is okay, Kirstin – I got it now.'

'Is it the one you mentioned?'

'Don't know, but I know a man who will. Thanks for thinking of me.'

'You're welcome.'

'Hey, you need something – you need to talk about anything – you call me, right?'

'Thanks.'

Kirstin Collins hangs up. She puts the painting back in the cloth it was wrapped in and ties string back around it.

Then she goes to Irish's desk and sits there. Just squats in his tatty old chair and swings it left and right, left and right. And she keeps on swinging until she feels a tiny bit better.

93

AMERICAN EMBASSY, LONDON

Bronty breaks from booking his Lundy trip and stands behind Mitzi to examine the digital copy of the painting. 'This is of knights,' he says disappointedly. '*The Ghent Altarpiece* shows several groups of people coming together to pay adoration to Christ. The missing panel is of judges, not knights.'

'Meaning this is, like, the worst forgery ever?'

He leans closer to the monitor and peers at the edges of the oil. 'I'm not an expert, but do you see this colouring here, around the edges? It's not right. These dark shades are out of character with the rest of the painting.'

Mitzi shifts her head and looks at it from different angles. 'Isn't that some kind of border?'

'It might be. Or, it could be evidence that there was once another painting over the top of it. One that's been stripped away.'

'The judges, you mean?'

'There have been rumours in the past about the panels. During restoration work, it was suggested there was a painting underneath at least one of them. Certainly, that would fit with the way the folding canvases show different scenes when the altarpiece is opened and closed. And remember this is the work of two men, firstly Hubert van Eyck, then his brother Jan.'

Mitzi has to trawl her memory. 'You know this crook Deagan showed the painting to Christie's – to a bunch of art experts – and they said it was a fake. They must have looked at the same things you're staring at and dismissed them as baloney.'

Bronty's still focused on the image, studying every brush stroke. 'Maybe at that time the painting hadn't been stripped back.'

'I can ask Kirstin to check in the files.'

He pulls up a chair and sits alongside her. 'The altarpiece is a really important piece of work. Which is why everyone from Napoleon to Hitler tried to steal it. The triptych is regarded by many as the first major painting of the

Renaissance, the forerunner of realism and certainly the greatest oil of its time. So to put these knights in there, to give them credibility, to immortalize them as a major presence in the Adoration of the Mystic Lamb was hugely significant at the time.'

Mitzi's almost afraid to ask the question. 'Why? They're just knights.'

'No, they're not. Like I said, van Eyck had already painted a panel of knights fitting that description. This is different. Look more closely.'

'That one in the middle isn't – you know who?'

Bronty nods. 'It might well be. And if it is, those knights gathered around and behind him are of the Round Table.' He pokes the monitor with his fingertip. 'Look here and you can see a circular emblem on their shields and three golden crowns on the flag behind Arthur.'

Mitzi's not looking. Her eyes are on something else. 'Holy shit, have you seen this?' She taps the screen.

Bronty studies a background figure of a priest, shown on horseback, carrying a bible and a cross. The crucifix is identical to the one they have a sketch of. The one Amir Goldman was killed for.

A knock on the office door turns their heads.

It opens and Annie Linklatter stands there, timidly, holding an envelope. 'This is the DNA profile you've been waiting for, ma'am.'

94

LONDON

It's been an unusual day for Angelo Marchetti.

No alcohol. No coke. No gambling.

The Italian has stayed clean for almost twenty-four hours and has spent the time getting his head together. Devising a way to stay alive and start a new and untroubled life. The key to it all is recovering the original memory stick. He can use this to leverage Gwyn into a situation that will make him vulnerable to Mardrid. Without it, he's a dead man.

Sophie Hudson said a lot before she died. She named the cops investigating the Goldman shooting and gave up the fact that she handed the memory stick to a woman from the FBI.

Mitzi Fallon.

Marchetti is staring at a head and shoulders squad shot of the lieutenant as he works from his hotel room. She's in full LAPD blues and looks too momsy to press his buttons. He prefers slimmer, younger women with bigger breasts and longer hair. That said, she's clearly an exceptional investigator, with the emphasis on *ex*.

Ex robbery squad. Ex homicide with an ex-husband.

The briefing note he's got shows her life almost has as many screw-ups in it as his. She's short of money and has two young daughters to look after.

Those are all the facts he needs to know.

For now.

95

AMERICAN EMBASSY, LONDON

The single glossy sheet looks like a weird heart-monitor graph with uneven columns rising and falling. Certain parts of the readout show dark pairs of numbered codes.

Mitzi's seen hundreds of genetic fingerprints, but Bronty hasn't.

'What am I looking at?' he asks. 'I know it's Dalton's DNA, taken from the water bottle you stole—'

'Appropriated.'

'I stand corrected – that you *appropriated* from Gwyn's office. But how do you make any sense of this?'

'You don't,' says Mitzi, taking the print off him. 'You just find a match for it. Juries love DNA. They don't understand it either, but they know it's the blueprint of a human being, they know we're all different and they trust that genetic fingerprinting is accurate. That's all that matters.'

Bronty is still intrigued. 'I get all that, but can you explain the science?'

'Kind of. I saw it ten years ago before automation, now it all happens in a machine but the process is similar. The lab pulls DNA out of a single cell they've swabbed – in our case that would be Dalton's from the water bottle. Enzymes are used to isolate the critical sections. Those parts are zapped with electricity. This separates them into unique pairs and patterns, then the whole thing is transferred onto a physical print.'

'That's really all it is?'

'Essentially, yeah. But like I say, it's all done by machines now. You ask some professor and he'll tie your mind up in knots with *dioxy-this* and *ribonucleic-that* and stories about *hyper-variable satellite somethingorothers*, but in the end, yeah, it's the way I said.' She goes back to the desk and taps on her computer. 'What I'm gonna do now is use our case file database to compare Dalton's DNA profile with the profile we got from the blood in the diner at Dupont Circle.'

'And if they match, then Dalton is Deagan's killer?'

'That's a jump too far. We still can't prove Deagan's dead – for the moment, he's down as a "missing-presumed". One thing for sure, though, it would irrefutably put Dalton at the place Deagan was seen alive.'

They watch the database churn through its records and wait.

'I worked out once that I spend sixty minutes a week just waiting for computers to process stuff,' says Mitzi. 'Four hours a month, forty-eight hours a year. That's a whole damned working week a year just waiting.'

There's a ping and the screen freezes.

Two separate sets of columns are displayed. One is superimposed over the other.

The word MATCH punches the middle of the frame.

'Well, looky here,' says Mitzi. 'Seems like I get to go see our new British friends again while you're off on your sea trip to Spooky Hollow.'

96

CAERGWYN CASTLE, WALES

CNN plays on one of the screens in Owain's private office; Sky News and Bloomberg are turned low on two others. All are running post-bombing interviews with government ministers and defence experts.

Owain mutes them all as a call from Gareth Madoc comes in on an encrypted line.

'Gareth, how are you?'

'Better, and so will you be. I have some good news.'

'Nabil?'

'No. He's still lying low. But we got to the girl.'

'And from your tone, it sounds as though she's cooperating.'

'She is. Zachra Korshidi's father Khalid is the principal fundraiser and trustee of the local mosque, and it's one of the biggest in the States.'

Owain is momentarily distracted by a bottom-of-screen caption on Bloomberg saying the price of Mardrid stock has fallen two per cent after he bought a company in Colombia *alleged to have links to Farc, the left-wing rebels.* He makes a note on a yellow jotter, then apologizes. 'I'm sorry; I just had to write something down. Is this girl's father only a financial player, or is he operationally active as well?'

'If not operational, then certainly influential. Khalid Korshidi is chairman of New York's Sharia Council and is known as a hard line fundamentalist. Zachra says he's too controlling and egotistical to take a back seat to anyone on anything. She's sure he knows everything that's going on.'

'And there's no love lost between them?'

'None at all. She hates him. Wants to get as far away as possible.'

'Then we need to help her, but do you really think this is going to lead us to Nabil and who he reports to?'

'Our girl says she knows Nabil. I showed her a photograph and she instantly ID'd him as someone who had come regularly to her house over the past year, usually alone or with one other man. Her mother served tea while he talked with her father in the front room. Usually, when they'd finished, they'd say they were going to the mosque and drive off together.'

Owain pieces things together. 'That means Khalid has Nabil's trust. Time is against us, Gareth; we can't afford to simply tail the father and hope we hit the jackpot.'

'I know. I've asked her to copy his cell phone directory. I've given her a reader. And she's going to put a tracker tack into a heel of his shoe. If he sees it, he'll think he just stood on a bit of metal. Apparently, he only ever wears an old black pair, so we should be on him easy enough.'

'Can we get eyes and ears in the house, preferably in this front room?'

'She's nervous about that, but I'll push her again once we've got the tracker in play and we start working his phone.'

'Do it within the next twenty-four hours, Gareth. Myrddin is in a sweat and you know what that means.'

'Visions?'

'Bad ones. The worst I've known him have.'

97

CALEDFWLCH ETHICAL INVESTMENTS, LONDON

Mitzi takes a black cab over to the CEI offices, while Bronty heads for a train from London to Ilfracombe and then, if he's lucky, the last ferry out to Lundy.

Mitzi hates boats. She gets seasick just lying in a bubble bath. Nic Karakandez, her ex-partner in the LAPD, had a boat and regularly took the girls out on it, but she always declined and went grocery shopping or holed up in the harbour coffee shop with a book. Karakandez was a great cop and a more-than-decent guy. Handsome enough for her to have a serious crush on him. Had she not hung on to the remnants of her tattered marriage, life might have been different and he might not have spent all his money on that old tug of his, jacked in his job and set off to sail the seven seas.

She thinks about him and the whole world of might-have-been as she waits in the vast CEI reception full of expensive wood, antique leather and people talking English with accents she's only ever heard on TV.

A glass-fronted lift slides into view and gradually reveals Melissa Sachs's elegant black shoes, suntanned legs, fashionable orange skirt, white frilly-cuffed shirt and finally a head of perfectly cut shoulder-length dark hair.

By comparison, Mitzi feels like a beaten up bag lady as she heads her way.

'Lieutenant Fallon, I'm most surprised to see you here.' The PA flashes a friendly smile but her eyes are full of questions. 'We don't have any meetings with you in the diary, so how can I help?'

'I need to speak to your boss and to George Dalton.'

'I've no idea where Mr Dalton is. I understand you have some numbers for him so you could try those, or go through the embassy.'

'It's easier to communicate with the dead than get an answer from an embassy. What about Sir Owain?'

'Not here, I'm afraid. He's gone to his home in Wales and will be working from there for a few days. Would you like me to give him a message?'

'Yeah, tell him I'm coming to see him.' Mitzi starts to head to the exit.

'That's not a good idea.' Melissa follows her. 'He has a strict policy on not mixing his personal and professional lives. I'll call him and ask him to get back to you with a time that you can meet in his office. That will be more convenient for everyone.'

'Listen, lady; your boss and his boy George are up to their very British stiff upper lips in a homicide. Now, I guess if that was made public, it wouldn't do either of their reputations any damned good.' She opens her arms and turns slowly in a circle. 'To say nothing of what it would do to the value of this *fine* company.'

'Lieutenant, I suggest—'

'Don't! Suggesting is a really bad thing for you to do.' She glares at her. 'Call your boss and tell him I'm mad as hell. So mad I'm gonna trek to the middle of freakin' nowhere to see him, and when I arrive I expect decent black coffee and honest answers.'

Mitzi doesn't wait for a reply.

Outside, the noise of London hits her like a slap. She's had enough of this case now. She wants to go home and nurse her sick daughter, wants to make peace with Jade, wants to hold her sister's hand, pour a glass of wine and help her sort her marriage out.

What she *does not want* is to be going to some country named after a mammal to get jerked around by Sir Lah-De-dah.

'Taxi!' She walks in the road with her hand held high.

A cab pulls over and a window slides down revealing a

bald-headed old Londoner in a Chelsea shirt. 'Where do you want to go to, Mrs?'

'San Francisco.' Mitzi pulls open the door. 'But take me to Dean Street, and hey, buddy, just 'cause you hear an American accent, don't think you can go the long way round and make a mug outta me.'

98

SAN FRANCISCO

Tess and Chris Wilkins appear to be your typical childless couple. Married for twelve of their fifteen years together, they've put on a little too much weight and grown lazy with age. Their money comes from a modest business that involves collecting, refilling and reselling ink-jet cartridges and it's successful enough to afford a semi-decent four-bed in a semi-decent LA suburb.

San Francisco is a place they know and love. In the past, they've done all the touristy things from driving the Bay Bridge to sailing out to Alcatraz and watching the sun go down while eating the world's best shrimp gumbo on a deck at Fisherman's Wharf.

Chris has dark, hippy biker hair and a big curly beard. He's thirty-nine years old, stands six-two and crushes the scales by three hundred pounds. Tess is three years younger, five inches smaller and a hundred pounds lighter. She was once a cheer-leading blonde who could do the splits, but those days have long gone. Her hair is now a frumpy charcoal colour, needs layering and a good four inches cutting off. She tells friends she'd do it but Chris is a bit of a caveman and likes her to keep it 'long 'n' natural.'

Taylor Swift plays on the radio of the six-berth RV they rented at the airport. They've brought a lot of stuff with them: snacks, drinks, a whole closet of clothes. The twenty-seven-footer is just about right for their many needs.

Chris pops another couple of pieces of gum as the six-litre V10 roars up a long San Franciscan hill. 'We anywhere near, yet?'

His wife screws the cap back on the bottle of Coke she's been swigging and checks the sat-nav stuck to the wind-shield. 'Another mile or two before you turn off, then about the same again.' She pulls at the top of her pink T-shirt and fans air down into her cleavage. 'You think the air-con is working in this thing?'

'I put it on hot, so you'd have to take your top off.'

She laughs at him and rolls it up just below her breasts. 'I take this off while you're drivin' we're gonna end up in a ditch.'

'Sounds good to me.' He wobbles the wheel playfully.

'Dead I mean.'

'Now that don't sound so good.'

'Seriously, can you get any more chill out of those vents?'

Chris thumbs the fan button but it's as high as it'll go.

'There's somethin' wrong with it. May as well wind down the window and let the wind blow back that fine hair of yours.'

She gives him her sexiest smile, lowers the passenger door glass and leans back against the headrest.

Chris enjoys a glance at her long locks being wind whipped off her pretty little cheeks. He wants to pull over and jump her right here, right now, with the big RV blocking the highway and everyone honking their horns in a ten-mile tailback.

'Eyes on the road, darlin',' she says from behind big black shades. 'Drive nicely and as soon as we get parked up, I'll sort out that little pecker problem you have there.'

99

SOHO, LONDON

Mitzi tips the doorman. She worked hotels in her teens and remembers all too well how much she depended upon the generosity of guests to beat the minimum wage.

She enters the coolness of the hotel and walks past the front desk to the lifts. Her mind is on making arrangements to get over to Wales as quickly as possible. As soon as that's done, she's going to wrap things up and head home.

'Excuse me, Mrs Fallon,' says a fat-faced man in a smart suit. 'I am the hotel manager, Jonathan Dunbar.' He hands her a business card as the elevator announces its arrival with a ding.

'Please, after you.' He gestures for her to enter the box of polished steel and mirrors. 'Let me accompany you to your room.'

She steps in and studies him suspiciously. 'I've been here over twenty-four hours, I know where my room is.'

'Of course you do.' He presses the button. 'I would just like a *discreet* word with you, if possible.'

The elevator jerks its way up. 'I don't do discreet,' says Mitzi. 'Discreet can be translated in all languages to mean cover up, fuck up or shut up. It's my least favourite word in the whole world. Except maybe "overdue", that's probably a full shade shittier than discreet.'

Dunbar sees his own face in the mirrored walls and it's full of apprehension. This woman is going to be trouble when he tells her what he has to tell her.

The lift pings. Doors slide open. He puts a hand through the gap and smiles. 'Here we are.'

'Is that an affliction that you've got?' She steps past him.

'Pardon?'

'Your habit of stating the freakin' obvious. Is it some kind of disease you've picked up?' She jams a keycard into her door slot and pushes it open. 'Look, *here we are*, again.'

'May I come in for a moment?'

She sees he's genuinely worried about something. 'Sure. But don't even think about giving me some crap about charging a higher room rate, or say my credit card's been declined.'

'It isn't that. Not at all.' He shuts the door behind him. 'I'm afraid the mistake is entirely ours. Mine, to be more precise.'

'Really?'

'Earlier today we were visited by two police officers who asked to search your room and Mr Bronty's. They were from the terrorist unit – I mean the *counter*-terrorist unit – the police obviously don't have a unit of terrorists. Only they weren't.'

Mitzi looks confused. 'They weren't what? They weren't cops, or they weren't anti-terror cops?'

'They weren't cops. Police, I mean.'

'So what were they, and why did you let them into our rooms?' She glances around to see if anything has been stolen.

'The real police say they must have been confidence tricksters of some kind. Very professional ones because they had official-looking ID.'

'Jeez, that must have taken them all of twenty minutes to download from the internet.' Her mind is on the memory stick sitting safely in her purse, but she checks her trolley bag to see if anything else has been taken. 'If stuff's missing, your face is going to end up a bigger mess than mine.'

He shifts nervously and watches her search the small bag.

Mitzi squashes clothes down and refastens it. 'You got lucky; what little I have is still there.' She looks at him like she does when one of the girls has pulled a brainless stunt and the other has snitched on her. 'Didn't you think of calling the station house and checking things out before you let them in here?'

'No, I'm sorry. I didn't. Not until afterwards.'

She rolls her eyes. 'For the record, Dumbo—'

He corrects her, 'Dunbar, not *Dumbo*.'

She smiles, 'No, I think I was right first time. For the record, Dumbo, *checking* only ever works as a precautionary measure. That means *before* something happens.'

He feels himself redden. 'I know. I'm very sorry. To make up for your inconvenience I'd like to have some champagne sent to your room—'

Her mind is locked on the incident. 'These so-called cops, they have names?'

'Yes, they were DCI Mark Warman and DS Penny Jackson.'

She scribbles the names on a pad by the bed.

'There really are officers with those names at Scotland Yard, but they weren't in your room.'

'You're doing that thing again.'

'I'm sorry.' He smiles thinly. 'Obviously they weren't in the room.' A thought hits him. 'Did you have anything in the wall safe?' He looks towards the open door above the mini-bar.

She nods solemnly. 'Cartier bracelet. Rolex watch. Some diamond earrings I bought at the Elizabeth Taylor auction. Not much.'

Dunbar's face is white.

'Relax. I had nothing in the safe.' She checks in the bathroom. Her toothbrush, paste, cleanser and pads are all still there. She shouts out to him, 'You said they searched my colleague's room – have you told him?'

The manager looks embarrassed. 'I'm afraid he checked out

while I was out of the hotel and we don't have a forwarding number for him. Perhaps you could have him call me?'

'I'll talk to him later. Now, if it's all the same with you, I'd like you to leave. I've gotta make some calls, then I'm checking out.'

'I understand. I'm very sorry.'

'You think you can keep strangers out of my room for the next hour?'

'I'm sure we can.'

'And you mentioned champagne.'

He relaxes a little. 'I did.'

'Make it whisky. The best you have and send cake with it, the most sinful and fattening your chef has baked.'

'It will be our pleasure.' He heads for the door, feeling relieved. 'Thank you for being so understanding.'

'Oh, I'm still a long way from understanding, so tell the front desk that when I check out, I expect a discount. The kind that will make me feel *discreet* all the way back to California.'

100

NEW YORK

For several minutes, Zachra Korshidi stands in silence and watches her father sleep in the back room of their Bronx row house.

His rickety chair is positioned near the dirt-streaked sash window that overlooks the small yard where her mother tries to grow olives. It seems that the warm afternoon sun and the large meal he's just eaten have conspired to send him into a deep slumber.

Zachra looks at the food splatter in his grey beard and on his white dishdasha and hates every inch of him, right down to the cheap rubber-soled shoes he has left in the hallway near the front door.

She has been sent to collect her father's dirty plate and take it to the kitchen for washing. But her mind has turned to more important matters. In her pocket, she touches the tiny tracker tack. All she has to do is jam it into the heel of his shoe.

She listens closely to the rattle of her father's snores and feels her heart tighten with anxiety as she leaves the room and heads over to the footwear. Her mother is running water in the kitchen, plates clatter on the metal drainer. She puts her father's tray down and moves quickly. The tack is less than the length of her small fingernail and she almost drops it. One end is needle sharp, the other rounded.

The rubber heel on the brogues is rock-hard. Try as she might, she can't force it in.

The floor of the hallway is made of old boards so she puts her foot in the shoe and uses her weight to press the tack into the rubber. The pin sinks in but the heel clacks noisily against the wooden board. Zachra takes off the shoe and looks at it. The tack is in.

'What are you doing?'

Her father's voice spins her round. He is in the doorway staring at her.

She picks up the other shoe and the tray. 'I came to collect the dishes and on the way back saw your shoes were dirty.'

He moves towards her, his eyes full of questions.

Zachra studies his hands. Fists so familiar to her. 'Please don't hit me. You told me it is *sunnah* to keep one's clothes and footwear clean. I was going to polish them for you.'

He knocks them from her hand. 'Take the tray to your mother. Never touch anything of mine unless I tell you.' He watches her move past him and then slaps her hard across the side of the head.

The blow makes her ear explode with pain and leaves it buzzing but she doesn't cry. She won't give him the satisfaction. Not now. Not ever again. Zachra hopes the Americans catch him. Catch him and kill him for what he did to Javid and what he would have let happen to her.

101

SAN FRANCISCO

Coyote Point is a big spread of park and woodland, barely ten miles from the city airport, jutting proudly into San Francisco Bay.

Chris and Tess Wilkins set the RV down on an approved

site. They turn on the radio, shut curtains and make their big old bus rock and roll for a full hour and a half.

Afterwards, they shower and while Chris barbecues steaks under the veranda, Tess clears a batch of paperwork and makes calls. They eat outside on a fold-up table and chairs saying hi to people drifting by, then they share a few beers with a couple of old-timers to the left of them, seniors from Wyoming who've been coming to Coyote for twenty years.

After dinner they walk through a grove of eucalyptus trees down to the edge of the water where otters and bobcats scuttle in and out of their habitats.

'We get time, we should go see the zoo,' says Tess. 'The leaflet I picked up says they've got a big aviary there as well.'

'You seen one zoo, you've seen them all. Besides, you know how I feel about cages.'

'You shouldn't. Bars are in your mind. Think you're free and you are free.'

'You ain't never done time, little Miss Philosopher, so that's easy for you to say.'

'Well, you ain't never doin' time again, so you better learn how to start sayin' it.'

'Let's start by not even talkin' about this shit.'

'That's fine by me.' She squeezes his hand. 'I love you, baby.'

'Love you too, sweetcheeks.'

'You think we've been out long enough?' She swings his hand up and down like a pendulum.

He sees a cheeky smile on her face. 'More than.' He unfolds his fingers from hers and grabs her ass. 'Let's make that bus rock some more.'

102

NEW YORK

SSOA operatives Bradley Sullivan and Jessica Lanza are parked in separate cars at opposite ends of the street where Khalid Korshidi lives.

They're both equipped with tracker monitors, following the movement of the target tack that Zachra inserted into her father's shoe.

Sullivan is mid-twenties and dressed in denim jacket and jeans, Big Bang T-shirt and Jesus sandals. Lanza has shoulder-length dark hair and could pass as his mother. She's in dark slacks, beige top and a long cardigan that hides her Glock.

Six hours pass before they get to communicate.

'Eyeball one. I have target on the move and in my line of sight.' Sullivan starts the engine of his old Buick Encore.

'Eyeball two. Gotcha and ready to go.' Lanza guns up her Toyota Avensis and puts her coffee carton back in the cup-holder on the dash.

Korshidi heads across the road to where he parked his

battered Transit and within a minute is in the traffic heading south.

Lanza and Sullivan follow him out to the I-95 then down as far as Jerome Avenue, where they expect him to turn left onto East 161st and then head towards the Yankee Stadium, the area where Antun had been meeting Nabil.

He doesn't. He hangs a right on 176th then dumps the vehicle in a corner lot and walks a few hundred yards to the metro station.

Sullivan gets caught in traffic but Lanza reads it better. She pulls over and by the time Korshidi is disappearing down the steps into the station, she's only twenty yards behind him.

He heads straight for the Four train. As he steps into the carriage he glances back to make sure he's not being followed.

Lanza pretends to adjust what looks like an iPhone in her hands but is actually a highly advanced tracker monitor. The carriage is packed and broiling. They ride for almost half an hour before he gets off at Utica Avenue.

Out on the street, Korshidi walks north. After a block Lanza's pleased to see Sullivan's Buick pass her and stop near the junction with Beverley Road. By the time she gets there, her partner's out on the street and she's able to slip into the unlocked car and take the weight off. More than anything, it's a relief to turn on the air-con.

Sullivan's foot follow goes on all the way past Tiden and down to Snyder, where Korshidi turns left and crosses the road. The whole area is populated by low rent stores. Everything is here, from second-hand clothing to stolen tools, phone unlocking and dope dealers.

Korshidi heads down some basement stairs near a barber's shop and Sullivan hangs back to avoid being spotted by whoever might open a door for him.

Lanza passes him in the Buick and pulls up twenty yards away on the other side of the street. There they both vanish into the shadows.

The waiting game has begun.

103

SOHO, LONDON

It takes Mitzi two thick slices of chef's cheesecake to forgive Dumbo and stop freaking out about having her room tossed while she was at the embassy. Even after using a hand scanner to check for electronic bugs and deciding it's clean she's still nervous.

The bottle of thirty-year-old single malt whisky the manager sent up is now being shipped to Kirstin Collins to crack open at Irish's wake. She'll make sure she calls on the day and checks on the kid.

Mitzi licks the last of the cake from the fork and finishes reading Vicky's report on the Gwyns. The girl done good. All the stuff about King Arthur is weird but maybe Gwyn is some kind of enthusiast or collector. Collectors are always crazy. And rich crazies will often kill if things don't go their way.

She calls Donovan and updates her on the events of the last twelve hours then asks to be bounced to Vicky, who picks up after the second ring. 'HRU, how can I help you?'

'Hiya hon, it's Mitzi.'

'Hi, Lieutenant. How are you?'

'Feeling about as raw as newly cut beef. Hey, I just called to say you did a great job on those profiles.'

'Thanks. I found it all fascinating. It's like Sir Owain and Lady Gwyn are a modern-day Arthur and Guinevere.'

Mitzi laughs. 'Don't get carried away. I think all English lords and ladies live privileged lives like that and I ain't so sure he's a knight in shining armour.'

'Of course. I didn't mean morally, it's just with all the historic connections.'

'Yeah, that's a bit strange, don't you think? And what about the guy he took legal action against?'

'Mallory – I put his numbers on the briefing I sent you and I spoke to him. He says he knows things that would make your hair curl.'

'That's not a look you want to see. What's he know?'

'He wouldn't say. Not in person. I think it's because of the injunctions.'

'I'm heading out to Wales tonight, so I'll look him up. Can you get Travel to find me somewhere near Gwyn's estate?'

'Sure.'

'And send me a proper address for Caergwyn Castle. I just searched for it on Google and couldn't find the place.'

'Will do. I looked on our standard satellite maps and it doesn't show up there either.'

'How can that be?'

'I checked with intel and they say it's probably because there's a no-fly zone there.'

'Military restrictions?'

'Seems that way. The SAS use the countryside for manoeuvres. This castle appears to be in the middle of their training grounds.'

Mitzi thinks out loud. 'A knight conveniently surrounded by an army.'

'Kings, castles and legends,' says Vicky, almost too excitedly. 'I wish I was there to see it all.'

'I'd gladly swap places. Mail me the details soon as you can. I'm gonna check out and hire a car.'

'Back to you ASAP, Lieutenant.'

Mitzi hangs up and looks long and hard at the memory stick containing the Arthurian data.

It brings back all the nervousness about having her room snooped. This is what Warman and Jackson, or whoever they are, tossed her room for. What cost Sophie Hudson her life. And what's certain to cause more bloodshed. She knows she has to do something with it. Something more secure than just put it back in her purse

104

SSOA OFFICES, NEW YORK

Gareth Madoc sits behind a glass desk in a secure penthouse office on Sixth Avenue.

He's listening to Jessica Lanza on a comms feed. 'About an hour ago, Khalid Korshidi ditched his car, caught a train out to East Flatbush and entered what looks like a safe house.' She can't help but sound optimistic. 'Now get this: he's just been joined by Nabil Tabrizi.'

'Have we got a listen in?'

'Not yet. The building is in a position we can't hit with a parabolic.' She looks out of the windshield of the Buick and down the street to where Sullivan is crossing over. 'Sully has gone to play the jacked-up druggie looking for a quiet place to shoot up. He'll drop a syringe down the steps to the basement entrance. With any luck he'll get a recorder on the glass, then we have to pray the technology works.'

'It usually does.'

'Yeah, well, I'll stop sweating when "usually" becomes "always". I gotta go. Back to you soon.'

'Stay safe.'

'You too.'

There's a click and she's gone.

Madoc turns his thoughts to Zachra. The fact she tagged her father means she's onside. Now is the make or break moment. She has to get listening devices into that back room where her father hangs out. If she does, he's ready to write that ticket she wants for a new life.

He dips into his jacket pocket, takes out an untraceable cell phone and sends a text message: *Goin shopz tomoz, wannacum? Shrn.*

It's code to have Zachra call him straight away. If her parents saw it, she'd be able to explain it as being from her friend Sharron.

Across the room is a video wall with feeds to more than fifty domestic and international outposts. Behind him is an electronic wallboard, upon which is mapped key operations and the deployment of manpower and resources.

The burner beeps and he grabs it.

The return message says: *Calluin5.*

He takes the phone and walks to the window while he waits. The seconds weigh heavy. People forty floors below move like ants on the sidewalks.

His burner rings.

'Yes?'

'I've only got a minute.' Zachra sounds nervous.

Gareth gets to the point. 'Those mini-cams I gave you. You *have* to put them in place. Right this minute, while your father is out. Do you understand?'

'When can you get me out of here?' She sounds desperate.

'As soon as we record your father saying something we can act on.'

She pauses for a minute. Her mother is in there cleaning the house, no doubt looking for her. 'I have to go.'

'You *must* do this, Zachra. For your own sake, you have to do it and you need to do it right now.'

105

SAN FRANCISCO

Chris Wilkins is out on a long, meandering daytrip on his own, in a Toyota sedan he rented first thing this morning. The RV would have been no good for what he has in mind. He takes the 101 to Interstate-80, cruises San Bruno, Brisbane and Bayview before hitting South Beach, Oakland Bridge, Emeryville and Walnut Creek.

Around midday he grabs a third-rate hamburger and a cold beer in a place buzzing with flies and bar bums. After freshening up, he rolls on and off the 680, through Danville and San Ramon before cutting into Castro Valley and then over the Bay via the San Mateo Bridge.

By the time he hits the freeway back to Coyote Point, he's close to exhausted. But it's been worth it. He's found the surprise he's been looking for.

He cracks a wide smile when he pulls up outside the RV and finds Tess stretched out on a striped fabric fold-up chair with a book across her suntanned legs.

She tips her shades as he approaches. 'Tough day at the office, baby?'

'Somethin' like that. My back is killing me. Seats in that rental are so bad they'd give a ghost spinal problems.'

'Come inside, I got something that will take the pain away.'

She takes his hand and leads him up into the RV. She clunks the door behind them, wraps her hands around the back of his grizzly-bear neck and kisses some life into him.

He lets his fingers wander and she gently eases him away. '*That's* not what I invited you in here for.'

'It's not?'

'No.' She points to the open laptop on the galley table. 'Feast your eyes over there.'

Chris taps the spacebar to clear the screensaver and studies the Facebook page and its new postings. His eyes light up. 'You're the best, sweetcheeks. Simply the best.'

106

WALES

A glance at the digital clock on the dash of Mitzi's blue Ford rental tells her she's been on the road for three hours and still has a quarter of her hundred and seventy-five miles to go.

Vicky had added a helpful footnote to her briefing, mentioning that Wales has more castles than any other country in the world but so far, Mitzi hasn't seen any, let alone the one she wants to find.

'Goddamned British drivers!' She rides her horn at a giant yellow tractor crawling behind a road full of sheep.

A ruddy-faced old farmer in a green Barbour gilet and flat cap turns on his high seat and glowers back.

It's another fifty minutes before she gets past and the sat-nav chirpily announces, *'Turn left and you have reached your destination.'*

'About freakin' time.'

She takes the unmarked turning and finds herself driving a rutted dead-end of a dirt track.

'In fifty metres you will have reached your destination.'

'Where?' Mitzi peers in anger through the windshield. 'You crazy piece of crap, where's my castle?'

A black and white chequered flag pops up on the sat-nav screen and waves jubilantly as the Ford bumps in and out of potholes and stops at a hedge and fence.

'You have reached your destination.'

Mitzi pulls the handbrake on. 'Jee-zus! You stupid, stupid machine!'

'You have reached your destination,' repeats the voice defiantly, then offers a new screen and the chance to gamble on a fresh destination.

She gets out of the car so that she doesn't pull the damned thing off and beat it against the dashboard.

Skylarks flap from surrounding birch trees and the air is fresh with scents of long grass and wild flowers. It's nice to be out of the car. Far across the fields, there's a dense forest around a hill. She's willing to bet a first-class flight home that Caergwyn Castle is hidden in the thick of it.

Mitzi returns to the car and checks the address and details that Vicky gave her.

She's entered all the strangely spelt names correctly and the postcode is right. Ideally, she wanted to see Gwyn tonight and force a face-to-face with George Dalton. But right now she doesn't fancy driving around like a lost tourist for another hour. Vicky's notes show that Rhys Mallory, the man Sir Owain took legal steps to silence, lives just two miles from where she is.

She enters his address in the navigation system and presses the touchscreen.

'Make a U-turn when possible and take the next right.'

'You'd better be right.' Mitzi scorches the screen with a glare as she starts the car and follows the instructions.

Ten minutes later, she's bouncing down a farm track towards a solitary detached stone cottage. She parks behind a beat-up Land Rover Defender that looks like it's never been washed and gets out. As she flaps the door shut, a dog barks out of view.

A scruffy, silver-haired man in filthy brown overalls appears, with a black and white collie at his heels.

'Can I help you?' His voice is coated in a thick Welsh accent.

'Professor Mallory?'

He looks her over. 'Who are you?'

'I'm a lieutenant with an FBI unit that specializes in religious, historical and unexplained crimes.'

'FBI, eh?' He wipes his hands on an oily rag and takes the glossy ID card she's offering. He examines it with amusement and hands it back. 'This is a long way for the Eff-Bee-Eye to come.'

'It certainly is. I'd like to speak to you about Sir Owain Gwyn.'

'Really?' His eyes widen. 'Now that's funny, isn't it? You want me to talk about the very thing I'm legally not allowed to talk about. How do you suppose we do that, then?'

'How about we have one of those conversations that afterwards we both deny ever took place?'

'Off the record, you mean?'

His habit of answering her questions with a question starts to grate. 'Yes.'

He waits a second and then nods his assent. 'Follow me round the back of the house. You might as well have a cup of tea while we're not having that conversation.'

107

WALES

Instead of tea, Mitzi settles on a glass of lemonade made by Mallory's wife, Bethan. She's a dumpy brunette with streaks of red in her waist-length hair and has breasts that sag beneath a long, chin-to-toes black dress, broken by a necklace of multi-coloured beads.

'It's awesome,' Mitzi says appreciatively. 'I could have done with this two hours ago, when I was halfway between here and London.'

Bethan looks pleased. 'Would you like something to eat? We have rabbit stew on the stove.'

'No, I'm good, thanks.' Mitzi dreads to think what rabbit might taste like.

The professor's wife takes this as her cue to leave the American with her husband in the cosy glass lean-to built on the back of the cottage.

Mitzi sits on a brown fabric settee that has an old ginger tomcat perched on the other armrest. She puts her glass on the terracotta floor tiles and gives her host her full attention. 'So, Owain Gwyn – what can you tell me about him?'

'He's a liar, a deceiver, a duplicitous denier of the truth. No friend to history. No ally of openness.'

Mitzi's taken aback. She didn't expect such an outburst. 'And what *exactly* would he be lying about?'

'His whole life is a lie. Him and his wife and that mad old man who lives with them; none of them are what they seem.' Mallory leans forward, his brown eyes shining. 'What do you want with him? Why have you come over here to snoop around and ask me about him?'

She knows she has to provide more than a standard

brush-off. 'We have a homicide in the States that has links to one of his staff.'

His eyes widen. 'To Gwyn?'

'No, to his staff. Sir Owain is not a suspect.'

Mallory sits back and assesses her, much in the way he did students when he was a lecturer. 'Do you know what patronymic means?'

'I think so. It refers to the practice of descendants taking the name of the father.'

'That's exactly what it is. Williamson, for example, would suggest son of William. Names and heritage are important, Lieutenant. Especially Owain Gwyn's.'

'Why particularly his?'

'Because that's what he wants to cover up.'

'I don't understand.'

'My research and my book, the one he stopped being published, told the truth about him and King Arthur, the links to his family, the secret activities of his company and how governments turn a blind eye to what he does.'

'You mean he's cashing in on the Arthurian legend?'

He laughs. 'No, no. This is much more important than mere commercial exploitation.' He can see that she doesn't have a clue. 'Let me explain. There are three commonly held views as to who King Arthur might have been. Firstly, a Roman soldier, left behind to help the Britons fight the barbarians who flooded the country when the Romans left in the sixth century. Some say he was Ambrosius Aurelianus, others Lucius Artorius Castus. The centurion Castus has even been associated with a cavalry unit that worshipped a sword embedded in the earth.'

'This would be Excalibur, the famous sword in the stone?'

He smiles, 'That's probably just misunderstood history, as most Arthurian legend is. Back in the Dark Ages, heavy broadswords were made by pouring molten metal into stone casts. If the cast was good, then when it cooled a child could easily pull the sword free and it was said to be fit for a king.'

'And the legend of the lady in the lake – her giving Excalibur to Arthur?'

'More historic misinterpretation. When kings died in those days their bodies were put on pyres and their swords offered to a water goddess to protect them in the afterlife. Ambrosius, incidentally, is said to have been buried at Stonehenge, a structure that according to some legends was created by the prophet Merlin.'

Mitzi tries to steer away from what she suspects is a bottomless pit of superstition and myth. 'You said there were *three* views of who Arthur was?'

'Yes. The second is that he was a Romano-British warlord called Riothamus. I believe Riothamus is a Latinization of the Brythonic personal name *Rigotamos*, meaning "king-most", "supreme king" or "highest king". As well as fighting valiantly against the Goths, Riothamus is thought to have crossed the channel and fought his final battle in a field in Burgundy – one that has great resonance to the Arthurian legend. That place was Avallon, with two l's – one more than Avalon, the place legend has it that Arthur was laid to rest.'

Mitzi's fast-reaching bored. 'All fascinating, but what has the ambassador and his family got to do with this?'

Mallory is determined not to be rushed. 'To answer you, we must go back to AD 500 and the story of the Welsh warrior Owain Ddantgwyn. He was a great leader and back then such fighters associated themselves with beasts. For example, you've heard of Richard the Lionheart?'

'Of course.'

'Well, Owain Ddantgwyn was known as the Bear. The Welsh word for bear is Arth, while the Latin name is Ursis. It's easy to see how he came to be called Arth-Ursis and that got shortened to Arthur.'

He gives her a second then continues, 'Historic record has Owain Ddantgwyn – which as I'm sure you agree is not a long way away from Owain Gwyn – referred to as "the once and future king". This is a phrase you will constantly hear associated with Arthur. Well, Owain had a son and his genealogy can be traced into the medieval period, where a more familiar and noble name emerges as direct descendants.' He pauses for maximum effect. 'You know the Spencers?'

'As in Diana, Princess of Wales, daughter of Earl Spencer.'

'Indeed. And the twisted roots of royal genealogy don't stop there. Look into the family history and you'll see that William was given the middle name Arthur, just as his father Prince Charles was.' He examines the American with curiosity. 'Are you aware that the title "Prince of Wales" is always given to the heir to the British throne?'

'I guess you know that I'm not.'

'Well, it is. And it dates back to post-Roman and pre-Norman times when the most powerful Welsh ruler was also taken to be the true King of the Britons. In the twelfth century, a man named Owain Gwynedd stopped using the title King of Wales and called himself Prince of Wales. As a detective, I presume you are drawing some conclusions here.'

Mitzi tries not to be angered by his condescension. 'You're saying that our modern-day Sir Owain Gwyn is a direct descendant of King Arthur.'

He looks exasperated with her. 'At least that.'

Mitzi frowns, 'What do you mean *at least*?'

For the first time since they met, he grows uncomfortable. 'For God's sake, look at the damned evidence. The bear is on his heraldic arms, as is the round table and the triple crown of Arthur.'

'Professor, I have a cousin in Texas who is a Scottish lord. He bought the title online because he liked the idea.'

'It's a stupid comparison. Owain Gwyn bought no title. This man was and is—' He stops mid-sentence and looks pained to hold back the remaining words.

'What?'

'I can't say. Even in a conversation that never took place.' He nods irritably to the slate clock on the wall. 'It's getting late. You must go and I must get on.' He sighs as he raises himself from his chair and ushers her towards the back door. 'History knows more about Owain Gwyn than the modern world does. Be careful in your dealings with him.'

She stops in her tracks. 'What do you mean by that? You think he's a danger to people.'

He tries to explain. 'Imagine Jesus Christ was on earth, but he didn't want to be discovered. Imagine history had been written to hide his existence. Would you see it as your duty to expose him? And if you did, would you think such disclosure might put your life at risk, Lieutenant?'

108

WALES

The evening sky is lit by a falling scarlet sun as Mitzi books into the Norton. The guesthouse is an imposing sandstone manor and her bedroom has a panoramic view across the valleys and a never-ending soundtrack of fast-flowing streams beneath her window.

While she runs a bath to soak off the aches of the long day, she calls Bronty and finds he's just got off the ferry in Lundy.

'I'm exhausted,' he says over crashes of breaking sea and squawking gulls. 'You can get to heaven quicker than reach this place.'

Mitzi laughs as she tests the bathwater and adds more hot. 'I promise you, *Wales* was as difficult to reach.'

He looks around the jetty. 'I think I just saw seals in the water. Grey seals – eight, maybe ten feet long.'

'Stop sounding like you're having fun. I've had a day from hell and couldn't even find Caergwyn Castle.'

'How can you miss a fortress?'

'Believe me, out here it's easy. When you call me on a secure line I'll tell you what Mallory had to say about the ambassador.'

'Will do. The light's virtually gone here, so I'll take a look around the island in the morning and then get back to you.'

'That's fine. Sleep well.'

'You too.'

Mitzi ends the call and checks the bathwater. It's now hot enough to boil a lobster. She runs the cold full blast, then kicks off her clothes and calls her daughters.

No one picks up.

She gets the answerphone for a second time.

Ruthy has no doubt taken them all out for the day. She'll call again after dinner.

She eases herself into the water. It feels too good to remain silent. 'Aa-a-h, that's *soo-o* good.'

The guesthouse has provided her with little bottles of bath foam, body scrub, shampoo and hair conditioner. Mitzi uses the lot. It feels great just to be lying in a big pool of soapy spa bubbles and smells.

Her phone rings.

She looks across the other side of the bathroom, and sees it on the shelf over the sink. Too far away to reach.

The water is working its therapeutic magic and for a moment she thinks about ignoring the call.

'Damn it!'

She climbs out and takes a gallon of water with her.

'Fallon.' She grabs a white towelling robe from behind the door.

'Lieutenant, it's Owain Gwyn.'

'Hang on.' She puts the phone down and quickly pushes her arms into the robe and ties it up. 'Sorry, I was just getting out of a bath.'

'My apologies for disturbing you. Outside your hotel, there is a black Range Rover and one of my men. When you are ready, please get in and you'll be brought straight to my home.'

'I thought I'd come by in the morning.'

There's no answer.

'Sir Owain?' She looks at the phone to see if she's accidentally cut him off.

She hasn't.

He's hung up.

109

WALES

An ice-blue quarter moon hangs above the Range Rover as it speeds down unlit country lanes.

Mitzi snatches a grab-handle as they hit a bump and she

clears the back seat. 'What's wrong with this country? I thought the Romans laid roads for you?'

The driver doesn't answer. He hasn't spoken since he checked her name at the guesthouse and held the vehicle's door open for her.

'Any chance of slowing down? You know, maybe just below warp speed so we get there alive?'

Again, there's no reply from the broad-shouldered man in the front.

She settles back as best she can and listens to her stomach grumble. Now she wishes she'd accepted Mrs Mallory's rabbit stew.

Lights appear in the distance. The 4 × 4 crunches to a halt. Through a gap between the front seats, she sees shadows inside a gatehouse. A man comes out and walks to the driver's side.

The silent lunatic behind the wheel slides down the window and shows his ID. A flashlight shines in her eyes. 'Hey!' She puts up her hands to block the glare. Darkness returns. There's a tap on the roof and the vehicle crunches gravel. Metal gates clank shut behind them. The tyres rumble more smoothly now. They're on asphalt but the road is unlit. Mitzi peers out into the darkness. Sheep appear in the headlights like a crop of woolly rocks.

The luminous fingers on her watch tell her it's half past ten and they've now been driving seven minutes along the driveway. That's as long as it used to take her to drive from her old house in LA to the mall.

The soft yellow lights of Caergwyn Castle appear in the

velvet night. The building is uplit by powerful ground beams. She sees syrup-coloured sandstone walls, soaring towers and crenulations that run like a gap-toothed border in the sky.

The Range Rover stops and the mute driver gets out and opens her door.

She stands for a moment in the cool evening air, picks up the smell of lavender and pine. It's easy to imagine kings and queens living here, being waited on hand and foot, dining in fine halls and celebrating glorious battles and conquests.

Metal clunks against metal. Heavy bolts slide behind the huge, arched oak entrance doors facing her. A round-faced servant dressed in a smart black suit strides out. Behind him hurries a younger man in cream-coloured trousers and a red jacket.

'Good evening. I am Alwyn, Sir Owain's butler. Please follow me.'

He leads the way inside.

She's struck by an array of new scents. Brass polish. Silver polish. Marble polish. Thick, waxy wood polish.

'Sir Owain said to show you to the library.' Alwyn opens a door and stands to one side.

Mitzi steps in and double-takes the endless walls of books. 'Look at the size of this! Man, has he never heard of the Kindle?'

110

CAERGWYN CASTLE, WALES

The butler leaves Mitzi staring in amazement at what appears to be a cathedral filled with books.

The oak-beamed library is two storeys high and its top level is an octagonal gallery reached by spirals of wooden staircases almost fifty yards apart. There are twenty stone archways on either side of the room, all creating deep alcoves filled with twenty rows of shelving. Sliding ladders are propped against each of the racks so books at the top can be more easily reached.

Along the centre of the stone floor stand various large display cases, all showcasing ancient folios. Only now, as Mitzi wanders the cool, musty room does she note the surveillance cameras, flashing red lights and sensors of a very sophisticated alarm system.

On the far wall is an impressively large oil of a medieval battles. The canvas covers more than three hundred square feet and in the foreground, the body of a fallen king is being carried away by soldiers. Under a shimmer of almost heavenly light, a fully robed bishop is picking up his crown.

There's another painting, a fraction of the size, above the door she just came through. It's a portrait of a man with long hair and a moustache, dressed in a black cloak with a white ruffle collar and a large black, floppy bow tie. He has brooding, dark eyes that strongly remind her of Sir Owain.

As though cued by her thought, the door beneath the portrait clicks open and the ambassador walks through. He's dressed in black trousers and a crisp white open-necked shirt worn beneath a black cashmere jumper. 'Lieutenant Fallon, how are you?' He steps forward and offers his hand.

She shakes it then points to the painting. 'I'm fine, Mr Ambassador. I was just looking at the portrait. An ancestor, I presume?'

'That's Saint Richard Gwyn; the library is named after him. Please walk with me, there are things I wish to show you.'

She tags alongside. 'Saint as in a real saint, or as in a surname, like David St John?'

'As in real saint. He was martyred – executed in the sixteenth century for an act of high treason, otherwise known as refusing to say Jesus Christ wasn't the Son of God. He was hung, drawn and quartered – you know what that is?'

'I guess after the lynching they drain the body then cut it up?'

'Not quite; the drawing is pre-mortem, not post. It involves tying the condemned man to a horse then dragging him from his prison through the streets until he is in agony. Then he's carried up the scaffold and hanged until almost dead. He is cut down and emasculated – his testicles cut off. Then they disembowel him, sever his limbs and sometimes his head. The entrails and genitalia are burned in a public fire, the skull spiked and displayed. The four limbs – the 'quarters' – would either be nailed in prominent places in the city, or dispatched to different corners of the country.'

'Jeez, and I thought Californian executions were gruesome.'

'Britain has a past more brutal than most.' He stops walking and turns to her. 'But it's the present and the future you should be afraid of. Unfortunately, you're caught in the middle of something you shouldn't be.'

She fixes him with a challenging stare. 'Please don't patronize me. Getting into the middle of things, as you put it, is the nature of my job.'

'Perhaps, but I suspect we're talking at cross purposes.'

'How so?'

'You think I'm referring to your homicide investigation.'

'And you're not?'

'Not directly.'

'Then enlighten me.'

'I will.' He paces along the library and gestures at the upper floor. 'Every book in this room is a first edition and almost all are priceless. Some are the only ones in existence. Others are so rare, experts in their field don't even know they exist.'

'And I suppose that includes the Camelot Codex?'

He ignores the question and taps the glass of a display case. 'This book here is the oldest illustrated bible in the world. It's older than the Garima Gospels, recovered from Ethiopia and older and much finer than the Book of Kells created by Celtic monks.'

Mitzi looks down at a large volume lying open on an ornate brass stand. It is the size of a giant, thick atlas and the pages are covered in lavish illustrations and copperplate handwriting.

Owain swipes an electronic card across a sensor on the side of the cabinet and lifts off the glass cover. The air fills with a tobacco-like fragrance caused by the mass of musty pages and ancient wood they've been bound in. 'This is the Arthurian Bible. It is written on the best of velum, a form of stretched and dried sheepskin.'

She inspects the pages as he continues. 'The animal's hair was removed by soaking the stripped skin in lime and excrement and then scraping it with a semi-circular knife called a Luna. The skin was then tensioned on special frames and cut to size by velum-makers. It is a real art.' He touches the sides of the book. 'More than two hundred blessed lambs were slaughtered to make this book.'

The main illustration staring up at her is that of a man who looks like a Roman emperor. He is shown in battle on horseback, only he's not holding a legion's standard but a large, gold crucifix identical to the drawing Irish had sent her. Around the horse lie corpses, skewered with pikes and swords.

'It represents God's never-ending battle for souls,' says Owain. 'The text was written by an order of holy men who guarded Christ for the forty days he walked the earth after his resurrection.'

She looks at him sceptically. 'I suspect you might have a tough time proving that.'

'I don't have to. I do not intend to sell the artefact; therefore, the provenance only matters to my family and me.'

She circles the book, inspecting the shape and texture from multiple angles. In places, she can even see hair follicles on the velum. 'I imagine the person who had this before you also once said that he had no intention of selling it, but he did.'

'Actually, you're mistaken. It's never been sold or stolen. Nor robbed from a grave, if that's what you are thinking. It was delivered into the hands of my family by Josephus of Arimathea when he came to Britain after Christ's death.'

Mitzi doesn't know whether to believe him or not. 'Joseph of Arimathea – as in the rich guy who persuaded Pilate to allow Christ's body to be laid in his own private tomb?'

'No, not Joseph. His son, Josephus. History frequently mixes them up. As it does whether the Holy Grail was a chalice, a sacrament salver or, as a few believe, a sacred and secret text written in the blood of Christ.'

'And are you one of those believers?'

'I am.' He turns a page and reveals a painting of knights riding across open green countryside.

It shows King Arthur and a priest carrying a bible and cross. Mitzi realizes it's identical to the one found on the Ghent panel in Bradley Deagan's apartment.

'To make this folio,' he adds, 'a metalworker applied pure gold leaf and silver to the capital letters that start each paragraph. A portrait painter of highest regard drew the figures, and the most accomplished landscape artist of the time completed the background illustrations.'

He turns over a leaf and it crinkles so dangerously Mitzi fears it may crack. On display now is a double-page spread of blood-brown script covered in a matt varnish cracked with time.

The ambassador reads her mind. 'In a distrusting moment

I had a scraping of the letter analysed. It is human blood and the carbon dating puts it in the first century. Every letter written here was done while the manuscript was wrapped in the sanctity of a tabernacle cloth blessed by St Peter. The quills the scribes used came from the tail feathers of birds that Christ himself had blessed before his death. And the wooden binding that holds the folio together was crafted by the carpenter Joseph, Jesus's mortal guardian.'

The script hypnotizes Mitzi. She can't understand a word of what's in front of her but she can tell that it has been painstakingly prepared and such care has to be indicative of a powerful message.

'The text,' continues Owain, 'begins in pre-Christian times. It starts with the birth of the world and the genesis of forces of good and evil. It describes the constant struggle for life and how out of the universal clash between hunter and hunted, oppressor and oppressed, one man has to step forth and become a just and honourable leader, a setter of standards and morals.'

He glides a hand above the pages in an almost reverential motion. 'These passages explain how that leader must choose followers and how those followers must be divided into disciples, men of words and knights, men of action.'

Owain folds back the pages, then replaces the glass cover and locks the case again. 'On the gallery above you are scrolls and scripts that pre-date the bible I just showed you. They are written in ancient languages such as Etruscan and they all carry the same message.'

Mitzi casts her gaze up to the top floor and then back to

where they are standing. 'And the other display cases, the ones on this floor – what do they hold?'

'They are also Arthurian works. They have all been copied into encoded script and kept digitally. Extracts of which have been stolen from me.'

'The Camelot Codex?'

'I believe that is what the person who made the copies is calling it.'

'And this is what Amir Goldman and his assistant Sophie Hudson were killed for?'

'It is. Lieutenant, do you still have this copy?'

'I do.'

'Then I must insist you give it to me immediately. It is an illegally made copy of a digital transcript of four of the books in this library.'

She feels a shift of mood. 'At the moment, that's not possible. It's an intrinsic part of my homicide investigation and it will remain so until the case is closed.'

'For your sake *and* your family's – you really must give it to me.'

She tilts her head and frowns accusingly. 'Say that again, because from where I'm standing, it sounded like a threat.'

'It is. While you are in possession of that copy, you are putting *your* life and that of anyone who matters to you in serious danger.' He dips his right hand into his pocket and produces a small black battery zapper, which he presses.

The room fills with the thunder of iron shutters closing off the doorway, the alcoves and staircase.

Within seconds, the library is transformed into a giant metal cell.

111

The display cases sink into armoured recesses until they are flush with the stone floor. Red lights flash. An alarm sounds.

Sir Owain walks calmly to an archway and holds his hand against a fingerprint scanner. 'This room is protected,' he explains to Mitzi. 'But sadly, you are not. I can give you security, the best in the world, but only if you return what is rightfully mine and you understand the causes that I am involved in and respect the reasons to keep them secret.'

He types a code on an alphanumeric pad below the scanner and the middle display case disappears below floor level. Lights flicker in the dark space and Mitzi sees stone steps leading down below ground.

Sir Owain walks over to her. 'Lieutenant, the threat to your life and those of your twins and your sister Ruth is not from me. It is from people who seek to hurt me and those who work with me for the greater good.'

'And who exactly are those people working for the greater good?'

'I hope, in good time to have you meet them – even become one of them. From what I know about you—'

'You don't know anything about me apart from a few names you'd find online and quite honestly, I'd like to keep it that way.'

'I know you've worked more than a hundred homicides, three of them serial killings. You've been lead detective on sixteen rapes and five child sex abuse cases, all of which resulted in successful prosecutions. In your earlier days, you cleared up more robberies than any other detective on the force.'

'Okay, you've had some private dick pull my service record. Big deal.'

'Your beautiful twins, Amber and Jade – they were born five minutes apart. From what I'm told, they were not your first pregnancies. You lost a child, a boy, during the first trimester. You hadn't told anyone about the pregnancy, so you didn't tell anyone about the loss. I believe you were back at work twenty-four hours after leaving hospital.'

Mitzi feels violated. Only her confidential medical and employment records could have shown him those facts.

'Your ex-husband Alfred has been unemployed since you had him sent to prison for the last in a long line of assaults on you. And he will probably still be out of work a year from now. Jack, the man your sister Ruth has thrown out of her house, yesterday engaged one of San Francisco's most aggressive divorce solicitors and right this moment he has investigators searching for easy ways to make sure she gets the worst settlement.'

'How do you know these things?'

'Knowing things is my business.' He gestures, palm open, to the staircase running below the library.

'You're joking, right?' She gives him a wary look. 'No way am I going down there with you.'

'You are not in danger from me, Mitzi. Far from it. You came here because of questions about an iron-age cross and a series of deaths. The answers are down there.'

'I'm still not going.'

Owain reaches into his jacket and produces a gun.

Mitzi backs off.

'Don't be alarmed. It's for you, not me.' He holds it by the short barrel and extends it. 'It's loaded.'

She snatches it and checks the magazine. It's a Glock 23 packed with .40 rounds. 'I thought hand weapons were banned in Britain.'

'They are. I have a special licence for that, and for many other weapons.' He turns his back to her and starts to descend the staircase. 'Please be careful; the steps are steeper than you might imagine and I don't want you to trip and shoot me accidentally.'

Mitzi watches him disappear and feels her heart pound. She looks around the sealed-off library, takes a deep breath and steps down into the darkness.

112

The stairs from the library lead into a long and wide stone tunnel dimly lit by recessed amber lights. Everything is watched over by innumerable ceiling-mounted surveillance cameras.

To Mitzi's surprise, there is what looks like a glass and metal security lodge ten yards ahead of her. Sir Owain is stood there, talking to two men in black uniforms. They are almost as tall as the ambassador and have holstered guns on their belts and automatic weapons racked on a wall behind them.

She stuffs the Glock he gave her into the band of her slacks. There's no point carrying it. It would be as much use as a peashooter against the level of firepower down here.

'Mitzi.' He calls for her to hurry up.

The men in black give her a polite smile as she walks past them and through a shuttered door they've opened for their boss.

To her surprise, there's a second set of stairs beyond the checkpoint leading to what at first glance looks like a chapel. A raised, candlelit altar covered in a white cloth stands thirty yards ahead of her. Behind it, a large wooden crucifix, complete with the sagging wounded body of Christ. As her eyes become accustomed to the light, she notices the cross is identical to the one she saw in Irish's drawing.

Now she sees the tombs.

Dozens of them. So many, that at first she they look like stone benches. Each of the sarcophagi is three feet high and topped by a marble sculpture of a knight in armour, complete with sword and shield. His arms are folded across his chest and lying over his heart is a small replica of the cross behind the altar.

'What *is* this?' asks Mitzi. 'Some kind of family crypt?'

'It's a knights' mausoleum.' He walks towards her. 'Not the only one in the world, but undoubtedly the most secret and secure.' He runs his hand over the smooth marble head of a carved figure. 'This, here, is my father. All down this side of the crypt, is my bloodline. Along the opposite side is my wife's.'

Mitzi surveys the rows of carved sarcophagi. 'And the rest – the ones in the middle?'

'They are the bravest of the brave. Centuries of men and women who secretly served their countries and gave their lives in the battle against evil.'

She walks around the back of a tomb and sees an inscription dating back to the thirteenth century. 'So all these dead folk, they're what, some religious militia?'

'I've never heard it called that before. We like to think of our movement as a circle of people who, like yourself, are dedicated to keeping the world safe. In medieval times they were called knights. These days we don't like anyone to know we exist, let alone call us anything. Anonymity is our strongest shield.'

'But what do *you* call yourselves?'

'Arthurians. We follow codes and principles close to those historians have attributed to King Arthur.' Owain walks on and Mitzi tails him until they stop just before the altar.

Four of the stone tombs have had their ornate lids removed and bodies are visible. As well as skeletons, each coffin contains photographs, jewellery, letters and mementos of the individual's life.

'This is all one family,' he explains. 'Son, father, grandfather and great-grandfather.'

She looks closer and sees they are all laid out in the grey tunics and tights she imagines knights wore beneath their armour. Three red lions run over cloth where hearts once pounded. Across the ripples of bony rib cages lie iron crosses of the exact type that started her investigation.

'The old gentleman who ran the antiques store in Maryland was killed by people trying to plunder and destroy the tombs of our knights in America. Three crosses like those you are looking at were stolen from our mausoleum near Glastonbury, inside the Meshomasic State Forest in Connecticut. I can take you there and show you, if you wish me to validate what I'm telling you.'

She looks across the bodies. 'No need. I believe you.'

'The man who robbed those tombs was once one of us. A trusted member of our group. Now, he seeks to destroy everything we stand for.'

'Why such a change of heart?'

'Money. Greed. Weakness and desperation. All the usual factors in the downfall of a man like him.'

'But how can a couple of stolen crosses represent so big a threat to you?'

'The people who are paying him want to destroy us. To do that they need to prove we exist. Exposing the graveyards is laying our history bare to the world. We cannot allow them to name the knights. Our order would die.'

Mitzi begins to see the dangers. 'So I guess you got injunctions on Professor Mallory because you feared he was also about to expose you?'

'Let's say that some of the links he was making were too close for comfort. He could have begun a chain reaction that we might not have been able to stop.'

'And the murders I'm working on . . .' – there's scepticism in her voice – 'are they all down to this mysterious grave-robbing ex-knight of yours?'

Owain knows he's being tested. 'Not all. George Dalton will be here in the morning and he will be able to discuss in detail the homicide you have connected him to.'

'And you think by bringing me down here, showing me all this and telling me those things, I'm going to view his answers – perhaps his admissions – in a different light?'

'That's exactly what I hope you'll do.'

'Then I'm afraid that despite all your research, you really don't know me at all, Sir Owain. In my book, murder is murder. No excuses. No escape. Not if you're a petty crook who made a mistake, or if you're a finely educated diplomat who really should have known a whole lot better. Now can you get me a ride home? My stomach thinks my throat's been cut and you don't want to see what happens when I get any hungrier than this.'

113

WALES

It's gone midnight by the time Mitzi gets back to the guest-house.

The night manager, a greasy-haired thin man, says there's no chance of anything to eat before breakfast.

'What kind of freakin' country is this? Life doesn't run nine to five any more – you should know that yourself.'

'I'm very sorry, madam.'

'Sorry doesn't fill my goddamned stomach.' She stomps upstairs to her room.

Everything in the minibar is ridiculously expensive.

She guiltily opens two packs of candy and a small bottle of white wine. Her completely unsatisfactory supper costs twenty English pounds. She daren't even convert it into dollars.

By the time she gets into bed, she's calm enough to call her sister. To her surprise, Amber is beyond excited because Ruth's promised to take them to the Bay Aquarium tomorrow, which apparently is made up of more than three hundred feet of underwater tunnels where you can see more than twenty thousand fish.

Mitzi would kill to see a fish. A big juicy trout. Grilled with a slice of lemon and maybe sides of fries and vegetables.

She finishes the call and turns off the phone and looks up to the heavens. 'You listening, God? I really need your blessing and some deep and decent sleep.' Just to make sure, she takes the last of the painkillers the hospital gave her and hunkers down beneath the sheets.

114

CAERGWYN CASTLE, WALES

Owain Gwyn pours a glass of Vieux cognac and carries it from the walnut cabinet at the back of his office to his desk.

On his monitor is an icon marked NIGHTBRIEF. For once, he finds the intel hard to digest. His mind is on other matters. Not just the Californian cop and her homicide crusade but also Mardrid, Marchetti, the terror attacks in the US and UK. Jennifer's pregnancy. Her relationship with Beaucoup.

His own mortality.

Time is running out. His time. He has to make sure the Order is in good shape to run without him.

The secure phone to New York rings and breaks him from his thoughts. 'Hello.'

'I hoped I'd catch you before you turned in.' Gareth

Madoc's voice is raw from working days without sleep. 'Our girl got a tracker on Khalid Korshidi.'

'Well done.'

'It gets better. He led us to a safe house out in East Flatbush. We got ears on the place, and it was a good job we had. There were already three other people in the basement. One of them was Imam Yousef Mousavi.'

The name is enough for Owain to put down his cognac. 'You're certain?'

'We've run voice recognition software on the recordings. We're ninety per cent sure.'

'Did anyone use his name?'

'No. But Nabil Tabrizi was there and he referred to him as Imam. Antun always believed Nabil reported to Mousavi.'

'Who was the other person? You said there were three others.'

'We don't know, but the imam was in overall command. He led the conversations and was most reverently spoken to.'

'The CIA and CTU would sell their souls just to get their hands on Mousavi, let alone anyone above him. Please tell me they spoke about something more important than the price of halal meat.'

'Trinity.'

'What?'

'That's what the "unknown" said. Hang on; I've got the transcript here. He said, and I quote: "*In forty-eight hours' time the Trinity will be no more.*" Then the "unknown" asked if they all understood what was being demanded of them. They said they did. After that everything quickly slid into prayers.'

'I'm just trying to make sense of this Trinity reference. Did the Americans get anything helpful from the men they locked up after the raid on Nabil's body shop?'

'I spoke to the CIA about an hour ago. They've got nothing so far.'

'Pity. Trinity sounds religious but it could mean three of anything. Remember that intelligence we had about al-Qaeda targeting sports stars?'

'I do, it was a hit list based on Forbes top earners.'

'See if we've got three stars together anywhere soon.'

Gareth makes a note to himself.

Owain has another thought. 'I'll get some of our analysts to draw up a matrix that shows the movement of all leading politicians, sports heroes and religious leaders over the next twenty-four hours.'

'At least you know the new Pope will be safe.'

'I hope so. I'll be with him in Wales for the first papal visit for more than thirty years and not even the Devil himself will be able to get through security down there.'

'I'm sure you're right.'

'Any developments with the Korshidi girl?'

'A little. I've pushed her to fit the recorders while her father is out. If he's as important as she says he is, then we may get lucky.'

'We need to.' Owain takes a long pause before continuing: 'Gareth, I sense that the next few days will shape our destiny –

mine, yours, Lance's and the Order's. If for some reason it turns out that I cannot – *how shall I say this?* – be around, then you and Lance must guide our members until the next of my line is ready to step forward.'

'Owain, I—'

'No, please let me finish. You have been like a brother to me, and I love you deeply for all your support, your friendship and loyalty. Consider me foolish and this unnecessary, but I just want to say thank you.' He leaves no opening for discussion. 'Now let's talk no further on this matter; I have cognac to finish and a bed to go to. Goodnight, dear friend, goodnight.'

115

WALES

Mitzi's dreams are filled with flashes of medieval knights on horseback, Irish's tumbling car and fish.

Millions of tropical fish.

Her daughters are swimming in the San Francisco aquarium with them. They're all down there together. Horses. Knights. Irish. His trashed car. The Ford's windows are busted. Fish and her girls are swimming in and out of the holes.

Somewhere above water, back in the real world, a phone rings.

Mitzi breaststrokes an arm out of bed and grabs it. '*Urmgh*,' is the best she can manage.

'Good morning, Mrs Fallon. It's the front desk. There is a driver waiting for you in reception.'

'What?'

'A driver, madam. From Sir Owain Gwyn.'

She squints at the bedside clock. 08.55.

'Crapolla. Tell him I'll be ten minutes.'

'Yes, madam.'

She bangs the phone down, flies to the bathroom and quickly showers and dries. A look in the mirror shows her black eyes have morphed into large purple stains. Make-up deadens the ugliness a little but nowhere near enough to completely hide them. She drags a comb through her hair. Attacks it with hairspray. Dresses in black slacks and an unironed grey top, then grabs a jacket and heads downstairs.

The same driver is waiting in reception. The one that says nothing and throws the vehicle around like it's a cocktail shaker. He smiles and walks outside.

116

LUNDY

It's rained all night and is still raining when Bronty sticks his head out of the tiny farmhouse where he's staying. It's not the kind of warm, light drizzle that makes you feel good to be out in it but torrential rain that soaks you to the skin and leaves you cold and shivering for the rest of the day.

The American hurries to the Marisco Tavern, the island's only hostelry and a place where a full English breakfast of bacon, eggs, fried bread and mushrooms costs less than a cappuccino in London.

Within minutes, he's pointed to a man breakfasting in the corner of the tavern's main bar, a ferryman from the Oldenburg called Dan Smallfellow. The old sailor is a personification of his surname. He's a tiny sparrow of a man, with a bent back and wisps of white hair that refuse to lie down on his mottled bare skull.

'So what do you want to know?' he says, after Bronty has introduced himself. 'Are you looking for oil, gold or legends? It's usually one of them things.'

Bronty is amused by his candour. He takes out a copy of the sketch of the cross seen by Sophie Hudson. 'Does this mean anything to you? Does it have to do with the island?'

Old Dan looks at it and takes a swig of tea. 'It looks Celtic but different. Like it belonged to a special sect or clan.' He puts the drawing down. 'So it's legends you're chasing. There are plenty of them here.'

'Like King Arthur and his knights?'

'You're a Yank, aren't you?'

'I'm American, yes.'

He takes a bite of toast. 'And you're trying to link that there cross with King Arthur and Lundy?'

'Is it a ridiculous suggestion?'

'Not at all. There are them that say the island is Avalon – Arthur's resting place.'

Bronty suspects he's being strung along. 'I thought that was supposed to be in England, near Glastonbury?'

'Propaganda. The English claim it's in England. The Welsh claim it's in Wales and the French claim it's there.' The ferryman looks at rain hitting the window. 'They are all liars when it comes to legends. They smell the tourist dollar and lie, lie, lie. Not for nothing is Lundy known as *Annwyn*, the gateway to the Otherworld.'

Bronty valiantly refrains from launching into a theological lecture about heaven. 'So if Arthur is here, where exactly would I find his grave?'

Old Dan slurps more tea before answering. 'That would be a secret, wouldn't it? Think of how King Richard the Third's bones lay for centuries beneath common ground in Leicester; perhaps King Arthur lies out here in an unmarked grave.' There's a sparkle in his eyes. 'Go and visit the Giants' Graves or the Celtic Stones – you might find him there. Or, look out to sea and figure if he were rowed out from shore and laid to rest with the fish and sunken ships.'

'I get the feeling you're making fun of me.'

He shakes his head. 'I'm not ribbing you. Everything is possible on Lundy. It's a place of magic. The longer you stay here the more you'll find I'm right.'

117

CAERGWYN CASTLE, WALES

Deer mooch at the edge of a copse of beech then scatter as a speeding Range Rover breaks the morning peace. Hares and rabbits skittishly head for cover. Fat sheep rise from slumber and plod damp morning grass.

The 4x4 stops by the main entrance.

Mitzi's out of the back before the driver can walk round to her door. She flaps it shut and without looking round, heads towards the castle.

'You're the American, aren't you?'

The deep male voice has come from nowhere.

She turns and is startled to see an old man, shrouded in long white hair, straggly beard and full-length black coat.

'Holy friggin' hell! Where did you come from?'

'I am Myrddin.' His skinny hand levitates towards hers. 'It is my pleasure to have encountered you.' His eyes roam her face and he remembers his vision at the Font of Knowledge – *two women, one known, one a complete stranger. Both in danger. Both will see death.*

She takes a long stare into his pale green eyes as she shakes his hand. 'Mitzi Fallon. In future, you should go easy with your surprise *encountering*.'

'Eyes tell you very little,' he says, disarmingly. 'If you are searching for the true nature of a person you should look instead to their mouth. The lips and tongue are the slaves of the brain; they are stupid and far more likely to make mistakes than the eyes.'

Unwittingly, she shifts her attention to his mouth. The teeth are plentiful, well-shaped and unstained. The lips youthful, plump and moist. All features more fitting a far younger man.

In return, Myrddin pointedly studies her. 'Your mouth is well used to truth. You are a good person, but it is not right that you are here.'

'I'm sorry, what did you say?'

'You seek the men who entered the Cave of Past and Present, those who slayed the Keeper of Time—'

'I seek *what*?'

'—you pursue them and also the silent brown beast that carries the disciples of Death.'

'Aah.' She gets it now. The poor old guy has a screw loose. 'Very nice to have met you, Mervyn.' She smiles politely and shakes his hand again. 'I have to go now and see Sir Owain in the real world, you take care.'

Mitzi wants to walk away but for some reason she can't. Her feet are so heavy she can't move them.

Myrddin lets her hand drop. His eyes narrow and those soft lips of his speak slow and persuasive words. 'You must return the shadow of knowledge. Give back the light of tomorrow or else you will cry endless tears.'

'Lieutenant!' The voice is Owain's.

She turns her upper body to find him.

'Good morning.' He walks briskly towards her. 'How are you today?'

Her feet free up and she stumbles forward. 'I'm, er . . . I just met Merv, here—' She turns back to gesture to the old man.

Only he's gone.

'Are you all right?' Owain takes her arm and steadies her. 'You look like you've seen a ghost.'

118

SAN MATEO, SAN FRANCISCO

Ruth Everett wakes with what feels like the mother of all hangovers. First comes the agonizing pain in her head. Then a whoosh of sickness, followed by the realization she is fully dressed and lying on the kitchen floor staring up at the ceiling.

But the worst is yet to come.

The moment when she remembers what happened.

The nice woman who had broken down outside her house . . .

. . . had attacked her.

She'd let her use a landline to call the vehicle rental company and while they waited for the breakdown truck, she'd started to make some coffee. She'd been stood at the window getting mugs out of the dishwasher when the woman stuck something sharp in her neck. That sneaky bitch had spiked her, slapped a hand over her mouth and then forced her to the floor where she passed out.

Ruth gets to her feet. Struggles to the sink to pour some water. She pictures what's she's about to find. Her purse will have been emptied of cash and credit cards. No doubt all her jewellery will be gone. Maybe even the car off the drive.

The twins.

She hadn't thought of them at first because she was so messed up by the drugs, but she does now.

'Jade! Amber!'

Her throat hurts as she shouts. 'Girls – where are you?'

They were on the patio when the woman rolled up. Maybe they've run to neighbours for help. She rushes to the hall. Looks in the lounge and TV room. There's no sign of a disturbance. No fight. Nothing stolen.

'Girls – you upstairs?' She feels dizzy as she hauls herself up the treads.

In the master bedroom, Jack's books are still piled high on the table next to his side of the bed, a page marker stuck a third of a way through a novel he never got to finish. Bracelets and rings shine out from a crystal jewellery holder in the middle of her dressing table. 'Oh my God.' She sinks on to the bed as reality hits her.

A note lies on the quilt.

It has a simple seven-word message.

'CALL THE COPS AND THE KIDS DIE.'

119

CAERGWYN CASTLE, WALES

Sir Owain guides Mitzi to a teak garden bench on a paved pathway a few yards from where he found her. 'Sit a minute, then I'll walk you inside.'

'I'm fine. And I'm not a dog that needs to be walked.' She looks out over the empty lawn. 'Who was that old guy and where the hell did he go?'

'It's complicated.'

'I bet it is.' Her cell phone rings. 'You mind if I take this?'

'Please.' He steps away to give her privacy.

Caller display says it's her sister. Probably unable to sleep and needing to rant about Jack and his wandering hands. 'Hey Ruthy, I'm kinda busy right now – can I call you back?'

There's a tense silence before she answers. 'Mitzi, it's the girls.'

She picks up the fear. '*What's* the girls?'

'They're gone. They've been taken from the house.'

'I don't understand. What do you mean?' She thinks of Alfie. Maybe he's picked them up without permission.

'I let this woman in . . .' Ruth starts to choke. 'She said her car had broken down – and while we waited for the rescue truck she stuck something in my neck.' She's almost unable to speak now. 'I just came round and found a note. It says if I call the cops the kids will die.'

Mitzi's heartbeat goes off the scale. 'Have you called them?' She has to remind herself to stay calm and act professionally. 'Who'd you call, Ruth?'

'Just you.' She breaks down now. 'Just you, that's all.'

'Okay.' Mitzi struggles to breathe and hears herself saying, 'Do nothing. Lock the doors, sit tight and let me get back to you.' She looks up at Gwyn. He's stood a few yards away, his back to her, his eyes fixed on one of the castle towers.

Could he have done this? A follow-through on the warnings he'd given her?

She pockets the phone and charges at him. Hits him square in the back. The blow knocks Owain forward but not down.

He staggers and turns to see her wide-eyed with rage.

'You motherfucking son-of-a-bitch. You think you can hurt my fucking kids?' She throws a raw right-hander.

He plucks it out of the air like he is catching a baseball tossed by a toddler.

Mitzi boots out at his legs. A crippling kick, hard enough to shatter a shin bone.

He leans effortlessly away from it. Gently twists her hand so the wrist and elbow lock and she is forced face down onto the grass.

Mitzi knows the manoeuvre well enough. If she shifts an inch her wrist will break.

He bends close to her face. 'I've done nothing to your children. Do you understand me?'

She doesn't answer.

His grip stays tight and his voice calm. 'Lieutenant, do you understand what I am saying?'

'Yes.'

'Okay.' He lets go of her arm and helps her to her feet. 'I'm very sorry I had to do that. Now please tell me what has happened.'

120

CALIFORNIA

It's a shack of a place. Way off the beaten track. Made from cheap clapboard and is little more than a big shed divided into a living room and kitchen, two bedrooms and a bathroom.

Just perfect for their needs.

'Kidnapping sure is thirsty work,' says Chris as he brings in a six-pack from the RV. 'You want a beer?'

The twins are laid out on the floor, back to back. Tess is sat opposite them in a cheap chair, with a handgun on her lap. 'Yeah, but get me a glass. I don't like drinkin' straight from the bottle.'

Things had pretty much gone to plan.

She'd stuck Ruth Everett with a sedative then called Chris, who'd been waiting in woods half a mile away. Once he'd gotten himself in position in the house she'd shouted the girls in from the patio, saying their aunt was sick. Chris had spiked them as easy as popping sausages on a BBQ.

Together they bundled them into the RV and headed out to where they're now having a celebratory beer.

Chris takes a tumbler from a cupboard, rubs a dishtowel in it to get rid of dust and froths out the Bud for the love of his life.

Tess gets on her knees, puts her fingers across the wrists of the girls and checks their pulses. Too much of the sedative and they die. Too little and they'll be a handful.

Seems from the throbbing vein beneath her fingers that she dosed them just right.

She checks their restraints again. Chris handcuffed and bound them, sealed their yaps with Duck tape and for good measure stuck loose, black hoods over their heads.

Everything's just tickety-boo.

She sits back down and takes the glass from him. 'Thanks.' Tess enjoys a long drink before putting it on the floor.

He looks down at the twins as he raises his beer. 'Pretty kids. It'll be a real shame when we have to kill them.'

121

CAERGWYN CASTLE, WALES

Owain closes the study door and listens carefully to Mitzi's account of how her children were abducted.

By the time she finishes, it's plain she's in need of some reassurances. 'As an investigator, you know the note means that the kidnappers intend to make contact with you. Probably sooner rather than later.'

Mitzi nods and stops biting a thumbnail. 'I need to call my boss and tell her what's happened. The FBI has a special unit that deals with this kind of thing.'

He gestures to a Victorian desk of golden mahogany. 'Feel free to use the phone. Though you may want to consider waiting another hour. I'm sure these people will reach out directly to you.'

'I can't wait.' She gets to her feet. 'I'm already crazy with worry. These are my babies. They're everything that matters to me.'

'I understand.' He gets up and walks over to her. 'I'll leave you while you make the call.'

She picks up the phone and hears no tone. 'How do I get an outside line?'

'Zero, zero.'

'Thanks.' Her fingers shake as she enters the numbers for her boss's direct line.

Owain walks down the corridor into the west wing. He passes through a full-body scan operated by two armed guards. Only then is he allowed into the suites of private offices that contain SSOA staff and the order's main data banks and network systems.

At a curved desk, topped with a fan of high-definition 3D screens, the ambassador talks to Lance Beaucoup.

'Lieutenant Fallon is in the guest office talking to her superior on the phone. Her children have been abducted.'

The Frenchman punches a button and Mitzi's voice pours out of a black speaker grille built into the desk.

She sounds strained. 'No, I haven't spoken to anyone but Ruth. We need to get a female officer over there to support her.'

'See it as done,' says her boss. 'Soon as you hang up, I'll talk to the Kidnap Unit and get traces set up on your sister's phones and your cell.'

'I have to tell their father.' Mitzi makes the announcement as much to herself as to her boss. 'He's going to lose it when he finds out.'

'Give me a location and we'll send an officer to wait outside his dwelling, then he can follow up as soon as you've told him.'

Owain signals to his colleague. 'Turn it off. I don't need to listen to any more of this.'

He kills the volume. 'You want me to put a team on it?'

'Straight away. Who was the young operative who did the background for me on Fallon and that Irish policeman?'

'Ross Green. He was working with Eve Garrett. They're both ex-cops who I'm sure will one day make Inner Circle members.'

'I hope you're right; we always need new blood. Put him on this – and her if she can be freed up.'

'I'll talk to Gareth and fix it.'

'And tell him to make sure they take care. You can rest

assured Mardrid is pulling Marchetti's strings and he's going to try to use Fallon's girls to pull ours.'

122

NEW YORK

An under-tens soccer match is finishing at the Met Oval in Queens, a public ground hailed as the oldest continuously used soccer facility in America.

Brooklyn Knights are two-nil up against Westchester on a pitch that boasts a skyline view of Manhattan and lies just a third of a mile and a three-minute walk from Zachra Korshidi's house. Stood among the small crowd of cheering parents is Gareth Madoc. On the opposite touchline are two armed members of his team. Six more are stationed along the approach roads to the ground.

Zachra is twenty minutes late for their secret meeting and Madoc is getting nervous. South of the pitch, he sees the shadowy shape of a black burqa slide through a patch of trees. He whispers into the transmitter clipped to the cuff of his baggy brown pilot jacket. 'Standby. We have target approaching from south side.'

Bodies move in the crowd. Unseen hands click the safety catches off their weapons. Zachra may be being followed; she may not. No one is taking any chances.

Madoc makes sure she sees him, then wanders away from the cheering parents and up a bank heading back to the streets. He slips into the shade and watches.

In one hand she carries a brown paper bag bearing the Burger King crest, and in the other a half-empty beaker of cola. Through the slit of her black niqab he sees her fearful eyes flicking everywhere.

'You okay?'

The covered head nods.

'Anything you can tell me?'

'My father ordered my mother and me out of the house. He said he'd be receiving a very important guest and we were not to be there to shame him. We had to clean the back room, then he told us to stay away until he calls.'

'Did you ask how long that might be?'

A laugh tumbles through the head cloth. 'You don't *ask* my father things. You just do what he tells you.'

'Did you manage to fit the devices I gave you?'

Zachra doesn't answer. She lifts her cola, forces a bent straw into the slit in her headdress and takes a long drink.

Madoc watches the liquid rise and notices the knuckles of her right hand are swollen. He glances at the bag held in her left hand and sees her other fingers are also damaged.

Zachra catches his stare. 'He beat me for being in his room. The back room where you wanted me to go. He made me kneel like a dog, then stamped on my hands.'

Madoc's heard enough. 'We need to take you to hospital.'

'Hospital can wait.' There's steel in her voice. She throws

the finished cola into a trash bin and lifts up the Burger King bag so he can see it. 'I'm taking *this* somewhere quiet to eat.' Before she turns and walks away, she adds, 'And yes, your camera and microphones are now hidden in his room.'

123

CAERGWYN CASTLE, WALES

Mitzi puts the phone down and sits in stunned silence. The door opens and Owain walks in with George Dalton.

It's just her luck that the man she has most wanted to interview turns up when she can least afford to talk to him.

'I heard about your daughters.' Dalton looks genuinely sympathetic. 'I'm very sorry about what has happened.'

She addresses the ambassador. 'I need to leave right away and catch a flight back to California. Can you tell me what's the nearest airport?'

He shakes his head. 'That's not necessary. My helicopter will get you to Heathrow and from there I have a jet that will fly you across the Atlantic.'

She looks shocked. 'That's very kind. Thank you.'

'There's no need to thank me. Please excuse me while I make arrangements.'

Mitzi watches him go. Her eyes settle on Dalton. If

nothing else, she's going to throw one question at him before she leaves. 'Did you kill Bradley Deagan?'

He takes a long beat before he answers. 'Sir Owain informed me that you know a little about our cause. About the *good* we try to do.'

She strides into Dalton's space. 'I have your DNA.'

The consul's face reddens.

'I lifted the bottle you drank from when we met in London and ran it through the labs. Guess what? It matches the DNA found mixed with Deagan's on the washroom floor in the All Night All Right diner off Dupont Circle.'

He thinks for a moment. 'I'm not sure what you are surmising from that. I have already told you that I was there.' He looks unconcerned. 'The bathroom would have been filthy. I imagine there was DNA from a hundred other people as well.'

'Bad luck there. It had just been cleaned. The hygiene rota was signed ten minutes before you came in for your bleed.'

Dalton licks his dried and nervous lips. 'Last time we met you said you had surveillance footage and that was a lie.'

'You were at that diner with a man you had followed all the way from a crime scene.'

'You could be lying now.'

'I'm not.'

Owain walks back into the room. 'Pilot says he'll be ready for take-off in about twenty minutes.'

'Thank you.' Mitzi turns back to Dalton. 'Come on, George; you and I both know you killed Deagan and hid his body and vehicle somewhere. Today of all days, save me the dance.'

Dalton glances at the ambassador, who gives him a telling nod.

Finally, he opens up. 'I tailed a brown SUV from the antiques store where the owner died. Deagan and another man pulled up a couple of miles away. They both went into the woods, but only Deagan came out. I followed him to the diner. He went in and ate. When he came out I asked him to return our property.'

'*Asked*?'

'Yes, *asked*. He could have given it me and nothing would have happened. He went crazy, pulled a knife and we fought. I got stabbed, he got killed.'

'And the body and the vehicle?'

'Must have got moved.'

She smiles in disbelief. 'You were doing well with the openness and honesty, until then.'

Owain steps into the conversation. 'From what I told you yesterday, you can imagine why we wouldn't want to be caught up in a homicide investigation. It's imperative that George's admission – and everything else I confided in you – stays between us.'

'I'm sorry, Sir Owain. My job isn't to keep secrets, it's to disclose them.'

'I really hope you don't do that.' He glances at his watch. 'We should get you down to the helipad; the pilot will be about ready.'

Mitzi's cell phone rings.

Her heart jumps. The display says: 'Number withheld'.

She presses the accept button. 'Mitzi Fallon.'

The voice is electronically distorted and chillingly slow. 'Which of your daughters do you love most?'

The words make her light-headed. She sits on the back of a leather sofa to steady herself. 'What do you want?'

'The codex. If I don't have it within twenty-four hours, I'm going to kill one of them. You can choose.'

124

FBI HQ, SAN FRANCISCO

CARDT, the FBI's Child Abducted Rapid Deployment Team, has an office two floors below HRU. Donovan rings unit boss Bob Beam, fills him in and says she's on her way down with one of her lieutenants.

Within five minutes, she and Eleonora Fracci are sat in a briefing room.

Beam is late forties and looks like a college prof in his leather patched brown blazer and square-framed spectacles.

With him are two contrasting colleagues: a tall, broad man with black, soldierly hair and a petite, blonde woman in a grey business suit. He introduces them as they pull up chairs around the small table in the glass-walled room. 'This is

Damon Spinks. He'll lead the operational side of any recovery we get to stage. And this is Helena Banks; she's our psychologist and negotiator. She can talk the devil into singing in a church choir.'

Donovan reciprocates. 'My colleague here is Eleonora Fracci, one of our lead investigators. She works alongside Mitzi Fallon and I want her to be the link on this – to you, me and any other agencies we include.'

Beam writes her name at the bottom of the notes he made when the AD called him. 'Right now, everyone's in what we call the sit-and-shit mode. It's the most unnerving phase there is. Given the warning that the kidnappers left, we can't get a full team to the house the girls were taken from because the unsubs might be watching.'

Spinks jumps in to give a little reassurance. 'I've got an unmarked surveillance helicopter flying high and sweeping surrounding areas. We're also asking for real-time satellite access and rollback replays, but we'll be lucky to get them.'

Donovan blows a sigh. 'What about traces on the house landline and family cell phone numbers?'

'Those we can get,' says Beam. 'You know the game, though. The kidnappers will use burners and ditch them straight after a call.'

'Worth a shot.'

'Always.' He rolls the pen across his fingers as he thinks. 'And you figure the girls might have been taken because of this case their mom's working?'

'That's right. She's handling two homicides connected to

an old cross and a memory stick taken from an antiques store near Washington DC.'

Beam makes notes. 'What's on the stick?'

'Coded information.'

He looks interested. 'As in spies?'

Donovan shakes her head. 'We don't think so. Seems to be something else. Fallon didn't go into great detail.'

'Then she needs to.' He looks at Eleonora. 'Can you call her and get the full picture for me?'

'*Si.*' She dips into her voluminous Fendi bag and produces a clutter of photograph frames. 'I took these from her desk. I thought you'd need photographs of the girls.'

'Thanks.' He takes them and carefully lays them on the table. 'Nice kids. I hope we can keep them that way.'

Helena, the psychologist, picks up one showing the girls with their mom at Disney. They're all wearing mouse ears. 'Can you tell me something about the family? It would be good to get an idea of how the girls might be acting right now.'

'Not sure how much we can help,' answers Donovan. 'Fallon's new to the unit. Came from LAPD Homicide after a messy divorce and brought the kids with her.'

'Their father is a bum,' adds Eleonora.

They all give her a look that demands further detail.

'I checked on her a little. He used to beat her. One day she beat him back, called the cops and filed for divorce.'

'Good for her,' says Helena.

'She's a tough cookie,' adds Donovan. 'That's part of why I wanted her on this unit.'

'She'll need to be,' says Helena. 'Her girls, too. Let's hope some of Mom's survival instinct has rubbed off on them.'

Beam is examining a seaside shot of a younger Mitzi carrying twin toddlers, one on each arm, into the sea. 'Any chance of Fallon trying to solve this on her own?'

Donovan thinks out loud. 'She called it in straight away. Means she's trying to do things by the book; she wants us involved.'

The psychologist smiles sceptically. 'Make no mistake – a mother will do anything to save her kids. And one like Fallon will only go by the book as long as she believes the book is worth it. After that, then there isn't a line she won't cross.'

125

CAERGWYN CASTLE, WALES

Mitzi hangs up.

Owain and George Dalton stare expectantly at her.

She's almost in a trance as she talks. 'I have to hand over the codex within twenty-four hours or they'll kill one of my girls.' She almost breaks down. 'But hey, I get to choose.'

The ambassador guides her to a nearby sofa. He knows there's no point lying about the dilemma she's in. 'What you decide to do now is critical. Unfortunately, as you have two daughters, they *will,* if necessary, kill one of them, to increase their leverage.'

Mitzi stares at her hands. It's a long time since she's seen them shake. She looks up at the tall Welshman. 'Once these sons of bitches have got what they want, they're most likely going to kill them both, aren't they?'

He knows she's right. 'What instructions did they give you?'

'Said again not to phone the cops. I'm gonna get a call within the hour telling me where to go. I told them I was in England and they said they knew that. Then they hung up.'

'You said England?'

'Yeah. Why?'

'You're not in England. You're in Wales. It means they know you crossed the Atlantic and came to London, but not that you came out here to see me.'

'Or,' adds Dalton, 'it means they don't know they are separate countries.'

Owain sees tension on Mitzi's face. 'I'll stand down the helicopter. Given the developments, you're better off here than anywhere. Certainly, there's no point flying you back to the US.'

'I'm not sure about that.' She becomes visibly more nervous. 'I want to be as close to the girls as possible.'

'I understand. But what if by travelling you miss vital contact with the kidnappers?'

She sees his point. 'I don't know. I'm not thinking straight. Give me a minute.'

'What are you going to do about the FBI? Are you going to tell them about this call?'

'I have to.'

'Keep in mind that we're better placed to help than they are. If they make one slip, then you know this gang will kill your daughters and flee.'

Mitzi chews a nail. 'The bureau have a standard trace on my phone. They'll have picked up that I received a call.'

'They haven't. There's a communication shield around the castle. It makes it impossible for anyone to track your location or listen in.'

A thought hits her. 'Were *you*? Were you recording and tracking that call?'

'We were, but the kidnapper's location is masked. There are anti-trace software programs that make it look like calls are coming from hundreds of miles away from where they are made. We can break it down, but it'll take time.'

She looks desperate. 'I don't have time.' Her phone rings. She looks down and sees that it's Donovan's direct line. 'This is my boss. I have to take it.'

'It's up to you.' He touches her arm. 'You have to decide whether to trust the FBI, who've been dealing with kidnappers for decades – or us – an organization that's been doing such things for thousands of years.'

126

FBI HQ, SAN FRANCISCO

Sandra Donovan explains that she's with Fracci and is putting her on speakerphone.

'Mitzi, it's Eleonora.' The Italian leans over her boss's desk and talks into the spider-shaped conferencing unit. 'We're going to do everything to get your children back, I promise.'

'I know you will. Has anyone called the local precinct?'

Donovan answers. 'No. They're in the dark and we're keeping them that way. Have you fixed a flight?'

She hesitates. 'I thought I might stay here for a while and see if the kidnappers make contact. I don't want to be mid-air if they call. Have you got any breaks?'

'Not yet,' says the assistant director. 'We're figuring this woman who approached your sister was working with at least one man, probably more. Eleonora's just spoken to Ruth and she said she thought she had a Californian accent.'

'Ruthy is smart on accents; she used to be a teacher and could pick out exactly where every kid came from.'

'We're going to work on a sketch too. We can do a lot over a secure video link to Ruth's home computer. It's not as good as being there with her, but it's close.'

The Italian leans towards the mic again. 'We got a trace on your husband. He'd been in a bar brawl and spent the night in a cell in Oakwood. The custody sergeant knows you from way back and is about to kick him out without charge.'

Mitzi huffs in exasperation. 'Alfie never changes. I'll give him half an hour, then call. Can you have someone look out for him?'

'We will,' confirms Donovan. 'We've met with the Child Abduction Response Department and they need to go through your case. I've asked Eleonora to get the files from Vicky and bring them up to speed. I know this is tough but can you think of anyone who might bear a grudge and be behind this – guys you've locked up, gangs you've crossed?'

'I don't think so. I'm pretty sure this is down to whoever killed Sophie Hudson for the memory stick she took from Goldman's store.'

'Which you've still got?'

'Yeah, I've got it all right.' She can feel Owain's eyes on her. 'It's in a place where no one's gonna find it.'

'If you're right,' says Donovan, 'this stick is what you're going to have to trade for your girls.'

'I know. And to be clear, evidence or no evidence, if it means I get the girls, I'll trade it in a blink.'

Eleonora senses the call's about to wrap up. 'Can you have Bronty call and bring me up to date?'

'He's not here. He's following some religious leads on Lundy.'

'Lundy? Where is that?'

'Off the west coast. I'll have Bronty contact you.'

'No, leave it. I'll call him. You have enough to deal with.'

'Thanks.' She finishes the conversation and looks around.

Dalton and Sir Owain have left the room.

In their place is the tall, thin, white-bearded man she saw in the garden.

127

LUNDY

The storm the weathermen predicted is now battering the tiny island.

Most of the thirty people who live here are holed up inside cottages in the south, but Bronty is braving the elements, in an all-too-thin waterproof borrowed from the tavern.

So far, he's come across the remains of a granite quarry, scattered farm buildings, a small camp site, a couple of dozen holiday cottages and that's about it.

To many people Lundy would be hell, but not him. The peace and seclusion bring a spiritual satisfaction he's not felt outside of the seminary.

As well as the Giants' Graves where skeletons up to eight feet tall were said to be found, Old Dan listed other places with rich historical or religious connections. They come with exotic names, like Needle's Eye, Devil's Slide and Shutter Point, but for now he's making do with a rain-lashed walk along the low stone walls of Beacon Hill Cemetery. Like many graveyards, it's been built on the highest available peak, the point ancients thought closest to the gods and the heavens.

Bronty takes a slow look around. He gazes out over the sodden green pastures to the endless miles of surrounding waves. Somewhere out there is the confluence of the Bristol Channel and the Celtic Sea, a mixing of great waters and stirring of untold myths and legends.

As the minutes pass, he becomes aware that all that separates him and his homeland in America is water. He looks around and remembers the ferryman's remarks that to ancient Celts this must have looked like the end of the world.

The rain stops. Grey clouds shift. Shafts of sunlight warm his face. There's a glorious wind-free silence. Then comes the sound of screaming birds, flapping high and wheeling across the brightening sky. He makes a visor out of his hand and picks out herring gulls, starlings and blackbirds.

He lowers his gaze to the glistening grass and spots the graves. Four isolated standing stones you wouldn't give a second glance if you didn't know their history.

He walks closer.

The severely weathered pillars remind him of the Celtic crosses that adorn Cornish and Welsh churchyards. He struggles to read the inscriptions. On one, he makes out the letters OPTIMI, which is similar to the Latin male name Optimus. Another looks like RESTEVTAE or RESGEVT, which could be the female name Resteuta or Resgeuta. The third and fourth are even harder to discern. One looks like POTIT, or it could be PO TIT and the other IGERNI, TIGERNI. He wonders if it was originally Tigernus.

'If only the dead could tell their tales.'

Bronty turns to see a redheaded woman in a yellow anorak and black waterproofs studying him. 'I'm Geraldine Brummer.' She puts out a hand. 'And I'm guessing you're Mr Tomlinson, from the National Trust?'

'No. No I'm not.' Bronty shakes her hand anyway. 'Jon Bronty. I'm – err – just an American visiting the island.'

'Oh, I'm sorry. My mistake. I'm from Natural England. We manage the marine conservation and I've come out for the diving.'

'I guess if you're a diver then the rain doesn't bother you.'

'Actually, I love the rain. Makes me feel more alive.'

Bronty's phone rings. 'Excuse me for a minute?'

'Sure.' She smiles understandingly. 'You're lucky to get a signal.'

He smiles back and turns away to take the call. 'Hello?'

'It's Eleonora. Can you speak?'

'Hang on.' He walks away from the woman. 'Go on.'

'Mitzi's children have been abducted.'

'What?'

'They were taken from their aunt's home in San Mateo. I'll go into everything afterwards. Right now, I need you to give me a full brief on her case, everything you and she found and anything you think might help us.'

128

CAERGWYN CASTLE, WALES

Mitzi almost loses it when Myrddin appears barely a yard from here. 'Hellfire, Mervin, where did you come from? You shouldn't go creeping around like that.'

The old man approaches her, his face full of kindness. 'I have come to give you strength.'

'Excuse me?'

He takes both of her hands before she can back away. Holds them as intensely as he holds her stare.

She feels a strange sensation in her fingers. It rises into her arms and chest like a deep bass note. Mitzi tries to remove her hands from his, but they're locked there, as heavy and immovable as her feet were in the garden. A deep warmth spreads through her.

'Close your eyes for me.'

Normally a guy would get a crack for a line like that, but Mitzi doesn't feel as though she can stop herself doing as he asks.

'Slip back in time. Think of the moment you gave birth to your daughters. Remember how in your weakest physical time you created the greatest of all things. Remember their first breaths and cries. How they felt when you held them. How you felt, when you kissed their faces and touched their skin. Remember that magic.'

Myrddin takes her hands and places them behind her back as though they are cuffed together. 'See your children. See them as newborns entering the light of the earth for the first time, being carried towards you, about to be placed in your arms for the first time.'

Mitzi wants to speak but she can't. Her mind is flooded with the exaltation of motherhood.

He puts his leathery hands on her shoulders. 'Kneel.'

Her legs bend and the cold, hard floor touches her knees.

'The ground gives you strength. It renews you, absorbs your fears and from it you grow.' He pushes a little harder on her shoulders. 'Lie.'

Mitzi slumps the rest of the way, conscious now of the floor, of the cold against her side and face.

'The ground gives you energy and protection. It feeds you when there is no food and hides you when there is nowhere for you to be hidden. Those looking at you will see only your physical form. Your spirit will be below ground, protected and nourished like the roots of a thousand-year-old tree.'

Mitzi feels like she's having an out-of-body experience. She knows she's being subjected to some form of hypnotism but at the same time it feels so empowering she has no urge to fight it.

'When you get up you will be strong. So strong that no man alive will ever be able to cut you down. When you stand and hear your name, you will not remember that you spoke to me or even recall that I was here. But when the time comes, when you are bound or pained, you will remember your power. Now unclasp your hands. Feel the ground. Thank it for becoming your friend. Kneel on it and worship it. Stand proudly upon it, as the greatest tree in a forest stands, and then open your eyes.'

129

LUNDY

A white flag with the red cross of St George flutters against the blue-grey rain-soaked sky. Beneath the square stone tower upon which it stands is St Helena's church and at the foot of it, the forlorn figure of Jon Bronty.

The former priest has just finished briefing Eleonora and is trying to get through to Mitzi. All his calls are tripping to her voicemail. An economical recording tells him for the third time, 'It's Mitzi; leave a message and a number and I'll get back to you, thanks.'

'Hi, it's Bronty. I just heard the news. I'm so terribly sorry. I'm going to finish up here and get back to the mainland as quickly as possible, but I don't think the next ferry is until tomorrow. I wish you much strength and I shall pray for you and your girls.'

He hangs up and slips inside the church to deliver on his promise.

The church is much grander and more impressive than the grey slate and harsh stone exterior had hinted at. The warm red brick of the interior and old dark wood pews feel familiar and welcoming to him.

There's a quaint chancel with a transept vestry to one side, Purbeck marble colonnettes with alabaster carvings depicting the Last Supper. In front of him is a large lectern carved from wood in the shape of an eagle, an old stone pulpit and square baptism font. A modest red-clothed altar stands near a stained-glass centre window depicting the crucifixion. He walks over and kneels before the god he walked out on. It wasn't a loss of faith in the Supreme Being that saw him quit, but a lack of belief in himself and his worthiness to wear the cloth.

He prays that Mitzi's children will be safe and quickly reunited with their mother, that the experiences will leave none of them scarred and that she and all her family will have the strength and belief to get through the ordeal without any lasting damage.

It's a lot to ask for.

He opens his eyes, looks up at the gleaming brass crucifix on the red altar cloth and feels at home. The church. The island. The people. Everything feels right to him. He could live here. This tiny land, of apparently so little, offers so much more than people can easily see.

As he gets to his feet and turns around to leave, he sees Geraldine Brummer praying quietly at the back. For a moment, he realizes he came to Lundy with a head full of questions and he's going to leave with answers – but maybe not the ones he was looking for.

130

CAERGWYN CASTLE, WALES

Owain returns with his wife and Lance Beaucoup. To his surprise, Mitzi is stood trance-like by the far window.

'Lieutenant.' He raises his voice to get her attention. 'This is my wife, Jennifer, and my colleague Lance.'

She comes alive. 'I'm sorry, I was miles away.' She takes Lady Gwyn's hand. 'Mitzi Fallon.'

Jennifer adds a reassuring hand to the one being shaken by the detective. 'You must be worried sick; let's sit together and talk awhile.'

Owain drifts towards the door as his wife comforts Mitzi. 'Please forgive me; I have a call in the office that I have to take.'

The ambassador returns to his study where George Dalton is on the phone, talking to Gareth Madoc in New York.

'Owain is here,' says the consul. 'I'll put you on speakerphone.'

The ambassador sits in his desk chair. 'Gareth.'

Madoc comes straight to the point. 'Khalid Korshidi has just met with Ali bin al-Shibh.'

'Bin al-Shibh in America?' Owain instantly pictures the man tipped to lead al-Qaeda one day. 'You're sure about this?'

'He mentioned the CIA black site that he was held at en route to Guantanamo. The voice and facial match we've run came back with one hundred per cent confirmation.'

'A creature like this doesn't crawl out from under the rocks unless there's a major target.'

'Three targets,' says Lance. 'Hence the code word Trinity. He's running Yousef Mousavi and Nabil in the US and no doubt someone else, someplace else.'

'Any idea where?'

'No. He only mentioned the US, but he confirmed dates.'

Owain hopes he's wrong, 'Tomorrow?'

'Yes.'

'Timings?'

'No. We didn't get that lucky.'

'Any sense of whether they are fixed for the same day, same hour, or consecutive days?'

'Afraid not.'

'Damn.' He tries to look beyond his frustration. 'What's Korshidi's role?'

'He's a bigger player than we thought. Part of the smart new regime that al-Zawahiri constructed post-bin Laden. Seems he's handling all the publicity because right now he's unfurling banners and is preparing to shoot a video message with al-Shibh.'

'Can we intercept the upload?'

'Better than that. We have eyes and ears in the room – we'll be able to see it being recorded.'

Owain gives Dalton a look that shows how impressed he is. 'We're going to have to share this intel with the Americans. I suspect Mardrid's money is behind all this. As soon as you have the tape and some more solid information I'll contact Ron Briars at the NIA and give him the heads-up.'

'Understood.' Madoc focuses on the video feed fizzing into life on a monitor at his desk. 'Looks like we're in "go mode" here. I'll get back to you shortly.'

The line drops.

Owain kills the speakerphone and turns to Dalton. 'Three separate attacks, all within the next twenty-four hours. What do you think?'

'Unusual but not impossible. Did you see the matrix of VIP movements that the Watch Team put together for you?'

'I did.' The ambassador pulls it up on his computer screen. 'I spent much of the early hours of this morning looking at it and narrowing it down.'

The consul gives his opinion. 'The most obvious hit seems to be the new Pope. The pontiff has long been a moving target for all manner of groups and individuals, but with no ultimate success.'

Gwyn remembers Paul VI almost being stabbed by a Bolivian artist, John Paul II being shot in St Peter's Square and Benedict, the last Pope, being attacked during Mass on Christmas Eve. 'I see your point, George, but you know as well as I do that papal security is so tight that tomorrow when the Holy Father visits Wales he will undoubtedly be the most protected man on the planet.'

'Maybe they'll go for the old Pope *and* the new one?'

'That's a terrifying thought.' Owain pictures the security inside the Vatican. 'Benedict is well protected in retirement by the Swiss Guard, but I shall talk to them and flag the possibility.'

Dalton's thoughts have moved on. 'What about the US president? He's always a target.'

Owain remembers the matrix. 'He is in New York tomorrow at a fundraising concert for those affected by floods and hurricanes. Give me a third target.'

'God's banker,' says Dalton. 'Marco Ponti. The newly appointed CEO of the Vatican Bank will be holding his first board meeting with a committee of cardinals in Rome. Compared to the Popes and the president, he's a soft target, but high-profile enough to be on a hit list.'

Owain pulls a face. 'Why kill the Vatican banker *and* two Popes? The statement that all Christians are evil isn't enhanced by shooting a banker. Nor, come to think of it, does the US president fit into a true religious trilogy.'

He's about to re-examine the Watch Team's list when the study door opens and his wife walks in.

Jennifer sees he is worried and is sorry that she has to add to it. 'The policewoman – she's taking another call from the kidnappers.'

131

Mitzi leans over a desk, pen in hand, notepad just below it. 'I'm listening.'

The voice on the other end of the phone is the one she's heard before. Male. Deep in tone. Electronically slowed down and distorted. 'Do you have the files?'

There's no hesitation in her answer. 'Yes.'

'Good. Be in Borough High Street, Southwark by seven. Come alone. And be in no doubt: we will know if anyone is with you.'

Owain and his wife enter the room as she scribbles down the instruction. 'I need to speak to my girls.'

There's the sound of the phone being put down. Movement away from the receiver.

'Mom, I'm all right.'

The sweet pain of hearing Jade's voice sucks the air from Mitzi's lungs.

'They haven't hurt me. I'm all right, Mom.'

'Baby, it's all going to be okay.' She feels tears sting her eyes. 'Honey—'

There's a click and the kidnapper is back on the line. 'Be there and have your phone on, or it will be the last time you'll hear her.'

'Amber.' Mitzi shouts the name out. 'I talk to Amber, or there's no deal.'

A distorted laugh rolls down the line. 'You don't say what happens.'

Mitzi digs deep, finds the courage she's looking for and cuts the kidnapper off.

She feels herself shake.

An antique clock ticks twice in the heavy silence. Mitzi realizes she's holding her breath and lets out a long sigh.

The phone rings.

She answers in a split-second. 'Fallon.'

A young girl's scream can be heard. It's long and piercing. The cry isn't of someone frightened. It's of pain. Mitzi's eyes tear up as the scream becomes muffled. It's followed by the sound of someone being dragged away. Then, the noise of a chair being knocked over.

'M–om,' Amber's voice fills the line. It's broken, weak, barely audible. 'They've c–ut me – Mommy!'

The phone goes dead.

Mitzi feels the world sway. Her stomach turns. She grabs the waste paper basket beside the desk and throws up.

Jennifer rushes to her side. Owain pours a glass of water for Mitzi and gives it to his wife. He stands back and waits until the American has composed herself, then he pulls a chair up close. 'Are you okay?'

Mitzi takes a tissue from Jennifer. 'I'm sorry for the mess.'

'No reason to apologize. We have to talk about what to do now, how to respond to them.'

'I know.' She wipes her eyes and nose.

'I presume you intend to give up the memory stick. Do you have it with you, or is it somewhere else?'

'It's with me. Very much with me.'

'What do you mean "very much"?'

'It was small enough for me to do what drug mules do. I swallowed it. They want the stick, they're going to have to take me as well.'

132

NEW YORK

Ali bin al-Shibh bears more than a passing resemblance to the late Osama bin Mohammed bin Awad bin Laden, his hero. He's every inch as tall and equally thin. His facial features are so similar that there is speculation that the thirty-five-year-old is one of the terrorist's twenty-plus children.

As he stands in Khalid Korshidi's back room and wraps a white turban around his head, he looks exactly as he intends to – a chilling reincarnation of al-Qaeda's founder.

'I am ready,' he announces with a final adjustment of the headpiece.

'Please, take the seat.' Korshidi guides the bearded leader to a stool in front of a cloudy backdrop of male faces, what the terror group calls 'The Martyr's Wall'. It includes bin Laden, his former number two Saeed al-Shihri and renowned propagandist Samir Khan, who was killed in a US drone strike.

'I'll only be a moment.' Korshidi adjusts small portable lights and returns to the digital camera he's mounted on a tripod. He puts on a pair of headphones, lifts the sound level a little and hits a button. 'The camera is recording.'

Bin al-Shibh's eyes close. His head tilts down and hands raise in adulation as he starts his message. 'All praise is due to Allah, who built the heavens and earth in justice, and created man as a favour and grace from Him. And from His Law is retaliation in kind: an eye for an eye, a tooth for a tooth and the killer is killed.'

The terrorist sits straight and his dark eyes burn into the centre of the lens. 'People of the West, of capitalism, of false gods, of evil, you were warned. You were offered the Solution and you ignored it. Islam opened its doors and you turned away. You were given chances to avoid unwinnable wars and still you spilled the blood of our children. With it dripping from your infidel hands, you asked your priests to celebrate your innocence and heroism. The wise among you must have known that a Day of Reckoning was coming.'

The camera shot tightens and his bold eyes dominate the frame. 'Al-Qaeda is the Reckoning. We are sent by Allah to destroy your false gods and false lives.' The aggression dies from his face. 'Take up the Koran, turn your backs on the Catholics and Jews and their lies about the Prophet of Allah Jesus. Do this and you will be saved. All praise is due to Allah, who awakened His slaves' desire for the Garden, and all of them will enter it except those who refuse. Whoever obeys Him alone in all of his affairs will enter the Garden. Whoever disobeys Him will have refused and will perish.'

He lowers his hands and locks his eyes on the lens. 'You

were warned. You have been punished and will be punished again.'

133

FBI HQ, SAN FRANCISCO

Beam and his team pull together their basic Child Abduction Response Plan. While Helena Banks works on a psychological profile of the kidnappers, she has a geographical analyst map out the most likely exit routes from Ruth's house.

Kay Podboj, a bright young academic fresh from Quantico, has been studying mileage, terrain and the location of airports and seaports. She approaches her boss's desk with a folder full of aerial photographs and a face that says the early findings aren't good.

Helena looks up from her own jottings and recognizes the signs. 'That bad?'

'Maybe worse.' She spreads out the shots. 'The Everett ranch is in a prime position. Must have cost a fortune. It's remote but within striking distance of all major roads. They could have gone anywhere.'

'Show me the most likely anywheres.'

'Here.' She fingers the first photograph. 'The San Mateo Bridge is five miles away and on the other side is five thousand acres of the Eden Landing Ecological Reserve.'

'Isn't that just salt ponds?'

'Mainly, but a whole lot of reclamation work's been done. There are plenty of places to hide and miles of airstrips to fly from.'

Helena shakes her head. 'I don't think they've flown. Not yet.'

'I agree. They could be out at West Waddell Creek State Wilderness. It's an hour from the snatch point and has six thousand acres of dense redwood and Douglas fir to give them good cover.' She glances at a map on the wall. 'An hour would also get them out to Napa.'

'Jesus.'

'Yep, the Lord himself and all his disciples could hide out there and never be found. It's eighteen square miles of sparsely populated valley. South is bad. Within two hours they could have reached Austin Creek.'

'How big's that?'

Kay looks at the map again. 'More than twenty miles of countryside, with camp sites and remote cabins all over the place. The girls were taken late at night, right?'

'Not so late. We guess between nine and ten. They'd come back from a day at the aquarium. Their aunt had been clearing up after dinner and they were outside playing a board game when the unsub pulled up.'

'Okay. My point is this – the kidnappers did the pro thing. They knew within an hour of the snatch they'd have cover of darkness, meaning they could drive further in a shorter period of time because there's less traffic and fewer cops on the road.

There are also fewer night flights and they would know that the authorities would be able to quickly search overnight manifests for planes leaving California.'

'I buy all that, but so what?'

'Well, driving far at night means you have to know where you're going and you must already have a place to go to. One owned or rented.'

'Not owned,' insists Helena. 'They wouldn't mess on their home lawn.'

'So, we're looking for a rented safe house, lodge or cabin somewhere out in the wilds. Ideally, they'd go for something a good hour from the ranch but not too far from an airport.'

Helena nods. 'I agree. Once this is finished, they are going to fly. Possibly out of the country rather than just the State.'

Kay taps several of the pictures in front of her boss. 'Then for me, the most likely exit airports are Oakland, Half Moon and San Fran International.'

Helena makes the first cut. 'I'd rule out Half Moon. There are a lot of private planes and hangars there, but the coast guard, air ambulance and Medevac also fly from that old strip and I think the local sheriff as well.'

'That leaves San Fran and Oakland.'

The psychologist crosses to the map on the wall. Oakland sits almost directly across the Bay from San Fran and she knows in recent years it's become a booming airport with hundreds of flights per day across the States, Mexico and Europe. 'Let's start here,' she says decisively. 'Give me a geo profile on where the kidnappers would hide out in this area.

I'm going to recommend to Beam that this is where we centre our resources.'

134

SSOA OFFICES, NEW YORK

Gareth Madoc watches a replay of the al-Qaeda footage in the office of Troy Hemmings, the chief analyst from the SSOA's North American Watch Team.

The former Harvard graduate is a thoughtful, bespectacled man who always wears a white shirt under a brown or black jumper and matching slacks. Today is a brown day and he crosses his suede shoes under his desk as he hits pause on the remote control in his hands.

'Well?' Madoc is anxious for his expert opinion.

'It's interesting for three reasons. First, it is Ali bin al-Shibh saying this and not al-Zawahiri. It means there must have been some power shift, otherwise Ayman would have been making this keynote, not one of his more promising lieutenants.'

'Maybe al-Zawahiri is trying to take more of a back seat. He's old now and perhaps recognizes the need to have a younger man front the organization.'

Hemmings nods. 'That's very possible. He's extremely bright and undoubtedly was the brains behind bin Laden.'

'But is al-Shibh really ready to step up?'

The analyst takes a second before answering. 'Yes, I think so, especially with Ayman al-Zawahiri and other grey beards behind him. Mokhtar Belmokhtar was expected to fill that void, but he got killed in Mali.'

'Old one-eye was a good hit.'

'Certainly was. Did you recognize anything familiar about the opening and closing of al-Shibh's speech?'

'Educate me.'

'Back in oh-seven, on the sixth anniversary of the 9/11 attacks, bin Laden released a video entitled *The Solution*. It was a long message made directly to the American public. He told them to abandon capitalism, condemn their government for military involvement in Iraq and Afghanistan and cleanse themselves by joining Islam.' Hemmings points to the freeze frame of al-Shibh on the monitor. 'This guy opened and closed with almost verbatim quotes from that speech. Just as Obama borrowed from Kennedy, he's borrowed from bin Laden.'

'So you think al-Shibh is being cast as the new bin Laden?'

'That's what it seems like to me.' He warms to his theory. 'This address of his is *very* clever. It's going to win the support of the old guard as well as new recruits. If al-Shibh's Trinity operation is successful this video will signal the resurrection of al-Qaeda.'

It's not a thought that sits well with Madoc. 'You said there were three reasons why this speech is important. I'm hoping the third is a clue to where any impending attacks might be.'

'It could be. I'd like to watch it a few more times before giving you a definite answer, but it seems to me that post the appointment of a new and more likeable Pope they're turning their anger on religious leaders and intend to make them targets rather than government buildings or members of the public.'

'What about the attacks on Grand Central and the Eurostar?'

'Distractions. Attention-grabbing distractions that are merely steps towards the big event, the one that will be most historically remembered.'

The SSOA leader is sceptical. 'How can you be so sure?'

'I can't, Gareth. I can't ever be *sure*. But look at the speech. It was full of religious references. Praise for Allah. Condemnation for those who turned their backs on Islam. Reminders of old sayings such as "an eye for an eye" and "kill the killer". At least twice he mentioned the worshippers of false gods and then there was that plea for people to turn their backs on the Catholics and Jews and all the lies about the Prophet Jesus.'

The analyst clears the video from his computer screen and types a command in a search box. 'And don't forget this.' He leans back so his boss can see.

A folder marked 'Fatwa' appears on screen and out of it comes a document entitled 'World Islamic Front Against Jews and Crusaders'.

'This was published under bin Laden's name,' says Hemmings, 'but everyone knows Zawahiri was the author, just as they know no other terrorist on the planet has launched as many successful assassinations and terror attacks as he has.' He turns to Madoc. 'Al-Shibh is following in his footsteps. He's restarting an age-old war – the Holy War.'

135

LONDON

Sir Owain's helicopter flies him, Mitzi and George Dalton to London. They pick up the south bank of the Thames around West Kensington and follow it down to a private helipad east of Vauxhall.

A black cab takes them the final three miles to Southwark. The taxi and the two nondescript cars in front and behind it are all owned and manned by members of the SSOA.

Mitzi barely speaks as they head past the Elephant and Castle roundabout and down the A3 for the final part of the journey. Her mind is filled with the sharp sound of Amber's screams. She plays nervously with the thin silver chain around her neck and the steel Rolex pinching her wrist. Both pieces of jewellery contain hidden microphones, receivers and tracking devices. Further trackers are concealed in her silver stud earrings and the heels of both shoes.

Dalton is sat next to her in the back of the cab. Owain is on a flip-down seat opposite them and is keen to settle her nerves. 'George and I will get out in a moment and the cab will drive to the middle of the High Street and park. Stay inside until they call you. Don't forget to 'pay' the driver when you get out – they may be watching. The cab will go and wait around the corner and be ready to collect you.'

She nods hesitantly.

'Remember, we have a lot of good people already out walking this street or sat in cars. There's no way you'll ever be out of our sight.'

'Thanks.'

He turns and talks to the driver. 'Colin, pull over when you can; we need to be on foot.'

The cabbie indicates left and slides the old black taxi into a bus stop.

Mitzi watches the two men get out. They shut the door, shake hands and part like friends going separate ways.

Two minutes later, the cab is drawing to a halt again. Mitzi checks her phone for what must be the hundredth time. It's on. Fully charged. The mute button hasn't accidentally been pressed. She hasn't missed a call.

Seven o'clock comes and goes.

So does ten past.

And twenty past.

Five minutes later it rings.

'Fallon.'

The distorted male voice gives her a simple instruction: 'The George Pub – walk through every room. We will find you.'

136

FBI HQ, SAN FRANCISCO

Bob Beam, Damon Spinks and Eleonora Fracci are studying a 3D map on a wall monitor in the briefing room. They look away as Helena Banks walks in and takes a seat at the long table.

Beam explains that he thinks the search should concentrate on an area east of San Francisco Bay. 'This particular rectangle of dense forest lies within a forty-minute drive from the ranch where the girls were abducted.' He traces a hand across the monitor. 'The grid that's marked runs horizontal along the 580 from Castro Valley to Dublin, then vertical down the 650 from Dublin to Sunol, horizontal across the 84 to Niles, then up from Niles along the 238 back to Castro. It takes in a lot of public parks and places to hide. You've got Hayward Memorial, Pleasanton Ridge, Recreation, Garin and Dry Creek. That's more than a hundred square acres of land.'

Helena doesn't agree with his strategy. 'I think you're off. Concentrate the search there and you could make a big mistake.'

'Why?'

'Our geo profile suggests the kidnappers struck at night because they wanted to drive long, not short.'

'Makes sense,' says Eleonora. 'They are professionals so they would know to strike when people are most tired and law-enforcement resources are weakest.'

Helena continues, 'We estimate that they drove for a minimum of an hour. Which, if they went through the back roads, would take them up to Shepherd Canyon Park, or if they mixed freeway and minor roads they could get as far as Mount Diablo.'

Spinks looks pained. 'Diablo is what, twenty thousand acres?'

'At least,' confirms Helena. 'If you take into account the surrounding lands, you're closer to a hundred thousand.'

'And it's high,' says Beam, warming to the idea. 'Diablo is about three thousand feet above sea level. If you hole-up in a cabin out there you can see people coming for miles.'

'We like it because of Oakland,' adds Helena. 'Both Kay and I think Oakland is the chosen evac point. We believe that when it's over, they'll ignore San Fran International and try to get out from there.'

'How far is the airport from Diablo?' asks Eleonora.

'Forty miles. It'd take them about an hour to get there.'

Beam studies the map on the monitor and the original grid he'd marked out. It no longer seems as viable as it did. 'Okay, let's prioritize our actions in the area that Helena suggests. But listen, that *doesn't* mean we totally ignore anything that comes in pointing to other zones.'

'I've already asked for camera footage from San Mateo Bridge,' says Eleonora. 'And from Bay Bridge too, in case they took a scenic route.'

Spinks has a bonus for them. 'I called a friend running a helicopter flight business out at Camp Parks. He's promised to help out, under the cover of running tourist trips, so I'll give him locations near Diablo to scout.'

Beam checks his watch. 'We need to get moving. Let's have search teams briefed and out within the hour; I'll fix for some of our people to start searching for rentals – cars, lodges, houses and whatever else is out there. Everyone get praying; we need a break and need it quickly.'

137

LONDON

Mitzi hands over ten English pounds to the cab driver. She walks along Borough High Street and through large green gates announcing, 'The George – London's only surviving galleried coaching inn and the home of fine cask beers'.

The hostelry is a long three-storey building painted in white and black. Two of the upper storeys have wooden galleries from which dangle flower baskets. Mitzi passes over a large cobbled area filled with dozens of drinkers at rough wooden tables.

She enters through a side door near a sign showing St George slaying a dragon. People are squashed into a warren of tight downstairs rooms. The noise is so loud she's scared of not hearing her phone. She holds it up so she can see the flash of any incoming calls as she pushes her way through an old bar with hard bench seating into one that looks even older and less comfortable.

Both areas are brimming with either bemused tourists or drunken Londoners. Some have food on tables, others are stood drinking.

The next room is more modern – a long and bright bar of blonde wood, gleaming brass pumps and blackboards offering fresh food. The crowd hanging here looks more family orientated, with mums, dads and kids grabbing the best tables by the windows.

Her phone rings.

'Hello.'

No one answers.

'Damn!' Mitzi looks at it accusingly. Only two of those little signal lines. The reception must be bad.

She moves into a hallway to get better reception.

After five minutes and no call, she climbs a set of paint-chipped stairs to a series of uneven floors and private function rooms. Several people pass her. None have the alertness she'd expect of someone involved in a kidnapping.

By the time she finds the Gallery Bar, she's uncomfortably hot and orders a glass of mineral water with ice. While waiting, she hears tourists discussing how Shakespeare and Dickens used to drink here. Given how long it takes to be served she wonders if they're still around.

She takes her change and is dropping it in her purse when the phone rings again.

Mitzi almost drops her cash as she answers. 'Fallon!'

Again, there's no pick-up.

She scans the bar. No one is looking at her. The place is full of regular-looking thirty-somethings, a few business types and a group of young guys in the far corner. None of the waiters or waitresses is paying her any attention.

Mitzi tries to stay calm. She sips the drink at the bar. After ten minutes she starts walking again. Back downstairs, she puts her now-empty glass on a table and goes to the only place she's not yet visited.

The restroom.

It's cold and smells of damp plaster and cheap air freshener. She uses a stall, then washes her hands. The mirror above the sink gives a cruel reminder that her face is still bruised and her panda eyes now bloodshot.

She waits patiently for a thin brunette in black jeans, matching waistcoat and white T to finish drying her hands under a noisy wall-mounted blower.

Their eyes lock. Mitzi glances towards the door. An athletically built woman, mid-thirties with short blonde hair, has her back against it.

In her hand is a gun.

The brunette smiles, holds out a palm and waggles her fingers. 'Give me the memory stick.'

138

Owain Gwyn slides into the shadows of a thin passageway off the main street, just down from The George and takes the call. 'Gareth, I'm on foot and in public, is this urgent?'

'It is,' confirms Madoc. 'I've this minute sent you a digital file. It's of the al-Qaeda video that's just been shot.'

Owain watches a silver Mercedes halt near the pub entrance and two burly men slip out. 'Do we know the targets?'

'No. It was a revealing speech, but not in that kind of way. I had Hemmings watch and he thinks the main target is likely to be a religious leader.'

The men disappear into the pub but the Merc stays on double yellow lines, its hazard lights flashing.

'We've been over this. I'm not willing to approach the Vatican with a view to cancellation unless you can give me more specific intel.'

'I can't do that. Not at the moment.' On his desk monitor, Madoc sees al-Shibh thank Korshidi and prepare to leave the house where they've been filming. 'Our new friend is on the move, so I'm going to have to go. Before you dismiss the risk completely, please look at the recording and make your own mind up.'

'Okay, I will.' Owain watches the Mercedes pull away from the kerb and head down the street towards London Bridge. 'I'll find time in the next hour.' He glances at his watch. It's even later than he thought. 'The Pope is already in Wales, but his first public appearance isn't until the morning. If he's in danger, that's when any attack will come.'

139

LONDON

Mitzi ignores the big blonde with the gun and gets in the face of the wiry brunette by the row of basins. 'You ain't getting anything. Not until Amber's at a hospital being treated. Only when I know that, when I can call her and talk to her, do you get what you want.'

The brunette scowls. 'We're not here to negotiate.' She nods to the blonde guarding the door.

Mitzi feels the persuasive jab of a gun in her side. She smashes her left heel into the big woman's right knee, hooks a hand around the back of her neck and slams her head into the edge of a sink. There's a sickening thunk of skull bone on ceramic and Mitzi knows she's unconscious by the time she hits the floor.

The brunette thinks of grabbing the spilled gun.

'Go ahead,' says Mitzi. 'If I needed a weapon I'd have brought one.'

The bathroom door opens and two men appear. They're unmistakably 'muscle'.

'She's got a fractured skull.' Mitzi nods to the comatose woman. 'I heard it pop. Best get her to a hospital before the brain bleed's too bad.'

The brunette turns cardiac-red. She grabs the gun and points it with shaking hands. 'Now give me the stick, you fucking bitch.'

'Calm down, honey.' Mitzi raises her hands. 'Things are already screwed here. You've gotta get some focus.'

'Give me the fucking stick!' She pushes the gun towards her.

'You want it, lady – you're going to have to pick it outta my poop.'

The brunette looks lost.

'I swallowed it.'

One of the guys smiles, steps forward and grabs her hands. He loops a plastic tie around her wrists and pulls it skin-nipping tight.

Mitzi goes with the flow.

The other muscle drapes his sweatshirt over her hands to conceal the cuffs, then bends over the injured blonde. 'She's totally out of it. I'll do what I can and follow in a minute. Take the mouthy bitch to the water and don't wait for me.'

140

LONDON

Owain and Dalton are sat in the cab monitoring developments via the pendant microphone around Mitzi's neck.

'We've got boats on the Thames,' says Dalton. 'Both east and west of London Bridge pier.' He taps on the glass screen dividing them and the driver. 'Colin, get off the High Street and head down to the Thames; they're moving her. I can hear street noise – they must be coming outside.'

Owain stares through the front windshield as the cab pulls into the traffic. 'It's about a third of a mile from the pub to the pier – they could walk that in less than five minutes. If you see a silver Mercedes on last year's plates, it could be a follow car.'

'Got it.'

'My money is on them going east.' Dalton follows a signal from Mitzi's tracker on a laptop map of London. 'Over here,' he points to the right of the screen, 'near the Millennium Dome.'

Owain isn't convinced. 'Maybe.'

The consul presses his case. 'There's a lot of open land and unused buildings down there. Remember, Mardrid's company bought into the post-Olympic regeneration boom.'

'I know, but he also owns properties around Chelsea Harbour, Battersea Park and Kew Gardens.' As he talks,

Owain dials the operations room at Caergwyn Castle. 'Lance – Fallon is on the move. Do you have a visual on her?'

Beaucoup is sat in front of a bank of monitors showing feeds from cameras in cars, people on foot and a helicopter hovering high over the river. 'Eye in the sky has got her. She's with one man and a woman almost at London Bridge pier. They're side by side and she has something over her hands, probably to cover some cuffs. I can see a small boat moored there.'

'What kind of boat?' asks Dalton.

He squints at the screen. 'Six or eight berth, built more for speed than cruising.' He recognizes it now. 'It's the same type the marine police use, a twin-engine Targa capable of thirty to forty knots.'

'What have we got on the water?' asks Owain.

'We have a big water slug of a canal boat, fully spec'd with operational equipment and rescue team. And a Hustler Rockit with twin Mercuries that will clear a hundred knots in the blink of an eye.'

'Only use the Hustler as a last resort. Once that thing cuts a wave, we'll have river police all over us. Let's take this one nice and slow. How are we doing on the American side?'

'The FBI are all over Fallon's sister's ranch in San Mateo. They sent agents out there disguised as maintenance men and I'm told they've done a full forensic search but have no fingerprint or DNA matches with known criminals.'

'Hardly a surprise,' says Owain. 'This is the work of top-end pros, the kind with no previous—'

'Marchetti!' shouts Beaucoup. 'I just saw Angelo Marchetti on the pier. He's with a party that got off the boat.'

141

SAN RAMON, CALIFORNIA

Mount Diablo fills the rear-view mirror as Eleonora Fracci parks her Chrysler Crossfire in the lot of a small mall. She's working her way through a list of people who paid cash on short, last-minute holiday lets and car rentals.

In front of her is a spread of fast-food joints, nail parlours, a grocery store, upmarket Chinese restaurant and a bar.

It's the bar she's interested in. That and the two guys twenty yards ahead of her who just disappeared inside.

An hour ago, Eleonora had driven past one of the target properties and seen a hulk of a man arguing with a woman in her thirties. He got to the point where he was done shouting and decided a punch would win the argument for him.

Eleonora had wanted to stamp on the brakes, get out and teach him a painful lesson. Only she would have blown her cover. While she was waiting and cursing, two more men came out of the rundown old shack and pulled the big guy and the battered woman inside.

The Italian was left looking at what was on the driveway and is now on the lot. A People Carrier with blacked-out windows. Perfect for four adults and a couple of teenage girls.

Eleonora waits until Mitch Conway, her assigned backup pulls up in his Chevy. She tosses her jacket in the back of the Crossfire and heads inside.

The bar is dark and moody. There's a long slab of hardwood with saloon-style mirrors and shelves behind it. Neon signs on the wall advertise Bud. A jukebox plays country.

'Mineral water,' she says to a middle-aged bartend.

'Yes, *ma'am.*' His eyes register his interest in her shapely figure. 'You want anything to eat? We got the best chicken in the valley.'

Her smile says she's going to pass on that.

Eleonora takes her BlackBerry out and busies herself with mail. At least that's what she hopes it looks like to the two guys on stools a few feet away. Without looking up, she knows their eyes are all over her.

The door opens, light spills in and she hears Mitch order a beer and ask where the washroom is.

The bartend puts down her drink. 'You don't want the chicken, I'm sure we could do something special for you.'

The comment is enough to prompt the woman-punching hulk into joining in. 'Pretty sure *I* could do something very special for you, honeycakes.'

His friend laughs.

Eleonora puts her phone down. 'No food thanks, I'm just waiting for a girlfriend.'

Hulk hitches his stool towards her. 'I'm Jake and this here is Randy.'

His buddy chimes in. 'You know what they say, Randy by name . . . '

'You guys local?' she asks.

'Hell no,' says Jake. 'We're from Fresno. Just come over for some fun.'

She sips her water and leaves her lips glisteningly wet. 'What kind of fun?'

Jake's eyes turn greedy. ''Bout any kind we can get.'

Eleonora leans back and blatantly checks him out. 'And what do you big, muscled men do for a living?'

'Meat packers.' He nods to his colleague. 'Randy here is about to open his own business.'

'Love to show you *my* meat sometime.' He breaks out laughing again.

She's heard and seen enough. Professional criminals don't pick up women in the middle of a job. Nor do they *not* wear watches. Jake has the sleeves of his checked shirt rolled up and his arms are tanned, with no sign of a timepiece ever being around any wrist. But both him and his jerkoff buddy have marks on their fingers where their wedding bands were. Most likely, they're away on a boys' holiday. Hunting, shooting, fishing and whatever else they can get. The woman she saw was probably a hooker, stupid enough to grab their cash and get passed around.

Eleonora takes a final sip of her mineral water and puts a five-dollar bill down to settle the tab. 'Sorry, guys. I have to go.'

'Hey, not so quick, babe.' Jake grabs her arm as she gets up.

'Get your hand off me.'

He doesn't take the hint. 'C'mon, sit down baby.'

She pulls her arm but he holds tight.

Eleonora smashes an elbow into his face.

He grabs his broken cheekbone and lets go of her.

She snags the barstool and pulls it from under him.

Hulk hits the floor spine first.

She slips out her gun and trains it on him. 'Follow me outside and I'll kill you. And if I ever see or hear of you hurting another woman, then I'll find you and break more than just your face.'

142

LONDON

Armed men hustle Mitzi off the quay and along the back of the bobbing boat. They squeeze her into a covered cabin and force her to sit on a narrow padded bench.

Through a window, she sees a young blonde man in a red T-shirt pull a thick rope back down onto the decking. The craft's noisy engine coughs into life. The floor vibrates and the Targa pulls out into the choppy grey river.

A good-looking man with trimmed beard and long black hair comes into the cabin and sits on the bench opposite. He unfastens the jacket of his shiny blue suit and smiles at her. 'Welcome on board, Mrs Fallon.' He stretches his hand out and rips the silver necklace from around her neck. 'A woman like you shouldn't wear such cheap jewellery. Earrings too. Glad I didn't miss those.' He grabs both studs and forces them out.

Mitzi yelps as her flesh tears.

Marchetti grabs her wrist and unfastens her watch. He opens the back door of the boat and throws everything into the inky water. 'That's better.'

He returns to the bench and looks towards his men. 'Someone give me a blade.'

Mitzi watches one of the thugs produce a knife for gutting fish.

Marchetti takes it and nods towards the brunette. 'My friend here tells me you've swallowed the digital files. So why don't I just use this lovely piece of steel, cut you up like a tuna and take it out your guts?'

Mitzi doesn't flinch. 'Because of the mights.'

He screws up his eyes. 'The what?'

'I *might* be telling the truth and *might* have swallowed it. Or, I *might* have stored it or mailed it somewhere. Kill me and you've only got a fifty per cent chance of being right. Release Amber, let her get treatment at a hospital, and I *promise* I'll tell you the truth.'

'You *promise*.' He laughs, then lunges forward and stabs the tip of the blade under her right collarbone.

This time she can't hold the scream back.

Marchetti keeps the steel wedged there. Far enough in to cause excruciating pain but not so deep as to start a fatal bleed. 'Give me the stick!'

Shock hammers her chest.

'Give it me!'

She stares through him.

Marchetti pulls back the blade and punches her face.

Mitzi feels her already damaged nose break again. Blood rushes through her nostrils. Lightning flashes in her head. The boat lurches to the right and she doesn't have the strength to stop herself falling to the floor.

The boards smell of teak oil and soap. That's the last thing she remembers before she blacks out.

PART FOUR

143

LONDON

As the waves of unconsciousness ebb away Mitzi feels a burn in her right shoulder where she'd been stabbed. Any deeper and she'd have bled out. There's a dull pulse in the centre of her face where her nose has been re-broken. But it doesn't feel as agonizing as it should. She guesses they've given her a shot of something.

Even without opening her eyes, she knows her hands are tied behind her back and she's sat upright on a hard metal chair, the kind that folds up and can be easily moved. Her ankles have been bound and the lack of sway means she's no longer on the boat. She guesses the shot was a sedative that kept her quiet while they moved her from the river.

In the blackness beyond her closed eyes, she hears a woman cough. It's probably the brunette and there's no doubt at least one man with her as well.

She smells fresh cigarette smoke and sawdust. The air on her face is cool but not cold. From the way sounds come and go, she believes she's in a medium-sized room rather than a big open space like a warehouse.

'You want tea?' asks the woman.

A man answers. 'Yeah, if you're making.'

Heels clack across bare boards. Tap water spurts then pounds the metal of a kettle. An electric switch clicks. Mitzi guesses they're in a private house, office or apartment that is still being built, decorated or renovated.

'No milk, that okay?'

'You got sugar?'

'Yeah.'

'Then three sugars to make up for it being black.'

Mitzi keeps her eyes closed and counts her blessings. They haven't killed her. Her daughters must still be alive. She's still figuring out the significance of them moving her, when she hears a door click open and a man speak. 'She should be awake by now.'

The voice is that of the man with the knife. Mitzi hears him walk towards her. She braces herself.

He puts a hand across her mouth and pinches her nose to block off the airway.

She splutters for breath and finally opens her eyes.

Marchetti squats so he is on her level. 'Hello again.'

Mitzi looks beyond him. The room is an apartment; she was right about that. The lights are on, meaning it's night-time. The place has been freshly plastered. There are dust covers everywhere. Sawn floorboards. Tins of emulsion and gloss paint are stacked in a corner.

'Any idea what this is?' Marchetti holds a black baton-like object in his hand.

She focuses on it. 'A metal detector.'

'Clever girl.' He steps back. 'Get her up.' He hands the security wand to the brunette. 'Check her out.'

The muscular guy pulls Mitzi off the chair. 'Spread your legs.' He laughs. 'I bet it's a while since someone said that to you.'

'Get on with it,' shouts Marchetti.

The brunette turns on the scanner and runs it up the inside of Mitzi's legs.

'Her stomach,' booms Marchetti. 'For God's sake, it's going to be in her stomach or bowels, not her thighs.'

The woman reddens and switches the paddle to the torso. She moves it slowly and gets a beep off Mitzi's belt. The muscle unfastens it and pulls it from the loops around her slacks. He unclips the top stud, pulls down the zip and rips open her shirt. The brunette moves the paddle over bare flesh and down to one side, where she gets another beep.

'Well, well, well.' Marchetti sounds pleased. 'Seems you might be telling the truth after all.' He turns to the muscle. 'Sit her back down.'

Mitzi watches him walk out of her line of sight. 'Like I said, release Amber and I won't leave you in any doubt about whether what's in my guts is what you want, or just a blank stick.'

'Clever,' he shouts. 'It buys you a little more time because you know I have to check it and therefore I won't just slice you open.' She hears him running water, then he appears with a mug and passes it to the brunette. 'Hold this until I'm ready.' He pulls open a box of tablets, tosses the cardboard and pops out all the pills from the two metal foils. His eyes light up as he looks at Mitzi. 'This is going to be messy.' He grabs her hair and pulls her head back. 'Open your mouth.'

She keeps it closed.

He chops his fist on her broken nose.

Mitzi screams in pain.

Marchetti forces the laxatives through her teeth and keeps her head tilted back. 'Water!'

The brunette pours the contents of the mug into her mouth. Mitzi gags. Tries to spit the tablets out.

Marchetti holds his hand over her mouth until she swallows. Mitzi hangs her head forward and wheezes for breath. Marchetti yanks her head back again and forces another handful of tablets over her tongue. This time she doesn't have the air or willpower to fight. As soon as the water hits her lips, she starts to swallow.

He wipes his wet hand on her and walks away. As he reaches the door, he calls back to his minions. 'Put her in the closet so she doesn't make too much mess.'

144

LONDON

The laptop on George Dalton's knees shows video feeds from the helmet cameras of the armed response units on the barge on the Thames.

The big old slug of a boat has crawled up to the quayside and moored below the approach to the select development where Mitzi Fallon is being held.

'Tac response is ready.' He turns to Owain: 'We're getting parabolic microphones trained on the building, we should have audio any minute.'

'Good. Keep the men on standby,' says Owain. 'We have to maximize the chance of getting to the girls before they go in.' He calls Madoc to catch up on developments across the Atlantic.

'Gareth, can you speak?'

'Not for long.'

'How are we doing on finding the Fallon kids?'

'Ross Green and Eve Garrett have identified some suspects. They're pro teams that Marchetti or Mardrid are indirectly linked to. We need time to get a fix on where they are right now.'

'Time is the one thing we don't have.'

'I know. I've got six tac teams out in the Bay area, spread both sides of the water, but it's a big space. To be honest, without top-notch intel on faces and places, we're going to draw a blank.'

Owain has already contemplated that bleak outcome. 'If it goes badly, Gareth, I don't want these animals leaving California in anything but a box.'

'Understood. Is there anything else?'

'There is. I've decided we can't let al-Shibh and his followers run until the morning.'

Madoc winces. 'We have a really good chance of identifying all the key members of this reconstructed cell.'

'I realize that, but without knowing who their target is, let alone the location and time of the attack, it's a risk we can't afford to take.'

'I just need a little more time. Let it run until al-Shibh takes us to wherever he's going to lay his head tonight.'

Owain stands firm. 'We can't. I'm sorry.'

Madoc blows out a long sigh but doesn't argue. 'Okay. How do you want to play it? You going to call Ron Briers at the NIA?'

He wants to soften the disappointment to him. 'Do you have someone on your "Tried and Trusted" list who you'd like to give a boost to?'

'Yes, I do. Several people.'

'Then you call it in. Always good to help those on the way up.'

'Thanks, I appreciate that.'

'No need. Just make that call to your guy and make it soon.'

'Will do.'

Owain turns off the phone.

'We've got sound,' says Dalton. 'It's muffled but I can hear Fallon. She sounds in a bad way.'

145

LONDON

The brunette spreads newspaper on the floor of the built-in closet. Her muscled friend strips Mitzi waist down, throws her into the space and shuts the sliding doors.

Being treated like a dog hurts almost as much as her busted nose and wounded shoulder. Gradually comes the added grief of extreme stomach cramps caused by the pills. Mitzi suffers in silence for as long as she can, then shouts through the blackness, 'You guys best get me to a john. And quick.'

There's a bang on the doors and the muscle shouts back, 'You just do your mess in there, little doggie, and hurry the fuck up.' He gives the wood a kick as he steps away.

Mitzi feels lower than low. Time is running out. She shifts sides to try to release the growing cramps. In the blackness she remembers the words of the strange old man at Caergwyn Castle. In her weakest moments she's capable of the most amazing things.

Pain drains from her wounds and stomach. The thumping

in her head stops. She's able to distance herself from the torture, slip through an imaginary trapdoor and hide away and grow strong.

Mitzi pictures her babies. Remembers them being handed to her in the hospital bed. The soft touch of their faces. The wonder of kissing their cheeks for the first time. The surge of protective, maternal love. A love so strong she'd kill if she had to.

The closet doors slide open. She blinks as light floods her space.

The brunette puts her hand to her mouth and looks like she's going to be sick. 'Oh my God, what a fucking mess.'

Mitzi feels no shame. No embarrassment. Whatever happens next, she won't give in. Won't give up. Won't let her girls down.

146

NEW YORK

Joe Steffani of the NIA recognizes the incoming number on his desk phone and picks up straight away. 'Let me guess,' he says in his Bronx accent, 'you're calling to keep me from my kids and you're gonna ruin my evening?'

'Ruin it or *make* it?' says Gareth Madoc. 'Depends how you interpret the news I'm about to give you.'

'Ha freakin' ha. So, what exactly have you got for me, my strangely well-informed foreign friend?'

'Ali bin al-Shibh.'

'Shut the fuck up.'

'Seriously. He is here in New York.'

Joe feels his stomach flip. 'You sure of this? You got eyes on him or something?'

'Eyes and ears. We're so close we could floss his pearly whites.'

The NIA man grows suspicious. 'Why?'

'*Why* doesn't matter. He just recorded a video message in the home of a senior mosque figure; now he's in a car with a couple of bodyguards heading to JFK. Once he's there, I guess he'll go to a private hangar and vanish.'

'Motherfucker.' He pulls his jacket off the back of his chair. 'You got hook-ups for me?'

'Will have by the time you've called a team together. You'll need other units too. At least four. We've got tails on the cell's bomber, commander and associates.'

'Jeez! You and your cowboys have been keeping things from us, Gareth. Naughty, naughty.'

'I consider myself told off. Once you're up and running we need to talk face-to-face.'

'You bet your ass we do.'

Madoc hangs up. A screen on his desk shows Zachra Korshidi re-entering the place she calls home. He hopes to God that when everything starts happening he can get her out of there, alive.

147

FBI HQ, SAN FRANCISCO

CARDT psychologist Helena Banks opens the door of her boss's office. 'You got a minute?'

'That's all I've got.' Bob Beam waves to a chair. 'I just heard from Spinks. He struck out in Walnut Creek. The single guy who hired the big shack came up kosher. Turns out he'd split from his wife but still went to the cabin he'd rented for her and their three kids. He'd figured he'd paid for it so he might as well use it.'

'Should have sub-let it,' says Helena. 'He'll need all the dough he can get for maintenance. I've been thinking about vehicles.'

'Go on.'

'We talked again to Ruth Everett and she said she saw a sedan at the bottom of her drive. It was part of why she bought into the woman's story about being alone and broken down.'

'We went through this.' He pulls a file from a tray stack on his desk. 'Only two dozen single women renting sedans in the last week and they all paid by credit cards.'

'I know. But I had research run rentals again and guess what, we have a guy who rented an RV at San Fran International and also a sedan in San Mateo.'

Beam feels his heart jump. 'You got a name and address?'

She puts a yellow Stick-It on his desk. 'Chris Wilkins, married man, has a business in LA.'

He peels off the paper. 'Name and address check out?'

'Yep. He exists. So does his business. House isn't his though – it's rented and the company is a mom-and-pop affair on an industrial estate. Type you could walk away from in a blink.'

'Record?'

'None.'

'Wife?'

'Teresa. Tess.'

'You got a picture of him or his lady?'

'Not yet. We're pulling some from licensing and Homeland Security.'

'Rap sheets?'

'None. Not so much as a write-up for speeding.'

Beam goes back to the root of what he guesses sparked her interest. 'Why would someone hire a sedan and an RV?'

'Unusual but not unheard of,' answers Helena. 'RVs are good accommodation but only crawl and are hell to park. Sedans get you around faster and more comfortably. What's strange, though, is that they have no kids, so you'd think motels or hotels would be more to their liking. On top of that, Wilkins rented them both separately and from different firms. It's not the kind of thing most people do. Folks want to strike a deal, get a two-vehicle discount.'

'Maybe the sedan was an afterthought and perhaps the wife can't drive?'

Helena gives a knowing smile. 'Oh but she can.'

'She can?'

'Both the RV and sedan went over the Oakland Bay Bridge around ten p.m., which is about the same time Ruth Everett was regaining consciousness on the floor of her kitchen.'

148

LONDON

The covert cab parks in the dark adjacent to the SSOA barge and less than five hundred metres from the development block where Mitzi is held.

Owain Gwyn's cell phone rings. 'Yes?'

'It's done.' Gareth Madoc sounds deflated. 'I've told my NIA contact and he's on his way over here. He already has a team meeting with Lanza and they're circling al-Shibh as we speak. I guess before dawn all our targets will be closed down, though I suspect it'll be tough to stick them with charges.'

'Don't be depressed. We had to choose between trying to catch everyone red-handed or ensuring no one gets hurt.'

'I know. I just wanted this to be one of those times we managed both.'

'We saved lives. Hang on to that.'

'I will. My guy's here, so I've got to go. Before you ask, I've nothing new on the Fallon girls but I promise I'll call you the instant I have.'

'Thanks. Let's talk later.' Owain hangs up and turns to Dalton.

The consul updates him. 'We've got a two-man team on the roof. They've heat-scanned the surface and she's being held in a top-floor room on the western side.'

Owain casts his eyes up into the darkness. 'Are you thinking of going in from the roof?'

'Not unless we have to. I want to get a listening device on the window; the feed from the parabolic microphones isn't as good as I hoped. We're going to lower an invisible camera as well, a fibre optic one that won't be seen in this light.'

'Do we know what Marchetti is doing?'

Dalton covers his earpiece and listens. 'I don't think he's in the room at the moment. I've picked up three voices. Fallon's, a woman's and a man's.'

The ambassador glances at his watch. 'I'm going to have to leave you. The Vatican hasn't returned my messages and even when they do, I'm sure I know what the answer will be.'

'They're not going to call off tomorrow.'

'No, of course not, it's too late. Which means I have to get to Cardigan and re-examine the security.'

'I'm fine here, don't worry.' He taps the computer monitor. 'We've got all our best men on this job; we'll get Fallon out safely.'

'I know you will.' Owain leaves his seat and opens the cab door. His private car is just a few hundred yards away. 'Try not to kill Marchetti. I really want some quality time with our old friend.'

149

LONDON

Beneath the pitch-black sky Angelo Marchetti stares out at the bright lights of the city. In front of him lies the watery vista of the Thames Barrier and to his right the glass-and-steel forest of Canary Wharf.

When the penthouse he's in is completed, Mardrid will sell it for millions, no doubt to some rich Russian or Arab. Right now, the whole development is nothing more than bare floors, walls and ceilings.

In his jacket pocket is a rolled up cloth that contains a hypodermic, some clean needles and enough heroin and cocaine to keep any decent rock band high for a month. The temptation to shoot it all into a big juicy vein is almost irresistible.

On a wad of paper towels is the memory stick his team just recovered from the Californian cop.

She's been lying to him.

The stick isn't his. It's smaller, thinner, lighter and empty.

The question now is what to do with her.

Fortunately, Mardrid is not yet on his back. But within a day or two, he will be. And Marchetti knows that if he can't deliver the details of the knights' graves, then he might as well dig his own.

He grabs the wad and useless file and strolls into the other room.

As per his orders, the woman's out of the closet, cleaned up and sat down.

Marchetti grabs another fold-up metal chair and settles opposite her. He holds the memory stick in front of her red and battered eyes.

'Where's the real one?'

Mitzi focuses on her girls. Imagines them running to her as toddlers, sweeping them off their feet, holding them tight.

Marchetti shouts this time. 'Where – the – *fuck* – is – it?'

She finds just enough saliva for her lips to work. 'Get Amber to a hospital and I'll tell you.'

He shakes his head in amazement. After everything he's done to her, how can she not be broken? What more has to happen for her to simply give in?

He knows the answer. She won't. He's seen people like her before: iron-willed, unflinching. Not so very long ago *he* had been such a person.

Through the window opposite, the sky starts to lighten. He knows dawn will come within the hour and with it intensified efforts in the US to find the girls.

'All *right*.' He sounds exasperated. 'I'll release one of your little bitches. *I'll fix it.* But I promise you this.' He steps closer, his eyes wide with rage. 'If you fuck with me – if you don't *instantly* give me what I want, then I will make you watch your other daughter die and it will not be a merciful death. It will be a slow and painful *scream-for-mommy* death, worse than anything you have ever seen or imagined.'

150

CALIFORNIA

Chris Wilkins honks his car horn as he approaches the hideout, knowing that forgetting to do so could result in a face full of lead.

Tess opens up. A Glock 29 dangles from her right hand; an assault rifle is only a grab away. From his face, she knows something is eating him. 'Everything okay?'

He takes one long look at the girls. They're still bound, gagged and hooded but are now separated. One is sat in a chair, her feet tied to the legs and her hands to the back. The other – the injured one – is on the floor, her legs raised and hand bandaged.

'In the back.' He nods to the kitchen.

Tess bolts the door and follows him into the adjoining room.

He lets out an anguished sigh. 'He wants us to free one of the girls.'

'He what?'

'The cut one. Says we have to take her to a hospital as far away as possible and leave her there with instructions to call her mom's cell phone straight away.'

She shrugs. 'We can get her to call from anywhere. It doesn't have to be a hospital.'

'I didn't tell it right. She *has* to call from the hospital, so her mother can check she's there.'

'Okay. I get it. Smart bitch.'

'Where's the best medical centre?'

Tess shrugs. 'No real idea. I'll look online. There'll probably be ones at Oakland and San Ramon.'

'Have a look east. Find something as far away from here as I could make in an hour.' He nods at the girl. 'How is she?'

'No real trouble. Bled like a haemophiliac after you cut her fingertip off with that carver and she's been whimpering like a kitten ever since.'

He goes to the fridge and pulls a beer. 'You want one?'

She takes a bottle and pops the cap. 'I don't like this. Don't like it one bit. You let the other side call the shots and it leads to trouble. Especially if the other side's a Fed.'

151

FBI HQ, SAN FRANCISCO

Sandra Donovan makes sure the door to her office is shut. It's a precaution she always takes when she's about to receive a call as important as the one being put through.

The director of the FBI wants to talk privately to her.

The light on her desk phone flashes. She snatches up the receiver, 'Yes, sir.'

Peter Lansley's noted as the kind of boss who likes to warm up a conversation. That's before he drops a bucket of ice down your pants. So she's not surprised to hear him start with small talk. 'How are you, Sandra? I've not seen you since the VICAP conference in Quantico.'

'I'm very fine, sir. Thank you for asking.'

'Good presentation that day – you certainly got some of the old timers thinking. I'm calling you about the Fallon case; there's something I need to tell you off the record.'

'Of course, sir.'

'In a moment you'll receive a call from a man who will give you two code words: Tole and Mac. That's Tango, Oscar, Lima, Echo. And Mike, Alpha, Charlie.'

'I've got it, sir.'

'Good. Because after that, this man will give you some information and believe me, you'll be able to trust it. He's a platinum-quality source. The intel we've had from him has never once been wrong. *Never*, Sandra.'

She notes his emphasis. 'This information, does it come from our side of the line or the other side, sir?'

There's a hint of laughter in his voice. 'Our side, Sandra. Very much our side. I told the caller that you could be trusted to deal directly with him. Don't let me down.'

'I won't, sir.'

The line goes dead. Donovan returns the receiver to its cradle and wonders what the hell anyone outside her team or Bob Beam's squad can tell her about the kidnapping of Mitzi Fallon's kids.

She doesn't have to wait long.

Her secretary buzzes through. 'I have a man on the phone.

He says Director Lansley will have spoken to you and you'll be expecting this call.'

Her eyes widen in anticipation. 'Put him through, Sylvia. Put him through.'

152

CARDIGAN, WALES

As Owain's helicopter sifts air over Cardigan he thinks how, centuries ago, this had been the starting and stopping point for hundreds of ships and thousands of sailors. It supported a booming shipbuilding industry, a thriving trade in wool export and a buoyant local community.

Not any more.

Once the river silted up, the big boats stopped coming and economic rot set in. Nowadays it's a small town with a population of less than five thousand. Tourists tend to be either of the history or religious variety. They visit the eleventh-century castle or St Mary's, the twelfth-century church that houses the Catholic national shrine of Wales, a statue of the Blessed Virgin known as Our Lady of the Taper and Our Lady of Cardigan.

The shrine is the focus of the new Pope's visit, the first to Wales for over thirty years. A cause for national celebration. And Owain's first port of call.

Rain clouds shroud the break of dawn and temperatures

are almost frosty as a limousine picks him up and heads across town. Alongside him is Carrie Auckland, a former MI5 high flyer who has been heading his European VIP protective units for the past five years. The forty-two-year-old is kitted out in a black bomber jacket, matching combat pants and sneakers.

She shifts her wiry, athletic frame and tries to reassure him that everything is going to be fine. 'Every hour of every day, we check bins, drains, post boxes and vantage points along the papal route. There's not a house, apartment, store or garage we haven't turned over. There's no chance of an attempt on his life.'

'There's always a chance, Carrie – that's why I'm here.'

'Unnecessarily, I hope.'

'Me too. Don't for one moment think my early arrival is a vote of no confidence. As far as I'm concerned, you're the best in the business.'

'Thank you.'

'It's just that the Watch Team insists there will be an attempt on the Holy Father's life and an extra pair of hands is always useful.'

'Watch have been wrong before.' She hands over a manila folder filled with briefing sheets.

'Many times. And I hope they are today.'

'The first document is the papal agenda,' she explains. 'The second, a list of people who will meet the Holy Father or be close to him. I've talked to Vatican security and either you or I will never be more than a few yards away. The third is a profile on the pontiff and his travelling habits. The fourth, an analysis of—'

He cuts her short. 'Too much, Carrie – just give me the highlights.'

'Okay. Well, this is the first time a Pope has been in Wales since 1982. He's visiting Cardigan, Swansea and Cardiff before arriving late in Westminster for Mass in the morning, then a flight to Belgium to bless a further restoration of *The Ghent Altarpiece*.'

'We'll talk about Ghent later. Just focus on Cardigan for the moment.'

'The village is easy for containment. I think between ourselves, the Vatican and security services we're locked down safe. The church goes back to the twelfth century but it's been extended, modernized and a place developed for the shrine.' She points to the folder. 'The schematics are all in there. You'll see that it's a difficult area to cover, so we've had to be extra vigilant there.'

'Good. You seem very well-prepared.' He relaxes a little. 'From a security point of view, what are you most worried about?'

She smiles. 'The unexpected. The nature of life is that something unexpected always happens.'

153

FBI HQ, SAN FRANCISCO

Sandra Donovan slides two photographs across her desk. One of a man and one of a woman.

Bob Beam picks them up. 'What are these?'

'Just sent to me via an untraceable server.'

He smiles. 'There's no such thing as untraceable.'

'Really? Go talk to the tech boys. I just said the same thing to them and they laughed in my face. They'll bore you rigid with explanations of how these JPEGs got pinged through every IP server in Asia before arriving here.'

He holds up the pictures. 'And these people are?'

'Gerry and Susan Stanhope. Paul and Sharron Glass. Steve and Sarah Dopler. Or more familiarly, Chris and Tess Wilkins. According to a trusted source, they're behind the Fallon kidnapping.'

He stares at the round face of the man and the chiselled cheeks of a blonde woman. 'We came across the same name when checking out rentals. What's the source?'

'I can't say, but it's good.'

'Can't or won't?'

'Can't. It came to me via Lansley.'

His eyes widen. 'Anything other than pictures to go on?'

Donovan rests her hands on the desk. 'Apparently, there's a select group of former soldiers already hunting the Wilkins couple.'

'Mercenaries?'

'I don't know who's paying or controlling them, just that Lansley says we can trust them. The man who called me supplied a list of all the locations that they're searching.'

He shrugs. 'So what am I supposed to do?'

She flips a sheet of paper to him. 'These are places they say they can't get to for the next hour. Maybe you can prioritize these addresses as part of your ops?'

'For the record, I don't like working on intel I don't know the provenance of.'

'Noted.'

He snatches it from her. 'Eight different locales. Great.'

'It's better than we had, Bob.'

He scrapes back the chair, stands and waves the paper at her as he heads for the door. 'This is going to end badly. Remember I said that.'

'Make sure it doesn't and—'

He slams the door.

'—*don't* slam the door!'

154

STOCKTON, CALIFORNIA

The sixty-seven-mile journey takes Chris Wilkins an hour and forty minutes.

He drives west into Danville, south to Dublin and then east through Tracy and north up towards Stockton.

About a mile away from the town's General Hospital, he pulls off the freeway, takes a left and parks near the Chinese Cemetery. He puts a hand across the top of the passenger seat, turns and looks into the back of the Toyota where Amber is tied up beneath a blanket. She hasn't been given any painkillers or sedatives for more than three hours because he needs her to be lucid when she gets into the emergency room. The lack of drugs means she's distressed and is moaning so much he wants to clip her.

'We're about there. I'll have you in a hospital in a few minutes. Remember, you get them to call your mom right away. Not after treatment – right away.'

Before restarting the engine, he uses a new burner to call London. 'The girl will be inside San Joaquin Hospital in Stockton within ten minutes. Call me when she's connected with the mom, then I'm gone.'

'I understand,' says Marchetti.

'You'd better. And don't go forgetting that extra risk equals extra payment.'

'Don't worry about your money.'

Chris kills the call and dials Tess. 'I'm there and about to go in.'

'Good luck, baby. Love you.'

'Love you too, sweetcheeks.' He hangs up, checks the time and his gun. Three hours from now, he'll be catching a flight to Vegas from Stockton airport. Either that or he'll be running for his life, because once Amber's made the call to her mother, he's going to kill her. Then he'll call Tess and she'll kill the other one.

After that, they'll both be gone.

So far gone, it'll be like they never existed.

155

SSOA OFFICES, NEW YORK

It's so long since Gareth Madoc has eaten, his stomach sounds like a damaged washing machine. He unwraps the sandwich his secretary has brought him. It's his favourite pastrami with mustard on rye and it's an inch from his mouth when his desk phone rings.

'Hell and damnation.' He drops the food back on its greaseproof paper and picks up the call. 'Madoc.'

'Don't sound so crabby; it's Steffani.'

'The pick-ups all worked out?'

'Yeah, even better than that. I owe you one.'

'You owe me *several* and don't you forget. Spill the details.'

'Bin al-Shibh's face was a picture. Never saw it coming. He was in a private hangar at JFK about to board a Lear. We had him boxed like a dog.'

'Any shooting?'

'No. Came without a tear. We have him at CTU under interrogation. Mousavi and Tabrizi are a different story.'

'More troublesome, I guess.'

'You guess right. Tabrizi is a fit boy. We took him at the house your people had been sitting on, but he fought like crazy. Had to break his face and some ribs before he gave up. Mousavi we took down in a cheap diner over the east side, when he went to the men's room. Can you believe this – he had one hand on a concealed gun even while taking a leak.'

'It's what you call being tooled up.'

'Ha freakin' ha. My agent wasn't laughing – the fucker shot him in the foot *and* pissed all over him.'

'He okay?'

'Yeah, the injury's the kind that'll fade but the story won't.'

'What about Malek Hussan?'

'Made us on the street and ran for it. After fifty yards, he had to stop and give up. Poor fuck nearly wheezed himself into a heart attack.'

'Korshidi?'

'Just this minute swept him up. He's playing it smart, alleging discrimination against him and his mosque. He'll change his tune when we run him the tape he made of al-Shibh.'

'Now you've got him, I'm going to take his daughter out of circulation; she was one of our main sources.' As an afterthought he adds, 'Maybe we'll scoop up her mother too. Can you help with a safe house if necessary?'

'Least I can do. We've got a place in Greenwich. It'll be good for a day or so.'

'Thanks. I guess none of them have given up the location of the planned explosion?'

Steffani laughs. 'That's the second guess you've got right. I'll call you if anyone sings, but don't hold your breath, buddy.'

156

SAN JOAQUIN HOSPITAL, STOCKTON

It's bedlam in ER.

Charge Nurse Betty Lipton's working a double and has just had a surgeon and two nurses call in sick.

Theatre is backed up with all manner of injuries. A lumberjack who chain-sawed a thigh bone. Two separate road traffic incidents with complicated crush and skull injuries. And a father of two who tried to blow his own head off with a handgun.

'Nurse!'

She ignores the shout from the rows of the walking wounded.

'Nurse!'

She looks up from her computer. Several people are stood peering at something. No doubt a collapse.

'Nurse!'

'Okay! Save your blood pressure, I'm coming.' She rounds the desk and heads over. Plastic seats are pushed back.

Someone's out for the count at the back of the room.

'Move to one side, give me some room.'

On the ground is a teenage girl. She's wrapped in a Tartan car blanket that someone's pulled open. Her legs and hands are bound. There's a gag in her mouth.

Stapled to her chest is a note.

'DON'T CALL THE COPS.'

157

SAN JOAQUIN HOSPITAL, STOCKTON

Amber Fallon is lifted onto a gurney and rushed into a treatment cubicle. Nurses check vital signs, they hook up drips and unwrap blood-stained bandages around her hand.

Outside the curtain, Betty Lipton hands the note to hospital administrator Ann Lesley, and brings her up to speed. 'Kid's called Amber Fallon. She's got a partially severed finger and is wiped out. Says she has to call her mom straight away or her sister gets killed.'

Lesley reads the note. 'You think she's genuine, or is this a clinical case of attention grabbing?'

'Munchausen is always hard to tell. I guess we make the call to her mom and find out.'

'I want to see her first.'

Betty leads the way into the cubicle.

Amber is propped up on a pillow and looks frightened. She jabbers as soon as she sees them, 'I have to call my mom – the man said.'

Lesley lifts a handset from a wall mount. 'What's her number, honey?'

'It's in my pocket.' She can't get at it because her hand is still being cleaned up. 'It's not my mom's cell but one that the man said she'd be on.'

Betty gets it for her and hands it across.

'What man do you mean, honey?' Lesley checks the digits on the note and enters them.

'The one who took us. He said if I don't call straight away, he'll kill Jade.'

'Jade's your sister?' She hits dial.

'Yes.' She sounds close to breaking.

The number rings out and is instantly picked up. 'Hello.'

'This is Ann Lesley from San Joaquin Hospital. Who is that?'

'Lieutenant Fallon – do you have my daughter?'

She's surprised the mom is a cop. 'Yes, I do. Amber's just being treated by some of my staff. Mrs Fallon—'

Mitzi cuts her off. 'Lady, I don't have time for questions. Give me the main number of your hospital, so I can call back and confirm you are who you say you are. Please do this right away – a lot of lives depend on it.'

'The number you need is four six eight, four seven hundred. If you're calling from out of Stockton the area code is two zero nine. Tell reception to put the call through to ER and they'll route it to me.'

'Is she okay?'

'She's fine, Mrs Fallon. She's in safe hands now.'

Mitzi feels like she's going to cry. 'Thanks.'

The administrator hangs up, ducks the curtain and shouts to the triage desk. 'Call switchboard and say they're about to get a call for me. It's urgent and needs to be put through immediately.'

Lesley looks around the waiting area as the nurse calls the

operator. ER is jammed to bursting. She wishes there was somewhere she could shift all these patients to.

She re-enters the cubicle and looks at the young girl on the bed. Poor kid is stressed out and, judging from the whiteness of her skin, pretty bled out too.

She takes a tissue from a box at the side of the bed and wipes tears welling up in the corners of Amber's reddened eyes.

The phone on the wall rings. Everyone stares at it.

Lesley snatches it from the cradle. 'Hello.'

'It's Mitzi Fallon. Are you still with Amber?'

'Yes, Mrs Fallon.'

'Then for God's sake get her somewhere safe and call the—'

The line goes dead.

Amber looks up at the administrator. 'What did Mom say?'

She puts a reassuring hand to the girl's face. 'She says you're not to worry. Everything's going to be fine.'

158

FBI HQ, SAN FRANCISCO

'San Joaquin Hospital – Amber Fallon has just been admitted to the ER.'

Bob Beam looks up from his desk at Assistant Director Donovan. 'Your source again?'

She corrects him. 'Lansley's source.'

His instinct is to check. Always check before you deploy. He picks up his desk phone. 'Get me the administrator at San Joaquin Hospital in Stockton. I'll hold.'

The AD lets out a sigh of frustration. 'You need to get a team there, Bob, and you need to do it quick.'

He puts his hand over the mouthpiece. 'I need to be sure, Sandra. Post budget cuts mean we have too few people and once they're gone they're gone.'

His secretary comes on the line. 'Putting you through now.'

A woman's voice follows. 'Ann Lesley; who am I talking to?'

'This is Special Agent Robert Beam from the FBI in San Francisco. Can you confirm for me that you've just admitted a young girl called Amber Fallon?'

The line goes silent for a moment. 'Agent Beam, do you have a number I can call you back on to verify you are who you say you are?'

'Jesus Christ, lady, I don't have time for this—'

'A number, please.'

'Five, five, three, seven four hundred and make it fast.' He slams down the phone and looks up at Donovan. 'She wants to check who I am.'

'Checking can be so annoying, eh?' She's red-faced with anger as she flips out her phone and taps in a number. 'Eleonora, it's Sandra Donovan. Get yourself to San Joaquin Hospital in Stockton. Run the lights. Mitzi's daughter Amber has just been admitted.'

Beam is about to argue when his phone rings. 'H'lo.'

'Agent Beam?'

'Yes.'

'It's Ann Lesley. We do have Amber Fallon. She's with me right now and she's a very frightened young lady—'

'We're going to get some agents out to your hospital, ma'am.'

'She was left in ER with a note pinned to her chest saying the police were not to be called. She claims her sister is in great danger—'

'We know about that, ma'am. Thank you for your help.' He glances down at the two face shots Donovan gave him. 'Can you tell me, was she with a man or woman? A big man, round faced with dark hair, or a woman, probably blonde hair, quite pretty?'

'No, sir. She wasn't with anyone. She'd just been left here.'

'Can I talk to her?'

'Not right now. We've given her a sedative and need to get her X-rayed and treated.'

'Call me when you're done.' He hangs up and turns to Donovan.

The AD's gone.

'Shit.' He bangs a hand down on the desk.

159

LONDON

Marchetti's slap knocks the phone out of Mitzi's hands.

There's wildness in his eyes. It's a look she's seen before. Usually on the face of a murderer or rapist she's hunted down. Sometimes on that of her ex-husband.

Marchetti grabs her by the throat and squeezes hard. 'One daughter freed. That was the deal.' He shows a smartphone in his other hand. 'Now, do you want to watch the other one being chopped up, piece by piece – or are you going to give me my fucking memory stick?' He lets go and leaves her spluttering.

Mitzi struggles to get her breath.

Marchetti gives her a second then grabs her by the hair and lifts her head. 'Where is it?'

'Dean Street.'

'Be more specific.'

'I bagged and wired it. Sealed it in an evidence bag and hung it down a street drain outside the hotel where I stayed.'

Marchetti sizes up a punch, one to teach the bitch a lesson.

There's a blinding flash. Smoke.

The brunette screams.

There's gunfire. Pistol shots. Pop. Pop. Pop. The raw stutter of semi-automatics. Blue and orange muzzle flashes in the dark, smoky haze.

Then silence.

160

LONDON

George Dalton watches the tac teams on split-screen feeds on his laptop.

Soon after the team leader and his right-hand man go through the window, four SSOA operatives take out the front door of the apartment and come in as back-up.

Once the shooting stops, Dalton switches to the single night-vision camera on the helmet of the team leader. The viewing frame fills with a pea-green sea as the former marine crunches his way over shattered glass, splintered wood and bodies.

The first corpse to come into focus is one of the body-guards. He's bleeding out in a classic dead man's sprawl near the doorway. A Glock rests in his loose fingers.

Next to him is what remains of a thin, young woman. Most of her face and chest have been chewed away by the bullets of an MP5.

The body of a second bodyguard is against the foot of an adjacent wall, legs stretched out, back against a doorframe. It looks to Dalton like he's been shot as he came in from another room.

The leader's camera tracks across to the centre of the foggy room. Two SSOA men are bent over Angelo Marchetti.

Dalton speaks into a microphone. 'Leader One from Base: is he alive?'

'This is Leader One – that's a negative Base. Target is not alive.'

'Shit!' Dalton remembers Owain's request to have 'quality time' with their former colleague. 'And Fallon?'

The team leader swings his head so the camera shows her. Mitzi's chair is upturned. She's lying on her back. Her knees point at the ceiling. The operative moves close.

Dalton hears the American's voice. 'About freakin' time. Help me off this damned chair. Get me a phone, or by Christ I'll make an even bigger mess than you just did.'

161

SAN RAMON, CALIFORNIA

Eleonora Fracci has Mitzi in mind as she guns up the Crossfire and burns rubber out of San Ramon. Specifically, it's the moment they met in the squad room and Fallon showed them a framed shot of her daughters at Disney. She'd never seen anyone look at a photo as proudly as Mitzi had. More than anything, she wants to see a new frame there – one showing Mitzi and the girls with Mickey. Hell, she might even go with them and take it herself.

She drives with one hand and finger-punches the address of San Joaquin Hospital into the sat-nav stuck to her windshield. The display tells her she's fifty miles and fifty minutes away. '*Idiota!*' She's confident she'll do it in thirty. The old six-speed Chrysler has a three-litre turbocharged V6 under its brilliant red hood and its limiter has been removed.

By the time she hits the 1-680, she's topping a hundred and fifty. San Ramon Central Park. Bishop Ranch Open Space. Athan Downs and Dublin Hills are all just a smear against the Crossfire.

Then the traffic backs up.

At the Donald D. Doyle Highway, the road becomes a parking lot. Drivers hammer horns. Local radio says there's a pile-up on the intersection with the Arthur H. Breed, the freeway she needs to use.

Eleonora flips on her sirens and lights. Traffic is fender-to-fender. It takes ten minutes for her to get off at Dublin Boulevard and run a road parallel to the blocked freeway.

There are stacks of red tail-lights up ahead. Others seem to have had the same idea. She hits the lights and sirens again. The sat-nav says she's coming to the end of the Boulevard and needs to re-join the freeway in less than a mile.

Eleonora picks up her radio and calls Donovan. 'I'm stuck in traffic. It's really bad.'

'How bad is *really bad*?'

She looks again and flinches. 'I could still be half an hour away. You best get a local cop to the hospital until I fight my way through this.'

Donovan doesn't answer, but Eleonora's certain she hears her boss swear, just before she slams the phone down on her.

162

SAN JOAQUIN HOSPITAL, STOCKTON

Chris Wilkins is counting seconds.

His instructions from Marchetti were very clear. Take the girl to the hospital and wait there. If he didn't get a call within half an hour, kill the kid and get Tess to do the same with the other one.

Not that he minds.

Murder had always been on the cards. He'd just never imagined doing it in a hospital in Stockton.

He pumps a hospital vending machine for coffee and checks his watch.

Two minutes.

If he doesn't get a call in one hundred and twenty seconds he's going to walk back into ER, find the girl and put a bullet in her head. He's already dumped his hired sedan in case they get a trace on it and has broken into a car on the staff lot and left it ready to hotwire.

Sixty seconds.

The coffee tastes like crap. He drops it in a trashcan and heads to a washroom. He goes into a stall, takes a leak and removes his black flight jacket. It's a reversible one. Once he turns it inside out, it's red and looks strikingly different.

The digital watch on his wrist beeps.

Time's up.

He checks his gun and steps out of the stall. There's no one else in the washroom. He calls Tess. 'It's me.'

'Hi.'

'No call. Do it.'

She hesitates. 'Okay.'

The mirror over the taps throws back the reflection of a hardened killer. One who's wasted plenty of people. But never a kid.

He tells himself there's a first time for everything and heads out the door.

163

CALIFORNIA

Tess Wilkins looks across the shack's open lounge to the young girl bound and hooded on the sofa.

She knows what she has to do and knows the risk of not doing it. Dead captives tell no tales. Live ones cause trouble.

She goes into the crummy bedroom and gathers what little stuff she and Chris have in there. She jams clothes into a rucksack, then walks to the bathroom.

Toothbrushes, paste, soap, hair dye, shaving gear and hair-spray get swept into the bag as well.

In the kitchen, she empties the pedal bin onto the floor.

There isn't much in it, just some fast-food packages and hand wipes. Under a microscope, though, there'd be enough DNA to send both her and her beloved to the Big House. Tess spreads everything out, then goes to the five-gallon jerry can that Chris left by the door. She pops the cap, hauls it as high as she can manage and sprinkles gasoline.

Tess sloshes the fuel liberally in the kitchen, bedrooms, bathroom and then pauses as she enters the lounge area. There's an order to things and she doesn't want to mess up.

She puts the can down, takes the rucksack outside to the RV and throws it in the passenger side of the cab. She slips the keys into the ignition and pauses for a second to think of anything she's missed.

There isn't.

She plans to walk back inside, put a cushion around her gun, and then shoot the kid in the head. After that, she'll empty the rest of the jerry, light a match and torch the place to get rid of any forensic traces. While the shack's burning she'll be driving. Before it's even extinguished she'll be at the airport. With any luck, by the time they start asking the serious questions, she'll already be back in LA mixing a cocktail for Chris.

All she has to do now is go back inside and pull the trigger.

164

FBI HQ, SAN FRANCISCO

Sandra Donovan has no choice but to call Stockton's Chief of Police. What she'd most like to do is locate whatever squad car is nearest San Joaquin Hospital and get the officers sent over there as fast as possible. But there are protocols and chains of command to respect.

The chief assures the assistant director that he fully understands the urgency of getting officers there until her agents arrive. As soon as she hangs up, he stresses the very same point to his deputy, who in turn undertakes to get on the case straight away.

The deputy calls his watch commander who then alerts his two strategic operations commanders. And so, fifteen minutes after Sandra Donovan's call, a cruiser eventually rolls out of Police HQ in East Weber Avenue bearing senior patrolmen Darren Ratcliffe and Tony Emery.

As they hit the freeway they are less than fifteen minutes away from the hospital, more like ten if Emery puts his foot to the floor, like he usually does. Only yesterday, he got a reprimand for driving too fast and dangerous, so he's not going to be dumb enough to make that mistake again.

165

LONDON

Two of the tac team carry Mitzi out of the apartment block and into a private ambulance.

Dalton rides with her and calls for a clean-up squad to put the building back the way it was, before they sprayed it with thunderflashes and bullets.

He finishes the call and leans over Mitzi. 'Stupid question, but how are you feeling?'

'Like shit in a blender.' She thinks of what she just said. 'Scrub that. I never want to hear the word *shit* again.'

'We have a hospital near Temple. Doctors are on standby to check you out.'

'I don't care. I just want to speak to my girls.' She tries to sit herself up and falls back, wincing with pain.

'Relax. I've called the FBI and they've got people on their way to Stockton where Amber called you from.'

'Have you found Jade?'

'Not yet. We still don't know where she is, and nor do your colleagues. But we're working together on it.'

Mitzi's spirits sink. The whole point of her going in there and surrendering to those damned people, was to buy the time necessary to recover *both* her girls. She looks to Dalton. 'You got a phone?'

He holds one out.

'Call that hospital for me; I have to talk to Amber.'

He gets reception, then ER, then the administrator and finally Mitzi's daughter. 'Amber, hold on, I'm going to put your mom on the line.' He passes the handset to Mitzi.

'Baby, is that you? Are you all right?'

'I guess.' The teenager is sat beside Betty Lipton waiting for a doctor. 'My hand aches in a really weird way. It's like all my finger's still there and someone's squeezing it in pliers or something.'

Mitzi feels her heart break. 'Be strong, honey. Have they given you anything for the pain?'

'Yeah, they're being real nice, Mom.' There's an awkward silence and then she adds, ' Mom, I'm sorry about what happened. They just grabbed us – I had no time to shout to Jade or—'

'Baby, you've got nothing to be sorry for. You're safe now, that's all that matters. I'm still in London but I'll be on a plane real soon and with you in less than half a day.' She looks to Dalton for reassurance and he gives her a silent nod.

'I love you, honey. I love you so much and I'm coming home to look after you and make sure you are all right.'

'I love you too, Mom.' She can't hold back the tears now. Tears of relief. Tears of trauma.

'Don't cry, sweetheart, you just hang in there now. Get some rest and do whatever the doctors tell you. You hear me?'

'Yeah. Yeah, I do.' She blows her nose on a tissue the nurse passed her. 'Mom, is Jade all right?'

‘She’s going to be fine as well.’ She looks up at Dalton but this time there’s no reassuring nod. ‘We’re Fallon women, aren’t we? And you know us girls always come out winners.’

166

SAN JOAQUIN HOSPITAL, STOCKTON

There’s an empty seat in the ER waiting room, three rows back, four seats from the end. Chris Wilkins slides his big frame onto the grey plastic.

It’s the perfect place to sit and watch.

He hears names being called. Sick people hobble into curtained cubicles to see exhausted medics. Trolleys pass, bearing horizontal patients and vertical drip stands. Minute by minute the scene repeats itself.

He watches and listens. Finally, he sees her. A nurse has an arm around Amber and a suited woman is on her other side, guiding her down the corridor.

Wilkins drops the newspaper he hasn’t been reading and tags along. Overhead signs signal different departments. He hangs back to avoid being seen.

Part way down a corridor they head into an area marked X-RAY.

Wilkins walks slowly along the passage and stands in the doorway. The department is jammed with people waiting to be scanned. The woman in the suit speaks to the receptionist and they're told to go straight on through.

Wilkins steps into the corridor and checks his escape routes. Either back the way he came, or through a door marked Emergency Exit. By his reckoning, the latter will bring him out close to the staff parking lot and the car he's broken open.

He walks into X-Ray reception and keeps his head down and face away from the nurse behind the desk.

As he approaches the closed theatre doors, he hears her call after him, 'Excuse me, sir. You can't go in there.'

He pushes a door open.

Two women turn and stare at him. His eyes flit across the room. The Fallon girl isn't there. He can't see her anywhere.

A nurse approaches him. 'You need to wait outside, sir.' She puts her right arm on his shoulder and tries to usher him out.

He shakes her off. 'Where's the girl? The girl you were with?'

The comment sparks the suited-woman into life. 'Who are you?'

He shifts his jacket so they see his gun. 'I'm a federal agent. I've been sent to protect her.'

They both look relieved.

'She's just using the washroom,' says the nurse. Her face lights up as over his shoulder she spots her returning. 'Here she is now.'

Amber catches the nurse's eye. And a glimpse of the man. She recognizes him instantly.

He starts to turn.

Amber grabs the handles of a wheelchair by the door and runs it hard into him. Extended metal foot rests smash into his shins. Wilkins loses balance and falls.

'It's him!' screams Amber. 'The man who took me.' She runs from the theatre.

Wilkins has lost neither gun nor focus. He scrambles to his feet. The charge nurse bars the doorway.

Wilkins shoots her in the chest and steps over the body.

There are screams all around him. He shuffles out into the waiting room, his right ankle burning with pain. Scared patients jam up the reception. 'Get the fuck outta my way!' He raises the gun and they clear his path.

In the corridor, he catches sight of Amber running through a mass of people. He lets off two high shots and they bring down part of the ceiling. Everyone but the girl hits the ground. An alarm goes off behind him. He ignores it and tries not to rush his shot. She's twenty yards away weaving left and right. Smart kid.

But not smart enough. He squeezes the trigger.

A roar bowls down the corridor.

Amber throws up her arms and falls face first.

An alarm goes off in front of him. More people spill into the corridor. They're coming from all directions. He has to get out of there. Has to make it to the parking lot and the waiting car.

Wilkins snatches another shot at the fallen body and runs.

167

LONDON

More than anything, Mitzi wants to shower.

She lets the hospital medics stitch up her shoulder and give her a booster jab, then she grabs a luxury white robe from a brass hook on the back of an expensive oak door and tells them all to scram.

The en-suite bathroom to the private room where she's being treated has one of those waterfall showers that she's seen in expensive hotels.

Mitzi turns it on full, dips her head under the warm water and stands there with one hand on the wall to make sure she doesn't slip or pass out. Once she's acclimatized, she grabs shampoo and pours out enough to soap a field of sheep.

Her face is greasy and tender. Blood has dried and clogged inside her nostrils. For almost a minute, the water runs red while she cleans herself up. Inevitably, she gets her shoulder-dressing wet. She's too sore to wash anything below knee height and too stiff to raise her legs. Right now, she'd pay a thousand bucks for someone to scrub her feet.

The cubicle glass is completely steamed up by the time she gingerly steps out and eases her battered body into the fresh-smelling white robe.

With some difficulty, Mitzi manages to towel surplus water off her hair and opens the door to the hospital room.

Dalton is stood there.

'Holy fuckola!' She puts a hand to her heart. 'I thought you Brits were supposed to have real good manners.'

He knows there's no kind way to break the news. 'I'm afraid your daughter Amber's been shot. She's in surgery fighting for her life.'

Mitzi doesn't take it in. 'No, that can't be. I spoke to her. I called her on your phone. That's not—'

'The man who abducted her went into the hospital and shot her. He killed a nurse, too.'

Her legs turn to jelly. She puts a hand on the wall but her knees fold and she collapses against the side of the bed.

Dalton rushes to her side. Tries to pick her up.

She pushes him off. She's on her knees and she can hear herself praying to a God she's not sure even exists.

He stands patiently next to her. Waits for the moment when she's ready for him to help her up and then hurt her some more by telling all the details.

168

SAN JOAQUIN HOSPITAL, STOCKTON

Fresh alarm bells sound as Chris Wilkins hits the horizontal metal bar on the red door and kicks open the Emergency Exit.

He'd hoped to catch the kid clean. A quick kill in a quiet

corner of the hospital, then slip out while people were still in shock. Now he's leaving in a hail of alarms and he's not sure he's done enough to finish her. Even worse, he's noticed a security camera on the way out that he didn't see on the way in.

By his reckoning, unless he's away from the hospital grounds and out of sight within the next ten minutes he's going to end up in a police body bag. He walks briskly around the building and turns sharp right. At least his sense of direction is good. The staff parking lot is straight ahead. Within five strides he sees the Ford he's broken into and left ready.

He skids down a short grass bank, clatters into a green Chevy and clambers around the back of it. When he gets to the blue Ford he yanks open the driver's door, tumbles in and pulls it shut. He sits and drips sweat while checking the windshield and rear-view mirror.

So far so good.

He wipes his brow with his forearm and jams the cables together. The engine growls. Before driving off, he takes another beat to compose himself. This isn't the time to make stupid mistakes. He has to appear just like any other driver. Law-abiding. Careful. Maybe shocked by all the noise and activity around him.

He pulls on his safety belt and adjusts the rear-view. People are spilling out of the building. The panic is starting. He stays calm. Drives slowly around the lot and onto one of the hospital's service roads. Coming up to the exit he sees a police cruiser screaming towards him. Its rooftop blues are flashing disco crazy.

Wilkins coolly indicates. He pulls over and gives the squad

car maximum room to blast past. Other drivers in front and behind follow suit. He's lost in the crowd.

Once the cruiser has gone he tags behind the car in front and leaves by the main exit.

Now he has to think.

For the next half-hour, the cops will be glued up gathering details. It'll be all about the nurse and the Fallon girl. Gradually, they'll get their shit together and pull pictures of him from the CCTV and wire them to patrol cars across the county. Soon after that, someone at the hospital is going to report their car missing and then the Ford will be useless.

A red Chrysler Crossfire with police lights strobing its grille flashes past him.

Wilkins has a bad feeling. Local cops don't drive cars like that.

It must be Feds. It means it's no longer safe to catch the flight Tess has booked him on. He'll have to try another airport, or find a new way out of the country.

169

CALIFORNIA

Tess Wilkins puts the jerry can in the RV and returns to the shack. Her hands stink of gasoline. She goes to the sink, soaps and scrubs.

She dries on a hand towel, tosses it on the floor and walks to the grubby sofa. She picks up a stained cushion and wraps it around the muzzle of her pistol.

Less than two feet from her, Jade Fallon is curled up against the other arm of the furniture. The kid's hands are still tied behind her back, her mouth taped and head hooded. She's so motionless that Tess guesses she's asleep.

Or dead.

Maybe she suffocated. Tess watches the youngster's chest and sees it slowly rise and fall.

Pity.

If the girl had been dead, she'd just burn the place and be gone. In the last few minutes, she's been growing squeamish. Even gotten to wondering if she could let the kid live. The proposal still appeals to her conscience. But not her sense of self-survival. And Tess Wilkins is ruled by self-preservation.

She swallows hard, lifts the muffled gun and looks away as she shoots Jade in the head. It's louder than she expected. Like an echo. The recoil more powerful than she'd imagined.

Then the pain and realization kick in. She's not only fired a shot, she's been shot.

Fire spreads through her chest and back. Tess stumbles and sees a small, thin woman in the doorway, hands outstretched and a gun clasped between them.

She must have got a round off at the same time.

Tess Wilkins coughs blood as she hits the floor. At least she killed the kid. It's one less witness against Chris.

170

SAN JOAQUIN HOSPITAL, STOCKTON

Eleonora Fracci follows the screams.

She finds two lone cops in X-ray playing King Canute with a tidal wave of panicking patients. She flashes her shield at the older police. 'I'm looking for Amber Fallon, a teenage girl, daughter of a colleague.'

He shakes his head. 'She's in ER – they're operating.'

'What happened?'

'Guy busts into here, shoots a nurse, chases the girl down the corridor and pops her before he cracks a fire exit and disappears.'

'How badly hurt is she?'

He shrugs. 'I dunno. Bad, I guess.'

Eleonora notices blood pooled in the doorway to the X-ray room. As she gets closer she sees the body of the nurse. It's been turned. There are smears on the floor where someone tried to save her. Bloody footprints lead away. They're small. A woman's, not a man's. No doubt made by someone professional enough to have known that once death was certain the body would have to be left in situ for the cops and ME.

Eleonora looks at the gunshot wound. It's left of chest and looks like it was made from no more than three feet away. It takes a special kind of animal to kill like that. One that's killed before. One that feels nothing when he looks into the eyes of another human being and takes their life.

She makes the sign of the cross and says a quick and silent prayer for the dead woman's soul, then she heads back to the cop. 'Did anyone get a description of the gunman?'

He points to a camera above the reception desk. 'We're searching the tapes. That little baby should have a clean shot of him.'

'That's what I want,' says Eleonora. 'A clean shot at this bastard.'

'There's a queue,' says a tall, dark-haired man who has appeared just a few yards from her.

She looks at him suspiciously.

'I'm Ross Green and I guess you're Agent Fracci.' He jabs a thumb over his shoulder to the corridor. 'Can we talk outside?'

171

CALIFORNIA

SSOA agent Eve Garrett drags the woman's body off the sofa so she can get to the girl.

Blood seeps from the black hood pulled tight over Jade's head. She grabs the drawstring, unties it and carefully pulls off the cloth.

Jade is unconscious and unresponsive. Her mouth still taped.

Eve guesses there's a wound around the temporal or parietal bones on the left side of her head. She pulls off the tape, puts her fingers into a river of red and feels for a pulse.

There isn't one.

She puts her hand to Jade's mouth and can't feel any breath. Eve's not ready to give up. She presses the button on her radio. 'I need paramedics and I need them Superman fast.'

Control has her coordinates so she doesn't waste time waiting for a reply. Eve digs out a Swiss Army knife from her pocket and uses the blade to sever the thick plastic band around the girl's wrists. She picks her up, lays her on the floor and checks her airway before she starts CPR.

Two beats in, Eve spots the muzzle-flash burns on the cushion. She can't help but wonder what kind of woman could execute a young girl like that. Death was too good for the bitch.

She checks again for a pulse. There still isn't one.

'Goddamn it, come on!' She starts another cycle of chest compressions. 'Don't give up on me, girl.'

Eve knows that the statistics are stacked against her. CPR seldom saves the lives of people shot and bleeding like this.

But there's always a chance.

The wound is fresh, less than five minutes old, and that means there's a slim hope of saving the brain from damage and keeping the heart pumping.

Sweat pours down Eve's face. Muscles in her wrists and arms ache. But she doesn't stop.

The door to the shack has been hanging open ever since she walked in. Through it she hears the thwack of helicopter blades. 'They're coming, honey,' she whispers to Jade. 'The paramedics will be here any minute.'

Dust blows in the doorway. The hum of rotors makes the floor vibrate.

She looks up and sees two medics. One has a defib machine, the other an oxygen kit and medicine case.

172

CARDIGAN, WALES

Inside the church of Our Lady of the Taper, one of the dog handlers respectfully calls an *all clear*. A watching inspector gives a thumbs-up. Another handler and his sniffer dog weave in and out of rows of seats.

Owain leaves them to it and walks the building on his own. He knows everyone is going to be searched and no one can get in here without prior vetting and electronic scanning. But he has a bad feeling – the kind Myrddin taught him never to ignore.

The service is being filmed, relayed to crowds outside and broadcast live to the world, but only three camera points have been allowed and none are on the altar. Covert but armed police are stationed at all three points and at the sound control desk. All the televisual crews have been thoroughly validated and will be body-searched each and every time they pass through the church.

Owain walks outside and watches officers direct onlookers to strategic areas behind street barriers. There are two cordoned-off sections specifically for photographers, journalists and camera crews. Over his head a trio of police helicopters circle high, wide and near.

Carrie Auckland walks through a checkpoint. She's now more suitably attired for a church service, in a knee-length blue dress with high neckline.

As soon as she reaches him she breaks the news. 'The Vatican helicopter has just touched down and the Guard are making the transfer to the Popemobile.'

'How long?'

'Ten minutes. No more.'

173

SAN JOAQUIN HOSPITAL, STOCKTON

Eleonora makes Ross Green stand outside her car while she checks with Donovan that he is who he says he is, some PI from a hotshot international company she's never heard of with special clearance from the FBI director to work on the case.

She rings off and shrugs. 'My boss says you can help.'

'Glad I passed the test.' The SSOA operative leans against Eleonora's Crossfire. 'The shooter is called Chris Wilkins, aka several other false names. We believe his real identity is Charlie Wood, an unspectacular name for a very special breed of killer, kidnapper and all round bad guy. He's married to an equally obnoxious waste of human DNA called Theresa Wood, née Tobin.'

'And how do you know this?'

'It's my job to know it. Like I said, we're on the same side. My colleagues are trying to help your colleague, and right now Wilkins is getting away.' Ross dips into his jacket pocket and pulls out a fold of paper. 'He's booked on a flight out of Stockton in an hour. My betting is that after all this heat he's going to skip it.' He sees her going for her phone. 'I've already got someone at the airport. And at Byron and Livermore Tracy and Camp Parks. Then I'm blown. Fresh out of personnel.'

'And you want me to fix cover at the other airports?'

He nods. 'I have a feeling he'll try for a small private plane out of the state, then go international for a while.'

'I can do this. I'll call my office again.'

'Good. Then give me your cell number and I'll get moving. I see anything I'll call you.'

She pulls a card from her jeans. 'Where are you going?'

'South.'

'Mexico?'

'Uh-huh. If he drives hard and straight, it's six hours, max. I have to cover all bases.'

174

CALIFORNIA

The airlift from Mount Diablo to the John Muir Hospital helipad takes only a few minutes.

Eve Garrett flies with Jade. She stays until paramedics roll her into the ER. As the surgery doors shut a mortuary crew trundles past with a gurney to pick up the corpse of the female kidnapper.

The SSOA agent cleans up in a washroom and is about to make herself scarce, when a stubble-faced young medic in scrubs catches her arm. 'You best hang on; the sheriff is going to want a word with you.'

She shakes him off. 'Don't touch!'

'My bad.' He lifts a hands apologetically. 'Just doing my job.'

The brunette dips into her pocket and produces a false ID. 'I'm a PI. His office already has my number.' She starts for the exit.

'Wait!'

She turns and scowls.

'*Please.* Is there anything you can tell me about the shooting – anything that might help us treat the victim?'

She stops and gives what little she's got. 'You're still well within the Golden Hour. I was there when the shot was fired.' She mentally chastises herself. 'If I'd been seconds earlier the kid wouldn't even have been hurt.'

He eases up on her. 'Paramedics said you did a good job. Gave her a fighting chance.'

'Did my best.'

He clicks a pen and prepares to write on a clipboard. 'How long did you have to work her heart?'

'Five, six minutes. Felt a whole lot longer.'

'It always does.' He makes a note. 'How soon before they got oxygen to her?'

'Less than ten. I was still working her when they arrived.'

'That's good. A lack of oxygen to the brain is always our biggest fear.'

'You said fighting chance – you think she's gonna make it?'

He weighs up how to respond and in the end goes for honesty. 'Usually a head wound is the kind of trauma you don't get over.'

Her face falls.

'That said, the shot wasn't straight on.' He bends his wrist to demonstrate. 'The kid has lost a lot of scalp and bone but no brain.'

'So she'll be okay?'

'I can't say that. Giving CPR and getting oxygen to her so quickly are big pluses though. At the moment, they're dealing with shock and swelling, so she's a long way from okay. That said, she's hanging in there and if she's a fighter then anything's possible.'

'She's certainly that. We done here?'

'We're done. Thanks.'

Eve takes her cue and hightails it out of the main entrance.

She spots a taxi rank and grabs a ride back to the shack. With any luck, there'll be something there that gives her a clue as to where the other kidnapper is.

175

CARDIGAN, WALES

The plate on the uniquely customized Mercedes Benz M Class reads SCV 1 – *Stato della Citta del Vaticano* – and even by the pace of country traffic, it's moving disruptively slowly.

Slowly, but perfectly on time.

It takes exactly ten minutes for the armour-plated Popemobile to make the journey from the improvised helipad off the A487 into the crowd-packed streets of Cardigan.

The Holy Father watches the adoration from behind four walls of bulletproof glass and warmly acknowledges as many onlookers as he can.

Invisible rings of security are already in place as the famous white vehicle stops. The Vatican's Swiss Guards are closest, the

British secret service next and then Owain's SSOA operatives. There's a deafening cheer as the new Pope appears at the back of the vehicle and descends hydraulically operated steps into the cool Welsh air. He smiles and looks around before kneeling and kissing the earth.

As the pontiff rises, the cheering reaches a new crescendo. He walks towards a prearranged spot where a seven-year-old boy and eight-year-old girl are waiting in newly bought school uniforms.

The Pope bends to talk to them. There's an explosion of camera flashes. He accepts a bible from the boy and a bouquet of flowers from the girl. More camera flashes. A tidal wave of cheers. Clapping sweeps him along a red carpet and into a protected entrance.

Owain takes out his phone and calls his wife.

She doesn't pick up.

He leaves a message. 'Hi, it's nothing special. I'm at the church and about to go in, so will have the phone turned to silent.' He pauses, then adds, 'I love you, Jenny. Love you more than you'll ever know.'

'Touching,' says a voice behind him.

Owain's blood runs cold.

He turns, and sees Josep Mardrid barely a yard away. 'What are you doing here?'

The suntanned face oozes a gleaming smile. 'I wouldn't have missed this for the world.' He makes the sign of the cross. 'I'm a very religious man.'

'You're the personification of evil.'

Mardrid looks pleased. 'I'll take that as a compliment.' He studies the ambassador's face. 'I love churches and graveyards, don't you? So much history and ritual. Secrets buried beneath ground. Hidden but so close to disclosure. You understand what I'm alluding to, don't you?' He smiles generously. 'I have one of your knights' crosses, Gwyn. The first of many that I plan to collect.'

'I'll take that as an admission of theft, though that's the least of your crimes. By the way, they won't let you keep a cross where you're going.'

Mardrid laughs and fastens the middle button of his jacket. 'Sorry I can't stay and chat but I have things to do – history to make.' He tips his head. 'I'll be sure to return the cross. When I bury you.'

Owain calls Carrie Auckland as he watches his old enemy drift towards a party of Spanish diplomats. 'Josep Mardrid is here.'

'What?'

'He's with the Spanish contingent around the front of the church.'

'I'll have eyes on him in a minute.'

Owain signs off and joins the flow of dignitaries filing into the church. As he walks down the centre aisle, he recognizes English, Welsh and Italian ministers, the deputy head of MI5 and the *Oberst*, the Commandant of the Swiss Guard. There are TV celebrities that he can't put names to and by the look of it, there's also a small block of local parishioners.

Mardrid.

He can't take his mind off the man. He's here to 'make history'. He'd sought him out to brag about it. And mention the cross. Owain looks around and can't see him.

He takes his place on the front pew. Out of the corner of his eye, he sees Carrie Auckland briefing two of her undercover operatives.

The temperature in the church is becoming uncomfortably warm. He glances at his watch. Five minutes until the start of Mass. His attention drifts to the big bronze statue of the Virgin Mary and baby Jesus. When Pope Benedict blessed it, back in 2010 during his visit to London, it was designated as the Welsh national shrine. Today the new Pope will follow in the footsteps of Pope John Paul II by blessing a candle and inserting it in the taper holder in the Virgin's right hand.

The phone in his pocket silently vibrates with a text message. He slides it out and discreetly reads the screen.

'Jade Fallon shot in head. In surgery. Suspect Tess Wilkins now dead. Eve.'

Owain returns the phone to his pocket. The doors at the back of the church clunk closed. Organ music strikes up. People stand and straighten out their best clothes.

The greatest Mass that Wales has ever witnessed is about to begin.

176

CALIFORNIA

Chris Wilkins decides it's time to ditch the Ford. He's already run it longer than intended.

Stockton Airport lies less than fifteen minutes from the hospital. He'd hoped to have dropped the car there and been out of state before anyone even started looking for it. After the shootings, it's too risky.

The road ahead offers nowhere for him to pull in and grab new wheels. He turns his burner on and calls Tess for the third time.

There's no pick up.

They've been together for more than a decade and he's never had to call three times to reach her. Wilkins turns off the phone, slides down the window of the Ford and tosses it. Through a side mirror, he sees it hit the blacktop and bounce into grass.

He'd put the first two unanswered calls down to the complication of killing the Fallon kid, torching the place and getting out of the area. Now he knows it isn't that. Tess is a pro. She always understood the importance of following the plan and either phoning in or being around to take the call. He's trying not to think the unthinkable, to imagine she's been caught – or worse.

With Stockton no longer an exit option, he considers finding a small airport and paying cash to a hick pilot to get him out of State, but there's a good chance the cops are going to be all over those kind of landing strips.

He rules out a run to Canada, even though Vancouver is only a fifteen-hour haul from Stockton and if he went a more roundabout route, he could hit Winnipeg in under a day.

As soon as he gets new wheels he'll head south towards Mexico. Not down the fast lanes of the interstate where the cops might come hunting and the traffic cameras could pick him up. He has another route. One so windy and obscure, he's certain God himself wouldn't be able to find it.

177

NEW YORK

Joe Steffani drives across town to meet with the brass in the NIA. The radio is up high and so is the sun. It's been a hell of a successful day and he should be happier.

Locking up five major terrorists should pretty much make his career, and that's going to bring the kind of security, salary and pension that will set him up for life.

But he's not.

What's eating him is that if Gareth Madoc is right, there are going to be three terror attacks in the next twenty-four hours and one of them will be right here in New York City. That's why the top brass want to see him in person.

From the checks he's just done, al-Shibh, Korshidi, Tabrizi, Hussan and Iman Yousef Mousavi are still saying nothing.

The traffic in Lower Manhattan is worse than ever. Steffani's Jeep grinds to a dispiriting halt part way down Wall Street. He shakes his head in dismay. There's still enough time to get to his meeting but only just.

He stares around him, bored and impatient. A cute blonde in a Lexus to his left looks him over. Some idiot is trying to get a hot-dog cart through the traffic and is drawing horns. Down a side street looms a church an ex-girlfriend of his used to go to. Its neo-Gothic spire used to soar above everything. Now it's dwarfed by the buildings around it. Such is progress.

The traffic finally moves and he loses sight of it.

Then something hits him.

And the jigsaw of clues comes together, almost like a miracle.

178

CARDIGAN, WALES

No one does theatre better than the Catholic Church.

Not for them, understatement, nuance or humility.

The way Owain sees it, *any* Catholic Mass is a grand affair, but one including the Bishop of Rome is the religious equivalent of a Cirque du Soleil premiere.

There are so many lit candles Cardigan could put Las Vegas in the shade. The opening act, a central procession of the entire ecclesiastical cast, is breathtaking. Finest silk and cotton vestments. Priceless golden incense burners and chalices. Intoxicating scents of frankincense and elevated voices of heavenly choristers.

All a distraction from the most important thing of all.

The Holy Father's safety.

An army of well-regimented altar boys in crisp, black-and-white cassocks and cottas is usurped only by a legion of lavishly robed priests, bishops and archbishops who have insisted that they too must have a place centre stage. But none compare to the sumptuous sight of the new pontiff.

He is dressed in layer after layer of antique vestments. Each drips with symbolism as old as Christianity itself. A uniquely designed pallium, ornamented with red crosses that represent the blood of Jesus, is fixed to his chasuble with three gold pins, representing the nails with which he was crucified.

Owain notices a fanon, a shawl of alternating gold and silver stripes and a subcinctorium, a strip of fabric embroidered with a cross and the same Agnus Dei, Lamb of God, as featured in *The Ghent Altarpiece*.

Over the Holy Father's left arm is a maniple, a band of priceless silk made of intertwined red and gold threads, symbolizing the unity of Eastern and Western Catholic rites.

Most striking of all is the long, open-fronted cope that the Pope is wearing: red, fringed with green, deliberately evocative of the Welsh flag. The Holy Father walks to the lectern, raises his gaze to the packed and hushed congregation, then greets them in stilted Welsh: '*Bendith Duw arnoch* – the blessing of God be upon you.'

All hearts rise.

All except one.

The appearance of Josep Mardrid has shaken Owain Gwyn. Deep inside the house of God, he feels the force of evil stirring.

179

SSOA OFFICES, NEW YORK

The call from Joe Steffani leaves Gareth Madoc slack-jawed.

Being a foreigner, he simply hadn't made the connection that his New Yorker contact has. Now it makes sense.

Perfect sense.

Madoc is gone from his desk in sixty seconds and gets himself down to Lower Manhattan via Metro rather than the car-jammed road.

At the intersection of Wall Street and Broadway, he sees what had got Steffani excited. There, as big as big could be, is the explanation of what Mousavi had meant when he was secretly recorded at the al-Qaeda safe house saying, '. . . *the Trinity will be no more.*'

Everyone thought it was a reference to three separate targets, but it wasn't.

It was just one.

A National Historic Landmark. A place where people took refuge from flying debris when the first tower collapsed during 9/11. A building connected to the ancient kings and queens of England.

Trinity Church.

The sanctified bricks and mortar represent the long-standing special relationship between the Church of England and God-fearing America. Forged when the first stone was laid in the seventeenth century and strong enough to survive two rebuilds and more than three hundred years.

New York's finest, cops from the financial district, are out in force turning people away, setting up barricades and trying to push sidewalk traffic further and further back.

But it might be too late.

Madoc catches a glimpse of Steffani on a phone. He's walking away from the church, towards the graveyard where, among others, lie Founding Father Alexander Hamilton, the first US treasury secretary, and Robert Fulton, developer of the world's first steamboat.

Trinity is the perfect target. It destroys history as well as lives.

'Hey, Joe!'

Steffani looks up and acknowledges him.

Madoc wanders over and waits until he finishes the call.

The NIA agent clicks off his phone and turns on his smile.

'We came up trumps, buddy.' He points to the tower. 'Up there are twenty-three of the biggest bells in thc US. Half were replaced recently by a company from England. There was a service engineer in there yesterday, fit the description of Malek. The bomb squad just found several pounds of his handiwork packed beneath the decking boards.'

'It's defused?'

Steffani nods. 'It certainly is.'

Madoc allows himself his first smile for a long time. 'I've got someone to call, someone who's going to be very relieved to hear that.'

180

CARDIGAN, WALES

The Gospel reading passes without so much as a stumbled syllable.

The pontiff ends by reminding everyone that in 1982, when John Paul II became the first reigning Pope to visit Wales, he called on the young people of Britain to begin 'a crusade of prayer'. He adds, with almost passionate emphasis, '*That* crusade needs to be renewed. The enemies we face today are more insidious and demanding than ever. We must become increasingly united and devoted in our worship of the Lord, Jesus Christ, Our Saviour.' He lets the message sink in, then adds, '*Bendith Duw ar bobol Cymru!* – God bless the people of Wales!' The cheers of the crowds outside can be heard through the church walls.

The Pope leaves the lectern and heads towards the sacred statue for the final part of his heavily stage-managed Mass – the lighting and blessing of a new taper.

Owain's phone buzzes in his pocket. He palms it so it can't be seen as he reads the message. 'Target was "Trinity" the church in NYC. Bomb defused. GM.'

Tension flows out of his shoulders. His worries about the Pope have been for nothing. He'll call Gareth as soon as the service finishes.

Around him, expectation builds among the assembled congregation. A cherubic acolyte walks self-consciously across the altar. In his uncomfortably outstretched hands, he carries a long, narrow box fashioned from dark hardwood and fastened with a large clasp bearing the Papal insignia. It comprises the crossed silver and gold keys of Saint Peter, the triple crown of the pontiff showing his roles as supreme pastor, teacher and priest and most importantly, at the top of the clasp, a distinct cross on a globe, signifying the sovereignty of Jesus.

The Pope opens the box and removes a virgin candle, brought directly from Rome.

A second acolyte appears, somewhat older than the first and with steadier hands. He carries a long candle lighter, made of wood and brass. He waits patiently to one side.

Slowly, reverently, the Holy Father places the candle in the holder in the right hand of the Virgin Mary and then turns for the lighter.

Inexplicably, the acolyte drops it.

The clatter of brass sends a shockwave through the church. Security men tense. Hands dip into jackets.

But nothing has happened. Nothing but a dropped prop on the ecclesiastical stage.

The boy picks up the ceremonial instrument. A kindly priest moves towards him and beneath his robes, finds a lighter.

There's a click and a hiss of an incongruous Zippo. Once more the flame intended for the ceremony is lit.

The Holy Father appears unperturbed. He waits patiently for the priest to retreat, and calmly takes the lighter from the red-faced young man.

All eyes are on the candle in the statue's hand.

All except Owain's.

He is scanning the church. He glances behind him and looks back to the altar.

The Pope ensures the candle is burning brightly. He hands the brass lighter back to the acolyte and blesses the shrine. There's a reserved but definite smile on his face as he turns and addresses the congregation.

Owain doesn't hear what he says. His mind is on the candle. It's the only thing he didn't personally check. He's sure it will have been examined by the Swiss Guard, but *he* didn't check it.

He reminds himself of Gareth's message. The attack was

planned in New York and it's been thwarted. The crisis is over.

Yet doubt remains.

He looks again at the candle and at others in the church. It's thicker than some, longer than others, smaller than most. The flame is the same as those around it. There really isn't anything unusual about the column of wax, except that it has just been blessed by a man Catholics believe is the holiest person on the planet.

The door at the back of the church creaks. Someone is trying to leave without disturbing the Mass. It's an odd time to go. There are only a few minutes left of the service.

The exit is controlled by the Swiss Guard. They wouldn't let anyone leave. Not now. Most likely one of them has stepped outside.

Why?

Owain fears he knows the answer.

The candle could contain a core of C4, a pliable and stable explosive that isn't detonated by flame. Whoever is leaving may be about to trigger it remotely using a shockwave detonator. It's the kind of play a military man, someone like a Swiss Guard, would make.

He hesitates. Tells himself to stay still, or he'll just make a fool of himself.

But he can't.

He breaks from the pew of dignitaries and rushes the altar. There's an outbreak of gasps.

Two robed priests try to block him. He knocks them away.

He has to get himself in front of the candle. At best, he'll look an idiot. At worst, he'll block the blast.

He extends a hand and shoves the Holy Father clean off the altar.

Outside, on the giant screens, and on televisions across the world, millions watch in horror.

The bomb goes off.

Stone, glass and flesh fill the morning sky.

PART FIVE

181

CALIFORNIA

The SSOA Gulfstream flies sub-supersonic but takes only seven hours to get from London to the landing lights in San Francisco.

Mitzi has been in a state of shock all the way. Her brain refuses to accept that both her daughters have been shot and are still fighting for their lives.

Bronty and Dalton have flown with her. Her FBI colleague is mumbling about a woman diver he met who thinks underwater caves off Lundy's shores might contain Arthurian tombs. Mitzi couldn't give a damn.

Nothing matters any more.

Nothing, except being with Jade and Amber.

Despite her physical and mental pain, she knows she still has to talk confidentially to Dalton. There are things he must be told.

As soon as Bronty goes to the washroom, she slips into the seat alongside the consul. 'I want you to know that as far as

I'm concerned, the Goldman case is closed. I appreciate you flying back here with me, I really do. And I know it's not just because you have your codex back.'

'It's not.'

'I know.' She gives him a reassuring smile. 'We're done. Everything I heard and saw while I was in your country is forgotten.'

'Thank you.' He looks relieved.

'The truth is, *I'm* done as well. I'm planning on handing in my shield and gun.'

'That would be a loss.'

'I don't think so. If my girls live, then maybe I get a second chance at being a good mom.'

'Mrs Fallon, I'm sure you're a very good—'

'Please – *don't* patronize me.' She gives him a scalding look. 'And don't call me Mrs Fallon. Go back to Britain and carry on doing whatever it is that you do. You and your secret knights have taken vows to be a power for good. So, you have my admiration, my support and my silence.'

He pushes his luck. 'I know Sir Owain harboured thoughts that you might join us.'

She shakes her head. 'Not me. I'm sorry.'

Bronty returns to his seat and Mitzi and Dalton fall silent. An in-flight announcement tells passengers to buckle up for landing.

The plane wheels drop. Mitzi feels the pressure build in her head. She shuts her eyes but there's no relief. Just two faces.

Jade.

Amber.

If they die she doesn't know how she'll live with herself. The doctors said Amber took a bullet in the hip and another in the back. Mitzi didn't even dare ask about paralysis. Everything from that moment onward seemed distant and blurred, as though it were happening in a fog.

The plane lands and taxis to a stop. She's vaguely aware of hands helping her down steps. The noise in the terminal splits her head. The cool, middle-of-the-night air makes her shiver as they wait for the limo to pick them up.

Mitzi smells new leather as she slumps in the back seat. Cars, lights and buildings flash by her side-window. She looks out into a world that she no longer feels part of.

Bronty sits alongside her in the back of the Jaguar. Dalton is in the front, talking about her on his phone, as though she's not there. And he's right. She isn't. She picks up that her ex-husband has been informed of the girls' injuries and is travelling over from LA.

She pities him. Not for a long time has she had a kind thought for Alfie Fallon but right now, she feels for him. Fears for him. As low as he is, this period of his life is going to drag him even lower.

'We're here.' The voice is Bronty's.

Car doors open.

She feels Dalton's hand on her right arm. Feels the touch of the fingers that surely killed a man at a Dupont Circle diner and set her off on a journey that ended with her daughters almost dead.

Mitzi pulls away from him and steps out into the darkness. A polite babble of voices breaks out. She looks at the sprawling front of the San Joaquin Hospital and wonders where Amber is.

Someone calls to her. Donovan is here. Others, too. Vicky the researcher, hand in hand with a tall man she doesn't know.

And Ruth.

That bum of a husband, Jack is right alongside her. They've all turned out. Her sister tries to catch her eye, but Mitzi looks away. Not now. She's not ready for reconciliation and all the questions that go with it.

Not yet.

She takes a beat and decides to say something before someone else tries to. 'I don't want to be rude. I'm really grateful everyone turned out so late. But could you all just leave me the fuck alone? Just while I visit my daughter and try to behave like a mom – and not like a cop.'

182

NORTHERN MEXICO

It's been a long drive. The drive of his life. But he's made it.

Larry Petty, a man previously known as Chris Wilkins and originally christened Charles James Wood, slides the rental car down the tight driveway of the house and squeezes on the brake. The dash tells him the outside temperature just hit 106 degrees, so he leaves the air-con running, unbuckles the safety belt and sighs with relief as it zips back over his shoulder.

For a moment, he just wants to sit and enjoy the fact that he's stopped running. That he's alive. Safe and free. It's taken him more than twenty-four hours, two stolen cars, a bus and train ride, plus the use of his one remaining false ID to get here.

Quite a feat.

There were moments when he wondered if he'd make it. Times when he realized that Tess hadn't. He'd pulled to the side of the road and sobbed himself in half. Convinced himself that she'd been arrested. Nothing worse. That she was sat somewhere laughing at the cops and saying jack shit to them. But then he'd heard her death on the news and his world had fallen apart.

The whole journey has been spent with one eye on the road and the other in the mirror looking for cops. He'd gambled they'd focus on airports and freeways and he'd been right.

From Stockton he'd taken the long and winding back roads until he hit Fresno. Out there, he'd stolen a Chevy parked in a car-share pool and worked minor roads to Bakersfield, where he picked up a bus to Flagstaff. He found his way to a train station and bought a ticket to Mexico.

Now he's about to grab a shower, heat up a pizza bought at a gas station and crash out in the two-bed row house he's rented down by the Sonora River.

He turns off the engine and steps out into the baking heat. The neighbourhood looks upmarket and smart. Brightly painted houses are stacked next to squares of burned grass and the odd slab of tarmac to park on. Nothing special, but it's neat. There's no trash. No graffiti. No gangs out on the streets. It's the kind of place he can blend in for a day or two.

When he's rock-bottom sure all the heat has died down, he'll catch a plane out of Garcia International and start over. Life goes on.

183

SAN JOAQUIN HOSPITAL, STOCKTON

The doctors tell Mitzi that Amber is going to live.

They also tell her it's too soon to define what quality of life she'll have.

The bullets have ripped tissue, caused trauma and chipped bones. Recovery will be slow. Long. Painful.

The consultant, a big man with white hair and kind eyes, says, 'She's still unconscious, Mrs Fallon, but her vital signs are good and I expect her to come round any time soon.'

Mitzi pushes for good news as he takes her to the recovery room where Amber's resting. 'She's going to walk again, right?'

He smiles. 'We're really hoping so. Right now, we just need

her to regain consciousness and start talking to us. Then we can run tests.'

They turn a corner and in the corridor Mitzi sees a hard chair staked outside a room. There's a familiar figure crumpled uncomfortably on it.

Eleonora Fracci looks up, bleary-eyed.

'How long have you been there?' Mitzi asks.

'All the time. I stay until you arrive.'

The Italian stands up and straightens herself out.

'You really look like shit,' says Mitzi, then opens her arms to her.

They both hold tight and try to squeeze the pain away.

When they break, Mitzi takes the Italian's hands in hers. 'Thank you for being here, for looking out for my daughter.'

Eleonora nods. 'I wish I could have done more.'

She nods to the door. 'I'm gonna go in and sit a while.'

'Then I take a shower, so I look less like shit when you come out.'

Mitzi smiles and enters the darkened room. The first thing she notices is the beep of the machines. That and the fact that Amber's dressed in pink flowery PJs. She'd go crazy if she saw herself.

Mitzi slides into the seat by the bed and goes to take her hand. She sees the bandage around the severed finger and almost cries. Her head fills with the screams she heard down the phone. Amber's words – '*They've c–ut me – Mommy!*'

Mitzi lifts the hand and gently kisses it. 'It's gonna be okay, baby. Your mom's here now and everything's gonna be okay.'

184

CARDIGAN, WALES

Sir Owain Gwyn's grapheme under-armour soaked up most of the blast.

But not all of it.

Not enough of it.

The C4 concealed in the candle was remotely detonated just as he lifted it from the right hand of the Welsh national shrine. Because the ex-Guardsman was so large, he absorbed enough of the force to save the pontiff and all surrounding clergy.

But not himself.

The blast took off the front of his face and the top of his head. If he'd been a few seconds earlier – if he'd managed to pull the candle tighter to his body, then maybe he'd have survived.

Lance Beaucoup guides Lady Gwyn down the aisle of the Church of Our Lady of the Taper. Once her husband's remains had been taken back to the private family chapel at Caergwyn Castle, she insisted on being taken to the spot where he spent his last moments. Throughout the journey she'd replayed the message he'd left on her phone: 'I love you, Jenny. Love you more than you'll ever know.'

Somehow, the world's press has learned of her visit. Local police have shut off the streets in an attempt to give the widow of one of Britain's most distinguished knights a little privacy.

And, of course, Beaucoup has deployed enough SSOA men to make doubly sure the area is safe.

Laid outside the church are hundreds of bouquets, all carrying messages of condolence, praise and respect. Among them, wreaths from the Pope, the British prime minister and the American president.

As Lance and Jennifer enter the nave, they notice the back pews are still covered in masonry dust. The normally vibrant church light is muted because so many windows have been blown out and boarded up. The front pews have been removed and stacked at one side.

To the front of the chapel, there are heaps of rubble, wood and glass in different piles and Beaucoup's expert eyes detect where the bomb squad have been, where they have inspected and where they still intend to carry out further examinations.

The deputy chief constable and two senior officers are only yards away in case they can be of assistance. But Jennifer doesn't need them to point out where her husband had died.

Her heart guides her to the fatal spot.

She takes her arm out of Beaucoup's and looks into the eyes of the man her husband chose as her lover, the man destined to look after her when this terrible moment arrived. 'Could you ask everyone to leave? Just for a minute. I'd like to be alone with my thoughts of him.'

185

NEW YORK

The quiet backstreet in Greenwich Village is filled with overhanging trees and birdsong. Gareth Madoc checks for a tail as he zaps the central locking on his Range Rover and crosses the road.

He walks a full block and a half to the safe house where Zachra and her mother Nasrin have been since Khalid Korshidi was lifted by the NIA. He speed-dials a number on his encrypted cell.

SSOA agent Dana Levine answers. 'All clear for you to come up, sir.'

Madoc lets his eyes drift to the upstairs window of the dainty row house and sees a curtain cracked and Levine looking down on him. He climbs six stone steps to the big door and presses the buzzer.

One by one, he counts the bolts and bars sliding back. Five in total. Finally, the door opens.

'Hi there,' he passes the giant form of Ritchie Handsworth, the second SSOA agent stationed in the safe house.

'Morning, sir.' The agent shuts the door and locks and re-bolts it.

Madoc takes the uncarpeted stairs to the large back room. Zachra and her mother are sat watching TV, a rerun of an

Oprah show about dealing with broken homes. Both are dressed in casual Western clothes. The younger woman turns and her face fills with delight. 'Mr Madoc – I didn't know you were coming.'

He smiles back at her and dips into the jacket of his black suit. 'I've got something for you.' He hands over an envelope and a separate folded sheet of paper.

Zachra takes them and gives him a suspicious stare. 'What are these?'

'Look for yourself.' He adds the reassurance she needs. 'It's nothing bad.'

Her eyes sparkle as she rips open the envelope. 'Momma, look. Plane tickets to London. A chance to start again.'

Madoc realizes he's never seen her happy or relaxed before. He adds the more important detail. 'You need to study the single sheet I gave you. It tells you your new identities, where your new home is and your new bank account. The house is a modest terrace on the outskirts of London, but you'll be safe. It's paid for and it's yours for as long as you want. The bank account has ten thousand pounds in it. It should help resettle you while my people get you both jobs.'

Zachra throws her arms around him and kisses his cheek. 'Thank you. Thank you so much. You have no idea what this means to us.' She glances at her mother and then back at him. 'You've given us both our lives back. It's like being reborn.'

'You're very welcome. You're an enormously brave and talented young woman, Zachra. If anyone deserves to be reborn it's you.'

186

JOHN MUIR MEDICAL CENTER, SAN FRANCISCO

An FBI helicopter takes Mitzi the fifty miles from San Joaquin to John Muir.

It's almost dawn when staff in the Neuroscience Intensive Care Unit lead her to where Jade is recovering.

A foot from the door and alongside a wall sign that says NO PHONES, hers rings. 'Sorry. I need to take this.'

The two nurses drift back to their station.

'Hello.'

'This is Eleonora.' She takes an emotional breath. 'It's your daughter—'

Mitzi puts her hand on the wall and feels faint. The pause is too long for it to be good news. She should never have left Amber's bedside.

'She has regained consciousness.'

'What?'

'She is awake and talking.'

'Oh, my God.' Mitzi slides down the wall and sits on the floor. The relief makes her heart hammer and tears flow. 'How is she?'

Eleonora laughs. 'How is she? She is like a little Mitzi, that's how she is. She is already complaining about her clothes. You want to talk to her?'

'Oh yes, yes please.'

'I put her on.'

The phone becomes a swirl of crackles and clunks.

'Mom.'

'Baby.'

'Mom, are you all right?' Her voice is post-op raspy and drowsy.

'I'm fine, sweetheart. Don't worry about me. I'm visiting Jade and I'll be back to see you soon.'

'Is she okay?'

Mitzi gets to her feet and tries without luck to see through the bedroom window. 'Yeah, I think so, baby.'

She picks up on her mom's worry. 'Jade will be okay. Jade's a Fallon girl and like you said, Fallon women are winners, right?'

Mitzi feels a rush of pride. 'Yeah, we are, baby. We're winners.'

'Mom . . . '

'What, honey?'

'Did you see the PJs they put me in?'

She laughs. 'Yeah, I did.'

'Yuuck!'

'Don't worry, I'll bring new ones.' She hesitates. There's a question eating a hole in her head. One she has to ask. 'Can you feel your legs, honey? Is everything working?'

There's a long pause.

Too long for Mitzi's liking. 'Amber, can you feel—'

'Mom, stop nagging. I'm just wriggling my toes and checking like you asked. Yeah, I'm okay, but I really hurt a lot and I think I need to pee.'

Mitzi laughs again. 'You go pee while I see your sister, then I'll call you back. Deal?'

'Deal. Oh, and Mom, *pleeease* don't forget the PJs.'

Mitzi finishes the call and enters Jade's room.

The curtains are closed and the place is cast in a grey shade that smells of antiseptic. Her good mood has gone. A nurse has tried to disguise the brutality of the head wound but there's no hiding the swelling. The sight of it breaks Mitzi's heart.

Over in the corner is a single wardrobe. Placed neatly outside it are the Prada trainers Jack got her. She remembers feeling bad when that ass-groping pig bought them. Now she'd do anything to see her walk in them again.

She moves slowly along the bed. Jade looks deathly pale. It's so wrong that she's this close to death. Her life was only beginning. She was becoming a beautiful young woman. Albeit a headstrong, outspoken, feisty, never-let-it-lie, always-right, never-back-down, pain-in-the-ass of a daughter, but still a beautiful young woman.

Mitzi sits on the bed and takes the teenager's hand, just as she'd done with her sister barely an hour ago.

Jade's fingers are cold. Her nails are painted with Pink Bliss. It's not her colour, but Amber's. They must have been getting on. Before the world stopped and everything turned into flies and hit God's windshield.

She keeps hold of Jade's hand. Presses it to her face. Rests her head on the bed. Keeps her skin and her daughter's bound together. The last time it was like this was fourteen years ago in a maternity ward.

Mitzi closes her eyes and sees light pushing the curtains. Tiredness crashes in. The pains, stresses and strains all become too much for her. She dozes. The black tide that swims over her is healing and soothing, like a hot, dark bath.

Mitzi wakes with a jolt. Her face hurts. It feels like it's been pricked or scratched. Almost as though Jade has clawed her cheek. She looks down. There's blood on her daughter's nails.

Mitzi sits up. She puts her hands to her face. There's fresh blood on her fingertips. She tells herself she's imagining it. It can't have happened. She brushes hair from Jade's face. 'Baby, can you hear me?'

There's no response. But there is something different about her.

'Jade, it's Mom. Can you hear me?'

There *is* something different about her. Mitzi just knows there is. She looks again at the blood on her own hand and on Jade's fingers.

Her frown is back. Jade is frowning. Mitzi's seen it a million times. There's no mistaking that furrowed, sulky brow.

'Nurse! Nurse!' She almost screams the building down as she runs to the door. 'Hel-fucking-lo! Are there no freaking nurses anywhere in this goddamned place?'

One appears at the far end of the corridor.

Mitzi rushes back inside.

Jade's eyes are open. The tone on the monitor has changed. Her mouth moves.

Mitzi can't hear anything. She rushes to her daughter's

bedside. 'Sweetheart—' She stops just inches away, scared that touching her might ruin the fragile recovery.

Jade speaks in a hoarse, slow voice. 'Mom – please shut the fuck up – you're *embarrassing* me.'

187

NORTHERN MEXICO

Chris Wilkins showers, then does a final check around the house before hitting the sack.

He sets the burglar alarm. Tests the locks on all the windows. Slips a Glock into a cabinet in the bathroom and another under his pillow. Precautions he and Tess always made whenever they settled somewhere new.

He thinks of her as he turns the lights off and slips into the cool sheets. If she was here, they'd curl up together and not part until they were breathless, their energies spent.

Deep inside, he knows she's dead.

If she was alive and free, she'd have sent an email to one of their secret accounts. He's checked and she hasn't. If she'd been arrested, she'd have called their lawyer. She hasn't. Even though there's nothing on the news, every atom of his body is telling him she's gone. At some point, when his anxiety about being caught has gone, then he's going to fall apart. And afterward, when he's pulled himself together again, he will wreak a most bloody vengeance on those responsible for her death.

But for now, comfort comes in the form of rest. After being cramped in cars, buses and trains, it's a relief to stretch out on a soft bed. The air-con has a hypnotic whirr that helps him drift into the first stage of sleep. He tosses and turns. Kicks off the sheet. Sinks deeper into slumber.

It's been so long since Wilkins has done anything more than nap, that he doesn't stir at first. Not when the smoke alarm goes off. Nor when fumes creep up the stairs.

He wakes with a jolt.

Some sense has been triggered. He sits upright. His head aches from sleep but he knows what's happening. The house is on fire. He grabs the gun from beneath his pillow. Rushes to the bedroom door. The blaze is in the hallway. It's thick with smoke and orange flame. Too dense for him to run through it.

Wilkins shuts himself in and goes to the double windows in the bedroom. He untwists the locks and pushes them open. There's a drainpipe to his right. If he grabs that, at most he has a drop of twelve feet. A twisted ankle is better than risking a rush through fire.

He stuffs the Glock in the back of his briefs and gets up on the window frame. He turns and dangles his legs outside. Shuffles so he can reach the drainpipe. It's a bit of a stretch but he makes it and swings himself out.

Bare feet find the brickwork and he eases himself into the dark night.

Then he feels a sharp pain in his spine. His grip goes and he falls like a sack of sand. Before he even hits the front yard, he knows he's been shot. The impact knocks the wind out of him but he ignores the pain and reaches for the Glock.

A second shot opens up his stomach. A third cracks a rib under his heart. A fourth pops the middle of the throat.

Off in the distance there's the siren of a fire truck. Neighbours are running from their homes.

Ross Green is already breaking down his sniper rifle. He'll be gone before the fire-fighters arrive.

He just wishes Sir Owain were alive so he could tell him the news.

188

CAERGWYN CASTLE, WALES

The private chapel in the castle grounds is deserted, except for Myrddin.

He hasn't left the cold, vaulted place of worship since Owain's body was brought in. Nor will he. Not until the ceremony that will carry him to Avalon.

Wrapped in a timeworn funereal cloak, he stands like a round-backed sentry at the feet of the man he considered a son.

As Myrddin commanded, there has been no attempt to

sanitize the effects of the blast. Owain's body lies before him, battle-raw. He sees the eviscerated skin, the shredded clothing and clumps of dried blood. To him, they are the ultimate medals of honour, pinned on a brave mortal frame that contained an even braver spirit.

'You live on, my child. You are immortal.' He touches the knight's feet. 'You are born again in your unborn son, just as you lived in the spirit of your father, your father's father and the generations that shaped our great land.'

There are no tears in the old man's eyes. They have been wrung dry by too many years of sorrow, too many sons to stand over and mourn.

He puts both hands together, as if in prayer and clears his mind of everything except the oath he is about to make. 'These promises I solemnly give unto you. I will watch over your wife as though she were my own blood.' He places his praying hands on the great man's chest. 'I will be the strictest guardian of the mind and soul of the man to whom you entrusted her welfare. I will ensure beyond earthly doubt that he keeps your lady's love alive so she may raise your child in the enrichment of its light and warmth.' His white fingers stretch over the heart that loved so much and now no longer beats. 'I will watch over your son, Arthur, as he grows in your features, speaks in your voice and acts in your spirit. And when he faces the challenges that await him, I will be there to protect and guide him, as I did you.'

Myrddin crosses Sir Owain's hands, so they lie in the position that befits a fallen knight. With a sigh, he bends to the cold stone floor of the chapel and raises from it the sacred object that will complete his oath.

Into the great man's hands Myrddin fixes, not a burial cross but a mighty broadsword. One that symbolizes everything his family and the Order stand for.

The tired, old augur steps back and kneels.

He gazes into the future and visualises the day he will guide another young man, one yet to be born, to the body of his brave father. It will be the moment he tells him the time has come to take up the Arthurian broadsword and all the power and the responsibility that goes with it. It will be the start of the new Cycle.

ACKNOWLEDGEMENTS

Little, Brown/Sphere – Jade Chandler for her great ideas and sensitive persuasion (especially about endings!). Iain Hunt for all the hard labor/labour in editing. Andy Hine, Kate Hibbert and Helena Doree for their mastery of foreign rights. Jo Wickham – publicity. Hollie Smyth – marketing. Nick Castle – cover design and direction.

LBA – Luigi Bonomi for his constant belief, expert advice and resilient good humour, Alison Bonomi for her eagle eyes and kind assistance.

Professor Guy Rutty MBE, Chief Forensic Pathologist, East Midlands Forensic Pathology Unit, University of Leicester, for his unique guidance and amazing thoroughness – any deviations from fact are down to me not him.

Everett Baldwin Barclay – Jack Barclay and team for the best company advice in the business.

Peter Robson – better known as Lundy Pete for all his help and patience with the scenes set on Lundy and its wonderful legends and history.

Last but not least, Donna, Billy, Elliott and Damian for being everything that matters in fact not fiction.